Collusion

Also by De'nesha Diamond

Parker Crime Chronicles
Conspiracy
Collusion
Collateral

The Diva Series
Hustlin' Divas
Street Divas
Gangsta Divas
Boss Divas
King Divas
Queen Divas

Anthologies
Heartbreaker (with Erick S. Gray and Nichelle
Walker)
Heist and *Heist 2* (with Kiki Swinson)
A Gangster and a Gentleman (with Kiki Swinson)
Fistful of Benjamins (with Kiki Swinson)
No Loyalty (with A'zayler)

Published by Kensington Publishing Corp.

Collusion

DE'NESHA DIAMOND

KENSINGTON PUBLISHING CORP.
www.kensingtonbooks.com

DAFINA BOOKS are published by

Kensington Publishing Corp.
119 West 40th Street
New York, NY 10018

All Kensington Titles, Imprints, and Distributed Lines are available at special quantity discounts for bulk purchases for sales promotions, premiums, fund-raising, and educational or institutional use. Special book excerpts or customized printings can also be created to fit specific needs. For details, write or phone the office of the Kensington special sales manager: Kensington Publishing Corp., 119 West 40th Street, New York, NY 10018, attn: Special Sales Department, Phone: 1-800-221-2647.

Dafina and the Dafina logo Reg. U.S. Pat. & TM Off.

ISBN-13: 978-1-4967-0586-0
ISBN-10: 1-4967-0586-6
First Kensington Trade Edition: May 2018
First Kensington Mass Market Edition: December 2019

eISBN-13: 978-1-4967-0587-7
eISBN-10: 1-4967-0587-4

10 9 8 7 6 5 4 3 2 1

Printed in the United States of America

This novel is dedicated to Mr. Nelson.
Thank you for a lifetime of memories.

Author's Note

Most of the action in the novel takes place in Washington, D.C., but certain liberties have been taken in portraying the city itself and its institutions. This is wholly intentional. The world presented here is a fictitious one, as are its characters and events.

PART ONE

Strange Relationship

Prologue

Hay-Adams Hotel, Washington D.C.
Eight days ago

*I*n the posh presidential suite of the five–star hotel, minutes from the White House, the new House speaker spent
his celebration night in a luxurious den of debauchery.
High off a potent designer street drug, Cotton Candy, he
fulfilled a lifelong ménage à trois fantasy with an ex-
lover and one of Madam Nevaeh's sexy escort girls.

When he woke, he was surprised to see his ex-mis-
tress preparing to leave.

"Where are you going?"

"Home."

"What?" He struggled to detangle himself from the
bed's soft linen. "No. Wait. Don't go."

"Why not? You still got company." Kitty referred to
the gorgeous cocoa-brown woman lying in a cocaine
high among a cloud of white sheets. "By the way,
where did you find her? She's stunning."

"Yeah. What can I say?" Kenneth Reynolds boasted,

his eyes glassy and his nose swollen with pink dust under it. "I'm Mr. Lucky tonight. I'm going to talk to Madam Nevaeh about keeping Miss Abrianna here on an exclusive arrangement." He brushed strands of hair from the despondent girl's face.

"Madam?" Kitty arched one brow while she tightened the belt on her trench coat. "You're paying for pussy now? Hell. I thought she was some chick that you picked up from one of those sleazy clubs you like so much."

He laughed. "I don't mind paying for the best." He met Kitty's gaze. "Not that you're not."

"Fuck you, Kenny."

"Where are you going?"

"Home."

Reynolds stood from the bed and reached for her, but she dodged his touch. "Aw, now. Don't be like that. I thought we were putting our little spat behind us?"

"Behind us? How? Are you pretending not to know what happens to my nomination to the Supreme Court if you impeach the president?"

He groaned. "Politics, politics, politics. Can't we have one night that doesn't involve politics?"

Kitty stood still while Reynolds slithered his arms around her waist. "Tonight is supposed to be a celebration. You're looking at the third most powerful man in the country . . . and I'm gunning for the man at the top."

"And fuck me, right?" she clarified, brows arched.

"C'mon, Kitty. Why are you killing the mood? Hmm?" Reynolds snuggled his head in the crook of her neck. "Don't you feel how much I've missed you? What we had together?" Kenny's dick hardened against her. "Why don't you take off that coat and come back to bed? Hmm?" He nibbled on her earlobe.

"So you get what you want and fuck me. Is that it?"

Reynolds groaned. "Look. You're a good judge. You'll eventually get your seat on the court."

Kitty laughed. "Are you fucking kidding me? These are once-in-a-lifetime appointments. Lightning doesn't strike twice. If you remove the president, then it's bye-bye to my nomination."

"That's not true," Reynolds whined, backpedaling to the bed. "As soon as we remove that asshole from the Oval Office, the vice president will uphold your nomination. We can impeach him and then confirm you with no problem."

"Right." Kitty slid her hand into her coat pocket and wrapped it around a gun.

"Contrary to popular opinion, Congress can walk and chew gum at the same time."

"Bullshit—or it would have been done before."

Reynolds exhaled and leaned against the headboard. "I don't know what you want. The House doesn't confirm judges. That's the Senate's job."

"Majority Leader McCullough is following your lead on this."

Reynolds chuckled. "You're giving me way too much credit." He reached over and groped the unconscious woman lying beside him. "I'm still horny." He cast his gaze back toward Kitty, surprised to see a gun leveled at him. After a few seconds, laughter rumbled low in his chest. "Now what are you going to do with that?"

"I'm about to make sure that I end up on that court . . . by getting you out of the way." Kitty clicked off the safety.

Too high to realize how much danger he was in, Reynolds laughed more deeply. "C'mon, Kitty. It's only politics. It's not personal."

"Politics is always personal," she said and pulled the trigger.

PART TWO

Chaos and Disorder

1

In the rich suburbs of Alexandria, Virginia, drug lord and political insider Zeke "Teflon Don" Jeffreys had gathered his friends and valuable political D.C. clients at his lavish home to celebrate his thirtieth birthday.

While he mixed and mingled, a motley crew of party-crashers was kidnapping his business partner-slash-lover, Madam Nevaeh, right from under his nose.

"Hurry! Load her up." Draya, dressed as a server for La Plume's catering service, opened the back doors of the van.

"We are going as fast as we can." Abrianna Parker, disguised as a male server, complete with a mustache and padded chest, banged the madam's head on one of the doors.

"Easy," Kadir Kahlifa, in disguise as a man twice his age, whispered back.

Annoyed, Abrianna banged the madam's head again. He frowned.

Abrianna shrugged. "I'm petty."

"Are you two for real?" Draya hissed.

Abrianna climbed up, still holding the front of Madam's body.

"Hey!"

Everyone froze.

"What are you guys doing over there?"

Abrianna, out of view, mouthed to Kadir, "Who is it?"

"Hey, I asked you guys a question!"

"Security," Kadir mouthed back.

Horrified, Abrianna glanced around for a weapon.

Draya spun. "Nothing. We're . . . grabbing supplies for the kitchen."

A large, lineman-shaped security guy waddled closer to the open van door.

Draya attempted to close one of the back doors to block his line of vision.

"But what the hell is that?" He gestured to the bag and leaned forward.

Panicked, Draya rammed the door into the nosy security guard's face, shocking him. However, she hadn't seen the drawn gun until it went off.

BANG!

Abrianna dropped Madam Nevaeh and screamed, "No!"

Instantly, the four-hundred-plus-pound man flew backward and slammed against the back of the house and then dropped like a stone.

Abrianna raced forward. "Draya, are you all right?" She gathered her friend into her arms. "Speak to me. Say something."

Draya lifted her shocked gaze. "How the fuck did you do that?"

Julian croaked, "Somebody tell me that I didn't see that."

Everyone stared at Abrianna, especially Kadir. "I, uh, uh—"

"It came from over there," a man shouted from the distance.

"Fuck. We gotta go," Kadir said, picking up Draya. "Get in the van," he ordered.

Everyone hauled ass.

Julian climbed behind Kadir and placed Draya in the back of the van along with Abrianna and Madam Nevaeh.

For a brief moment, Kadir's questioning gaze met Abrianna's, but then he slammed the doors shut—and raced to climb into the passenger seat. "Let's go!"

Julian jumped behind the wheel.

The van peeled off as an army of security goons rushed around the corner and found their unconscious colleague.

Rat-at-tat-tat-tat.

Bullets punctured the back of the van; a few ricocheted, forcing them to duck or dive for cover.

"What the hell?" Julian shouted, bringing everyone's attention to the police cars streaming onto the estate.

"Holy shit," Kadir said, incredulous.

Julian's foot lifted off the accelerator.

"Don't stop," Kadir shouted.

Julian hesitated on seeing the swarm of blue lights, but then slammed his foot back down on the gas.

The last two patrol cars swerved and blocked the van's exit.

"Don't you fucking stop," Kadir threatened again.

Julian tightened his grip on the steering wheel. When

they blazed closer and made it clear that the van wasn't stopping, the cops scrambled to get out of the way.

It was too late.

"Hold on!" Julian cried, closing his eyes.

BAM!

Everyone and everything slammed forward.

The two police cars spun like pinwheels in the van's wake.

Draya groaned.

"You guys okay back there?" Kadir asked.

Abrianna, sprawled beneath pans and supplies, pushed herself up and crawled to Draya.

Draya rolled onto her back. "What the hell, Jules? Are you trying to kill me?"

"She's fine," Julian said. "If Draya is bitching, then she's okay."

"Are they following us?" Abrianna asked.

The guys checked their mirrors. "Not that I can tell," Julian said, relieved.

"Yeah. Well. We better get off this road just in case."

"How is our other passenger?" Kadir asked.

Abrianna turned and moved over to the insulated nylon bag and stopped short. "Uh, guys . . ."

"What?" everyone asked.

"There's blood," Abrianna announced.

"She was hit?" Kadir asked, coming out of his seat to climb into the back.

Abrianna pulled the zipper down and opened the bag. "Damn."

Blood bloomed across the center of Madam's white dress, but Abrianna was certain that it was the bullet lodged in the center of Madam's forehead that had killed her.

Draya shook her head. "Well, I guess she won't be telling us shit."

———◦•◦———

Zeke Jeffreys hid his humiliation behind a stony mask while former police lieutenant Gizella Castillo gloated as they shoved his large frame into the back of a squad car. Once he was tucked inside and the door slammed shut, his black gaze zoomed to hers and transmitted the message that this game wasn't over by a long shot.

She knew that he was probably right.

His guests were equally humiliated but more outraged at having to be loaded up in the back of police vans. Many of them had no idea of Jeffreys's double life. They had no idea that while they were mixing and mingling, he was trafficking the designer street drug Cotton Candy. However, this time he had done so with undercover cop Steven O'Day.

Castillo had wanted to bring the drug lord down for years but had never been able to scratch the surface. Police Chief Dennis Holder, an ex-lover and colleague, had clued her in about the planned raid and permitted her to be here to watch the whole thing go down. Other than a strange shoot-out involving someone jacking a caterer's van, the raid had gone down smoothly.

Now she wanted to see about putting the screws to Madam Nevaeh, Zeke's business partner and rumored lover, about Abrianna Parker. Castillo had learned from Abrianna's best friend, Shawn White, that Parker had been working for the infamous madam the night of Speaker Reynolds's death. The first time Castillo confronted Nevaeh about this, she stonewalled her.

But Castillo had a bad habit of never giving up. Holder had often joked that she was like a bloodhound. She never deviated from a trail. Never. Plus, Castillo had a history with Abrianna Parker. Six years ago she'd led a team that had rescued Abrianna, Tomi Lehane, and Shalisa Young from the basement of madman and serial killer Craig Avery. Back then, Parker was a tough but scarred teenage runaway, who didn't stick around long enough to answer questions about her abduction.

It surprised Castillo when Parker blipped on her radar while investigating the new House speaker for Tomi Lehane, who was now a *Washington Post* reporter. It *shocked* Castillo when she realized that Parker was actually running from a murder scene.

After a near forty minutes of threading through the handcuffed crowd, Castillo couldn't find any trace of the madam when she was certain that Nevaeh had been in attendance earlier. For a fleeting moment, Castillo wondered whether the madam had been the one who'd hijacked La Plume's catering van, but then dismissed it when she overheard someone say they saw that it was group of servers.

Suddenly a group of officers scrambled to their cars.

"What's going on?" she asked, rushing alongside Officer Donovan.

"They found the van," she told her.

"From the shoot-out?"

"Yeah. Apparently it crashed down an embankment. The driver is deceased."

"What about the others?"

Donovan frowned. "Others?"

"Wasn't it a group of servers?"

She shook her head. "Dispatch only mentioned the driver."

Castillo's hackles rose. "Male or female?"

"Female."

2

The Bunker

In an unknown place in an unknown location in the bowels of Washington D.C., Douglas "Ghost" Jenkins, lifelong political hacktivist, pulled open the metal door of his underground bunker to see his old friend.

"Well, if it ain't Bonnie and Clyde," Ghost said, blocking the entrance to his hideout. "Or should I say Clyde and Clyde?" He cocked his head at Abrianna and took in her outfit. "Nice disguise."

"Thanks."

Ghost's gaze darted to Julian and Draya. "Damn, if every time I see you, man, your ass don't multiply. What kind of place do you think I'm running here?"

"Really? You're going to do this now? I have an injured woman. She's been shot."

Ghost straightened and glanced at Abrianna. "What? Again?"

"Not me this time."

Draya raised her good arm. "It's me."

Interest lit Ghost's eyes. "Well, hello."

Draya frowned.

"You're hitting on an injured woman?" Kadir asked.

"Is it my fault that women are always getting shot around you?" Ghost stepped back, allowing the small group to enter.

Hunkered down behind a row of terminals sat a skeleton crew of millennial hackers. Ghost introduced them as "the fellas" to Draya.

"Uh, nice to meet you," she said and then looked to Abrianna like *Who is this clown?*

"C'mon." Abrianna led Draya toward the bunker's back cot room. "I'll fix you right up."

Ghost smiled as he watched them walk away.

Arms crossed, Julian stepped forward to block Ghost's view.

"Oh. My bad." Ghost looked to Kadir. "How many people are you planning to tell about this place?"

"Chill. They're cool," Kadir said. "So what happened to you the other night? I thought you'd still be waiting to post bail."

"C'mon, playa. Am I the sort of person to give the cops my *real* ID?"

"They were putting you in the back of a squad car."

"Some rookie busting my chops. You know how they do. Of course, I hope you got rid of the van. I had to report it stolen."

"Yeah. We traded that one in for another one and then filled that one with bullet holes too."

Ghost chuckled. "That straight and narrow path you swore that you were on isn't looking too damn straight, if you ask me."

"You don't know the half of it." Kadir looked around and leaned in close. "What do you know about . . . telekinesis?"

"What?"

"You know . . ." Kadir shrugged, inched closer. "The ability to move shit with your mind. Have you ever known anyone who could—"

"KADIR!"

At Abrianna's shout, Kadir and Ghost took off toward the back.

In the cot room, Draya and Abrianna stood in front of a nine-inch TV.

When the guys couldn't see what the emergency was, Kadir asked, "Is everything okay?"

Abrianna shook her head and then pointed at the news broadcast on the screen.

"Federal Judge Katherine J. Sanders will be sworn in tomorrow as the eighteenth chief justice of the United States Supreme Court, enabling President Daniel Walker to put his stamp on the court for decades to come. Sanders's nomination had been slow walked, while the Republican Senate members waited to see whether the new speaker would pursue impeachment of the president. But with Speaker Reynolds's death, the Senate majority leader decided to move ahead with the confirmation."

Abrianna stared transfixed at the image in the corner of the screen. "That's her!"

"That's who?" Kadir asked.

She pointed. "That's the other woman from the hotel. That's Kitty!"

"Judge Katherine Sanders?" he thundered. "*She's* the one you think framed you for murder?"

"Yes! I'd know that face anywhere. It's her!"

"But why?" Kadir asked, puzzled.

"Didn't you hear the reporter?" Draya asked. "That

speaker guy was going to impeach the president. An impeachment meant no confirmation. No Supreme Court."

Ghost slapped a hand across his forehead and whistled. "Holy shit. The same judge who sent you to the clink," he said. "The *new* chief justice of the Supreme Court. Ha! Good luck taking her down."

"We're going to need more than luck," Kadir grumbled, ripping off his fake mustache. "We're going to need a miracle."

Ghost shook his head. "Yo, dawg. That road you are on just got more crooked than a muthafucka."

"No shit," Kadir hissed, staring at Judge Sanders's image on the screen until the telecast cut to a commercial.

Defensive, Abrianna glanced around the eclectic group and read doubt and disbelief. "You guys believe me, don't you? I'm not making it up. She's Kitty—the other woman at the hotel that night."

Draya pressed a hand against Abrianna's shoulder. "I believe you."

"Yeah. I believe you, too," Julian added, curling up only one corner of his lips. His eyes, however, avoided her gaze.

Abrianna's jaw hardened.

Julian explained, "It's just that . . . well, this is *huge*, Bree. The fucking *chief justice* of the Supreme Court? What the fuck are we going to do?"

Abrianna's body slumped. "I have no idea."

"Well. How about that?" Ghost said. "We're all on the same page with our heads up our asses. Great!"

Kadir cut his friend a hard look. "Chill."

"What? I'm stating facts. It's a miracle that every Uncle Sam soldier isn't pouring into this bitch and hauling our asses to jail right now. You're wanted for bombing the damn airport, and your new chick here is wanted for killing the third most powerful man in America. Firing squads were made for terrorists like you two." He held up a hand and added, "I'm just telling you how the media *is* going to spin it."

"And don't forget the dead bitch we left back in the van," Draya reminded them.

Shut up, Abrianna mouthed.

"Come again." Ghost cupped his ear and leaned toward Draya. "Dead body? What dead body?" He looked to Kadir. "What the fuck is she talking about?"

Kadir hedged.

"Mutha—come here! Let me holler at you for a moment." Ghost spun his boy by his shoulder and then shoved him out of the door.

Sighing, Kadir went along. Deep down he knew that he was wrong for springing this situation on Ghost. If the roles had been reversed, he would have gone apeshit.

Ghost hustled Kadir to the bunker's break room and slammed the door. It took another minute to calm down and choose his words carefully. "There is no point in my asking whether you've lost your damn mind because I already know that since you've laid eyes on that suicidal stripper, you've completely checked the fuck out of reality."

"Ghost, calm—"

"Ah, ah, ah." Ghost held up a finger and shook his head. "You've lost any right to tell me to calm down. I'm not the one whose face is plastered on the news as a domestic terrorist."

"Hold up," Kadir interjected. "You're wanted by the federal authorities too for political hacking."

"For *questioning* . . . and for something that they

can't prove *and*, more importantly, my mug shot hasn't debuted on a single wanted poster or news broadcast."

Kadir cocked his head. "Are you jealous?"

"Jealous? Who? Me?" He waved the notion off. "Don't be ridiculous."

Kadir squinted and read the truth in his face.

Ghost swung the conversation back to the matter at hand. "Who is the corpse?"

Kadir sighed.

"Please, please tell me it's not *the* president of the United States."

"Don't be ridiculous," Kadir said.

"Then who?"

"Remember the madam we raced across town to *talk* to?"

"You're shitting me," Ghost said. "She killed her?"

"No. Abrianna didn't kill her," Kadir snapped. "We . . . sort of *kidnapped* her."

"Oh. Well. That makes more sense. What's a little kidnapping every now and then?" Ghost shrugged with a straight face. "What the fuck, man? Snap out it!"

"We didn't have much of a choice since the woman cleared out of her estate. A friend of Abrianna was catering a party for the woman's boyfriend, so her other friend, Draya, created these disguises and we crashed the joint."

"To kidnap the madam?" Ghost clarified, following along.

"Right. Only . . . there was a hiccup."

Ghost crossed his arms. "That tends to happen when committing *federal* crimes."

Kadir glared.

"What happened?" Ghost asked, rolling his hand, wanting to get to the end of the story.

"Bruh, I'm still not sure. This guard showed up when we were loading the body up and I think . . ." Kadir glanced at the closed door and then crossed over to stand in front of it, to make sure that no one entered. He lowered his voice. "I think . . . Abrianna threw this four-hundred-pound guy up against the side of the house—*without* laying a finger on him."

Ghost stared.

"You think I'm crazy, don't you?" Kadir tossed up his hands. "I don't blame you. If I hadn't seen the shit for myself I wouldn't believe it either, but . . . there's no other explanation. I saw what I saw."

"Catering?"

"Yeah. We—"

"Never mind. Finish the story."

"Like I was saying. The guy startled us, and when he approached the van to see for himself what we were doing, Draya slammed the van door into his face and his gun went off."

"So that's how she got shot?"

"Right. But when the gun went off"—Kadir's voice went even lower—"Abrianna screamed and . . . this huge guy *flew* backwards. I mean literally up in the *air* and slammed into the side of the house, knocking him out cold. I've never seen anything like it."

Silence.

Kadir's hands fell to his sides. "You don't believe me."

"Believe what? That your hooker girlfriend out there has super powers? Sure. Of course, I believe you. Why wouldn't I?"

Kadir's gaze leveled on his friend. "I'm not bullshitting you, man."

Ghost evaluated Kadir and then took a deep breath. "Okay."

"Okay? So you believe me?" Kadir checked, surprised.

"I believe that *you* believe what you thought you saw."

Kadir ran that sentence back through his head. "But . . . you don't believe it happened?"

"Is it important that I believe it? Does it change anything?"

Kadir sighed. "I guess not."

A few minutes later, they returned to the cot room where the group waited.

"I'm not crazy," Abrianna Parker insisted.

Ghost folded his meaty arms while his black gaze centered on her. "I've only known you for a few days; I hope you don't take offense but I personally think you're batshit crazy and I don't want anything more to do with this nonsense." His lethal gaze sliced toward Kadir. "Look, bruh. We go *way* back, but this mess right here? I want no part of it."

Kadir squared his shoulders at the curt tone. Emotions warred across his face and, despite his own visible doubt, he defended Abrianna. "Why don't we hear her out?"

"Hear her out? She just said that the new chief justice of the Supreme Court—and your mortal enemy, I may add—*murdered* the House speaker of the U.S. Congress, the second man in line to the presidency. Do you know how fucking *crazy* that shit sounds?"

"No crazier than half the conspiracy theories that you've entertained over the years. All of which has you huddled down here in this underground bunker, hiding from the feds in the first place. Is what she saying really that hard to believe?"

Ghost opened his mouth but words never tumbled out.

Kadir arched a brow and cocked his head.

Ghost closed his mouth and then speared Abrianna with a look. "What happened to the madam? Wasn't she supposedly behind the conspiracy theory when y'all left here the last time? Who is it going to be next? The president?"

"Hey!" Kadir shoved Ghost, sending him careening into the nearest wall.

"Yo, dude!"

"Watch it," Kadir warned.

Julian crowded behind Kadir, ready to tag into the fight.

Tension layered the room while everyone else held their breaths.

Ghost backed down. "All right, man. My bad." He clamped his mouth shut.

Kadir glanced back over at Abrianna. "Please. Continue."

Abrianna battled her pride to get the rest of her story out. "Look, you guys already know the rest. It was my first night as an escort working for Madam Nevaeh. That woman showed up and introduced herself as Kitty. My john was happy when she arrived. They knew each other. We . . . partied . . . and when I woke up my client was missing part of his head and that Kitty bitch was nowhere to be found. I got out of there, but then gunmen showed up at my apartment. My best friend Shawn, who's still laid up in the hospital right now, took a hit, but I kept running until I jumped into your car, Kadir."

"Where they shot up my car and I brought you here the last time," Kadir finished the story for her.

"Right." She huffed. "Now. What are we going to do?"

Everyone's eyeballs ping-ponged around the room again. Clearly, none of them had a clue to what to do next.

Ghost sighed.

"Great," Ghost moaned.

Their gazes shifted around the room again.

Roger, one of Ghost's hackers, cleared his throat and drew everyone's attention.

Ghost's brows climbed to the center of his forehead. "You got something to say? Speak up."

Nervous, Roger cleared his throat. "Well . . . I take it that the media received the image of Abrianna from the Hay-Adams Hotel security surveillance."

Ghost shrugged. "Yeah, and?"

"Then Kitty, er, Judge Sanders should be on surveillance, too," Abrianna said, grinning.

Roger smiled. "Exactly."

Hope, the last emotion in Pandora's box, filled the room.

"But how are we going to get our hands on their surveillance footage?" Draya asked.

Kadir's handsome grin stretched. "How else? We *hack*."

However, hacking the luxury hotel turned out to be a more difficult job. Ghost and Kadir ascertained that it would require physical access to the hotel's security server.

"How are we going to manage to do that?" Abrianna asked.

"My guess is that someone is going to have to pose as an employee and break into their security department. Once in there, upload a custom malware to give us access to their digital files."

"That sounds simple, which means it's anything but," Abrianna said.

Ghost smiled. "Smart girl. I'd imagine posing as an employee would be difficult. Something as small staffed as a hotel, everyone would know everybody. Don't you think?"

"Well, it's a pretty big hotel with shops and restaurants—but getting near security . . ." Abrianna shook her head.

"Right."

Julian spoke up. "What if someone was applying for a job?" He had everyone's attention and continued, "I worked security once at a hotel, and our security department was near the human resources office. New hires passed by our department every day."

Ghost and Kadir smiled. "You're hired."

Julian blinked. "Me?"

"Yep. You're not on anybody's radar. And you have the expertise to get in the door." Kadir slapped Julian on the back. "First thing tomorrow you're applying for a job."

Julian looked sick.

3

The morgue

Zeke stood over Madam Nevaeh's dead body lying on a cold slab in the city's morgue. Rage boiled inside of him while he ground his back molars almost to dust. He didn't believe for a second that Tanya a.k.a. Madam Nevaeh carjacked the caterer's van and plowed through a pair of police cars during a shoot-out. That story didn't make sense. But one thing was for sure, he was going to get to the bottom of it.

"Sir? Is it her?" the morgue's technician asked.

Zeke gave a single nod and then watched as Tanya's beautiful face was covered up with a single white sheet. He lingered an extra second, making sure that his emotions were suppressed deep into his gut before sliding on his shades and exiting the morgue. In the hallway, his new pair of henchmen, Defoe and Spider, fell in step behind him while he marched out into the night and toward a waiting black Escalade.

"Where to next, boss?" the driver asked.

"Home."

"You got it, boss."

The doors slammed shut after everyone had piled inside. In the next second, they pulled away from the curb. Stone buildings, one after another, zipped past his line of vision without him really seeing them. He had one hell of a mess to clean up after last night's raid. No doubt that overreaching bullshit had scared many of his friends on K Street and the military complex from wanting to do business with him. He had to figure out some way to set it right. Then there was Castillo's smug ass. He'd long thought that police bitch was out of his hair, but clearly her pillow talk with police chief Holder meant that she would forever be a pain in his side. Plus, Tanya had told him about her showing up at her crib, asking a lot of questions about Abrianna Parker.

He sighed. Abrianna was another loose string floating in the wind that Zeke had to deal with. He had already taken care of her ex-boyfriend Moses. Really, putting a bullet in that shady muthafucka's head was doing them both a favor. It was because of Moses that Zeke had been able to con Abrianna into thinking that she was in debt to him for eighty grand. She had more than that saved in a safe deposit box at the bank, but her shady-ass boyfriend stole that shit from her, too. Of course, now she didn't know that Zeke had her money. Instead Zeke farmed her out to work off the debt with Madam Nevaeh.

That shit was a big mistake. On the first night on the job, the bitch killed her client. It wasn't just any client, either. He was the third most powerful man in D.C. To clear up the mess before she could lead the authorities back to his and Tanya's doorstep, he sent his goons

Roach and Gunner to her apartment to wipe her out. They critically wounded her friend but somehow Abrianna escaped and linked up with some terrorist muthafucka who blew up the goddamn airport.

Now Nevaeh was dead.

Shit. Shit. Shit. And more shit.

Arriving back at his estate, he was disgusted at the sight of the night's abandoned party. It was one more damn thing on his damn plate.

Zeke stormed through the front door and marched straight to his study. There, he slammed the door and whipped off his shades and peeled off his jacket. After tossing them onto a chair, he loosened the top buttons of his shirt and paced for a good five minutes, trying to think about what his next move should be.

One thing he wasn't worried about was the trafficking charges. Those would disappear out of the system with a single phone call. At least he was pretty sure about that. Should he get on the phone and start an apology tour or . . . his gaze zoomed to the hidden door on the other side of the room. He strolled over and pressed a panel that made a portion of the wall slide open. Inside was a wall of security monitors that covered every inch of his house. He took a seat and pulled up the recorded images from last night. With so many people, he didn't know what exactly he should focus on first. He settled on going back to the time he'd made his toast from the second-floor balcony. From there, he followed himself out into the backyard, where he'd last seen Tanya. Her displeasure with him was written on her face and in her body language. He couldn't hear her words but he remembered them by heart.

"Why the long face, Tanya? Aren't you having a good time?"

She rolled her eyes, but kept her plastic smile firmly in place.

He chuckled. "C'mon. It's my birthday. You're supposed to be nice to me."

His reasoning failed to move her.

"So it doesn't matter to you that after tonight I'll be one step closer to making all of our dreams come true? C'mon. Smile. Who wants to be a king without a queen?"

Smirking, Madam Nevaeh turned around in his arms and faced him. "You're always promising me the world."

"Don't forget the moon and the stars," he added.

Her smile strained. "And yet you can't manage to find and kill one measly stripper."

"Here we go again." Zeke sighed. Nevaeh had finally burst his sunny bubble. "How many times do I have to tell you that the situation is being handled?"

"Handled how?" she snapped. "You don't even know where that situation is right now. She may be in a federal interrogation room running her fucking mouth about our whole operation."

"Don't be ridiculous," he chided. "Abrianna Parker is nothing but a junkie street rat with no credibility. She can't prove anything because she doesn't know anything. And there's nothing concrete linking her to us, not even a money trail. We've never paid her a dime. She was just a woman who crashed a masquerade party and ended up killing a guest. I have eyes and ears everywhere. If and when she pops up, I'll cut her fucking head off."

"You're wrong," she said. "You forgot about her friend who came out to the house with her that day. Shawn."

"He's not a problem."

"For you! He's still alive and making threats," she said, heated.

Zeke jerked her closer. *"Lower your goddamn voice."*

"Let me go." She wrestled but failed to get away.

"If the kid had anything, he would have made a move already. But I'll take care of him, too. Now chill the fuck out, you're fucking up my vibe. We're supposed to be having a good time."

"How about you just have a good time without me?" Nevaeh wrenched herself free. *"And don't you ever manhandle me like that again. I'm not your property. We're partners. Business partners. Remember that."*

"Oh? Only business partners now, huh? It's that serious?"

"Damn right. At least until you learn not to break promises." She marched off.

Zeke watched her go, shaking his head. *"If I didn't love that old broad . . ."*

Zeke watched Tanya march away and chose the cameras that followed her back into the house. He noticed two servers from the party fall in line behind her and trail her through the house.

"What the fuck?"

Tanya headed up the stairs and went into the bathroom. The servers, one a dude, went in behind her. He realized then that there were indeed a couple of places he didn't have cameras. The bathrooms were among them. A minute later, two more waiters entered the bathroom.

Zeke sped up the tape to when everyone filed out, but this time lugging a large nylon bag that was big enough to carry a body. "Holy shit." He stopped the tape and zoomed in. *Who are these muthafuckas?* He didn't recognize any of them from his long list of ene-mies. Unfreezing the video, he watched this small group descend back through the crowd without anyone paying attention to what they were carrying.

He punched up one camera after another, following them all the way out to La Plume's catering van. One of his guys came on the scene. What unfolded next had Zeke hitting the replay button a couple of times. One server was shot, and somebody threw Tiny's big ass against the side of the house. But other than the chick who banged his head with the van's door, no one had laid a hand on Tiny. When Zeke gave up trying to fig-ure out that puzzle, he resumed the rest of the tape and saw that one server jumped back out of the van to at-tend the one woman who was shot. He questioned whether that server was really a man. Again, he froze the tape and zoomed in. *There is something familiar about that profile.* He sat there studying the images for long time, zooming in and out—then a name popped in his head.

"I'll be damned." A corner of his lips hitched up. "Hello, Abrianna Parker."

4

Above ground, Ghost stashed his uninvited guests at a warehouse apartment that belonged to his play cousin who allowed him to use it from time to time. The bunker was too small for the expanding band of misfits. The sleeping arrangements were that Draya and Julian slept in the master bedroom, Kadir and Abrianna took the guest room, and Ghost bitched in his sleep on the couch.

For the longest time, Abrianna and Kadir stared up at the ceiling and listened to each other's breathing. The intimacy they'd shared twenty-four hours ago was gone, replaced by a strained tension. Abrianna didn't want to admit it, but it hurt. It shouldn't. After all, they didn't know each other. They were strangers thrown together under extreme and dangerous circumstances. The one night they'd slept together didn't mean anything, she reasoned. It was sex. She knew better than to attach emotions to anything—to anyone.

Abrianna piled bricks around her heart but couldn't do anything about the tears soaking her pillow.

Kadir stretched his hand across the gulf between them, startling her when his fingertips brushed her arm.

She rolled her head toward him. Her gaze caressed his lean and solid frame before meeting his stare that twinkled in the dark.

"It's going to be all right," he whispered.

She doubted that, but said nothing. Nothing in her life had ever been *all right.*

He moved closer.

Abrianna watched him, willing herself not to meet him halfway. However, his body heat and fresh Irish Spring scent tripped her up. She hated herself for anticipating a kiss, hated her skin tingling in the wake of his touch.

"Who are you?" he whispered, brushing her hair back. "What are you?"

Abrianna didn't understand the question, and he didn't ask again. Instead his head tipped forward, and she lifted her chin. Their lips met for a sweet, decadent kiss that sent her mind soaring into the stratosphere. He crushed her body against his, transforming their heat into an inferno. All she had to do was to keep her emotions out of it, but as Kadir kissed and nibbled his way across and then down her body, emotions were *all* she felt. Every one of them jumbled together in a traffic jam close to her heart. She didn't want it to end. She would die if it ended.

Tenderly, Kadir entered her and rocked his hips at a slow, steady pace that sent ripples of pleasure throughout her body. As she neared climax, she wrapped her long legs around his fit waist and locked her ankles below his thrusting ass. Kadir pinned her hands above her head and then shifted his hips into overdrive. For the next hour, they flipped each other over into a dozen positions. By the time they collapsed, the sheets were shellacked against their sweat-slick bodies, and they were too tired to do any talking.

Hours later, Abrianna lay in bed with at least a gallon of sweat still pouring off her body. She struggled to remain still as Kadir slept inches away from her. He had no idea about her private hell, her raging addiction. For the past few days she'd ignored the beast inside. She had no choice. Now, her body demanded its fix, threatening to kill her to get it.

Head ringing, she rolled onto her side and even eased one leg out from under the covers, but then stopped.

No. Tough it out.

She sucked in a breath and willed herself to think of something else—anything else. She couldn't. It was hard to think when a jackhammer pounded at the back of her head.

It'll just take a few minutes go get a fix. No one will notice me slipping out of the apartment to find a corner boy. The oscillating fan above the bed sent a breeze that chilled the rivulets of sweat rolling off her body. When she turned her head toward the closed window, her wet hair remained glued against her face. *A few minutes.* She swallowed to produce moisture for her dry mouth, but failed. At last it all became too much. Abrianna eased her other leg out from beneath the sheets and climbed out of bed. Her absent weight caused the mattress's springs to shift.

Kadir groaned and rolled over.

Abrianna froze and trapped her breath in her chest.

Still half asleep, Kadir adjusted the pillow and then drifted back off.

Abrianna slipped on her panties and then grabbed the rest of her clothes by the door and slipped out of the bedroom. She sprinted to the bathroom down the hall and dressed. She couldn't move fast enough. Her hands shook, her head ached, and the knots in her stomach tightened until they felt like rocks.

Exiting the bathroom, the hinges squeaked loud enough to wake the dead. At least that's what it sounded like to her ears. Even the flooring conspired against her, creaking as she inched down the hallway. She needed money, but where could she get some? The last thing she wanted was to rummage through Ghost's shit. The muthafucka already didn't trust her. Stealing from him wouldn't help the situation. Minutes later, she found herself easing into the master bedroom where Draya and Julian slept. Draya was in the bed, and Julian was knocked out in a chaise near the window.

"Bree?" Draya whispered, propping herself up against a pile of pillows. "What are you doing in here?"

Abrianna eased farther into the room. "Heeey. How are you feeling?"

"I was *shot*. How in the hell do you think I feel?" Draya deadpanned. "You got me out here playing cops and robbers."

Abrianna's shoulders drooped. "Really? You're already playing the guilt card?"

"Yeah. So you better get used to it." Draya smiled.

Abrianna perched on the edge of the bed. "Real talk. You good?"

"Yeah, girl. It's not like my ass hasn't been shot before. Remember that time Shawn had the dumb idea of hitting Big Boi's trap house back in the day?"

Abrianna chuckled. D.C. street kids since they were fourteen, they'd been through a lot of serious shit. Robbing, dealing, and sometimes turning tricks to survive had created an unbreakable bond.

"Hey, look." Abrianna swiped some sweat from her forehead. "You wouldn't happen to be holding right now, would you? Or have some money?"

Draya studied her, noting how she couldn't keep still. "Your head?"

"Yeah. It's pretty bad."

Draya stared.

"Please," Abrianna added. "Don't make me beg."

Draya sighed and then crammed her hand down her pants pocket and pulled put a couple of packets.

Abrianna almost kissed her, but when she went to grab the coke, Draya placed a hand over it.

"Shawn would kill me if he ever found out I gave you this."

"Who the hell is going to tell him?"

Draya evaluated her. "When this is all over, you have to promise me that you'll get help."

"You got it." Abrianna made a grab for the drugs, but again Draya refused to remove her hand.

"I mean it, Bree. None of that lip service you're always giving Shawn. I'm talking about real doctors. The whole nine yards."

"Are you kidding me right now?" Abrianna said.

"Fine. Go and find your own damn drugs." Draya started to shove the packets back into her pocket.

Abrianna panicked. "Wait. All right. All right. I'll go."

"Promise me."

"I promise. Damn."

Draya gave her the packets. "You better make it last. It's all I got."

"Right. Got it." Abrianna sprung to her feet and rushed back toward the door.

"You're welcome," Draya hissed after her.

Julian stirred, but didn't wake up.

Abrianna made a beeline back to the hall bathroom and locked the door. She wiped down the bathroom counter while struggling to control her trembling hands. Next, she dumped and divided the drug into crude white lines. "Hurry, hurry, hurry," she mumbled under her breath.

The buzzing in her head spread toward her frontal lobe, causing her eyes to twitch.

The bathroom's doorknob twisted, and then a rap sounded on the locked door.

"Just a minute," she shouted and then bent over the counter and vacuumed a line into each nostril. The coke hit like a bolt of lightning. She gasped, but once the burn in her nose and the pain in her head vanished, euphoria spread throughout her body.

The shame of being a junkie would come later, but for right now, she needed this hit. Her mind tumbled over the madness she'd been through in the past week. The fight with her ex, Moses, the stolen drugs from their apartment, the seventy-two hours the Teflon Don gave her to pay for the lost bricks of pink coke—only to learn after that Moses had stolen her life savings from her bank. When she couldn't pay the Don, she was forced into Madam Nevaeh's escort service, where her bad luck continued.

Knock. Knock.

"Bree, are you all right in there?" Kadir asked through the door.

Abrianna slammed back to reality.

"Bree?"

"Yeah. I'm coming." Abrianna shoved the empty packet into her pocket and then washed up at the sink. "It's all yours," she said, exiting the bathroom grinning.

Kadir stared after her until she disappeared back into their bedroom.

With her head still floating on a cloud, Abrianna stripped out of her clothes and climbed back into bed. By the time Kadir returned to the room, she was fast asleep.

5

"In today's news, the FBI and Homeland Security remain on high alert for wanted terrorist suspects Abrianna Parker and Kadir Kahlifa." A still image from the hotel's security cameras of a disheveled Abrianna Parker, racing away from the scene of the crime in a ball gown and chinchilla coat, was posted over the TV journalist's shoulder. *"Ms. Parker is believed to be with a recently paroled federal prisoner, Kadir Kahlifa, who is also wanted for questioning in the Reagan Airport bombing."*

An old federal booking photo of Kadir popped up next to the freeze-frame of Abrianna's face. *"The two suspects were also involved in a high-speed gun chase near the Washington Highland area not long after the bombing. The chase was captured on camera and has since gone viral on social media. Many on Capitol Hill have speculated that the two suspects may be a part of a homegrown terrorist cell and warn that the country may see a surge of attacks in the coming days. Ms. Parker and Mr. Kahlifa are considered armed and dangerous. If anyone should see either of these two in-dividuals, the authorities urge you to contact the number seen at the bottom of your screen.*"

"Shut it off," Dr. Charles Zacher grumbled, snatching off his glasses and rubbing at his tired eyes.

His assistant, Ned, raced over to the television suspended in the corner of Dr. Z's office and powered it off. He spun back around, eager to respond to his boss's next command, but ended up waiting.

Dr. Z's pain went from his eyes to his temples. Clearly, he was about to have a shit-storm of a day after enduring a shitty night behind bars. He still couldn't believe he'd been swept up in a damn drug raid while hobnobbing with the nation's political and military elite. Lobbying was a part of his job as research and development director at T4S, a necessary evil to keep government security contracts flowing its way. But a raid? The whole thing was ridiculous, and it had taken forever for him to be processed and released. *Him.* A man of his stature and reputation. He was outraged and humiliated.

Once the silence had grown too long, Ned asked, "Would you like some coffee, sir?"

"As a matter of fact, I would," Dr. Z answered, anxious for the young man to get out of his sight so he could string two cohesive thoughts together.

"You got it, sir." Ned jetted out.

Dr. Z dropped his weight into his leather chair, his racing thoughts refusing to stop. He tossed his glasses onto his desk, and then his gaze wandered back to the blank screen.

The events of the past week hadn't been a part of his calculations. There was no way to calculate that a test subject would pitch herself off the roof of the St. Elizabeth Hospital and another one would go on the run for murder.

Zacher's professional neck was stretched beneath a corporate guillotine with the blade descending fast. His mind tumbled back through all the things he should have done. For example, he shouldn't have given Dr. Craig Avery free rein with those experiments, especially at the expense of such a high body count. However, the arms race to develop the super soldier was top priority for the Pentagon and every military force around the globe, and T4S was leaps and bounds ahead of their closest competitors. It was Dr. Z's job to make sure that it stayed that way.

Uncle Sam turned to private security firms like T4S to color outside the lines of wartime laws and international treaties—also to avoid political culpabilities and public backlash when it came time to put more troops into hostile territories. The vision of an army of elite super soldiers had been the well-worn plot of many science fiction books and movies for decades. Dr. Avery brought it closer to reality than anyone had ever dared to hope. The government salivated at the real possibility of having soldiers who were stronger than the average man or woman, ones who wouldn't rely on expensive robotics that blew holes into budgets or were vulnerable to hacks and wear and tear.

Unfortunately, Dr. Avery's methods had turned unconventional and then downright insane. Sure, the man had no problem developing serums that produced enhanced strength, but he was determined to go after the golden goose: psychokinetics. Avery believed that the mind could influence a physical system without physical interaction.

Dr. Zacher had had his doubts but, over time, he became a believer. However, there were hiccups. The people above Zacher's pay grade terminated Avery when test subjects kept dying. However, Zacher encouraged and aided Avery in continuing his experiments off the books and off the grid. Their new problem was acquiring new test subjects. Avery had solved the problem by snatching teenagers off the street. The kind of teenagers who wouldn't be missed when they disappeared.

Avery's subjects continued to die excruciating deaths and at an accelerated rate during his home experiments—all except three teenage girls, now two. Turned out there were people searching for the missing girls, including a determined police lieutenant, Gizella Castillo. She and her police team had rescued the girl's from Avery's basement. Avery was killed in the process.

For a few years, Zacher had believed Avery died a failure, until Shalisa Young killed her mother. In the trial, the young woman pleaded not guilty and insisted that she'd never laid a hand on her mother, but only *thought* about stabbing her mother. She claimed that she was shocked when a knife from the kitchen's butcher block flew across the room with deadly accuracy. The court found Shalisa Young insane, and she was transferred to St. Elizabeth Hospital, a federal mental institution, where Zacher and his new team studied and experimented on the girl, until she leaped off the roof.

Another one of Avery's survivors, or test subjects, Tomi Lehane now worked as a reporter for the *Washington Post*. Zacher kept an eye on her, but he hadn't been able to confirm any abnormalities. The only thing that had blipped on his radar was a 911 call from Lehane's live-in boyfriend a few years ago. Apparently, he thought Ms. Lehane had died in her sleep, only to wake once the paramedics arrived to haul off the body. Zacher didn't know what that was about, but it freaked the boyfriend out enough to move out.

The last test subject, Abrianna Parker, was someone Dr. Zacher was well familiar with, and was in frequent contact with, at least he was until recently. Bree, as her friends called her, believed him to be a kind, old, homeless man named Charlie that she'd met years ago in Stanton Park. She had no clue about his part in her abduction or that he monitored her abilities without her knowledge. She hadn't noticed the times he had spoken to her telepathically. The first time he thought of a question and she answered threw him for a loop. She didn't do it all the time, but most.

The buzzing in Dr. Zacher's head persisted. He opened his top desk drawer and pulled out a vial and syringe. Quickly, he moved to fill the syringe with a T4S experimental drug, but by the time he placed the needle into a well-used vein in his left arm, the buzzing was deafening. His hands trembled. The first stab, the vein rolled. Hissing, he tried again. The moment the drug hit his bloodstream, the buzzing vanished and the throbbing between his eyes ceased.

"Here you go, sir," Ned announced, smiling with a steaming cup of coffee. "Just like you like it: black, no sugar." He set the cup down in front of Zacher.

"Thanks," the doctor grumbled, tossing the syringe and empty vial into the wastebasket. As he rolled his sleeve back down, the phone trilled from the corner of his desk. He read the caller ID, and a knot of nerves sank to his gut.

Ned cleared his throat. "Would you like for me to get that for you, sir?"

Dr. Z speared him with a look before he snatched up the hand unit. "Spalding, you're in the office early," he greeted, injecting a long, well-rehearsed pleasantness into his voice.

Pierce Spalding, president of T4S, wasted no time laying in to the doctor. "Your and Dr. Avery's screw-up is still all over the news this morning."

"Yes, sir. I caught a snippet a few minutes ago," Dr. Z admitted.

"I was told that Avery's freak science experiments would never come back to bite us in the ass."

"Yes, sir. You were."

"Is your word no good?" Spalding asked.

"Yes, sir. I mean, no. Uh . . ." Zacher shook his head. "This is a minor blip. I promise you. Abrianna Parker will not be a problem."

A long pause expanded over the line, making Zacher uncomfortable. He tightened his grip on the hand unit.

"I like you, Zacher." Spalding shifted the subject. "I've always spoken highly of you. I believe in your vision. That's the only reason why I've followed you and Dr. Avery down this rabbit hole for better or worse. But if we have a test subject running AWOL, then—"

"That's not the case, Pierce. I'm on top of this."

Silence.

Spalding had a good bullshit detector, and Zacher was certain that his boss didn't believe a damn thing that he'd said. It was more likely that Spalding was evaluating how much rope to allot Zacher to hang himself.

"All right, Charlie," Spalding said. "I'll let you handle this, but if I get the slightest hint that Ms. Parker is about to blow up in our faces, I'll take care of her myself. Am I making myself clear?"

Zacher nodded. "Yes, sir. I understand."

"Good. And try not to get busted in another drug

raid while you're at it. I have better things to do with my time than erasing police records."

"Yes—"

Click.

"Sir?"

Dial tone.

Sighing, Dr. Z returned the handset back to its cradle.

Ned hovered at the door, waiting for orders. "Is everything all right, sir?"

"What do you think?" he asked without looking up. Zacher still couldn't gather his thoughts for a cohesive plan.

"Sir, your nose is bleeding."

"What?"

"Your nose." Ned pointed.

The doctor touched under his nose and, sure enough, it was bleeding. From the other corner of his desk, Zacher snatched two Kleenexes from a box and dabbed under his nose. "How about now?"

"Good, sir." Ned gave him two thumbs up.

"Is there anything else I can help you with?" Ned asked.

"Yeah." Zacher swiveled his chair and faced Ned. "Find Abrianna Parker before Spalding sends out a hit squad . . . if he hasn't done it already."

6

Gizella Castillo knew better than to fuck police chief Dennis Holder, but after witnessing the boys in blue bringing down Zeke "Teflon Don" Jeffreys, her emotions got the best of her. It was more than a year since they'd slept together, and the sex was mind-blowing. But by morning, regret had settled in her chest, and she was at a loss about how to disentangle her emotions again.

While lying in bed with Dennis's heavy arm draped across her body, she watched sunlight pry through the blinds and wondered how much longer she would have to stay like that. She hated cuddling. It wasn't her thing. It made her hot and uncomfortable.

Riiiinng.

Dennis groaned and then stretched for the phone. "Yeah?"

Thankful for the diversion, Castillo wormed from underneath him and got up.

"Hey, where are you going?" he whispered.

She shook her head and strolled naked to the adjoining bathroom.

"What?" Holder barked into the phone. "Say that shit again."

Gizella closed the door on his conversation and marched across the cold linoleum to the even colder porcelain throne to empty her bladder. The whole time, she cursed herself for staying the night. It would have been fine if Dennis could accept it for what it was: sex. But somehow Dennis had convinced himself that he was in love with her, and he would view last night as a sign of her succumbing to him and his still standing proposal.

She wasn't. *"Are you sure?"*

She flushed and then went over to turn on the shower. A minute later, Dennis barged in uninvited.

"Hey," she snapped when the cool air hit her.

"Hey, yourself." He reached around her. "You're going to have to share the water this morning. I got to get down to the precinct. They cut Jeffreys loose."

Gizella dropped the bottle of body wash. "What?"

Dennis knelt and retrieved the bottle. "Yep. He wasn't even arraigned."

"You're shitting me."

"Nope."

"Why?"

"That's why I got to get down there and find out." He rushed to lather up.

"I'm coming with you."

Dennis opened his mouth to argue back, but he saw in her eyes that it would be useless. After a seven-minute dance, trying to share the single showerhead, they left Dennis's place. However, by the time they got downtown, it was too late. The Teflon Don had lived

up to his name and had been released without so much
as a mug shot taken of him.

————⤙•⤚————

"I need my head examined," Kadir told his reflection in the bathroom's mirror. For the second time, he
was flushing his life down the toilet. *And for what? A
woman?*

Of course, Abrianna Parker was no ordinary woman.
She was, hands down, one of the most gorgeous natural
beauties that he'd ever laid eyes on. The first time he'd
ever seen her, she was stripping at the Stallion's Gentlemen's Club. The vision of her long legs and dangerous
curves swirling around that golden pole remained on
instant replay in his mind.

As he now stared at his reflection in the bathroom
mirror, he cut the bullshit and leveled with himself. He
had lost his mind, allowing himself to get caught up
with the sexy stripper-slash-part-time-female-escort's
fugitive madness, despite having his own FBI-slash–
Homeland Security issues. As his bad luck would have
it, one of his last Uber fares had been a pair of suicide
bomber brothers who blew up the Reagan Airport. The
airport security cameras captured his image when he
helped the men unload their luggage. Unfortunately,
Kadir being an American Muslim and ex-felon shot
him to the top of the Most Wanted list as a suspected
terrorist. He would have turned himself in to clear up
the misunderstanding, had Abrianna not dove into the
backseat of his car while a pair of psychotic assholes
were spraying bullets. Abrianna took a solid hit to her
shoulder and for a couple of days he feared that she
wasn't going to pull through. Praise Allah, she did.

The right thing to have done was to turn themselves

in to the authorities and then work to clear their names, but neither trusted nor believed in the justice system. Kadir, fresh off a six-year bid for political hacktivism, swore that he was going to keep his nose clean, especially with FBI agent Quincy Bell on his ass, hell-bent on putting Kadir back behind bars. Even if Kadir could clear his name in the airport bombing, he was now actively aiding and abetting a wanted woman. He would be subjected to the same time for murder as the actual perpetrator.

Now he had these new claims about Judge Sanders to deal with? Was he sure the seductress was innocent, or was his dick doing all the thinking lately?

"You need your head examined," he repeated. Kadir knew Judge Katherine Sanders too well. She was the ball-busting, no-nonsense judge who had sentenced him to seventy-two months behind bars. No matter how hard he tried, he could not imagine the pale and almost handsome-looking woman slinking around in five-star hotels, performing threesomes with members of Congress.

The idea was crazy.

Never put anything past anyone. Ever.

But wouldn't that include Abrianna Parker, too? *Can I trust her?*

After seeing that big security guard slam up against the side of that house, common sense should have had him racing for the door—but he couldn't have seen that, could he?

Maybe Draya had hit the guard with the van door harder than he thought. Maybe the guard was reeling back as he fired the gun. That made more sense, didn't it?

Kadir turned on the faucet, scooped up water, and splashed his face, but the cold failed to jolt sense into him. After drying his face, he left the bathroom and re-

turned to the bedroom he and Abrianna shared. However, when he entered, she jumped nearly ten feet and
spun around, putting her hands behind her back.

"What are you doing?"

"What? Nothing."

While the lie hung in the air, Kadir's eyes narrowed.
"What's behind your back?"

"Nothing," Abrianna lied again.

Kadir stormed forward. "What's in your hands?"

Abrianna backed against the wall.

He attempted to reach around her.

"I said nothing." She twisted to block his hands.

But Kadir had speed and latched onto one of her
wrists and jerked it forward.

An empty packet fell at his feet.

Kadir stared. "What the fuck?" He knelt and picked
it up.

"It's not a big deal," Abrianna explained.

Hurt and disappointment stabbed him in his back.
"Not a big deal?" he questioned. "Only a *junkie* would
say that."

She flinched. "Fuck you! I don't owe you an explanation. If I need to take something to . . . to settle my
nerves, then that's my business."

"Your business? Look around. For the moment your
business is *my* business, especially when it plays into
your credibility in accusing a Supreme Court judge of
murder."

"Fuck you! One thing doesn't have anything to do
with the other!"

"You can't honestly believe that."

"I told you the truth!"

"Truth?" he challenged. "Before the truth was that
Madam Nevaeh was behind all of this."

"I never said that Madam Nevaeh was in that hotel

room—only that I believed that she set me up to take the fall—which is *still* a possibility."

"So now the judge is chummy with a D.C. madam?" He stepped back, shaking his head. "This is like listening to Ghost tell one of his long-ass conspiracy theories when the truth is usually simple and staring you in the face."

Abrianna processed his words—twice. "Are you saying that you think *I* killed him?"

"C'mon, Bree. You said yourself that you blacked out! Isn't it *possible* that during your blackout you could've done it? I mean, why the hell not? You can throw a four-hundred-pound man across a yard. How hard could it be to pull a simple trigger?"

"What?"

"C'mon. I'm not fucking blind. That guard who shot Draya practically flew in the air."

Abrianna looked lost.

"Fine." He threw up his hands. "I'm imagining things—but you can't say that I'm wrong. You *could* have done it, couldn't you?"

The word *no* sat on her tongue, but she couldn't spit it out.

"See?" He waved a finger in her face. "You can't say it."

Abrianna crossed her arms.

"I'm out here risking my *life*—my friends' lives—for someone who, Ghost keeps reminding my dumb ass, I barely know."

"Oh. Well, let me help you out. I'll leave." She bolted around him and grabbed her clothes.

Kadir huffed. "That's not . . . where are you going?"

"Why the fuck do you care? All that matters is that your neck is no longer on the line." Abrianna crammed one leg after the other into her jeans and then snatched them up over her curves.

"Your leaving changes nothing. The genie is out of the bottle."

"Yeah? Well, I can take care of the rest from here."

"Oh, really? How? By getting more of your friends shot?"

"You don't give a damn about my friends. At least I can count on them to have my back." She jammed on her Timberlands. All that mattered was that she got out of this room before she suffocated. She'd be damned if she had to explain herself to this man. He was right about *one* thing. He *didn't* know her. He didn't know what she dealt with on a daily basis. Fuck him and the horse he rode on into her life. She didn't need a knight in shining armor to save her.

After lacing up her boots, she sprung up from the bed and stormed toward the door. "Fuck you. I'm out of here." She opened the door an inch before Kadir caught up and slammed it shut.

"You're not going anywhere. Calm the hell down."

Abrianna spun and shoved him. "Fuck you!"

Kadir flew backward and slammed into the wall, knocking out a chunk of plaster. "The hell?" He stared as if she'd sprouted a second head.

"I said that I didn't need your help," she seethed.

Kadir pushed away from the wall, his back aching. "Yeah? How long do you think you're going to make it out there with the entire federal government searching for you?"

"That's none of your concern."

"Stop saying that! It *is* my concern. Whether you like it or not, I'm involved now. I don't give a shit that you're pissed off because I'm asking you *real* questions." He rotated his throbbing shoulders. "Damn. You're strong."

Knock. Knock. Knock.

"What is it?" they barked.

"Is everything okay in there?" Ghost asked.

Kadir lifted a brow at Abrianna.

"Yeah. Everything is fine," she answered.

"Are you sure?" Draya double-checked.

Abrianna knew that they were still clustered behind the closed door. She exhaled and said more calmly, "I'm sure. We'll be right out."

Silence.

"I mean it guys. Everything is cool. Give us a few minutes."

"Okay," Draya said.

She heard them walk away and forced herself to meet Kadir's gaze. "Look. I can't prove I'm telling you the truth. And yes . . . I took drugs that night. I even know that I have a problem." She took a deep breath. "But believe me when I say that I *need* them to function. I've been through a lot of shit. And . . . I'm gonna get help—soon. But I'm not lying about that judge. She *was* there at the hotel. Somehow, I have to prove it. It's the only way that I'm going to get my life back. And . . . I'm going to need your help to do it."

7

Office of the Washington Post

Hunkered down at her desk, reporter Tomi Lehane had been going back and forth with the Department of Motor Vehicles for nearly an hour, feeling her patience wind to an end. "There's got to be a record of the license plate. I know that I copied it down right. Do you have another database for government plates?" She huffed and rolled her eyes as the woman on the other end of the line told her again how sorry she was that there was no record for the plate number that Tomi had given her. "All right. Thanks for your help." She dropped the handset back into its cradle and swore under her breath.

For the next few minutes, she told herself that she had made a mistake and she didn't remember the plate number correctly. The problem was that Tomi hadn't forgotten a name or number in almost seven years. Physical objects she often misplaced, but facts, figures, and faces? No. There was no way that she would ever forget the African-American man who'd approached her outside a news studio in a black Mercedes . . .

"Ms. Lehane?" the man inquired from the car.

She'd frowned, but kept walking.

"Ms. Lehane, I know that this is rather odd, but I was wondering if I could have a few minutes of your time?"

"For what?" she asked, marching.

"Just to talk."

"Talk about what?"

"Well . . . it's sort of a personal nature. It's not an appropriate topic of conversation to be shouting out of the window."

She stopped and so did the car. "I don't get into strange cars with men I don't know. Tell me what you want or get lost."

The man's smile widened while he spoke inside of her head. "I want to talk to you about the powers I believe that you and Abrianna Parker have developed over the past six years."

She stared at him, heart racing. His mouth hadn't moved, but she heard him clearly. "Well?" *she asked, pretending not to have heard him.* "Aren't you going to tell me what you want?"

The man's cocky smile dropped. "Can you not hear me?" *he tried again.*

"Look, buddy. I don't have all day."

"No. Of course not," he said aloud, his frown deepening. "There must've been some sort of mistake. I apologize for the inconvenience."

The window rolled up and the Mercedes pulled away.

A shiver went down Tomi's spine at the memory of

the strange encounter. On a notepad, she'd sketched the man's face from memory. All that was missing was a name. Who was this man, and how was he able to talk inside of her head like that? How did he know about her powers? *Powers.* She was uncomfortable with the word. It wasn't like she was some Marvel or DC comic superhero. She could do a few odd things—like move small objects with her mind—and maybe she was stronger than the average female, but she wouldn't use the word *powers.* Still. Who was he?

——⋄·⋄——

The black Escalade pulled up into the empty lot of La Plume restaurant and parked. From the backseat, Zeke rolled down his window and looked at the building, trying to ascertain whether anyone was inside.

"Are you sure that he's here?" he asked.

"Yes, sir. He arrived forty-five minutes ago," Spider answered.

"Good." Zeke slid his shades back on and opened the back door. The cool October wind whipped around and ruffled Zeke's jacket as he marched toward the back of the building with his two henchmen falling in line behind him. When he stopped, his men advanced forward and pounded on the door.

Zeke waited for it to open, and when it did, it was by a teenage boy with a mop in his hand. "Yes?"

Defoe shoved the teenager back, where he tripped over a large yellow mop bucket and crashed to the floor. "Where's that fat fucker of a boss of yours at?"

Scared, the teenager stammered, "I-in the prep room."

Zeke and his men moved deeper into the restaurant, having no idea where the prep room was. They didn't have to travel far, and it was impossible to miss the heavy set chef, poring over paperwork on a steel table. When the large man looked up, he blinked a pair of long faux eyelashes at them. Disgust churned Zeke's stomach.

Recognition registered in the man's face, followed by fear. "Can I help you?" he asked, stepping back. "We're not open."

Zeke removed his shades and glanced around. "Nice place you got here."

"Thank you."

Zeke moved around like a health inspector, pretending to be interested in the cleanliness of the place. The stalling tactic was to make the fat dude sweat.

"Uhm. What is this all about?"

Zeke sighed. "Your name is Tyrone Hollis, right? A.K.A Tivonté."

"Yeah." The chef glanced over his shoulder when Spider and Defoe moved behind him. Now he was torn on whom he should watch.

"You catered my party the other night, correct?"

Tivonté swallowed. "Yes. Was . . . there something wrong with the service?"

"No. Actually, the food was magnificent," he answered. "Many of my guests praised your services."

"Ah. Good."

Another block of silence lapsed.

"Are you looking to book another party?" Tivonté asked.

"No." Zeke sighed. "I want you to tell me where I may find your friend Abrianna Parker." He stepped in front of the big man and cocked his head. "She *is* a friend of yours, isn't she?"

The fat fuck lied, "I don't know who you're talking about."

"No? Wasn't she and some of her other friends working as servers at the party the other night? Hmm? I have to admit, the disguises were pretty good, but not quite good enough."

Tivonté shook his head. "I hired a lot of students from the CulinAerie School. I don't know everybody's name."

Zeke paused and weighed whether he'd gotten this whole thing wrong. Had Abrianna tricked this guy into hiring her for the party, or was he in on the whole thing?"

Tivonté shrugged. "I'm sorry. I don't know anything more than that, other than my van got jacked that night, too. Cost me a shitload of money."

Zeke's glare hardened. He didn't like the possibility that he could be wrong. He was looking forward to killing someone over Tanya's death. A long silence ensued, and then Zeke signaled his boys.

Spider and Defoe jumped the chef, pounding him into the floor.

Tivonté howled.

The teenager, who'd watched everything from the corner of the room, dropped the mop and took off running out of the back door.

The beating went on for a full ten minutes. At that point Zeke was bored. "All right. That's enough," he said.

Spider and Defoe stood up, huffing and puffing over the bloody body.

Zeke moved closer and squat down. "I'm cutting you a little break, fat man. But in case you *do* know Abrianna Parker, I need for you to deliver a message for me." He reached over and lifted the back of Tivonté's head. "Tell that bitch that I'm looking for her and she better hope the government finds her ass before I do." He released his grip, allowing the man's head to thump against the tile floor.

"Let's get the fuck out of here."

8

The five-star luxury Hay-Adams in downtown Washington, D.C., has an unparalleled panoramic view of the White House, Lafayette Square, Lafayette Park, and the famous St. John's Church. The beautiful Italian Renaissance–style building wasn't as busy as it normally was at this time of year. They were still dealing with the nightmare scenario of having the speaker of the House killed on their premises. There wasn't a police presence, but the hotel's security had been visibly beefed up.

"Are you ready?" Kadir asked Julian. They were huddled in the back of yet another van.

Julian pulled a deep breath. "It's not my first breaking and entering gig, but given the stakes involved I don't know how I feel about being labeled as part of a domestic terrorist cell."

"Ah." Kadir waved off his concern. "After poppin' your federal cherry by pulling off a kidnapping, this should be a piece of cake."

Julian chuckled.

"How close are we?" Kadir asked Ghost, who was behind the wheel.

"T minus five," he responded.

"Cool." Kadir huffed. He avoided Julian's gaze for a few seconds. He knew that he was being hypocritical assuring Julian about pulling this off while he wrestled with his own doubts and lingering questions about Abrianna.

"You and, uh, Abrianna have been friends a long time, right?" Kadir asked.

Julian shrugged. "Yeah. I guess you can say that. We grew up on the streets together."

Kadir nodded. "Has she always, like, been so strong? I mean physically?"

Julian hitched up a half smile. "So the fight this morning wasn't nothing, huh?"

"I never said it was nothing. But I certainly didn't expect that she could put me through a wall."

Julian chuckled. "Yeah. She might need to look into anger management . . . among other things."

Julian wasn't really answering the question. If anything, he was adding more. However, Julian must have read the frustration on Kadir's face and decided to cut him a break.

"You seem like a good guy," Julian said. "I mean you seem like you really care for Bree. She deserves a good guy for once. But fair warning, she's not going to make it easy for you. In fact, she's going to make it damn near impossible."

"Bree hinted about having a rough home life."

"That's putting it mildly—and nowhere near the tip of the iceberg."

Kadir frowned.

Julian drew a deep breath while he seemed to come to a decision. "Look. Bree will probably kill me for telling you this, but . . . do you remember the Craig Avery case about six years back?"

Kadir shook his head. He had had his own issues going on about that time.

"It was a serial murder case. Crazy dude was snatching teenage girls off the street and torturing them. They attribute thirteen deaths to him. Only three girls were rescued from his basement. Abrianna was one of them. So damaged is a little understated." Julian's attention went back to the USB drive in his hand. "So all I have to do is stick this into the drive, and it will take care of everything?"

Kadir didn't hear him. His mind was tangled up with the information that Julian had unloaded on him.

"Yo, man. You still with me?" Julian asked.

"Uh, oh. Yeah." He shook and cleared his head before going back over the directions.

"We're here," Ghost announced. "Ready to rock and roll?"

Julian blew out a long breath. "As ready as I'll ever be."

Kadir smiled. "Then let's do this."

<hr>

At Hadley Memorial Hospital, Castillo knocked on Shawn White's door and poked her head inside. "Mind if I come in?"

Shawn stopped picking over a tray of food and sliced his cool blue eyes in her direction. "It's a free country . . . supposedly," he said in an unfriendly tone.

Castillo held onto her smile and eased farther into the room. "So how are you feeling?"

"Better."

"Really?"

"I would complain, but what would be the point?"

"That's one way of looking at it, I guess."

She tried to gauge his mood and then couldn't think of an easy transition to the topic that had brought her to the hospital, so she cut to the chase. "Madam Nevaeh is dead."

"Oh?" Shawn said, unfazed.

"I take it that this isn't news to you?"

"You can take it as me not giving a damn," he said.

Castillo crossed her arms. "Without the madam, how is Abrianna ever going to clear her name?"

Shawn shrugged.

The change in attitude since the last time she'd visited him only deepened her suspicion. "Have you spoken to Abrianna recently?" she asked.

"No," he lied.

"Look, Shawn. I know how close you and Abrianna are, but this is serious . . . and dangerous. If you know where she is, you need to tell me. I can help her."

"How? You're not even a cop anymore. You're a private dick, sticking your nose where it doesn't belong."

Castillo's spine stiffened. "That may be true, but I still have very good connections on the force."

Shawn didn't respond.

"Seriously," she pushed. "What's the plan here? Sooner or later, one of those federal agencies will find her and, given the seriousness of the charges they're going to hit her with, the government is not going to care one way or another if she's brought in dead or alive. Her or the guy she's running around with."

Shawn sealed his lips and glanced up at the muted television set.

Castillo had been dismissed. She hung her head and huffed out a tired breath. Then a face came to mind, a face that she'd seen at Zeke Jeffreys's party. She had seen him before. Seen him here in this room. Lifting her head, Castillo narrowed her gaze on Shawn's gaunt face. "Maybe you're the wrong person to talk to," she said.

No response.

"Maybe I need to talk to the guy who catered Zeke's party the other night."

Shawn's face tightened.

Jackpot. Castillo was on to something. "Yeah. You know who I'm talking about. Big fella. He was here the last time I visited. It was also his van that was stolen. What's the name on the van? La Plume Restaurant? Am I right?"

The more she talked, the more Shawn's face tightened.

"My God. What did you guys do?" she insisted.

Silence.

"Has Abrianna been here since the last time I visited you?"

Silence.

"You need to start talking to me. Does Abrianna have anything to do what happened to Madam Nevaeh? Did she kill her?"

Shawn snapped, "Don't be ridiculous! Of course she didn't kill that woman. Your friends in blue did that."

"What?"

Shawn zipped his lips again.

"Shawn, talk to me. This situation is out of control. Abrianna may not have killed that congressman, but they most certainly can pin any death that transpired during a crime, like a police shoot-out, on her. It won't matter if *my friends in blue* pulled the trigger."

Shawn drew a deep breath and appeared to be evaluating his next words. "Bree just wanted to talk to her."

Castillo's brows lifted. "Talk?"

Shaking his head, Shawn changed his mind about having this discussion. "I think you should leave now."

"Shawn, you have to know that I want to help her."

Shawn's face marbleized. "That's the thing. I don't recall anyone ever asking you for your help."

———————————

Abrianna paced back and forth in the bunker, nibbling her nails down to stubs. The knots in her gut doubled. Here she was again, asking her friends to put their lives on the line. Shawn was still recovering in the hospital, Draya was nursing a bullet wound, and she herself ignored her own aching injuries. She didn't like leaning on them, though none of them complained. If the roles had been reversed, she would do the same thing for any one of them. Right now it all felt like it was . . . too much . . . too overwhelming.

"This is taking too long," Abrianna fretted. "Something has gone wrong."

Roger glanced up from his terminal with a reassuring smile. "They haven't been gone that long. Relax."

Abrianna stopped pacing. "Don't tell me to relax."

Roger threw up his hands. "Hey, I'm just trying to help."

"I'm sure you are," she said. Her grudge against Roger had developed last week when she'd caught him trying to cop a feel when she was passed out. After she put a gun in his face, he'd been trying to get on her good side ever since.

A computer beeped.

Roger smiled. "They're in," he announced, pecking away on the keyboard.

"Yeah?" Abrianna and Draya crowded around him.

"Okay. Let's see what we got here," Roger said.

"Let's hope that the hotel stores their digital video files for more than a few days."

Abrianna frowned. "What do you mean?"

Roger said, "I'd imagine hotels would store daily surveillance for a short time before erasing for new space on the server."

Abrianna's stomach dropped. "Shit."

His fingers flew across the keyboard.

"How long does it take to do something like this?" Abrianna fretted.

"It depends," he answered, shaking his head as he entered row after row of what seemed like random numbers and symbols.

"It depends on what?"

"On how good their security system is. Since it's not your average motel, I'd imagine this place dropped a mint on security. Their clientele would demand it."

"Are you any good at this?" Draya double-checked.

The other hackers, working at other terminals, snickered.

"What?" Abrianna whipped her head around.

Roger bragged, "I'm one of the best—next to Kadir and Ghost, anyway."

Abrianna smiled. "Yeah? Kadir is that good?"

"I know him by reputation. Word is there's not a system around Kadir can't get into. Total rock star. Ghost has been trying to get him back into the game to help lead the next revolution against the federal police state."

"Police state? You guys really believe in that conspiracy theory shit?"

Roger looked up. "Don't you? A Supreme Court judge murdering the speaker of the house; who else would believe that shit but us?"

"He got you there," Draya said, elbowing her.

Abrianna's cocky smile vanished.

"All right. What time did you and the congressman arrive at the hotel?" Roger asked.

"Oh. I don't remember. It was late." She hunched over his shoulder while he went through the stored videos.

Another twenty minutes and "Bingo," they said together. On screen played the surveillance video of Judge Katherine Sanders strutting down the hallway toward the Presidential Suite.

Abrianna grinned. "I got you, you bitch."

———— ❖ ————

Castillo returned to her car, pissed, more with herself than with Shawn because, at the end of the day, the kid was right. Nobody had asked her to put her neck on the line to help Abrianna Parker. The only job that she had been hired to do was to investigate the former Speaker of the House for Tomi Lehane. That job ended when someone blew back his scalp.

It wasn't like she didn't have a ton of cases sitting on her desk back at her private detective firm, the Agency. However, at the moment, spying on cheating spouses held zero interest for her. Then again, there were also the missing children's cases growing colder by the day. But for those, she had run headlong into another brick wall. The frustration of hitting one dead end after another was demoralizing.

"Let it go, Gigi." She huffed out a long breath and then shoved her key into the ignition. "If they don't want your help, they don't want your help."

She started the car and left the parking deck. Her cell phone pinged. She quickly whipped it out of her jacket to see a text message from Dennis, asking whether he would see her that evening.

There he was, getting all clinging again.

She sighed and tossed the phone into the passenger seat.

She was halfway back to her agency when thoughts of Madam Nevaeh being discovered in that catering van overtook her. Without a doubt, Abrianna and her friends had snatched the madam from that party. Whether the woman was a police casualty or Abrianna had exacted revenge on the woman was what Castillo couldn't decide.

"Let it go. Let it go," Castillo mumbled, her hands at ten and two. Another mile down the road, the nagging at the back of her head got the best of her. At the next light, she made an illegal U-turn, picked up the phone, and asked Siri for directions to La Plume.

Within minutes, she was turning into the lot when a speeding SUV charged toward her and clipped the corner of her vehicle and spun her back out into the street.

"The fuck!" In mid-spin, she was T-boned by another car. Castillo's unbelted body thrashed around behind the wheel like a rag doll. The side of her head shattered the side window.

A surround sound of squealing tires was followed by more jarring hits: a multicar pile-up. Then the car stopped. The pain came a few seconds later. Everything hurt. When she opened her eyes, the world was a blur. She blinked several times, but nothing changed.

"Lady, are you all right?" The voice sounded like it was up a very steep hill.

Am I all right? She made a quick mental check. Besides the blurred vision, the aching chest, and ringing head, she answered, "Yes. I-I think so." She tried to open the warped door, but couldn't.

"Stay put," the man urged. "My wife is calling for help." Castillo ignored him and exited the car *Dukes of*

Hazzard–style, broken glass and all. Halfway through, the guy decided to help.

"Careful," he kept repeating while she swung her legs out.

Once on her feet, she wobbled for a moment. Soon, she had her bearings. "What the hell?" she asked after an instant replay in her mind.

"We saw the whole thing," the guy said. "That jackass could have killed somebody," the man raged on her behalf.

"Did you catch the license plate number?" she groaned, rubbing the side of her neck.

"Sorry. No." The man cocked his head. "Hey, are you sure that you're all right?"

Castillo nodded and backed away. "Yeah. Yeah." She had a bad feeling.

"Whoa. Where are you going?"

Castillo turned from the man and jogged toward the restaurant. A vehicle speeding away like that was never a good thing; that sort of driving happens after a crime.

"Hey, lady!"

"I'm fine! I'll be right back! Tell the police I went inside the restaurant," she yelled over her shoulder.

"But, lady . . . !"

Ignoring the man, Castillo picked up the pace. Her jog became a full-out sprint. After finding the building's side door locked, she rushed toward the back, where she pounded on the door. "Hello! Hello!" She banged on it again to no avail. Panic rising, she ran to the other side door and caught a break. It was unlocked. She bolted inside, reaching toward her back holster.

"Hello? Is anybody in here?" She removed her weapon.

"Hello? I'm Gizella Castillo, private investigator. I'm checking to see if everything is all right in here."

Silence.

"Hello?" She inched torward the back kitchen. A strange sound caught her ear. She followed it. When she rounded a corner, she spotted a teenager huddled over a large bloody body on the floor.

The teenager looked up, tears streaming. "I'm sorry. I-I should've never let them in. I think they killed him."

9

Tomi entered Ray's Bar. Through its low lighting she spotted Castillo, waving from a booth near the back. As she approached, her eyes grew wide. "Holy shit! What happened to your face?" Tomi asked, settling into the booth across from the private detective. It took a while for her to notice the cast on her arm.

"It's okay, I'll live."

Their waitress arrived, smiling while placing a bowl of peanuts in the center of the table. "What can I get you? A Bud Light?"

Tomi blinked. "Wow. You have a good memory."

"A good memory means bigger tips." The waitress winked.

"A Bud Light will be fine."

"You got it. Gigi?"

"I'm good," Castillo said after evaluating how much she had left in her own bottle.

Once the waitress drifted off, Tomi addressed the ex-cop. "Okay. Talk. What happened?"

"Car accident."

"Oh."

"Yeah. I was following a hunch on the case."

"What case?"

"The Abrianna Parker case."

Tomi shook her head. "I didn't know . . . Why are you still working on that? I didn't hire you to solve a murder case."

"No. You hired me to investigate Speaker Reynolds. He's dead. You used my work to do that little story identifying Abrianna before we got her side of what happened."

Tomi frowned as she took Castillo's words as a slap in the face. "I was doing my job."

"Yeah. I get it." Castillo shrugged. "You weren't interested in getting the whole picture. I was. So I followed a hunch and went to the hospital the other day and paid a visit to Shawn White."

Putting her ego aside, Tomi asked, "Who's Shawn White?"

"A friend of Abrianna's who helped me back in the day to nail Craig Avery."

"Your Deep Throat," Tomi said. "I remember from the Lifetime movie."

"Yeah, well. Shawn was gunned down at Abrianna's apartment hours after I saw her fleeing the Hay-Adams and around about the time she was recorded on that car shoot-out video that went viral."

Tomi processed that information. "And? You went and saw him. What did he say?"

"Off the record?"

Tomi huffed and slumped back against the booth.

Castillo waited.

"Sure. All right. Off the record."

"He told me about Abrianna and the circumstances that led her to work for a D.C. madam the weekend Reynolds was killed. So I then went to talk to the madam."

"Really?" Tomi leaned forward, but then had to self-correct when the waitress returned with her beer.

"One Bud Light," she sang, setting down the bottle.

"Thanks." Tomi smiled and then returned her attention to Castillo. "So you went to see the madam?"

Castillo nodded. "Of course she denied everything. But Shawn had said that Abrianna was indebted to the Teflon Don, a drug dealer-slash-businessman who's acquired quite a lot of political friends over the years. I'd never been able to get anything to stick on him. Anyway, I was privy to a drug raid coming to his estate, and I made sure that I was there to see it all go down—but then all hell broke loose." Castillo quickly recapped the events at the party.

"Wait. You think Abrianna stole the van?"

"Right after she somehow managed to kidnap the madam from the party."

"But why?"

"Shawn thinks that Abrianna was set up."

Tomi's entire frame deflated. "Set up?"

Castillo nodded. "When the cops found the van, the only body inside the was the madam. And she was dead."

"Shit."

"Right."

"So I paid another visit to Shawn at the hospital. I had a feeling that he was holding out on me."

"How?"

"I think he's been in contact with Abrianna recently."

"Did he confirm your suspicions?"

"No. He shut me down."

"So you don't have any proof that it was Abrianna who stole the van?" Tomi checked.

"Just my gut."

Tomi shrugged. "Maybe this madam stole the van when she saw the place being raided?"

Castillo smirked. "Anything is possible, but it's more likely that she was snatched. I started thinking about one of the guys at the party. One I'd seen before. The caterer."

"The caterer?"

"Turns out that he is another one of Abrianna's friends. And it was his van that was stolen."

"So you think he helped her crash this guy's party?"

Castillo nodded while she took a swig from her beer bottle. "So I decided to go to his restaurant and see if I would have better luck getting any information out of him. However, when I got there this SUV was peeling out of the parking lot like a bat out of hell and clipped my car, which spun me back out into traffic. And voilà. I got the shit knocked out of me and I got this lovely new cast."

"Damn."

"Yeah. But I'm a hell of a lot better off than her friend Tyrone Hollis. I found him inside the restaurant barely breathing."

"What?"

"Yeah. He almost died en route to the hospital."

"But who?"

"If I was to place a bet, I'd put my money on Zeke Jeffreys aka the Teflon Don. I'm not the only one in this town who can put two and two together."

"So where is Abrianna now?"

"Still on the run. And she better hope that the feds find her before Zeke does. He's on the war path."

————◆————

The Bunker

Abrianna and her ragtag team replayed the video clips from the Hay-Adams over again. Each of them marveled at what they were seeing. Feeling vindicated, a smug Abrianna sat back with her arms crossed. She had proven that she hadn't made the whole story up about Judge Sanders, even though there had been times when she'd questioned whether the drugs she took that night might have fucked up her memory. However, there was no need to tell any of them that.

Ghost was the first to spit out an apology.

"Apology accepted," Abrianna said.

Draya asked, "What do we do with this information now?"

"We leak this shit to the news," Julian answered, shrugging. "What else?"

"What, in an email with our names attached? How do we know if anyone will play it? The media is as bad as the government."

Ghost perked up at Draya's declaration. "A woman after my own heart."

Julian butted in, "Something tells me that being a woman with two legs is all it takes to be 'after your own heart.'"

Abrianna and Kadir smirked.

"That's offensive," Ghost countered. "I don't discriminate against the disabled."

"All right, you two," Kadir cut in. "Don't start."

"Why don't we upload it to the Internet and watch

it go viral? Our site is as popular as Anonymous or WikiLeaks," Ghost suggested. "This kind of shit is what we've been trying to expose about these dirty bastards running this fucking country."

Abrianna thought it over. "I need more than a video. I need my story attached. Simply uploading this won't clear my name. If anything, it still leaves the accomplice angle open."

"You want to do an interview?" Ghost asked. "We can do that, too. We sit you in front of a camera and voilà."

"We need to go through something more official. The government considers you and your friends here a criminal enterprise," Abrianna said. "No offense."

"Offense taken," Ghost said, leaning back and crossing his arms.

"She's right," Kadir said. "She needs to go through a reliable source."

Ghost expelled a long breath, doing a lousy job of hiding his hurt. "All right. Like who? You got somebody in mind?"

Abrianna hesitated. "Actually I do. But I haven't spoken to her in a long time."

"A friend?" Kadir asked.

"Not exactly." She glanced over at Draya's frowning face. "But I think that she can be an ally."

Kadir remained intrigued. "And you think that she will run your story *with* these images?"

"There's only one way to find out."

"Who is it?" Kadir asked.

"She's a reporter for the *Washington Post*. Her name is Tomi Lehane."

10

The White House swearing-in ceremony for the new chief justice took place three hours after the senate voted 61 to 37 to confirm Judge Katherine Sanders to the Supreme Court. The conservative right wing was already throwing a fit over what they saw as a corrupt administration scoring another win on the margins. The president was riding on a spike in popularity due to his strong response to Washington's Reagan airport bombing. The president and Homeland Security kept the press updated on the city's manhunt for suspected domestic terrorist Kadir Kahlifa and his possible partner-in-crime Abrianna Parker.

Tomi and photojournalist Jayson Brigham arrived ten minutes early for the ceremony; it was a new phenomenon for the often absentminded and habitually late reporter. Tomi had wrestled with guilt ever since she'd identified Abrianna as the murder suspect in the paper. Her professional ambition had overridden any allegiance she had toward her fellow tortured survivor.

She should have listened to Castillo about doing more digging on the story before outing Parker, especially after no one had been there for Shalisa Young before she'd hurled herself off a roof.

Tomi was jarred back to the pomp and circumstance of the moment when the crowd around her broke out into applause.

Chief Justice Sanders shook President Walker's hand and then turned and beamed at the crowd of gathered friends, family, and reporters while cameras clicked away, Jayson's included.

Tomi's cell phone vibrated. Quickly, she scooped it out and frowned at the unknown caller identification. On the last ring before the call transferred to voice mail, she answered, "Hello." Unable to hear anything, she threaded away from the crowd to the edge of the East Room. "Hello."

Silence.

Tomi stuffed a finger into one ear. "Hello."

"Hello. Is this Tomi Lehane?" a woman asked.

Tomi's spine tingled at the familiar voice. "Who is this?"

"Are you Tomi Lehane, with the *Washington Post*?" the woman asked.

She hesitated, but her curiosity won out. "I am."

"I have some information that I think that you may be interested in."

Tomi's patience eroded. "Look, lady. I'm in the middle of something. If you're not going to tell me *who* you are or *what* this is about, I'm going to—"

"It's about who *really* killed that congressman at the Hay-Adams."

Tomi stiffened.

"Hello. Are you still there?" the caller asked.

"Who is this?" Tomi demanded.

"Look. I'm trying to clear my name, Ms. Lehane. And I think that you can help me do that."

Shock hit Tomi hard. "Abrianna?"

Silence hummed over the line.

Tomi waited her out.

"Can we meet?" Abrianna asked. "Alone?"

Tomi's reporter instincts kicked in, "Sure. We could do that. Where would you like to meet?"

There was a pause.

Tomi shrugged. "I know this little hole-in-the-wall bar over on—"

"No," Abrianna cut her off. "No crowds."

"Okay. Then where?"

"Stanton Park—midnight."

Tomi frowned.

"Do you know where it is?"

"Yeah. Sure. No problem. Midnight. Got it."

"No cops," Abrianna stressed. "If I see a cop, I'm out, and I'll give the story to someone else. Deal?"

"Deal."

———◆◆———

Abrianna signaled Kadir to end the call over the encrypted computer line.

He punched a key and then swiveled toward her to ask, "Are you sure that you can trust her?" he asked.

"I don't trust anybody."

Kadir placed a hand over his heart. "Ouch."

Abrianna grinned. "Except you guys, of course."

Ghost shook his head. "Ice cold, man." From behind his computer station, Ghost leaned back in his chair and crossed his legs at the ankle. "The real question is whether your reporter friend has enough juice to get your story printed. At least your version of it."

"My version? We have proof now." Abrianna gestured to the printed pictures from the Hay-Adams security video. There were clear images of Judge Sanders in her trench coat arriving at the hotel, riding up the elevator, walking down the hallway, knocking on the suite's door, and even pictures of Kenneth Reynolds inviting her inside. However, there was no picture more damaging than the one of the judge *leaving* the suite, this time with blood visible on her face and coat.

"Too bad there aren't any pictures of the judge with the murder weapon," Draya said.

"No. She left the weapon in the room."

"The police have it?" Kadir asked.

Abrianna shook her head. "I took it."

"That's . . . not good," Ghost said. "Where's the weapon now?"

She thought about it. "Shit. I left it in Kadir's car after I ran out of bullets during that shoot-out."

"Shit. So the cops have it."

"Wait. You used the murder weapon during another crime?" Ghost asked.

"I didn't have a choice."

"Well. We have proof that she was there," Kadir acquiesced, "but it could still put us in a she said/we said situation."

"Only the good judge hasn't come forward to place herself in that hotel room that night. A lot of people would wonder why," Draya said, being helpful.

Julian nodded, looping an arm around her shoulders. "I'd like to hear the judge explain being in that hotel room the night that guy was killed." He jabbed the date and time stamp on the photograph.

"And don't forget about the blood," Abrianna said. "She's covered in it."

"You're going to get a lot of questions about the time discrepancy," Kadir warned.

"I was knocked out," Abrianna defended.

"You mean you were high," Kadir corrected.

Their gazes crashed.

Ghost interrupted the brewing argument. "Still. If you are able to convince this reporter to run the story, a lot of heat is going to come her way. They'll want her source—probably will throw her in jail in order to get to you. Do you think that she'll be able to handle it, or are you ready to turn yourself in and trust the system?"

Abrianna bore the weight of everyone's stare. "I don't have a choice," she said. "This is the only card I have to play."

Ghost shifted his attention to Kadir. "What about you, bruh? Are you turning yourself in, too? None of this shit clears your names from that bombing."

Kadir pulled a breath and evaluated his situation. No way in hell did he trust the government. They were likely to toss his ass back into a cell, revoke his parole, and forget about him for a couple of decades.

Abrianna placed a hand over his, and he would almost swear that he heard her plea inside of his head. *Please. It's time to stop running.*

Kadir looked at her and then back at the waiting group.

Sighing, he dropped his head. "This shit gotta end some kind of way. May as well toss the dice now rather than later. Right?"

11

Zeke was smoking again. *Damn it.*

He had given up the bad habit years ago—when Tanya told him that she hated the taste of cigarettes when she kissed him, hated the smell that clung to his clothes and hair.

"Dust to dust. Ashes to ashes," the preacher finished, closing the Bible.

After the circle of mourners mumbled "Amen," Zeke watched as the top-of-the-line chrome casket that Zeke had paid a knot of cash for was lowered into the ground. The turnout was good. Tanya's working girls, recent and retirees, had traveled from far and wide to pay final respects to the woman who'd helped many of them to get through college, raise families, support aging parents, or simply become financially secure.

Zeke was sure that Tanya was pleased by the turnout. She was likely smiling down on her family of outcasts right now.

Fuck. Zeke rubbed at the tightness in his chest and

wondered why the hell his throat kept closing off his air pipe.

The crowd thinned as, one by one, the mourners tossed red roses down into the open plot atop Tanya's casket and then marched in a single file line back toward their vehicles.

Zeke lingered, pretending not to feel the sting at the back of his eyes. This shit hurt worse than he'd ever imagined. Hell. He'd lost muthafuckas before. Almost all of the homeboys he grew up with were either six feet under or shipped off to a concrete plantation. He had ex-girlfriends who'd overdosed, got sliced up while on hoe patrol, and one he'd put a bullet in the center of her head when he'd caught her stealing from him. However, none of them had him in his feelings the way he was right now.

Only one thing could fix this shit—and that was getting his hands on Abrianna Parker.

Sensing a set of eyes burning a hole into his head, Zeke looked over his shoulder and noticed one of Tanya's top earners: Angel. He was fairly sure that was her name. She stood morose and alone by the open grave, eyeballing him up and down.

He liked her look. She was a tall stunner with Coke-bottle curves and mesmerizing hazel eyes.

He signaled Defoe, and when the large bodyguard leaned forward, Zeke gave him instructions.

Defoe nodded and then strolled over to Angel and repeated Zeke's words.

Without lip or attitude, Angel fell in line behind Defoe and followed him over to Zeke.

"Hello, Angel. Thank you for coming out today." He took her hand and kissed it. "Tanya always spoke highly of you."

Angel's eyes swam with tears as she shook her head. "I'm so sorry. I feel like it's all my fault."

Zeke frowned. "What do you mean?"

Angel glanced away, shaking her head.

Zeke drew a breath but calculated that this situation was best handled with patience. He stood firm and handed her a handkerchief. He watched her cry for a full minute before he repeated the question. "What do you mean that you feel like this is all your fault?"

Angel sniffed and lifted her chin. "I told Abrianna about her friend in the hospital. He'd sent a private investigator to talk to Madam Nevaeh the other day."

Zeke stiffened. "You *saw* Abrianna Parker recently?"

Angel nodded. "She was camped out at Madam Nevaeh's last place with that guy that's all over the news."

Zeke's face heated.

Angel added, "They held me at gunpoint and then left me tied in a chair. It took nearly two days to free myself from that house."

"That's it?"

Angel nodded. "It's enough, isn't it? I know Abrianna had something to do with Madam's death. I know it."

Zeke's mind zoomed to Abrianna's friend who Roach and Gunner had left bleeding in her apartment. "Do you remember this friend's name?"

"Shawn," she said. "I met him when Abrianna came to the estate the first time."

Zeke nodded. "I appreciate you telling me this information. I'll check into it. See what we see and then let the chips fall where they may."

The Bunker

"Hey, guys," one of Ghost's guys spoke up and broke their private huddle.

"What's up, Wendell?" Ghost asked.

"Wasn't your friend's restaurant called La Plume?"

Abrianna, Draya, and Julian looked at one another.

"Why?" Kadir asked.

"There has been a lot of traffic about the place recently. They found the stolen van the other day with a body in it. They haven't released a name—and now there are reports about some guy at the restaurant being found by some ex-cop all beaten up."

"What?"

Wendell continued, "Yeah. He is in the hospital and is listed in critical condition."

"No," Abrianna gasped, rushing to Wendell's cluttered space to see what was on the screen.

"Tivonté," Abrianna gasped. "It's gotta be."

"A black SUV was seen speeding from the premises says one witness and caused a five car pile-up in front of the place." Abrianna shook her head. This can't be happening. All of her friends were getting hurt.

"We need to go," she said, bolting away from the computer.

Kadir blocked her path. "Wait. What? What about the meeting with the reporter?"

"I-it can wait. We can reschedule." She attempted to move around him, but he refused to budge.

"Move. Or I'll move you," she threatened.

"I have no doubt that you can, but I have to stress that you're not thinking clearly. We need to end this. Tonight. I'm sorry about your friend, but you can't help him right now. But you *can* end this nightmare about

Judge Sanders and that dead congressman *tonight*. Only then will you and your friends be out of danger."

Abrianna glared, but since she didn't shove him into another wall, he went on, "A few minutes ago, you were saying you wanted your life back. Well, this is how you do it."

"He's right," Draya said. "You go and meet the reporter, and Julian and I will check on Tivonté *and* Shawn."

"You will?"

Draya nodded. "Of course. It's too much of a risk for you to sneak into a hospital again. You can't flake out on that reporter. We got this. Don't we, Julian?"

"Absolutely. You go in."

After a long moment, Abrianna relented. "All right. But tell him . . . I'm really sorry. I didn't mean for any of this to happen."

Julian wrapped an arm around her. "Of course you didn't."

Ghost spoke up. "We're going to need a change of plan."

Kadir pivoted. "What do you mean?"

"Follow me." Ghost and his crew marched into another hidden room inside the bunker and then made a beeline toward a robust armory.

"The hell?" Abrianna marveled, entering behind him and Kadir. "Look at all of this. What are you preparing for—an alien invasion?"

"Wow," Draya said, pulling up the rear with Julian.

"Yo, man. I think that I may need to stage an intervention," Kadir bristled as he made a full three-hundred-and-sixty-degree turn in the armed room. "You have crossed over to the dark side. Ghost, what the hell is all of this for?"

Ghost ignored the question and unlocked the top drawer of a steel cabinet. Inside was a cache of handguns. He reached for his baby: a .45-mm Wilson Combat Tactical Supergrade. "Ah. Come to daddy." He kissed the barrel and beamed.

Abrianna and Kadir exchanged worried looks. The whole scene had the feeling of a bad vigilante film.

"Uh, is all of this necessary?" Kadir asked, forcing humor into his voice. "We're meeting a reporter in a park, not in Aleppo."

Ghost holstered the weapon and then put the metal box back into the steel drawer. "It could be a trap. You don't think that I'm going to let my buddy walk into a potential ambush, do you?"

Abrianna's gaze boomeranged around the glass-and-metal cabinets that housed a variety of military-grade weapons that would give an invading army pause.

"Your girl has already admitted that this reporter chick ain't exactly trustworthy. We might find ourselves in another hostile situation. Best to be prepared than not."

"That's not what I said," Abrianna corrected.

Ghost moved to an angry looking assault weapon hanging on a display wall. "It's really kind of a yes or no question. Either you trust this chick or you don't." He sliced his gaze toward Abrianna. "Which is it?"

Kadir did the same.

Under pressure, Abrianna bore the weight of their stares before sticking to the truth. "I don't trust her."

"There. You see? May as well go prepared this time. Or do you want to be in another situation where muthafuckas are shooting and the only thing that you can do is duck?"

Abrianna and Kadir shot glances at each other again; neither knew what to say when the crazy person made sense.

"I got the perfect li'l baby for you, Ms. Parker." Ghost strapped the assault weapon around his shoulders and marched over to another cabinet.

Abrianna eyed him wearily as he pulled out a Tiffany-blue handgun.

Ghost informed her, "This is a Glock 21 .45 caliber. Now I'm not crazy about vanity weapons—after all, a gun is a tool and not an accessory. But come here and see if you like the fit and weight in your hand."

Abrianna moved next to Ghost and took the gun. She wasn't a novice. She recognized the quality of the piece the second it was in her hand.

"Yeah. You like that, don't you?" Ghost gloated, watching her light up.

"It's all right." She shrugged, downplaying her approval.

"Uh-huh." Ghost looked at Kadir. "Don't worry. I got something for you, too."

"Nah. That's all right, bruh. I'm good."

Ghost frowned. "So you're cool with an ambush then?"

"We don't know it's an ambush. Besides, I still got my piece."

"You mean that piece of shit you got from some junkie? How much did that put you back, ten dollars?"

"Funny. It's solid and it works when I pull the trigger. That's all that matters. Besides, I'm not supposed to even have that. I'm still on parole, remember?"

Everyone laughed.

Ghost said, "It's safe to say that you've fucked that shit up when you went viral playing Bonnie and Clyde on the Internet. You may as well go out blazing with a pair of gasoline drawers on now."

Kadir grinned, but shook his head.

"C'mon. I know you're tempted, a sharpshooter like yourself? The itch never leaves your system. It'll take you back to our old military days."

"What?" Abrianna's attention shifted to Kadir. "When were you in the military?"

Kadir shrugged. "In another life."

Ghost laughed. "My man here has had nine lives. Don't let him fool you."

Baffled, Abrianna stared. "I don't remember you ever mentioning your being in the military."

"Surely you're not on my case about my not sharing my *whole* life story?"

"Ouch." Ghost mumbled, dropping out of the conversation.

Abrianna jutted up her chin, but conceded his point. She certainly knew a whole hell of a lot more about him than he knew about her.

"My bad," she said, dropping the subject.

Ghost tagged back in. "Actually, me and your boy met in the army."

"He's not *my* boy," Abrianna corrected, but regretted how petty she sounded.

"Well, whatever your complicated Facebook status is, Kadir and I met on our first tour in Afghanistan. We had more than our fair share of death-defying moments. Kadir saved more lives than I can count with his shooting. No wonder T4S ran to recruit him like an NFL draft pick."

"Oh, really?" Abrianna said, impressed. "T4S— where have I heard that name before?"

Ghost laughed. "It's the same company he went to prison for hacking."

"What the hell, man?" Kadir snapped. "Are you writing my autobiography?"

Ghost cheesed, but tossed up his hands. "You're right, man. My bad. Diarrhea of the mouth."

Abrianna said, "I enjoyed it. It was . . . illuminating."

"I bet you did," Kadir countered. "Anything you care to illuminate to us about yourself?"

Abrianna's grin turned into a smirk.

"Yeah," Kadir laughed. "That's what I thought."

Draya sighed. "Can we please get back to the matter at hand? What's the plan?"

"You're right." Ghost got serious. "Okay. This is the plan . . ."

<hr>

At midnight, Abrianna and Kadir were hunched low in the backseat of Roger's black Cherokee a block away from Stanton Park. Ghost and the rest of the crew kept radioing their positions in and around the park scanning for cops and federal agents. So far, the coast was clear when Tomi entered.

"Is that her?" Kadir asked.

Abrianna nodded and kept her gaze leveled on Tomi while she talked on a cell phone.

"Still think that you can trust her?"

Abrianna sighed. "There you go with that word *trust* again."

"You know what I mean. Do you think she'll print our story?"

"How could she not—sex, drugs, and murder on

Capitol Hill? Hell, I'm practically handing her a Pulitzer Prize."

Roger informed Ghost, "We have a positive ID on the reporter entering the park. Does anyone spot a tail?"

Ghost's voice rumbled over the Roger's walkie-talkie, "All clear."

Abrianna nodded, but didn't move.

"Are you ready?" Kadir asked.

Abrianna bit her bottom lip. She had no idea why she was stalling.

Kadir whispered. "Are you having second thoughts?"

Closing her eyes against the nice sensations his warm breath caused on the back of her neck, she admitted, "A lot is at stake."

Kadir nodded and then waited with her in the dead silence. After a while, his gaze crept back toward her. "You know if you don't want to do this—"

"I do," Abrianna said. "I have to clear my name. I don't want to be on the run from the federal government for the rest of my life. You?"

"It wasn't in my latest life plans. No."

"But?"

Kadir sighed. "*But* . . . I know how the government works. Once we come forward, we're not likely going to be met with open arms. Too many careers depend on this country being tough on crime. Now that we're labeled as a couple of terrorists, they're not going to want to admit they got it wrong."

"I get that," Abrianna said, her stomach twisted into one more knot. "But this is the only real chance we have. I'm hoping my . . . history with Tomi will afford us at least *one* ally."

"What *is* your history with this reporter? How do you two know each other?"

Abrianna pulled another breath and suppressed the old memories. "It's a long story," she responded.

Kadir frowned but didn't push.

"All right," she said suddenly. "Let's get this over with."

They scrambled out of the car and headed to the park.

———◆———

Sitting on a bench in in the middle of the night, Tomi reevaluated her sanity. Why was she waiting *alone* to meet a woman who was wanted for murder? Was a story really worth this? Had she learned nothing about putting herself in vulnerable positions? *Maybe I have a death wish.*

"Sorry to have kept you waiting," Abrianna said.

Tomi's hands flew to the gun tucked at her hip.

"Whoa. Whoa." Abrianna pulled the Tiffany-blue .45. "It's cool. It's just me, Abrianna . . . and my friend Kadir." She gestured to the man to her right who also held a weapon leveled at Tomi's head.

Tomi lifted a brow at the strikingly handsome guy with smoldering dark eyes. The images on the news didn't do him justice. "You two have me at a disadvantage. I thought we were trusting each other, Abrianna?"

There was a long silence before Abrianna lowered her weapon.

Kadir followed her lead.

Tomi's hand drifted away from the weapon. The enormity of the situation struck her hard. "You're the guy who blew up the airport," she said.

Kadir shook his head. "I'm the guy they're claiming *helped* bomb the airport. I didn't."

Tomi arched a brow. "So it's a misunderstanding? What about the video they keep playing on a loop?"

"I'm an Uber driver. I dropped off two customers at the airport, helped them unload their bags, and got a big tip. End of story. I had no idea that they were going to blow up the damn place."

"Then why didn't you turn yourself in and explain?"

Abrianna cut in, "Because I dove into his car with bullets flying at my head and he's been helping me ever since."

Tomi's gaze shifted between the two of them while she weighed what to do. She also took the opportunity to note the changes in Abrianna in the past six years. She had gone from pretty to a knockout, but there was a lot of pain radiating in her eyes. Tomi recognized that pain. She saw it every morning in the mirror.

"I brought you something." Abrianna reached inside of her jacket and pulled out a thick legal-size manila envelope and handed it over.

"What's that?" Tomi asked without accepting it.

"This is proof that I've been set up. I didn't kill that congressman. I wasn't the only woman there that night."

Dubious, Tomi took the eight-by-fourteen-inch envelope and turned on the small flashlight hooked on her keychain. It wasn't much, but she could get a good look at what she had.

Abrianna watched and waited for a reaction.

Tomi blinked. "Wait. This is . . ." She flipped through the photographs faster. After staring at the one photograph for a full minute, she looked up at Abrianna. "Do you know *who* this is?"

"I do now. She's been all over the news."

Tomi looked back down at the clear images of the new chief justice of the Supreme Court and swallowed. "All right. Start talking."

12

Chief Justice Katherine Sanders beamed at the president of her alma mater as she shook his hand on the stage's podium. The applause from the black-tie crowd made goose bumps march across her body.

"Thank you, everyone," she said into the microphone, still smiling. This was it. Her professional dream had finally come true. She'd done everything that she could to make sure it happened. Sanders's speech began with a joke and then breezed through the stack of index cards faster than she'd intended. She hoped the words didn't sound as jumbled to the audience as it did inside of her head. "Again, this is an incredible honor. Thank you *all* so much for coming. I hope I make you proud. Thank you."

The audience came to their feet. Sanders's grin expanded while she reveled in the moment. A face in the crowd made her heart skip and melted the smile off of her face. When she blinked, the face disappeared.

The school's president touched Sanders's forearm.

She jumped and then apologized when she saw that he was attempting to escort her off of the stage. She accepted his arm, but stole another look back into the crowd.

Abrianna locked gazes with the judge.

Sanders missed the first step off the stage and stumbled on the second, but recovered by the fourth. The crowd gave her an additional round of applause, which reddened her pale face.

Abrianna smiled and drifted away.

Paranoid, Sanders returned to her white-linen, guest-of-honor table, still craning her neck and skimming for another glimpse of her worst nightmare.

"This is for you," a server stated, slipping her a purple envelope with the name "Kitty" scrawled in calligraphy. Her heart skipped a beat while dessert was being placed on the table. Before she could think to ask the server who'd given him the envelope, she was gone.

Sanders made another futile scan of the crowd.

Kadir moved behind Abrianna and whispered, "It looks like Sanders saw a ghost."

"Nah. That's the bitch's natural coloring," Abrianna said.

Ignoring the chatter encircling the table, Sanders worked one of her French tips along the back of the envelope and pulled out a postcard-size photo of her being shown inside Speaker Reynolds's hotel room.

Abrianna grinned when Kitty gasped and shoved the photo back into the envelope.

Tomi said, "Guess that's my cue." She maneuvered around Abrianna and Kadir and then through a throng of guests who were making their way toward the dance floor.

Focused on finding the haunting face in the crowd, Sanders hadn't noticed her date, Larry, and slammed into him.

"Whoa. Where are you headed off to?"

Flustered, Sanders took another look around. "No . . . I . . ."

"Care to dance?" he asked, offering his arm.

"No. I . . . I need to go and powder my nose," she said, fluttering a smile and sidestepping him.

Larry frowned. "Are you all right? You look . . . off."

"I . . . I'll be right back," she said and raced off. Bursting through the door of the ladies' room, Sanders headed straight toward the four-sink vanity and urged her reflection, "Pull it together, girl. You're seeing things." She drew several deep breaths before her heartbeat returned to normal. There was no way that prostitute was there. *But what about the picture?*

The bathroom door opened, and a woman stepped inside. "Hello, Kitty. Congratulations," the woman said, beaming as she joined Sanders at the sink. "For your confirmation *and* your award."

Sanders's gaze raked Tomi up and down before she remembered to smile. "Thank you."

"I have to admit that I was surprised to see the president push for your confirmation right on the heels of a terrorist attack and the cold-blooded murder of Speaker Reynolds. Makes one wonder whether the president has his priorities in order."

Sanders's smile thinned.

"Then again, Speaker Reynolds stood in the way of your confirmation—despite you two being lovers." Tomi shook her head. "Ouch. That had to hurt."

"Who the hell are you?" Sanders growled.

Tomi's smile brightened as she offered her hand.

"Oh. I'm sorry. Where are my manners? Hi. I'm Tomi Lehane. I'm a reporter with the *Washington Post*."

Sanders ignored her offered hand.

"I'm running a story in tomorrow's paper about your *personal* relationship with the deceased speaker and revealing the fact that you were with him at the Hay-Adams the weekend he was killed."

Sanders's eyes narrowed as she held up the purple envelope. "So I take it that I have *you* to thank for this?"

"Actually that was a gift from Abrianna Parker, an old acquaintance of mine, who came to me with the most astonishing story about what happened that night at the hotel."

Sanders blanched.

Tomi continued, "It's a hell of a story. Care to hear it?"

Swallowing, Sanders squared her shoulders. "That hooker is a wanted murderer. If you're harboring her—"

"I assure you that Ms. Parker is prepared to come forward and turn herself in after the article hits the front page." Tomi smiled. "*Now* do you care to comment?"

"I don't know what the hell that woman told you, but she's a liar! And she's a wanted criminal."

"Yeah. Criminals tend to have the best stories—and this one is backed up with pictures and *video*."

Sanders's jaw hardened.

"I figure that it's only fair that I get your side on why you *never* came forward about your being with the speaker that weekend. And how you came to have all that *blood* splattered over your coat when you left."

"Lies." Sanders slapped the countertop before she jabbed a finger in Tomi's face. "You do *not* want to fuck with me, little girl."

Tomi raised a brow. "Is that on the record?"

"Fuck your record—and if you *dare* print a single word of that nonsense, I will *sue* you and your liberal-ass paper for every goddamn thing you got."

"Now *that's* a better quote. Mind if I use that one?"

"Go to hell!"

Sanders marched out of the bathroom and through the ballroom to where Larry held court, laughing with other diners assigned to their table.

"Ah. Here's the lady of the evening."

"We're leaving," Sanders snapped and glanced over her shoulder to make sure neither Tomi nor Abrianna was fast on her heels.

"Is something wrong?" he asked.

"Grab your things and come on!" She swiped the back of her hand under her nose and spun away from the table.

Larry scrambled to catch up.

Judge Sanders ignored Larry's battery of questions as she stormed out to the valet.

"So are you not going to tell me why you raced out of a dinner where you're the guest of honor?"

"The ticket," she insisted, stomping her foot impatiently with her hand out.

Larry retrieved the valet ticket from his breast pocket and held it up.

Sanders snatched it from his fingers and gave it to the young man at the valet booth.

"Thank you. It will be just a few minutes," the kid said before taking off. Once the car was brought to the curb, she and Larry climbed inside and headed home—in silence.

Judge Sanders's mind remained in a whirl during the ride, so much so that she hadn't realized they'd arrived at her place until Larry had climbed out of the car and rushed around to open her door. It was only when the night's cold air whipped in and frosted her face did she pull herself out of a cloud of worry.

"How about a nightcap?" Larry asked.

"How about a rain check?" she suggested instead.

Larry's face collapsed in disappointment. "Look. I don't know what happened tonight, but—"

"We'll talk later," she said, cutting him off and delivering a peck to his cheek. "Good night."

He sighed. "Good night."

At the door, she rummaged through her clutch in search of her door key and swore when she had to do it a few times before finding it. After jamming it into the lock, she waved goodbye to Larry as he pulled off. Kitty entered the house and punched in her security code on the beeping keypad by the door. Quickly, she peeled out of her coat and headed upstairs to her private office, where she beelined to the phone and dialed a private line at the White House.

13

The White House

"You have ten minutes," Donald Davidson said, taking the unwanted phone call. "What's the emergency?"

Sanders seethed, "The emergency is that the five-foot-ten, black prostitute that the most powerful government in the world seems to be incapable of finding, let alone killing, is now talking to the fucking press."

"What?"

"You heard me," Sanders snapped. "And the bitch has pictures."

Davidson's face hardened. "Explain."

"A fucking reporter with the *Washington Post* crashed my award ceremony tonight and asked me for a comment on a story she's writing for tomorrow's paper."

Davidson's face blanched. "How in the fuck? What reporter?"

"Some bitch named Tomi Lehane. She must be some rookie. I've never heard of her before."

Silence.

Sanders snapped, "Well? Aren't you going to say something? *Do* something?"

"And what exactly do you think I should do?" Davidson barked.

"I don't know, get someone on the phone at the paper. Stop the story!"

Davidson's laugh sounded like it burst from a broken tailpipe.

Sanders's anger grew. "What the fuck is so funny?"

"You've been in this cesspool of a city long enough to know that that's *not* how shit works. The minute anyone picks up the phone, that confirms whatever story they're writing, and it will drag the administration into the middle of it."

"The administration *is* in the fucking middle," she clapped back.

He glanced around himself to make sure that he wasn't being overheard, too. "Are you making a threat?"

"I'm at home, trying not to have a heart attack. *Something* has to be done. This story can't hit the papers. I will not be hung out to dry on this one, I know *that* much. If I go down . . ."

"Watch your mouth. Making threats is not smart."

"Neither is fucking me over. Now you fix this shit!"

⟶•◆•⟵

In a nondescript van with the headlights off, Abrianna, Kadir, and Ghost watched Judge Sanders as she entered her house and then breathed a sigh of relief when her companion drove off. That was one less person they'd have to deal with tonight.

An upstairs light turned on.

"How long should we wait?"

"I don't know. We're going to have to play it by ear.

We need to know if there is anybody else inside the house first. The last thing we want is more surprises."

In the back of the van, Ghost hunched over a weird looking laptop. After tapping a few keys, he said, "She's on the phone."

"How do you know that?" Abrianna asked, angling to see over his shoulder.

"Because I'm watching her," he answered.

"How?"

Ghost sighed, but Kadir explained, "He hacked into her computer's webcam."

"You can do that?"

Ghost and Kadir chuckled.

Kadir added, "We can do anything that the government can. We can take over your computer, phone, smart TV, game console, baby monitor, home security . . . the list is long."

"All right. Dumb question. *How* are you doing it?"

"If a device is connected to the Internet or radio frequency, it can be hacked."

Abrianna shifted uncomfortably. "Now I see why you hate cell phones."

Ghost stopped typing and looked up. "Heeey. Maybe there's hope for you yet."

"There's a home security sign." Kadir gestured toward the blue octagon placard planted in the front yard.

"You guys can disable it, right?" she asked.

"Looks like an ADT sign," Ghost said, rustling around in the back. "Easy peasy."

Abrianna arched a brow. "Love the confidence."

"Most home security networks still rely on old wireless communications from the nineties. Each company's systems may be different, but the *hardware* is all the same," Ghost said, fingers flying across the keyboard.

"Yeah." Kadir intercepted the conversation. "We simply jam the wireless radio system, which will suppress the alarms to *both* the residence and the monitoring company."

"I hear you talking, but it sounds like gibberish."

Ghost grinned. "All you need to know is that we can get you in and out without alerting the authorities."

Abrianna smiled. "Perfect." Adrenaline pumping, she reached for the door.

Kadir restrained her by the shoulder. "Let's double-check the wire."

Abrianna twisted back around and lowered her head to speak into the microphone. "Testing one, two. Testing."

Ghost gave a thumbs-up. "Ready to rock and roll, boys and girls."

"Good." Abrianna went for the door again. "The sooner we get this bitch on tape, the sooner I can go back to my shitty life."

14

The Truman Balcony

"We have a problem." Davidson handed the president his bourbon. "A *major* fucking problem."

"What is it now?"

"Judge Sanders."

President Walker frowned. "Apparently this means I'm going to need a double."

"I figured it was better to be safe than sorry."

Walker cast his gaze over the railing of the balcony and into the night. "Spit it out."

Davidson lowered into the chair next to the president. "A *Washington Post* reporter has gotten hold of some damaging surveillance footage that I'd been assured had been taken care of from Hay-Adams. Shit is about to hit the fan—or rather the front page in a few hours, complete with pictures."

"What the fuck are you taking about?" Walker asked.

Davidson took a deep breath and shared the bad news. When he was through, the president was enraged.

"Goddamn it!" He threw his drink. As it exploded like a bomb on the balcony, he sprung up from his chair and paced. "Fuuuck!"

"I know that I should have brought this to you sooner. But I figured the less you knew, the better . . . unless the situation got out of hand."

"Kitty?" the president said, incredulous.

Davidson nodded.

"Who is the reporter?" Walker asked.

Davidson reached into his pocket and scooped out the note he'd written down. "Tomi Lehane."

"Never heard of her," the president said.

Davidson's face morphed into white marble.

The president arched a brow. "Tell me there's a story that comes with that poker face."

"I've heard of her. You have, too."

"I have?"

"Yeah. She is a rookie reporter on the Hill, but she's famous for being a survivor of a serial killer some years back."

Something tickled at the back of Walker's mind, but he couldn't pull up the details. "Refresh my memory."

"The entire story about Dr. Avery is above my pay grade, but suffice to say that he used to be an employee over at T4S."

"No shit?"

"No shit. The thing is . . . Abrianna Parker, the prostitute we've been looking for in connection to Reynolds's murder, was also a Dr. Avery survivor."

"Muthafuck me." Walker wished he hadn't thrown his drink. "So these chicks have a history?"

"Quite a history," Davidson said.

Walker shook his head. "The minute I call the *Post* to stop the story, it'll drag *me* in into the mess. It's bad enough I put her on the court." He thought about it

some more. "Hell. They're going to drag me into it re-
gardless. This bitch can drag me down the drain with her.
The Congress will impeach both of us." He sighed as his
pacing picked up speed. "Nobody will believe I had nothing to do with this madness. Not on top of everything
else. My recent bump in the polls for handling the airport
bombing will disappear like that." He snapped his fingers. "Can the reporter or this Parker chick tie *me* to
Reynolds's death?"

Walker considered the question. "The actual murder? No. But if Kitty . . ."

"Starts lying through her teeth," Walker finished.

Davidson fell silent for a second. "What do you
want to do?" Davidson asked.

"I have options?"

"There are always options."

———◦•◦———

Zeke ordered Spider and Defoe to remain in the car
before he strolled into Hadley Memorial Hospital solo.
This wasn't the place to draw attention to himself. An
earlier call to the hospital got him the room and floor
number for Shawn White. He stepped into the elevator
along with a cluster of people who wore various degrees of sadness on their faces. No one liked visiting
the hospital.

One kid with his arms wrapped around his mother's
legs kept staring up at Zeke. The one time that he
glanced down, the chubby-cheeked kid ducked back
behind his mother's thick thigh and cried.

"Aww. What's the matter with you?" his mother
asked.

Zeke smiled as the doors slid open to his floor, and
he stepped out alone. In the hall, he glanced around
and then followed the signs hanging above his head.

The floor was virtually empty, except for the two nurses huddled behind their workstation. He breezed past without them looking up. When he reached the right door, he glanced around again and then slipped into the room. In bed lay a thin man with the face of a teenager. As Zeke approached, he noticed the man's blond hair sprayed across the pillow, his long, curly lashes, and his plumped lips. If it wasn't for the Adam's apple, the boy could pass for a girl.

Abrianna had an interesting group of friends.

Zeke stopped at the bed's railing and suppressed the urge to put a bullet in the kid's forehead and keep it pushing. What he needed first was answers. Gently, he reached underneath the man's head and removed the extra pillow. Once he had it in hand, he shoved it down onto the kid's face.

Shawn woke and thrashed beneath the pillow. Zeke counted to ten before lifting it and staring into the kid's brilliant blue eyes.

"Hello, Shawn."

Shawn drew a breath to cry out, but Zeke crashed the pillow back down again and the thrashing resumed. After another ten seconds, Zeke removed the pillow.

"Don't piss me off by doing something foolish . . . like screaming."

Shawn glued his lips together.

"Good. See? We already have an understanding. If this goes well, I may let you leave this place through the front door instead of the morgue. Do I make myself clear?"

Shawn swallowed, making his Adam's apple bob.

"I'll take that as a yes." He leaned closer. "I'm looking for a friend of yours: Abrianna Parker. Care to tell me where I can find her?"

With his breathing returning to normal, Shawn erased all emotions from his face.

"Ah. You're one of those loyal muthafuckas, aren't you?"

Shawn stared.

Zeke's lips twitched. "Now see? That's something that we have in common. When muthafuckas fuck with my friends, then I'll see you for it. But then when one *kills* my lady . . ." He shook his head. "There is nothing but hell to pay. You catch my drift?"

Shawn didn't respond.

"Has Abrianna been here to see you lately?"

Silence.

Zeke's fake smile turned downward. "See? You're already fucking up. I don't like repeating myself. Has that bitch been here?"

Silence.

Zeke crashed the pillow back down onto his face. Ten, fifteen—twenty seconds passed, but this time Shawn didn't fight back. Zeke whipped the pillow off the boy's face, and he immediately drew several deep breaths but still refused to say anything. Pissed, Zeke whipped out his pistol from his waist and crammed the barrel into the boy's mouth. "You think that I'm playing with you, muthafucka? How about I blow your shit wide open? Huh? Would you like that?"

Shawn's throat made gagging noises, his eyes remained wild, but his face remained cold as stone. He wasn't going to say shit.

"Fuck you, muthafucka!" Zeke clicked off the safety.

A sound outside the door wrenched Zeke's attention. He eased his finger away from the trigger when a voice drew closer. He clicked on the safety and glanced at the door. There were several voices now.

Zeke's gaze returned to Shawn. Those cool blue eyes reflected the kid's resignation to his fate. Zeke chuckled and removed the pistol from Shawn's mouth. Grudgingly, he respected the young man. "All right. To be continued." He slipped his weapon back into his back holster. At the door, two nurses entered and jumped at seeing Zeke.

"Oh, my! You startled me," one said, frowning. "I'm sorry but visiting hours are over."

"Yeah. I was just leaving," he said, and then glanced over his shoulder at Shawn one last time. "Catch you later." He winked and slipped out of the door.

15

After her call with Davidson, Kitty needed a drink. She was still in her Jimmy Choo pumps; her heels' staccato clack echoed throughout the graveyard-like silence of the house. She had gotten used to it since her husband's death seven years ago. Her two daughters were grown and off raising her grandchildren. Calls home came mostly on birthdays and holidays, contributing factors that had sent her spiraling into the married arms of Kenneth Reynolds . . . and others.

Mind spinning, Kitty marched to the downstairs wet bar. Tonight, she wouldn't bother with ice or even a glass. Instead, she grabbed her beloved Jim Beam and downed the brown liquor straight from the bottle. Despite the rush of fire that blazed down her throat, she chugged a good third of it before breaking for air.

In no time, she was lit, and her tornado of thoughts slowed. She had no idea what to do or what she expected Davidson could do about that damn news story. Maybe there would be another terrorist strike before the morning edition, allowing the scandal to be buried among another wave of fear and mass hysteria.

Sanders took another chug from the bottle. *Think. Think. Think.*

This couldn't be the way that her career ended. *Please, God. Not like this.*

Something moved in the corner of her eye, and Sanders's heart leaped in instant paranoia. *Someone is here.* Why didn't she switch on the lights when she entered the room? She attempted to dismiss her fear, but couldn't.

Abrianna smiled at the scared, deer-caught-in-the-headlights look on Kitty's face. Her hands itched to wrap around her pasty-ass neck. She had this bitch right where she wanted.

"It's you, isn't it?" Sanders asked.

"Were you expecting someone else?" Abrianna asked, stepping into the thin strips of moonlight streaming through the venetian blinds.

The silence roared.

Sanders set down the whiskey bottle, trying to figure out how to play this situation.

Abrianna's smile expanded.

"What do you want?" Sanders asked.

"Take a guess." Abrianna moved closer.

"Money?"

Abrianna laughed. "Hardly. Why did you do it?"

"Humph. If you're here, you already know why."

Abrianna nodded. "Congratulation, *Chief Justice Sanders.* Looks like you got what you wanted."

"I didn't get *everything* I wanted. You're still breathing."

"What can I say? I've grown fond of the habit."

Again, Kitty snickered. "You only know *half* the story. It wasn't *all* my idea to kill Reynolds."

"You're referring to your collusion with Madam Nevaeh?"

"Who?" Sanders blinked.

"C'mon. No more games. Madam Nevaeh—my former employer."

Kitty laughed and reached for the Jim Beam again. "You've got to be kidding me. I'm not talking about some damn pussy-peddler. I'm talking about the White House."

Abrianna froze, her profile illuminated by moonlight. "What are you saying?"

"C'mon, girl. How dumb are you? I'm not the only one who had something to gain by Reynolds's death."

The president of the United States?

Sanders snickered. "Betcha your reporter friend would love a sip of that tasty tea. The administration wanted to stop an impeachment and I wanted my seat on the Supreme Court. One hand washes the other. In case you didn't know: that's how shit works in this damn town." She exhaled. "And now you've gone and ruined everything. Had I known how resourceful and indestructible you were, I would've put a bullet in your head while you were passed out that night."

"But you needed a scapegoat. Me."

"Well, look at that: a hooker with a brain."

"Fuck you."

Sanders's right arm leveled above the bar, in her hand a .38 special. "I'm going to rectify that situation right now. I may not be able to stop that damn story, but I sure as hell can take you out." She pulled the trigger.

Click.

Abrianna laughed. "Aw. I think you need these."

She held up a handful of bullets and let them all fall to the floor. "I had some time to kill while waiting for you to come back downstairs. I figured that a chick known as iron balls on the bench would be a card-toting NRA member and had weapons stashed around the place."

"You fucking bitch!" Sanders launched toward Abrianna, her acrylic nails ready to strike.

Abrianna had been sitting ready, hoping this dumb bitch would do something stupid. Trick was going to catch hands tonight. The first blow was a right hook that lifted the skinny judge out of her expensive pumps and sent her reeling sideways over a coffee table.

Before Kitty could shake off the stars circling her head, Abrianna leaped. However, it was hard to land blows. Kitty was one of those windmill swinging and leg-peddling bitches. All that was in Abrianna's face for a few seconds were spinning body parts.

Abrianna's patience snapped. She put her head down and went in, pounding.

The fight went out of Kitty on the second punch, but Abrianna was deep in a red rage. She didn't pay attention to the sickening crunch of bone.

"Bree, stop," Kadir barked, jumping in and dragging Abrianna off the bloody woman.

Sanders gasped and wheezed as she scrambled away in true fear for her life. "It's you." She swallowed, pointing at Kadir. "The terrorist they're looking for in the news." She mopped at the blood pouring from her nose.

Kadir shook his head. "You don't remember me, do you?"

Sanders's brows crashed. "Should I?"

"Six years back?" he prompted. "You tossed me into a cell for hacking into your daddy's pet project T4S."

Sanders's eyes widened.

"Yeah. I thought that might ring a bell," Kadir said.

Sanders looked back at Abrianna. "Who *are* you?"

"I'm the bitch that's going to bring you down," Abrianna boasted, panting. She plastered on a smile and lifted her shirt to show the judge that she was wired. "Thanks for the confession." Abrianna stepped back. "I'm sure a whole lot of people will find this conversation interesting. We were only missing the motivation to accompany the video from the hotel's surveillance." She winked. "See you in the news. You know, when they slap the handcuffs on you and make you do that long perp walk in front of the cameras."

A sob broke from Sanders's throat as she dropped to her knees. "Oh God! I'm ruined."

"You're damn right." Abrianna backpedaled to Kadir. "Let's go."

Kadir lingered, shaking his head and staring at the broken judge for a few more seconds before he turned and left the house.

16

In the parking garage, Abrianna and Kadir climbed out of the back of the van and walked over to Tomi, who was waiting next to her car.

"I have a present for you." Abrianna held up a recorder with the digital voice file.

Tomi removed her shades. "Holy shit. You got it? A confession?"

"Yep. Prepare to have your mind blown." Abrianna pushed the play button. Tomi's jaw dropped and remained open while Sanders said Reynolds's murder led all the way to the White House.

Abrianna shut off the recorder.

Tomi made a grab for it, but Abrianna pulled back. "What gives?"

"This is going to clear my name, right?"

"Are you kidding me? This is about to make you—*us* the biggest story to hit this town since Trump and Putin." Tomi lunged again and snatched the recorder.

She clutched it like Gollum's precious in *Lord of the Rings*. "You have to come upstairs. Give me a real exclusive of what happened that night. My editor is up there, waiting. He wants to meet you."

"What?"

"C'mon," Tomi pleaded. "When I told him about this story, he looked at me like I'd grown two extra heads. He read my first draft and saw the pictures, but let me tell you, he's nervous. But *this*"—she held up the recorder—"is one hell of an insurance policy."

"Then you don't need me."

"I do. The story needs a face." She glanced at Kadir. "Needs *both* of your faces. This story clears you, Bree, but not you, Mr. Kahlifa. It'll help, especially if we show that you're a hero in all of this."

"Hero is pouring it on a bit thick."

"Not from where I'm standing," Tomi countered, grinning.

Abrianna lifted a brow and gave a *really, bitch?* stare.

The grin melted off Tomi's face.

Unaware of the silent conversation transpiring between the women, Kadir said, "I still have to turn myself in to the FBI."

"Yeah. You both do," Tomi admitted. "But not until *after* the story breaks. Then, I think you'll find law enforcement a little more cooperative."

Kadir guffawed. "Are you kidding me? We're about to tell the world that our president murdered a member of Congress and you think that will make the FBI more cooperative? In what world?"

"A high-profile case like this, you bet your ass. Without it, they could make you disappear."

Abrianna and Kadir shared dubious looks.

"Please. Don't disappear on me this time," Tomi pleaded.

Abrianna's nerves were frayed, but Tomi was right. She couldn't disappear like she did after the Avery case.

"C'mon." Tomi walked and gestured for her to follow. "It's going to be all right. I promise."

Abrianna hesitated.

Kadir moved behind her and pressed his hand against her back. "C'mon. It's almost over."

His words sank like a stone in her gut. Was he talking about them? Were they almost over? She hadn't given much thought to what *they* were or what they would be when this was over.

"So . . . you'll come up?" Tomi asked.

Abrianna sighed. "Lead the way."

Sanders's sobs racked her body long after Abrianna left. This was rock bottom. *What can I do? Where can I go?*

Envisioning the police handcuffing and parading her before the news cameras or her having to stand before a judge, a *lower* court judge after ascending to highest court in the land, was too much. *What will my daughters say? My colleagues? The world?* Sanders sobbed until she heard footsteps.

She lifted her head. "Davidson."

Dressed in black, he stood over her; in his hand, a silencer-tipped gun. "Goodbye, Kitty." He aimed.

"No. Wait!"

He tapped the trigger and blew a hole into the side of her head.

Office of the Washington Post

Abrianna's interview went on for hours under the watchful eye of Tomi's editor, Martin Bailey, and photographer Jayson Brigham. She kept some details out of the article. Details like *how* she became an escort and who she worked for. The police car chase to Madam Nevaeh, the kidnapping and the shoot-out with the police, hacking the hotel security cameras, and breaking into judge Sanders's home. Other than all that, she was completely truthful.

Exhausted, Abrianna sat next to Kadir with her head buzzing and sweat beading her hairline. After another hour, she was done.

"That's it," Tomi boasted proudly. She hadn't stopped typing since she sat down. Bailey edited as fast as she wrote. Together, they were a well-oiled machine.

Head pounding, Abrianna stood, but wobbled on her feet. "You have everything you need?"

"Everything *except* how you managed to get the hotel security video," Tomi said.

Abrianna smiled. "Sorry. I can't reveal our sources."

"Uh-huh." Tomi's gaze cut to Kadir.

Bailey said, "I called a good friend of mine, who happens to be a damn good attorney: Joseph Bowen. He has offered his services. He can also arrange for you to turn yourselves in to the authorities."

Abrianna and Kadir hesitated.

"Pro bono," Bailey added.

"And he's good?" Abrianna asked.

Tomi answered, "One of the best law firms in the city."

Abrianna glanced to Kadir, who shrugged. "Can't beat free."

"Haven't you ever heard that you get what you pay for?" she asked.

"In this case," Bailey said, "you're getting a hell of a bargain."

"Then he's hired," she said. "Hey. Do you have a bathroom around here?" She needed a bump, bad.

Tomi glanced up. "Uh, yeah. Go straight down this row of cubicles to get to the hall, and then go straight down that hallway until you reach the vending machines and hang a right. The ladies' room is the first door on your left."

"Thanks."

Kadir stood and offered, "Hey, I'll go with you."

Tomi and Bailey looked up then.

"I can manage. I don't need a babysitter," Abrianna said dismissively. She avoided his gaze as she rushed off. In the empty ladies' room, she entered the first stall and locked the door before digging out her last twenty-bag.

The stall door burst open.

Startled, she dropped the bag. "Fuck!"

"I knew it."

Both dove for the drugs.

"What are you doing?" she screeched. "Give me that back."

He growled, "You don't need this shit!" He struggled, playing keep-away while he dumped the contents into the toilet and flushed.

"Nooo!" Abrianna went ballistic, swinging away.

Her punches were like hammers, threatening to break his back.

"Goddamn it!"

Bang!

A geyser of water blasted him from the broken toilet bowl.

The small news team stormed into the flooded bath-room.

"What in the hell?" Tomi shouted.

Abrianna snapped out her rage and scrambled away from a fallen Kadir.

Bailey and Jayson disappeared, but returned shortly with a wrench to shut off the toilet's main line.

"Are you two all right?" Tomi asked, staring at the soaking wet couple.

"Yeah. Fine," Abrianna said. "Look, I gotta go."

"What?"

Abrianna took off.

"Wait. Where are you going?" Tomi chased after her.

"I'm tired. We're finished here, right?" Abrianna said, charging forth.

"Yes. I guess. I got everything I need, but . . . will you please slow down? Aren't you going to tell me what the hell happened back there?"

"Your damn toilet broke," Abrianna snapped. "Isn't it obvious?"

"You're not about to disappear on me again, are you?" Tomi fretted, keeping up. "You can't pull a Hou-dini on me here. Without you, I'm going to get a lot federal heat."

Abrianna turned; she was surprised to see Kadir marching along with Tomi. She jerked her gaze away from him. "I'm not going to bail. I'll be back tomor-row. We got to meet the lawyers . . . and then turn our-selves in, anyway. I just need a shower, clean clothes, and some sleep."

Tomi stared. "You don't look so well."

"Yeah? How would you look after a toilet exploded in your face?" She turned and punched the button for the elevator.

"All right. Then I guess I'll see you two tomorrow," Tomi said, though she wanted to add, "I hope."

The elevator arrived, and Abrianna and Kadir stepped inside, looking like drowned cats. Before the door closed, Tomi advised, "Try not to kill each other."

Abrianna and Kadir rode the elevator in silence. Their stubbornness continued during their jaunt to the parking deck. In the van, a grumpy Ghost roused from his nap and cursed them out for taking their sweet-ass time returning. "Why the hell are you two soaking wet?"

"It's a long story," Kadir said.

During the ride back to Ghost's play-cousin's warehouse apartment, he grumbled on about how fucked up it was that he'd somehow become the damn Uber driver shuttling them around town, risking his neck. When it was clear that he couldn't draw them into an argument, Ghost shut the hell up.

Abrianna and Kadir used separate showers, again irritating Ghost.

"Oh. I guess that means I got to wait to wash *my* ass, huh?"

Neither of them responded.

He tossed up his hands. "Just fuck me. I get it."

Abrianna stripped down and stood beneath a pulsing stream of water. It felt good for a moment, but her body rebelled for not getting its fix, and she was back out of the shower and bending over the toilet, soaking wet and hurling. Pain roared through her head. She collapsed to the floor and hugged the cool porcelain for dear life. Despite having little in her stomach, her abdominal muscles spasmed relentlessly. She begged everyone she could think of, even the God she didn't believe in, for relief. At some point, she passed out.

Soon after, Kadir's smooth baritone penetrated her cloud of pain.

"It's all right. I got you," he whispered lovingly. He slid a robe on her like he was dressing a baby doll.

Something cool was pressed against her head, and then she was lifted. She laid her head against his chest and sighed.

"What's wrong with her?" she heard Ghost ask.

"She's going to be fine," Kadir assured, carrying her to the bedroom.

"Are you sure? She looks like she needs a doctor."

Abrianna groaned and shook her head. "No. No doctors."

"Don't worry. I got this," Kadir said, settling her onto the bed. "I'll take care of her.

"Is she a junkie?" Ghost asked.

Kadir snapped. "Look, man. I *said* I would take of her. This doesn't have anything to do with you."

"Maybe I—"

"Ghost!"

"All right." Ghost held up his hands and backpedaled to the door. "I'll let you deal with it."

"Thank you," Kadir said tightly.

Ghost closed the door behind him, and Kadir turned his attention back to Abrianna.

"I-I'm sorry," she stuttered.

Kadir went to her. "You have nothing to be sorry for." He got her beneath the blankets. When she continued shivering, he raced out to find more. Once he had her buried beneath several blankets, he climbed into the bed and cocooned her.

"It's all right. We're going to get through this *together*," he assured, kissing her head. "I'm here."

Something about the sound of his voice lulled Abrianna into a peaceful mind space despite her body's rioting spasms. *Together*. She liked the sound of that. She liked the thought of him always being around, too. That would change tomorrow, but tonight, he was seeing her at her worst again, and he stayed. She loved that.

———◆◆———

President Walker woke knowing he faced a difficult day. Capitol Hill would be abuzz over the *Washington Post*'s story. After all, Sanders was his appointee. However, the staged suicide should stem the flow and keep the story from climbing higher up the ladder. Plus, Walker took pride in being a good actor. He had no doubts that he could convey the right balance of shock, remorse, and disappointment for the cameras.

By five-thirty, he and his select group of Secret Service men made it to the Mall for their daily morning jog. It was important for him to stick to his routine. In his head, he rehearsed words of condolence for the judge's family. He'd ask for an investigation. Congress would launch several; however, with Sanders dead, he was confident that no one could tie him to the speaker's death.

An hour later, Walker was back in the residence quarters of the White House, showering and preparing for his day. At the breakfast table, he kissed the first lady and settled down to eat and read the papers. He reached for the *Washington Post* first and regretted it.

THE MURDERER IN THE WHITE HOUSE

17

America was plunged into shock when Tomi Lehane's explosive article was published. The story was the breaking news on every news channel around the world. The stolen video from the Hay-Adams Hotel played on a constant loop. Calls flooded the *Post*'s phone lines, and Tomi's in box exploded. On social media, #Murdererinchief trended to number one and held.

Political pundits voiced doubts as to whether America's institutions would ever recover. One thing was for sure, Abrianna Parker, Kadir Kahlifa, and Tomi Lehane were the hottest story in the nation. Everyone wanted to interview them.

Everyone wanted a part in the political story of the century.

Everyone waited with bated breath for a response from the White House.

However, 1600 Pennsylvania Avenue was on radio silence. The daily briefing was canceled. By noon, there was still no word on whether the president would address the nation from the Rose Garden or the Oval Office. But sooner or later, President Walker would have to say *something*. Silence was only pouring gasoline on the fire.

All calls to Judge Sanders went unanswered, and by late afternoon, the world knew why.

Just breaking, recently appointed Chief Justice Katherine Sanders was found dead in her Alexandria home this afternoon. Her oldest daughter, who'd grown concerned when her mother failed to return her calls after this morning's blockbuster story about the judge's alleged collusion with President Walker in murdering House Speaker Kenneth Reynolds, discovered the body. Initial reports suggest a suicide, but officials have yet to rule out foul play.

#KillerJudgeSanders trended number two on Twitter.

It didn't take long for conspiracy theorists to get to work. Within minutes, half the country believed the country had a serial-killer-in-chief running the White House.

The two people who couldn't care less about the judge's death were Abrianna and Kadir. As they rode to the FBI headquarters with Tomi and her colleague Jayson, they heard the news of the judge's death on the radio. Abrianna knew the question circling inside Tomi's head. "No," Abrianna answered without waiting for her to ask. "I didn't kill her. Not that it didn't cross my mind, but the woman was very much alive when we left last night."

Tomi studied her and then said, "I never figured Judge Sanders to be the kind of person to take the coward's way out."

Abrianna jerked. "I've never understood that saying. Suicide is hardly cowardice. It takes a lot of courage to pull it off."

Kadir glanced at Abrianna, but she ignored his stare and continued with Tomi, "What? You think that she could ascend to the highest court in the land, only to crash down and become another number in the prison system?"

"You *knew* that she would do this?" Tomi asked, surprised.

"I didn't say that. I never gave a single fuck about what she would do."

Driving, Jayson pulled into front of the Federal Bureau of Investigation and parked. A mob of reporters rushed the car. "Whelp. We're here." He glanced back through the rearview mirror. "Are you guys ready to do this?"

Abrianna noticed Kadir fretting in his seat. She took his hand and squeezed.

Kadir smiled, at least he tried, but there were too many flashbacks to the last time he was in this building. He'd been thrown in a cell for six years. He didn't know whether he had it in him to do any more jail time, especially for something that he didn't do. This time he had a better set of lawyers. The *Post*'s editor, Martin Bailey, had referred them to a top-notch firm who'd leaped at the opportunity to represent them.

"Let's get this over with." Kadir opened his door and climbed out.

Abrianna, Tomi, and Jayson followed his lead.

The mob of reporters swarmed as the group made their way toward the front door.

"Ms. Parker! Ms. Parker," they shouted.

"Can you tell us your reaction to Chief Justice Sanders's death?" one reporter yelled.

"Is there anything that you want to say to the president?" another one boomed.

Yeah. He can fuck off and die.

They made it to the door and rushed inside, escaping the barrage of questions. The reporters stopped shouting when the door closed.

"Well. That was fun," Abrianna mumbled, removing her shades.

"Better get used to it," Tomi warned with a smile.

Attorneys Joseph Bowen and Marcus Johnson approached and introduced themselves. Behind them, a team of federal agents waited to take them into custody.

Kadir's gaze zeroed in on his old nemesis, Special Agent Quincy Bell, and his muscle-head partner, Roland Hendrickson.

They flashed Kadir humorless smiles.

"Long time, no see, Mr. Kahlifa," Bell said, removing his toothpick. "Welcome home."

PART THREE

Something Wicked This Way Comes

18

Cargill Parker read the *Washington Post*'s exclusive on his daughter at least a hundred times. He traced Abrianna's picture in the paper with his finger and was hit by a longing that surprised him. She had developed into a gorgeous woman.

Over the past six years, he had been impressed by Abrianna's ability to disappear into thin air. He'd lost count of the number of private detectives he'd hired over the years. Every one of them proved useless in the end. Once, he'd thought that mouthy lieutenant Gizella Castillo from the D.C. police department had hidden Abrianna. He had her followed, but that didn't pan out, either. Two years ago, he'd been convinced that Abrianna had been abducted again or had fallen prey to any number of dangerous vices on the streets and was dead.

Then, suddenly, she was resurrected. She was back in the headlines—this time wanted for murder.

That didn't surprise him.

Cargill placed a hand on the keloid scars across his

chest and closed his eyes. His mind zoomed back twelve years. Nine-year-old Abrianna stood at her brother's bedroom door, a gun smoking in her hands. Cargill remembered the smell and taste of his blood bubbling in his throat as he stared up at her from the floor.

She looked magnificent, a beautiful, avenging goddess sent to slay the dragon.

She failed.

He was almost disappointed.

Cargill opened his eyes and smiled. He wanted to see his daughter again. He would need to make it special if he was to impress her. He was curious to see whether Abrianna could still excite him despite having a woman's body.

He reached for his bourbon and climbed to his feet. He entertained thoughts about Abrianna as he walked toward the four-poster, king-size bed. With one hand, he unbelted his robe and exposed himself to Lovely, the eight-year-old Haitian-American girl who'd stopped pretending to be asleep.

She bolted up and scrambled to a corner of the bed.

"Ah. Ah. Ah," he said, setting down his drink on the nightstand. "You know how angry I get when you make me chase you," he warned. "You don't want to make me angry, do you?"

Tears filled the girl's wide-eyed stare. At that moment, she reminded him of Abrianna. "Tonight, I'm going to call you Abrianna, and I want you to call me Daddy."

19

Vice President Kate Washington stormed into the Oval Office. "We have to do something. The press is having a field day."

President Walker stopped pacing. "No shit. Tell me something I don't know." He raked his hands through his silver mane. "How in the fuck is this shit happening?"

"I don't know. You were the one who was supposed to be handling everything, remember?"

The president resumed pacing.

Kate glanced to Davidson, who shrugged, lingering for some kind of instruction. "Can you please give us a few minutes?" she asked.

Davidson looked to the president.

Walker waved him off like he was an irritating fly.

With a nod, Davidson exited the Oval Office.

Once alone, Kate folded her arms and unloaded on the president. "You can't stay locked in here forever.

We have a rabid press, and the entire White House staff is in meltdown mode."

"Will you please stop telling me shit that I already know?"

Kate shook her head. "I bet you also know what you *have* to do. The *only* thing that you can do."

Walker smirked. "You're fucking loving this shit, aren't you?"

"Me?" She thumbed herself in the chest. "You want to blame this shit on *me?* Do I need to remind you that you ignored my advice, thumbed your nose at the awesome responsibility of this office? Was it *my* fault that you and your Secret Service buddies couldn't keep your dicks in your pants on a presidential trip in Brazil? Was it *my* fault that your shenanigans were leaked to the damn press and given to the Congress for ammunition to impeach you? If none of that shit happened, Sanders's nomination would've never been held up in the first place!"

"And what? She wouldn't have had the excuse to go and kill the man?" Walker charged.

Kate shrugged.

"You're actually excusing Sanders's motive?"

"I never said that."

"You're implying it while that dead bitch is dragging me down the drain. Nobody believes that I didn't have shit to do with this."

Kate rolled her eyes.

"See? You don't even fucking believe me."

"That's because I know you. Go play that victim shit with the first lady because if you pull that bullshit with the public, they'll have your head for it."

"No. I can beat this."

Kate was incredulous. "If you don't step down, and soon, you will be impeached, and you *know* it!"

The president hung his head.

Kate read defeat in his posture and urged in a softer tone, "Step down, Daniel. It's over."

Walker lifted his chin, waltzed behind his desk, and buzzed his secretary. "Emma, get Davidson in here again."

Kate frowned. "What are you doing?"

He ignored her, and a minute later, Davidson returned to the office. "Yes, Mr. President?"

"I need you to do some hunting. I need everything you can find on this Ms. Abrianna Parker and everyone who's close to her. I mean *everything*. Leave no stone unturned."

Davidson nodded. "Yes, sir, Mr. President."

"Daniel, what are you doing?" Kate asked.

Walker smiled. "What does it look like? If I'm going down, I'm going down fighting."

Castillo's private investigating firm, the Agency, usually took cases spying on cheating spouses. Occasionally, companies hired her to do background checks, but what kept her up at night was her pet project: searching for lost children. Children who'd disappeared, without a trace. In recent years, she found some of them hidden in the seedy underworld of sex trafficking.

Since she'd founded the Agency, she'd recovered eight girls and three boys. Two of the girls were pregnant. All three boys were dead.

Staring up at her personal corkboard with the pictures of missing kids still pinned to it, Castillo realized that it was time to return her attention to them. Yet Tomi's exclusive interview with Abrianna Parker kept needling her. Castillo was shocked and wrestled with feelings of betrayal. Tomi didn't owe her anything—

let alone any confidence about breaking this story. However, Castillo had seen Tomi the other night, and the chick never said anything about having been in contact with Abrianna, let alone that she was interviewing her for an exclusive article.

She tossed the paper aside and retrieved the check that Tomi had given her for services rendered. She'd been hired only to investigate Speaker Reynolds. *What am I upset about?* Like Shawn White said, no one had asked for her help.

Castillo shook her head. Actually, that wasn't entirely true . . .

———⋙⋅⋘———

Six years ago

"What in the hell do you mean, she's gone?" Cargill Parker bellowed. The six-foot-three towering white man sucked all the oxygen out of the room. He was intimidating, and Castillo was not easily intimidated. It took a full minute for Castillo to even notice the nervous café-au-lait black woman cowering by his side.

An affronted Lieutenant Castillo attempted to calm the angry man who'd blown into the hospital like a tornado in search of his daughter. "Sir, please. You're upset. Maybe this conversation would be better down at the station?" she suggested.

Cargill's face glowed red as his eyes narrowed. "You're lying. Where is she?"

"Excuse me?" Castillo stepped forward, her hand landing where her service weapon was supposed to be, had she not been suspended hours earlier. She'd taken a huge risk in forging a judge's signature on a warrant for Craig Avery. It was a Hail Mary that cost a few of

*her men's lives, but saved the three teenagers huddled
naked in that madman's basement.*

*One teenager had left the hospital with her band of
friends before anyone obtained her full name or con-
tacted her parents. Now here they were, howling in
Castillo's face.*

*Quick for a man his size, Cargill grabbed Castillo's
arm and jerked her forward. "I don't have time to play
these games. Where are you hiding my daughter?"*

*"Cargill." The timid and well-polished woman at
his side placed a hand on his arm. "Please, darling.
Calm down."*

"Shut the hell up, Marion," he hissed.

Marion shrank as if he'd bitten her.

*Castillo warned, "Take. Your. Hand. Off. Of. Me.
Mr. Parker."*

His grip tightened.

"Or lose it," Castillo added. "Your choice."

*Sensing his intimidation tactics weren't working,
Cargill released her. "My apologies," he said gruffly.
"My wife and I have been through a lot these past few
months. We just want to take our daughter home and
put this whole madness behind us."*

*Castillo nodded, though she didn't buy the man's
bullshit for a second. Her mind zoomed to what the
doctor, who'd checked Abrianna over, had said about
the years-old bone breaks and scars on the teenager's
body. Castillo was now certain where those injuries
had come from.*

Marion asked, "Can we please see Abrianna now?"

*"Abrianna," Castillo repeated. It was a pretty name.
Up until then, the girl had only been known as Bree No
Last Name. The teenager, as well as her friends, had
been careful not to give that information. "Look, Mr.*

Parker, I wish that I could help, but your daughter left of her own volition about thirty minutes ago. I didn't even get a chance to finish interviewing her."

"Where in the hell did she go?" Cargill thundered.

Castillo shrugged. "I have no idea."

"You've got to be kidding me," he growled. "You people call yourselves professionals? Who's your supervisor?"

"Mr. Parker, your daughter was not under arrest. She was free to go."

"Free to go where? She's a teenager who'd been a prisoner of a madman. You didn't think to detain her until her parents arrived?"

"I'm sorry, sir. But—"

"You're damn right you're sorry. Your whole department is sorry." He turned and stormed away, leaving his wife behind.

"Please, excuse my husband. He can be very . . . passionate at times," Marion said, fidgeting.

Castillo's brows came close to touching her hairline. "Passionate?"

Marion's smile wobbled. "My daughter," she said. "Did you get to see her at all?"

"I spoke to her for a few minutes."

"And . . . how did she seem to you?"

"Damaged," Castillo answered. "I suspect that she's been that way for a long time."

Marion's eyes watered.

"I may be stepping a toe out of line, but you seem a bit damaged yourself."

"Marion," Cargill bellowed from halfway down the hallway. "Are you coming or not?"

"Yes, sweetheart. I'm coming," she shouted, and then addressed Castillo, "Look. If you're hiding her—"

"I'm not—"

"It's okay. I understand. She's right to stay away. It's best that she does."

Castillo frowned. "Mrs. Parker, if you're telling me that your daughter is in some kind of danger, then there are steps we can take to protect her—and yourself."

Marion laughed.

"Marion!" Cargill shouted again,

Marion backed away. "You don't understand."

Castillo moved forward. "Try me."

"You can't protect us. He's too powerful. But you can help Abrianna by keeping her away. Promise me you'll keep her away and that she'll be well looked after."

"Mrs. Parker, I—"

"Damn it, Marion!"

Marion spun around and raced toward her husband. "Here I come, sweetie," she sang like Mary freaking Poppins.

The strange encounter never left Castillo, mainly because she hadn't been able to do what Marion asked: make sure that Abrianna was well looked after.

According to Tomi's article, Abrianna had had a difficult life after leaving the hospital that night so long ago. She'd survived by hustling: drug trafficking, prostituting, stripping, and finally landing on being an escort girl for D.C.'s rich and powerful. Abrianna would rather do all of that than return to the lap of luxury with her billionaire parents.

What the hell happened in that house?

20

After a ten-hour FBI interrogation, Abrianna was released.

Kadir wasn't so lucky.

With the warning to remain in D.C., Abrianna and her attorney, Joseph Bowen, plowed through the reporters.

Once Abrianna climbed into Joseph Bowen's Mercedes, she hammered him. "Why isn't Kadir being released? Why are they holding him? Are they arresting him?"

"I don't know any more than you," the attorney said.

"They can't believe that Kadir had anything to do with that bombing, can they?"

"Maybe, maybe not. There are *other* factors at play."

"Like what?"

"Like his parole. Mr. Kahlifa had been captured on camera engaged in a speeding gunfight."

"He was driving. I was shooting," Abrianna exclaimed. "In self-defense."

"I know. However, the government can be hardasses. Plus, I got the distinct feeling Agents Bell and Hendrickson have a hard-on for Mr. Kahlifa. They aren't too eager to let him go."

———◆———

After listening to Kadir's story for the hundredth time, Special Agent Bell stretched back in his chair, sighing. "We got ourselves a problem."

"We do?" Attorney Marcus Johnson asked.

"We sure do." Hendrickson rolled and cracked the tension from his neck.

"And what problem is that?" Kadir asked, not amused.

Bell said, "I know that you got your dick hard to be hailed as the next American hero in this cockamamie story about the president, a hooker, and a murdering judge, but the wrinkle in your plan is that you violated your parole. Car chases, shoot-outs, and there are serious questions as to how you and Ms. Parker acquired that surveillance video from the Hay-Adams."

Kadir's features smoothed out into hard granite.

"I mean. You had to have *hacked* into the hotel's security system, right?"

Silence.

"That's a *big* no-no, not to mention a major violation to your parole." Bell laughed and waved a finger in Kadir's face. "Yeah. It *was* you."

"Maybe you should stick to what you can prove," Kadir hissed.

"I can *prove* you violated your parole." Bell stood and reached for his cuffs. "Mr. Kadir Kahlifa, I'm placing you under arrest. Stand up, asshole."

Marcus Johnson stood. "Now there's no need for that type of language."

Bell ignored the attorney to hiss into Kadir's ear. "I'm sending you back to your jailhouse girlfriends. They can suck you off like old times. If we hurry, I can have you back there before lights out."

"Fuck you."

"Fuck me?" Bell rocked back. "Nah, muthafucka. Fuck you." Bell head-butted Kadir and reeled him back a few steps.

Johnson jumped to his feet and shouted, "Whoa! Agent Bell!"

Pissed, Kadir lunged before his attorney could stop him.

Bell's sharp reflexes helped him land a punch across Kadir's jaw.

"Gentlemen! Gentlemen," Johnson shouted, scrambling. "Stop this!"

Kadir retaliated with a hard punch, rocking the agent's head back. Blood sprayed from the agent's lips.

Late, Hendrickson tagged into the battle with hands of steel.

Johnson raced and pounded on the door for help.

By the time more agents arrived, Kadir was knocked out cold.

21

Tomi Lehane's blockbuster story landed her on every cable news channel for multiple shows. In a furor, pundits speculated what this game changer meant and when the president would step down. *It was inevitable*, they said, but no one told that to the president. President Walker's supporters cast blame and suspicion on Abrianna, called her every name but a child of God. However, when the *Washington Post* uploaded the Sanders confession on their website, the naysayers were shut down.

Abrianna blocked out the noise. Today, Tivonté and Shawn were being released from the hospital. She woke early, disguised herself in a platinum wig and a pair of Jackie O sunglasses, and ventured to the hospital. She wasn't out in the streets a full minute before she was convinced that she was being watched. Scanning over her shoulder, she picked up the pace. Her paranoia had people on the street and the city bus eyeballing her.

At the hospital, Abrianna went to Shawn's room

first. A nurse was rolling him out of the room when she arrived. "Hey, diva," she greeted, removing her glasses and leaning in for a hug.

Shawn glowed. "It's about time!"

"I'll take him from here," she told the nurse, taking hold of the handlebars. "You have no idea how much I've missed you."

"You better have while you're out there enjoying your newfound fame," Shawn said.

"Ha. I'm off the grid. I'm still enemy number one with half of the country hating my guts."

"You know what I always say: You're nobody until somebody hates you."

"Amen." Abrianna chuckled. "Which room is Tivonté's?"

"He's up on the next floor."

Tomi was on yet another political show when Abrianna rolled Shawn into Tivonté's crowded hospital room.

"Hello, stranger," Abrianna greeted, beaming.

"Bree!" The group of friends shouted.

Tivonté beamed. "Come through, bitch. Come through." He opened his arms.

Tears brimming in her eyes, Abrianna rushed forward.

When Tivonté's arms wrapped around her, they were thinner than usual, but felt good. Her friends were her life, her treasure.

"Are you two about to make out?" Draya joked. "Do we need to leave?"

They laughed and pulled apart and wiped their eyes.

"Glad you made it," Tivonté said. "I thought your ass went Hollywood. Your name and picture is plastered everywhere. The thot that brought down a presidency."

"All right. I got your thot!" Abrianna rolled her eyes. "But I can't wait for this mess to blow over. Reporters are worse than bill collectors, if you can believe it."

"Now you're making shit up." Tivonté swatted her arm.

Draya cut in, "I, for one, am glad that some of the foolishness is over. Maybe we all can stop getting shot."

"I'm so sorry that I dragged you all into my chaos. I put you all in so much danger."

Tivonté waved her off. "Girl, please. My daddy beat me worse than this when I came out of the closet on my thirteenth birthday."

Shawn joked, "I'm jealous. I think she cried more for you lying in here than for me."

Abrianna shoulder-bumped Shawn. "Stop! I love you both the same."

"And we love you," Tivonté told her. "When a muthafucka comes for one of us, they come for all."

Draya nodded. "Yeah. I was joking about the whole getting shot thing. There's no one I'd rather catch a bullet for." The two hugged.

"Let me get some of that," Julian said, wrapping his arms around Abrianna. "If you ever need another get-away driver, I'm your man. The shit was kind of fun."

"That's because you weren't shot." Draya smacked the back of Julian's head.

"Ow."

Tivonté harrumphed and batted his eyes. "Next time y'all snatch somebody else's catering van when y'all are playing private eyes and kidnapping bitches, especially if it's dealing with that sick muthafucka Zeke leave me out. I hope you're still keeping an open eye out for his ass. He's gotta be slinking around here somewhere."

Abrianna rolled her eyes. "Fuck him."

"All right," Tivonté warned. "You know my grand-mother used to say, 'a hard head makes a soft ass.' They don't call him the Teflon Don for nothing."

Abrianna considered his words. "I'll deal with it later."

Shawn added, "Maybe you should see Castillo. She's still lurking around, too. But at least she's no friend of Zeke's, either. Maybe she can keep an eye out for him."

"A cop?"

"She's not a cop anymore, remember? She came by after you guys crashed that party, pissed as shit. But I really think she wants to help you."

Draya folded her arms. "I don't get it. Surely that dirty muthafucka Zeke don't think he's *still* getting those eight stacks from you. Not after all that you've been through."

"If so, he'll be waiting a long damn time."

"Let's hope not. But . . ." Julian hedged.

"But what?" Abrianna snapped.

Julian shrugged. "Has he ever written off a debt?"

"It was never my debt to begin with. Moses's ass owes him for those bricks, *and* he owes me for stealing my shit out of the bank. I'm not paying a muthafuckin' thing and I'll tell it to his face, too."

"Oooh. Look at the balls on you," Shawn sassed.

Tivonté harrumphed again.

"Oh. Spit it out," Abrianna said. Tivonté always had the juiciest gossip on the streets.

"Well, it's not concrete or nothing, but word is Moses's ass has already gone on to glory. Ain't nobody seen hide nor tail of his ass in a hot minute."

Abrianna's annoyance melted.

Tivonté continued, "People talking. Do you remember that hoe Simone? Moses moved in with her after you put his ass out?"

"Of course I remember."

"Girl, she been cryin' on every shoulder that'll hold still. Told everybody how violent you are and how you broke Moses's arm and then put him through a wall."

"He stole my money."

"Yeah, well. She ain't buying the story about the judge killing that congressman. As far as she is concerned, you're a cold killer."

Abrianna waved off the story. "I ain't worried about what that knock-kneed heifer got to say. Moses probably stashed my shit somewhere and, after he sold me off to Zeke, high-tailed his ass out of D.C."

Tivonté hedged.

Abrianna cocked her head. "But?"

"But, Mimi—you probably don't know her. She was Roach's side piece that stays out there in Forestville."

"Roach—Zeke's man?" Draya asked.

Tivonté smirked. "He *used* to be until Bree and her Arab superhero had that gun chase that's playing all over the Internet."

"So where does this Mimi chick fit in?" she asked Tivonté.

"Well. Mimi told my girl Sheena at the nail shop that Zeke had outmaneuvered Moses's double-dipping ass. Roach said that they stole Moses's supply. Moses never owed that eight stacks."

Floored, Abrianna blinked. "What?"

Tivonté nodded. "Uh-huh, chile. She also said that Zeke jacked a bag full of money before he put a bullet in Moses's skull." He threw up his hands. "I ain't saying I believe her, but it sounds like some shit Zeke would do."

"That muthafucka." Abrianna seethed. "He got those bricks, my money, *and* had me out here selling my ass?" She slapped her hand on the hospital tray table. Behind her, the suspended television exploded.

"Holy shit!"

Everyone dodged as shards of broken Plexiglas and electronic parts rained down onto the floor.

After the shock wore off, Julian laughed. "We need to hurry and get you out of here. This place has exploding televisions and shit."

Shawn frowned. "Your nose is bleeding."

Embarrassed, Abrianna swiped under her nose. "Damn it."

"Here." Julian picked up the box of tissues from the tray and handed it to her.

"Thanks." She snatched a few sheets and dabbed it clean.

Her friends' gazes darted among one another.

Abrianna's head buzzed. She couldn't make out their exact words, but she knew what they were thinking. "I'd quit if it wasn't for the headaches."

Draya sighed. "You promised."

"I know and I will. It's just that . . . they're so unbearable," she added.

Shawn took her hand. "Maybe you should see a doctor? It's past time."

He was right, but she feared what a doctor would tell her. She couldn't imagine that it would be anything good. "I'll . . . think about it."

Knock. Knock.

Abrianna and her clan looked up to a familiar face.

"Hello." Castillo crept in with a bundle of carnations. She stopped when her gaze crashed into Abrianna. Castillo stared as if she'd stumbled across Big Foot.

"C'mon in," Tivonté invited, smiling.

Castillo blinked and approached the bed with the flowers outstretched. "I hope I'm not imposing. I remembered that you said that you'd be leaving today, so I figured I'd stop by and give you these," she said to Tivonté, but never took her eyes off of Abrianna. "Hi."

"Hey," Abrianna said cautiously.

"What happened to your arm?" Julian asked.

Castillo held up her arm cast. "I was in a car accident before I found your friend here."

Tivonté sniffed the flowers. "Thanks, girl. I told you. After saving my ass, we're fam. For real."

Shawn nodded. "Yeah. I'm sorry I was such an ass to you the last time. And I'm damn sure glad that you ignored me and went by La Plume that day. Matter of fact, you've saved *two* of my friends now. You're definitely family."

"Wow." Castillo glanced back at Abrianna and smiled. "I'm glad I could help."

Abrianna cleared her throat and said, "I, uh, never thanked you for saving my ass back in the day. I'm sorry about that. Shit was kind of crazy then and, uh—"

"No need. I was—well, it sounds kind of cold to say that I was doing my job. It meant more to me than that, but—you're welcome."

Abrianna smiled. "Well, thanks for saving Tivonté, too. I don't know what I'd do without this knucklehead." She patted Tivonté on the back. "And if you're a part of their family, then it means you're a part of mine as well."

Castillo beamed.

Draya swiped her eyes and announced, "This calls for a group hug."

No one gave Castillo time to protest before five sets of arms nearly squeezed the life out of her.

A nurse entered the room, pushing a wheelchair. "It's time to go home, Mr. Hollis."

Everyone cheered.

22

Lights out.

On the top bunk in his cell, Kadir stared at the ceiling. His mind raced, but there were way too many coulda, woulda, and shouldas to count. He turned his thoughts to the other side of the world to Yemen. Had the news reached his family? Was his father hanging his head in shame again? Were his mother's tears soaking the pillows? The only member of his family who was proud was probably his twin brother. Baasim had long stopped being a fan of America's democracy and vowed to never return.

I should've gone home, too.

His father, Muaadh Kahlifa, had begged him when he was first paroled. He was sure the law wouldn't have chased him there. But in Yemen, Kadir would've had a different struggle. The country had been in the midst of a civil war since the Houthi rebels seized the government years ago. It wasn't the Yemen Kadir remembered visiting as a child.

Where does that leave me? A man without a country? he mused. *It leaves me in prison.*

"Open cell C-165," a guard barked.

Startled, Kadir sat up.

His cell number was repeated in the distance before a loud buzzer sounded and the metal door opened.

"You got a new roommate, convict." The guard's grin slanted.

Kadir ignored the guard and focused on the six-foot-six black dude ducking into the cell with steps that were as heavy as an elephant's. The man was as broad as a mountain with muscles that had muscles.

The guard chuckled, patting the big man on the back. "Now you two play nice and get along, especially you, Precious. The medical ward is complaining about patching up your cellmates. The last one nearly got shipped out to the morgue."

Kadir groaned.

"Close cell C-165," the guard yelled.

The order was repeated from the corresponding guard while Kadir and *Precious* sized each other up. After their door shut, the prison guard had one more message, "By the way, Kahlifa, Special Agent Bell says hi." He laughed and marched away.

Fuck.

A malicious grin wormed across Precious's thin lips.

Kadir hopped down, never breaking eye contact with the giant.

Precious rolled his neck, cracking the tendons, and then pounded his right fist into the palm of his left hand.

Kadir angled his body away from his aggressor and

planted his feet. Mentally, he mapped out the giant's vital organs, prime real estate when calculating how to take down an opponent. Every man's vulnerability was the chin; tap that hard enough and Precious's knees would fold. However, most fighters knew that, so the chin was also one of the most protected. Kadir had a good reach, but he doubted a clean shot would open to him.

Precious inched closer, bouncing side to side.

Kadir put up his fists.

"I'm going to enjoy this, rag head." Precious dropped his chin and went with a right hook.

Kadir dodged, dancing on his toes. After landing a punch against the giant's side, Kadir realized he was in trouble. The man was made of steel. Pain ricocheted up his arm, throwing him off his game, which opened him up for a solid punch to the face.

Kadir's lip split and sprayed blood across Precious's orange uniform, which pissed the giant off further.

Growling, Precious attacked, ending their graceful dance. The fight turned into an old-fashioned street brawl with Kadir dishing out as much as he received. After a six-year stint, this was *not* Kadir's first prison fight. Unable to outpower those steel fists, Kadir switched up and used his old high school wrestling moves, hoping to exhaust his attacker.

Kadir succeeded in getting Precious into an Anaconda Choke, an arm triangle chokehold from the front headlock position, a near impossible maneuver to escape.

Precious grunted and growled, but soon his body went limp beneath Kadir. He held on for a while longer, but to avoid catching a murder charge, Kadir released the big man and then scrambled back in case Precious was playing possum.

He wasn't.

Precious was out cold.

"Well, shit!"

Kadir whipped his head toward the voice. The prison guard had returned with a couple of buddies with clubs, and none of them looked pleased.

23

The White House

President Walker was on his third bourbon an hour before noon. He didn't bother to turn from the tall windows when he heard the angry march of his vice president into the Oval Office. "Well?"

"The House gaveled in Gary Everhardt as the new speaker. He sailed through with over two hundred and thirty-three votes. They are holding a press conference now."

Sighing, Walker drained his glass before moving away from the window to grab the remote. A panel in the wall slid to the side and revealed a television. The station was already programmed to C-SPAN, where Speaker Everhardt stood before a bank of microphones, monopolizing the screen.

"We are absolutely going to launch an investigation into what part the president of the United States played in the death of our former speaker and colleague Kenneth Reynolds," Everhardt announced. "I have no doubts that we will find enough evidence to impeach. I, along with millions of Americans, am horrified by the apparent lengths this president will go to maintain power. It's clear that speaker Reynolds was nothing more than a political pawn in this administration's dangerous obsession with power. My caucus and I are here to stand up to this dangerous criminal and see to it that he is removed from the power that he covets so desperately. Thank you."

President Walker powered off the television. "Oh God."

"Daniel—"

"Don't!" He wagged his finger. "Don't start!"

Kate plowed on, "Save yourself *and* the country the humiliation of a long, drawn-out impeachment trial," she pleaded.

No sooner had those words tumbled out of her mouth, Donald Davidson and Sean Haverty, chief of staff, strolled into the office.

Walker ignored Kate and shifted his attention to the two men. "Tell me that you got something."

Davidson crossed over to the president's desk. "Not much on Abrianna Parker herself, but you might find this interesting. It's about her *father*. You'll never believe this, but he's *Cargill Parker*."

Kate and Walker perked up.

"The oil and gas tycoon?"

"The one and only," Davidson said, handing over a folder. "Of course, he's also a Republican donor. He and his wife adopted Abrianna when she was five years old. She ran away from home at fourteen and got caught up in the whole Craig Avery incident. After she'd been rescued, she disappeared again."

"Humph. Another little girl lost story, huh? The public will eat that up. That's not what I want."

"That may be true. However, Cargill isn't a boy scout. On paper, he's a powerful and successful businessman," Haverty told him.

Kate frowned. "And *off* paper?"

"Off paper, we get into a dark rumor mill. About him and a secret society that he belongs to."

"Oh, God. More conspiracies," Kate mumbled.

"*Very* persistent rumors and conspiracies," Davidson insisted.

"Do tell."

"Mr. Parker is a member of an order called the Dragons Templar. There's not much known about them. However, there are rumors that have persisted about his private Lynnwood Club. Rumors that involve sex . . . and children."

Walker lit up. Davidson had handed him the biggest gift he'd ever received. "Really?"

Kate shook her head. "We are in a constitutional crisis and you two are talking about pursuing rumors? Am I getting this right? We're not going to get out of this bullshit by launching rumors and propaganda. None of that has ever been proven, right?"

Haverty said, "I don't think anyone has ever tried to prove them. Parker is *old* money, and that's one hell of a buffer."

"Right," Kate snapped. "That old money isn't going to suddenly disappear. We don't have time for this. Step down with dignity or let the Republicans humiliate you by tossing you out on your privileged white ass."

The office quieted while Walker paced.

Kate's patience thinned. "I can't believe that you're seriously considering this. It's beyond ridiculous."

Davidson hedged. "It *could* play to character. Not only to Mr. Parker's but also to the type of criminal environment his daughter grew up in. Then you could cast doubt on the authenticity of the surveillance video . . ."

"And even suggest that she coerced the confession before Sanders killed herself," Walker added, smiling.

"Was it a suicide?" Haverty asked.

"This is madness!" Kate refused to play along.

Davidson kept his eyes on the president. "So what do you want to do?"

Walker decided, "Throw the Hail Mary and pray that we get something that sticks. Go after the father."

Davidson nodded. "Yes sir, Mr. President." He exited the office.

Walker added, "Sorry, Kate. You're going to have to wait a little longer to get behind this desk."

"You're delusional." Kate spun and marched out of the Oval Office. She caught up with Davidson before he left the West Wing. "What in hell are you doing?" she hissed, tugging his arm to make him stop.

"What does it look like? I'm carrying out the president's orders."

"What you're doing is giving him false hope."

"So?" He shrugged.

"*So?* This is dangerous. He's going to drag us all down with him on this foolish witch-hunt. Stop encouraging this nonsense."

Davidson chuckled. "What do you care if he flails for a while? He's nowhere near the truth. Only you and I know about your and Sanders's murder scheme."

"Shhhh!" Kate glanced around and then pulled him into the empty Cabinet Room. "Lower your voice. Do you want someone to hear you?"

Davidson smirked. "All I'm saying, sweetheart is that you're going to get what you want sooner or later. Sanders gave you a big fucking gift by naming the White

House and not you personally. President Dumb-Shit thinks he sent me to knock off your one-time 'college-experiment' to clean up *her* mess. He'll never know that you convinced Sanders to kill Reynolds to get her through the Senate committee. So sit back, relax, and watch the show. Let him spin his wheels. He's not going to get out of this trap." He brushed a kiss against her stiff lips. "Kitty was just a college fling, wasn't she?"

Kate glared. "I'm not answering that again."

Davidson shrugged. "Just checking, because I know your gay husband doesn't give a damn."

"You're enjoying this."

"Absolutely, Madam President." He saluted. "Absolutely."

24

DARPA Conference Center, Arlington, VA

Dr. Charles Zacher took to the stage before members of the Defense Advance Research Project Agency (DARPA) and grabbed them with his opening: "Imagine a soldier who can outrun any animal on the planet, carry hundreds of pounds with ease. Communicate telepathically with his squadron, go weeks without eating or sleeping, or regenerate lost limbs on the battlefield, and be completely controlled, mind and body, by military technicians thousands of miles away. Does this sound like science fiction to you? If so, then you're not living in the *real* world.

"We are in a twenty-first-century arms race among a vast array of covert technologies that are presently under development. There will be a new kind of soldier, a genetically modified and artificially enhanced superhuman fighting machine that dominates the battlefields of the future. The engineering of these super soldiers is not only a top priority for the Pentagon, with black budget projects with classifications so high that not even the president of the United States has the clearance to access."

Dr. Zacher held every member at his conference at rapt attention. "We at T4S are the leaders in this race, and if you're here with our special invitation, then we believe that *you* are among the best of the best scientists, and we want you to be a part of our team."

For the next forty-five minutes, he led potential recruits through T4S's founding, accomplishments, and mission statement. During the Q and A, he was challenged by the new crop of engineers on the nefarious and questionable morality of some of the projects his company engaged in; those were from the liberal crowd. The other ninety percent of the participants were excited and enthralled with the company's possibilities.

All too soon, time was up. Dr. Z thanked the crowd for their time, and he exited the stage.

Ned met him and handed him a towel and bottled water. "You were great out there, sir."

"Thanks." He patted his forehead dry. "What did you think, Spalding?" Dr. Z asked without turning around to confirm his boss stood behind him.

Spalding chuckled. "You know that I've always believed that you're one of the best."

Dr. Z turned with a sardonic smile. "It's always nice to hear, though."

Spalding said, "Well, there you go." He folded his arms. "Walk with me."

Dr. Z handed the towel and water back to Ned and fell in lockstep beside Spalding. His boss waited until they cleared out of the main conference room and away from the loitering crowd in the hallway before he addressed what he wanted to talk about.

"Have you seen the news or read the papers?" Spalding asked.

"Yes."

"Then you should know what I'm about to say."

Dr. Z sighed. "You still want me to bring Parker in."

"I want you to bring them *both* in. Parker and the reporter—Ms. Lehane."

"Why?"

"Their propensity to always be in the news is making too many people nervous. The point of having lab rats is to be able to observe them in private. These two have a habit of being in the spotlight."

Confused, Dr. Z said, "You caught me a little flat-footed."

"How is that?"

"Well, I thought that the reason you wanted Parker brought in was because she may be exhibiting violent tendencies like Shalisa Young, but it appears that may not be the case at all. She was framed."

Spalding's smile tightened. "I understand. Over the years, you've grown quite fond of Ms. Parker. You've watched her grow up. Pretended to be a grandfather figure to her. So this order comes particularly hard."

"That's not it."

"No? Then enlighten me. What is the problem?"

"There's no problem."

"Really? Because this is the *second* time that I've given this order."

"We weren't the only ones who couldn't find her," Dr. Z informed him. "The entire federal government was looking for her and quite frankly . . ." He paused to take a breath. "I think that it's a mistake to grab her now. The type of scandal they're involved in makes it sticky to extract either one of them. I suggest that we wait until this whole political drama dies down."

"See. That's where I think you're wrong," Spalding said. "I think this is the perfect time for her to disappear. When she does, we have the perfect scapegoat to take the fall."

The light clicked on in Dr. Z's head. "You want to frame the president of the United States?"

25

Every bone is Kadir's body ached. Most nights he slept with one eye open. The guards made it a game to constantly find excuses to gear up and charge into his cell with clubs swinging. However, the more they punished him, the more he rebelled.

When he entered the visiting room, Abrianna's eyes rounded in horror. "Oh, my God! What happened to your face?" Abrianna demanded, "Who did that to you?"

She reached over the table to touch him but was reprimanded. "No touching!"

Abrianna jerked back and glared at the guard.

Kadir chuckled. "Kind of reminds me of the Stallion's VIP room when the bouncer wouldn't let me touch you during that lap dance. How do you like having the roles reversed?"

"Are you enjoying this?"

"Other than the pain and the swelling, yes. A little bit."

She sat back in her seat and folded her arms. "So who did it?"

"No one. I . . . slipped in the shower," Kadir grumbled.

She cocked her head. "Really?"

Kadir ignored her reaction. "How are *you* holding up?"

"Me? I'm fine. No bathroom tiles have jumped out and whipped my ass," she said.

"Consider yourself lucky." Kadir smirked.

Abrianna's annoyance ebbed. Even with a busted face, Kadir was handsome as hell. His black, wavy hair had grown a couple of inches. And a beard was taking shape that made his pretty-boy face look more mature. "The lawyers assured me that they are still working on getting you out of here."

"Good to hear."

"The government has nothing and they know it. The attorneys were able to get copies of your Uber records from the company. Thank goodness you logged that fare to the airport on your app. Also, they have a statement from a guy who lives in your apartment complex who backs up your story. He said that he was the one who sent the Al-Sahi brothers to your place when their cabs hadn't showed up to take them to the airport."

Kadir nodded. "Yeah. That's Mook. He's the neighborhood junkie. I don't know how much his word would hold up in court."

Abrianna agreed. "The problem they're having is you violating your parole."

Kadir expelled a long breath. "Yeah. I've been told.

They can make me serve the rest of my parole time in here."

"How long is that?" Abrianna asked.

"Two and a half years," he answered.

"You're shitting me," Abrianna said, eyes widening.

"I wish."

Guilt etched lines across her forehead. "My God. What have I done? It's my fault you're in here."

"Nah. Nah." Kadir shook his head. "Don't beat yourself up. I'm a man. I made my own choices."

Abrianna fretted. "I can't leave you in here after all you've done to help me. There has to be something that I can do."

"Don't do that," Kadir pled. "I don't want you working yourself up and worrying about me. I'm going to be fine. This is not my first time at the prison rodeo."

"Of course I'm going to worry about you. Are there no mirrors in that dangerous bathroom? Your head is shaped like an Oompa Loompa."

Kadir laughed and winced when pain shot up from his cracked ribs.

Abrianna gasped and reflexively took his hand. "What? What is it? What's wrong?"

"Nothing. It just hurts when I laugh." Kadir's smile wobbled as he tried to get comfortable again.

"Then stop laughing, because there's not a damn thing funny," she snapped.

"Hands," the guard barked.

Abrianna rolled her eyes and pulled her hands back across the table.

Kadir hitched up a grin, winking his dimples. "Ah. I'm starting to get the impression that you give a damn about me."

"Yes, I give a damn. You saved my life."

Kadir's smile expanded. "I'm glad that you came out to see me. The last time I was in . . ."

She frowned and then remembered. "Oh, I forgot. Your family moved to Yemen shortly after you were convicted."

He nodded, pleased that she'd paid attention to his pillow talk.

"But what about friends or your fiancée?"

His smile flattened. "I was actually referring to after Malala, uh . . ."

"Passed away." Abrianna filled in the blank, lowering her eyes.

"Before the car accident, Malala was great. She never missed a visiting day." He sighed and stopped rambling on about the woman who he'd always thought would be his wife. There was no reason to live in the past. "As far as my friends—well, you've met one of them. Is *he* the type of person to be rollin' up in a federal prison to give me a shout-out?"

"Good point."

Silence grew between them while each struggled to find a safe topic.

Kadir spoke. "Look. If I don't get out of here—"

"Don't say that."

"Please, let me finish," he said and then took a deep breath. "If I don't get out, I want you to promise not to blame yourself. I've had a lot of time to think about it, and there is *nothing* that I would change. I'm glad that I was there to help you when you needed someone." He placed a bruised hand back on top of hers. "I know you've been through a lot . . . much of it that you haven't been comfortable to share with me, but I want you to know that none of that stuff matters. You don't have to let the past imprison you."

Abrianna shook her head.

"I know that's ridiculous advice from a man who is actually in a prison," he joked. "But I'm not." At her confusion he explained by pointing at his head. "The real prison is in here. Never let anyone imprison your mind. That's the whole game. In here, we have the power of true freedom: our thoughts, our dreams, and our prayers. We mess up when we let muthafuckas live in our heads rent-free—telling you who you are or who you're not. What you're worth or what you're not worth. Stop it. You don't need anything to numb yourself or block out their voices. You have to kick that monster out of your head."

Abrianna stiffened. Had he given himself away? He'd tried not to betray Julian's confidence—but it was hard.

"I appreciate what you're trying to do," she said. "But you really don't know what the hell you're talking about. You can't imagine what lives in my head. You have no fucking clue how desperately I've tried to evict my 'monsters.' They have made it clear that they aren't going anywhere." A tear skipped down her face. "Me and the monsters are one and the same. For better or worse and 'til death do we part."

26

Two weeks later

Abrianna hid from reporters and moved in with Shawn in his two-bedroom apartment. "Welcome to my humble abode," Shawn said as Abrianna wheeled him inside. *"Mi casa es su casa."*

"Are you sure that you don't mind my staying here for a little while?" she double-checked.

"Of course not. It'll be like the old days."

She grimaced. "Jeez, I hope not."

However, within days it was a prison. She blacked out the windows and disconnected the landline, fearing the rabid media would find her. She did carry one burner cell phone from Tomi so she could keep in contact with her and her attorney, but Abrianna developed Ghost's paranoia about it and kept changing the phone every third day.

Today, when Draya and Julian joined them for brunch, they danced around her going crazy as a topic.

"Any news on Kadir?" Draya asked. When the group

leaned forward, it was clear it was *the* question that they'd been dying to ask. "Is he ever getting out?"

Abrianna's gaze lowered. "I have no idea. The FBI isn't saying jack shit."

"Surely they can't keep him indefinitely," Julian said. "The man is innocent."

"Yeah . . . but he violated his parole." She sighed. "Our attorneys aren't getting much. The feds got some kind of ax to grind."

"Damn. I'm sorry," Shawn said. "But it goes to show that no good deed goes unpunished."

Everyone agreed. The evening's festive mood waned.

Draya pointed to the muted television. "Why is *she* getting all the shine? Every time I turn around, there she is, cheesing and shit in front of the cameras."

Abrianna glanced over to the screen to see Tomi. "Everyone gets their fifteen minutes of fame."

"It's been a long-ass fifteen minutes," Draya grumbled. "I'm sorry. I know that she's your girl."

"I never said that she was my girl," Abrianna corrected. "She's just someone I know and thought could help me." She shrugged.

"Humph." Draya stabbed a piece of her cake. "The bitch seems like an opportunist to me. Is she doing anything to help get your man out of prison?"

"Kadir is not—"

"Chile, please. Don't fix your lips to lie. You forget that we know you better than anybody. You've been trying to hold up that long face for a while now. I'm exhausted looking at you," Tivonté said.

Abrianna glanced around. Her friends nodded in agreement.

Draya threw in an "Amen."

"All right. I don't know what we are," she amended. Then she nodded back to the television. "As far as I'm concerned, better her than me. Tomi keeps trying to get me to go on one of those shows, but the last thing I want is for those people to dissect every inch of my life. I already know how fucked up it is. I don't need the world's opinion."

Shawn's forehead wrinkled, a sign that he was thinking too hard. "Maybe you're looking at this shit all wrong," he suggested.

"What do you mean?"

"You're a hustler." He shrugged. "You know how to stay a couple of steps ahead of the game. Use them before they can use you."

Draya struggled trying to follow his lead. "And how do you suppose she does that?"

Shawn leaned back as if holding court. "Bree, you're the victim in all this—a pawn in a presidential conspiracy. When the world sees you—not looking like the hot mess you were racing out of that hotel; bat those big brown eyes and tell them how the government is *still* victimizing you *and* Kadir—you could mount pressure in getting him released. Tell everybody that they're refusing to release an *innocent* man as some sort of payback for bringing down a corrupt president. I betcha that'll work."

"Oh, I don't . . ." Abrianna shook her head, unable to process the idea of sitting in front of cameras and giving the world a peek into even a fraction of her life. It gave her heart palpitations.

"You do want them to release him, don't you?"

"Of course. I fuckin' owe him my life."

"Then you know what you got to do. But make sure it's one of those shows willing to pay *mucho dinero*." He lifted his glass. "You know how it is: Don't hate the player, hate the game."

The next day, Abrianna agreed to meet Tomi back at

Stanton Park. She also hoped to see Charlie. She hadn't seen him in weeks, and she was sure that he'd been keeping up what was going on in the papers. He was probably worried about her. But after an hour of sitting in the park, there was no sign of him. Now, she was worried.

"Hey," Tomi said, rushing the bench. "Sorry, I'm late. It seems like the whole world discovered all my contact numbers." She laughed.

"I'm not surprised. You're real popular on TV."

"The exposé shook the whole government. It's the story of the century."

Abrianna shrugged, unimpressed.

"I take it that means that you're still not interested in doing interviews?"

"The last thing I need is for the world to dissect my life. It's shit. I don't need anyone to confirm it."

"I wish you'd reconsider."

Abrianna rolled eyes behind her big glasses.

"If it's money . . . there are plenty of stations willing to shell out six or even seven figures to get you in front of the camera."

"I have reconsidered. I want to help get Kadir out of prison. My friends think my going on television could help mount public pressure on getting him released. What do you think?"

Tomi blinked. "I think that they're right. Seeing you will put a more human face on his plight."

Abrianna tilted her sunglasses down so she could meet Tomi's stunned gaze. "Fine. Can you set it up?"

"Of course. I'll get right on it."

Pushing up her glasses, Abrianna asked, "So what's going to happen to the president anyway? Why hasn't he stepped down?"

"Oh, he will," Tomi assured her. "There's no way that he can survive this. It's rather pathetic the way he's clinging to power. You can tell that his vice president is dying to plant her pumps in the middle of his ass and kick him out of the door."

"Okay." Abrianna sprung to her feet. "I gotta go."

"Yeah?" Tomi sounded disappointed. "Okay. You still have the cell phone I got you?"

"Yes. But I'm going to get a different one tomorrow. I heard that it's best to change them every three days."

"Why?"

"It makes it harder for big brother to track you."

Tomi smirked. "Don't tell me that you're a conspiracy theorist."

"After the kind of life I've lived? I'm now a card-carrying member."

Tomi shook her head. "Oh. Wait. I think I have a few of the interview offers that were emailed to me in my bag. You can take them back home and decide which ones you want to do." She opened her bag and pulled out a stack of papers. A sketch caught Abrianna's attention.

"What are you doing with a picture of Charlie?"

Tomi paused, looked at the sketch and then back at Abrianna. "Who's Charlie?"

Abrianna stared at the picture to make sure she wasn't imagining things. She wasn't. It was definitely Charlie. "First tell me why you have this."

Tomi shrugged. "He approached me a couple of weeks ago. Pulled up next to me in a black Mercedes. He said that he wanted to talk to me about . . . something *crazy*."

"Black Mercedes?" Abrianna laughed. "That's impossible. Charlie doesn't own a Mercedes. Hell, he doesn't even own a car. He's a homeless old guy that hangs out at this park. I've known him for years." She looked again. "Maybe he has a twin or something."

Tomi frowned. "He mentioned you."

"What?"

She nodded and took a deep breath. "This guy said he wanted to talk to me about some . . . *powers* that he believed you and I have developed over the past six years."

Abrianna fell silent.

Tomi cocked her head and studied her. "Do you know what he's talking about? Have you experienced anything . . . odd in the past few years?"

"I've experienced a lot of odd things."

"No. I mean like *special* . . . abilities."

Abrianna shook her head too fast to be believed.

"I have," Tomi confessed.

Abrianna's gaze swung up from the sketch.

"Small things."

"Like what?"

"Like . . . I can move things around . . . with my mind."

The hairs on the back of Abrianna's neck stood.

"What about you?"

Abrianna debated answering the question because, she realized, she was scared.

"You can, can't you?" Tomi saw that she'd spooked her. "There's something else."

"There's more?"

"At one point, the guy stopped talking with his mouth and I could *hear* him in my head. I damn near pissed on myself right there in the middle of the street."

"Sometimes I can hear people's thoughts," Abrianna blurted. It was a relief to say it out loud. "It's a constant buzzing at the back of my head. Day and night. Half the time I think that I'm going out of my mind."

Tomi frowned. "What do you do?"

Abrianna sighed. "Drugs, mostly. It quiets the buzzing."

The wind picked up, and the women shivered.

"Anything else?" Tomi asked.

Abrianna eyed her wearily. "You're not going to write about this, are you?"

"Not on your life," Tomi said. "I've busted my ass for the past six years trying to prove that I'm *not* a freak."

"Humph. A freak is all I know how to be." Abrianna's gaze fell back to the sketch and a wave of questions numbed any feelings of betrayal. "Who are you?" she whispered.

"You said his name was Charlie?" Tomi asked.

Abrianna nodded. "At least that's what he told me. But fuck. It could be anything. The old man that I know doesn't ride around in a Mercedes."

"With government tags," Tomi added.

"Government?" Abrianna shook her head. "None of that makes any sense."

"I can't find the lie in that statement." Tomi reclaimed her sketch. "How long have you known him again?"

"Six years," Abrianna shrugged. "He was the first person I met after I ran away from . . ." Abrianna's mind drifted back to the moment she'd met the homeless man. "Noooo," Abrianna groaned, not wanting to believe the obvious.

"What?" Tomi asked.

"The night I was snatched up by that sick fuck Avery, Charlie was there. Avery helped me get Charlie out of the middle of the road."

"You're kidding me."

Abrianna shook her head. As the tide of questions receded, that numb betrayal turned into anger. "How could I be so stupid? They were *partners*. They had to be! They said Avery was a doctor."

"A scientist," Tomi said, nodding. "That crazy shit he used to concoct down in that basement and injected us with wasn't for shits and giggles."

"We were fucking lab rats."

Tomi nodded. "It's the only shit that makes sense. Apparently this 'Charlie' befriended you in order to keep an eye out or monitor you. What do you guys talk about?"

"Nothing," Abrianna said. "We'd just shoot the breeze. Before this whole crazy shit with that congressman went down, I met Charlie five days a week for lunch in this park."

"*This* park?" Tomi looked around.

"Yeah. On the weekends, he said that he went to see about his granddaughter." Abrianna tossed up her hands. "That's probably more bullshit. Fuck!"

"Look. Don't be so hard on yourself. You couldn't have known."

"Please. I have a pretty good bullshit detector. Well, at least I tell myself that. But after Moses, Sanders, Zeke—shit. It's one more thing I'm fooling myself about. I have to go."

"What?"

"This is all too much," Abrianna said, standing. "I'll catch you later."

"Well, uh . . . remember to text me your new number."

Abrianna gave her the okay sign and kept it moving. But before she exited the park, she took another glance around, searching for Charlie. *Who in the fuck are you, muthafucka?*

━━◦◦◦◦━━

"Do you think that's her, sir?" Ned asked from behind the wheel.

Dr. Z watched Abrianna march as if she were going off to war. "Yeah. That's her," he said. "I'd know that walk anywhere."

"Do you think that she was looking for you?"

"Maybe." His gaze shifted back across the park to Tomi Lehane. She was the reason that he hadn't gotten out of the car in his disguise to approach Abrianna. Tomi would've seen straight through it and remembered him.

"So what do you want to do?" Ned asked. "Which one do you want to follow?"

━━◦◦◦◦━━

Abrianna felt eyes on the back of her neck as she marched toward the bus station. She glanced over her shoulder but couldn't detect anyone in the crowd paying her any attention. She turned back around, told herself that she was imagining things. But the feeling returned, and before long, she was turning around every third step.

Deciding to change direction, she dashed across the street, but halfway across, she heard, *"Abrianna."*

She jumped, spun.

A horn blew a fraction of a second before the front end of a car plowed into her. She bounced onto its hood, smashed into the windshield, and then rolled off and hit pavement, where she lay, knocked out cold.

━━◦◦◦◦━━

Kadir sprung up from his cot, panicked and disoriented. Heart racing, he looked around his cramped cell with a desperate need to do something. On his feet, he rushed the metal bars, yelling, "Hey! Guard! I need to make a phone call! Hey!"

Inmates in the surrounding jail cells snickered. "Oooh. He needs to make a phone call."

"Hey!" Kadir shouted, banged on the bar until an angry line of guards in riot gear storm-trooped toward him.

Kadir's hands came up in surrender. "I don't mean any trouble," Kadir said. "I need to make a phone call. I think my girl is in trouble."

More laughter.

The guards made an intimidating line in front of his door.

"Really, guys. I need to make a call."

"Open cell C-165!"

"Guys . . ."

A buzzer echoed throughout C-block. When the bars slid open, the aggressive guards charged inside the small space, clubs swinging. Kadir went down on the third strike. From the concrete floor, he attempted to protect himself, but after a dozen blows, he was knocked out cold.

27

The private and prestigious Lynnwood Club in Fairfax, Virginia, was the playground of Washington's political and financial elite who were bored with more conventional sports and couldn't resist indulging in their most deviant desires.

Cargill Parker, president of the Lynnwood Club, welcomed an old business associate in his private quarters on the top floor of his lavish club. He was dressed in a burgundy and black brocade robe with a monogramed P stitched on the left breast pocket. In his hands, he carried two brandy snifters, with the same calligraphy letter in the center. "Mr. Jeffreys."

Zeke accepted the offered brandy. "Thank you, Mr. Parker. I appreciate you taking this meeting on such short notice."

"You have information about my daughter?" he asked, moving toward a mahogany secretary.

"Yes. I have to apologize for my ignorance. I've known Abrianna for a couple of years. I had no idea that she was your daughter until I happened to see you on a news clip the other day."

"Well, it's not like there is a strong family resemblance, so I can see why my pale skin could have thrown you off," Cargill joked. "She's my adopted daughter."

"Yes, sir. Still. Seeing how long we've done business together, I feel some kind of way about it."

A corner of Cargill's lips hitched higher than the other. "If you're seeking forgiveness, then you have it." He opened a top drawer on the secretary. "Cigar?"

"Uh, no, sir. That's won't be necessary."

"Are you sure? Montecristo Number Two, the best."

Zeke caved. "I guess one wouldn't hurt."

"Excellent." Cargill waltzed back over and offered the box of cigars to Zeke.

"Thank you," Zeke said, taking the cutter and then accepting the small blaze of fire from Cargill's monogrammed lighter.

Zeke found the older gentleman's calm demeanor unsettling, and even though not much in this world scared him, there was something about Cargill's calculating green eyes that creeped him the hell out, too. He also knew what kind of sick bastard the billionaire playboy was behind closed doors. It wasn't hard to guess why Abrianna had run away from home.

Cargill sighed after exhausting the small talk. "So. Where *is* my daughter?"

"Currently, I . . . don't know."

Cargill transformed into white marble before Zeke's eyes.

"*But* . . . she was at my place a couple of weeks ago," Zeke added. "An uninvited guest, but she was there."

Cargill's interest returned. "Oh?"

"Yes. I, uh, don't want to dance around the subject, but you do know the type of business that I'm in and, like I said, had I known that you were her father, I would have brought this information to you sooner."

"Are you trying to tell me that my daughter was in your employ?"

"I, uh, yes, sir." Zeke swallowed and waited for the man's reaction. To his surprise, the older gentleman smiled and sipped his brandy.

"And how was she?"

"Excuse me?"

"You don't strike me as the kind of man who doesn't test the product before putting it out on the market. I'm asking whether you found my beautiful daughter up to snuff. I'd be disappointed if she or any of her training had fallen by the wayside."

This cold muthafucka here. Zeke toked on his cigar and, after blowing out a thick toxic cloud, he answered, "I unfortunately hadn't had the pleasure of testing the new product. She'd only been in my employ for one night."

"Ah. So she was working for you the night the congressman was killed? Your name was missing in the paper."

Zeke didn't respond.

"Okay. So you don't know where *Abrianna* is now?"

"No. But I'm fairly confident that I *can* find her."

"Oh?"

"I have eyes and ears everywhere."

"And since you're here, what is it that you want from me?" Cargill asked.

"I need to know if there's a reward."

Cargill smiled. "Absolutely."

28

Abrianna woke to sirens ringing in her ears. Pain was the second thing that she noticed. Her body drowned in it. She wanted to cry out, but she couldn't get her lungs to expand for enough air. *What the hell happened?*

"She's waking up," someone said above her.

"Hey, lady. Are you all right?" a man asked.

"What kind of question is that?" a woman snapped. "Did you see how hard that Mercedes hit her? It's amazing that she's still alive."

At the woman's words, Abrianna recalled the car horn as well as someone calling her name—only it seemed like it was in her head rather than on the street. That didn't make sense. She closed her eyes again and fell through a vortex of pain. Before she knew it, she was roasting in unrelenting heat. Her head filled with Avery's maniacal laughter. She wrestled to get away, but she was spinning over a flame that scorched her inside and out. Sanity was a distant memory, and torture became her master.

When she woke again, she was lying in the back of

an ambulance, a mask strapped across her face, but whatever was streaming through, it wasn't oxygen. The people hovering above her were dressed like EMTs, but something was wrong.

Get up! Abrianna attempted to move and drew the attention of the two attendants.

"Relax, Ms. Parker. Everything is going to be all right," one man said, pressing her back down on the gurney. "You were in a bad accident, and we're going to get you to the hospital."

"No." She shook her head and tried to push back, but she was weak, hot.

"We're going to need something stronger," he told the other attendant.

"No." Abrianna went to rip the mask off, but her arms were strapped down. *What the fuck?* With as much strength as she could muster, she yanked her right arm and ripped it out of the leather band.

"Fuck!" The guy went to hold her right arm down when she yanked her left one free.

"Hurry with that injection!"

"No, no, no," Abrianna repeated, but she doubted if they heard her through the mask.

The female handed over a huge syringe. "Here you go."

Abrianna's eyes widened. The image of another syringe in the hands of a madman flashed in her head. Terror seized her, renewing her push to get up.

"She's fucking strong! Help me hold her down so I can inject this shit."

The female attendant leaped to take hold of her arms.

Abrianna glared at the dripping needle as it came closer to her arm. A scream ripped from her throat.

The male attendant roared as he stabbed his own

right eye and the female flew back and crashed against the back door. Before Abrianna could stop screaming, there was a loud bang. The van swerved wildly, tossing Abrianna off the gurney. She crashed among the medical equipment. There was no time to get to her feet before the vehicle rolled. The interior light went out. She attempted to latch on to something—anything—but nothing was anchored. It was like being inside of a human dryer, around and around. It went on for forever, and when it stopped, it still felt like it was rolling.

The silence lasted only for a few seconds before gunfire rattled off outside of the van.

What the fuck? Abrianna sluggishly pulled herself up, rummaged around in the dark, trying to figure out which way was up. All the while, the gunfire sounded close. *Gun.* She patted herself down to see if she still had it. She did. The Tiffany blue .45, it was still holstered at her back. Heart pounding, she started to move. Two steps in, she tripped over the male attendant and cut her hand on something.

In the midst of the gunfire, a hammering on the vehicle came from her right.

"Bree! Are you in there?"

She froze. "Ghost?"

More gunfire.

"Bree!" The door wrenched open, and it was Ghost looking like a giant merchant soldier in body armor and rocking an assault weapon.

"In here," Abrianna said, relieved to see the big lug. "What the hell is going on?"

"Can you move?" He climbed into the bed of the van, turning on a powerful light clipped to the side of some sort of eyewear. It was enough light to make out the two bodies sprawled across the roof of the van.

Ghost grimaced at the guy with the hypodermic needle in his eye. "Goddamn."

"Fuck him," Abrianna said, accepting Ghost's hand to make her way over to him and then hop out of the van. She was instantly surrounded by Ghost's crew. "I don't understand what's going on or what you're doing here."

"What does it look like? We're rescuing you. The question is what in the hell does T4S want with you?"

"Yo, Ghost," Roger yelled from the top of the hill. "I'm picking up traffic on reinforcements. We have to get out of here, man."

"Got it." He grabbed Abrianna's arm. "Can you climb?"

"I-I think so."

"Good. Let's go."

They took off up the hill.

Pain ricocheted throughout Abrianna's body as she attacked the steep incline. Sweat streamed from her scalp to her rubbery legs, gluing her clothes to her body. Her heartbeat and breathing drowned out every other sound around them. Despite being on the verge of what had to be a heart attack, she willed herself to keep pace with Ghost.

Near the top of the hill, a loud buzzing swept across the back of her skull. Abrianna glanced over her shoulder and back down at the overturned ambulance to see a guy taking aim at them from the window of the overturned van. On instinct, she spun, firing off her blue .45. Her first bullet missed her mark by millimeters, but the second and third bullet exploded the gunman's head and pitched him backward to slump into the cab.

"Nice fucking shooting," Ghost praised, having spun around too late so he was left without a target.

"Boss!"

"We're coming," Ghost yelled. "C'mon."

They hustled to the top of the hill, where Abrianna took in the carnage of dead bodies in black littered on the street and hanging out of square-shaped utility vehicles.

"This way," Ghost ordered, racing toward an open-doored van.

Once they dove inside, Wendell stomped on the accelerator and burned rubber with the doors swinging.

29

Nervous, Tomi settled into the guest chair of her favorite evening cable show, *The Filibuster* with Joy Walton. Joy was an old school, hard-hitting journalist who regularly made news by pinning politicians down and knocking them off talking points. People either loved or hated her, and Joy didn't care which side of the pendulum you were on.

"And we're back," Joy told her audience. "Joining us this evening is *Washington Post* reporter Tomi Lehane. Her blockbuster story has not just the country talking, but the whole *world*. The President of the United States *and* the chief justice colluded to murder the House speaker of the United States. Congratulations and welcome to the show."

"Thank you. I'm happy to be here."

"Where to begin?" Joy laughed. "First, how did you land this incredible story?"

"Actually, it was plain . . . luck. Abrianna Parker reached out to me."

"Luck? You're being modest, aren't you? You and Ms. Parker do share a history."

Tomi sighed. "Yes. But as you also know, Abrianna and I hadn't seen each other in *years* . . . so it's simply that I was the only reporter she knew."

"Well, I've read the article, seen the pictures, and listened to the recorded confession online; the one question that I'm dying to know the answer to is *when* the public will get to meet this mysterious Abrianna Parker?"

"Ahh. That's a good question," Tomi admitted.

"Do you have an answer?"

"Yes. Soon."

The Bunker

Abrianna sat alone in the bunker's break room while Ghost and his crew gathered in the armory room, undoubtedly discussing whether they believed her not knowing why T4S, a powerful paramilitary force, had ordered her extraction in broad daylight. She did take exception to the word *extraction*. Last time she checked, hitting someone at full speed would meet any justice department's legal definition of attempted murder.

She kept replaying the scene in her head, or at least what she remembered. It frustrated her because she couldn't pinpoint anything other than her being paranoid before foolishly dashing across a busy street. The rest of it she didn't understand herself.

She pressed a hand against her forehead and sighed. It was no longer scorching hot, and her brain didn't feel like it was turning into scrambled eggs.

Abrianna heard Ghost's distinctive heavy footstep slap against the concrete floor. She straightened up in the tacky orange plastic chair and swept her curtain of sweat-drenched hair back from her face.

Ghost entered the room and stopped.

She waited with the back of her head buzzing, but she refused to turn around and face him.

At long last, Ghost moved from the door and over to the counter. "Care for some coffee?" He opened the cabinet and removed a red can of Folgers.

"No. But I could use some water."

He nodded and shifted direction to the refrigerator. "Here you go." He set the bottled water in front of her and returned to the coffeemaker.

Abrianna waited, but he was in no hurry to start the conversation. She snatched up the water and twisted off the cap.

When she was in the middle of chugging, he said, "There's a lot of shit that isn't adding up."

Instead of commenting, Abrianna drained the rest of the bottle and then smothered a belch behind her hand.

Ghost turned with an arched brow.

"Excuse me," she demurred, grinning.

He shook his head and poured coffee into his "Ghost in the machine"–inscribed mug before joining her at the table. "T4S is a private paramilitary security firm," he began. "They get to do all the fun things that the Constitution won't allow the federal government to do. They are part intelligence and part private military with black budgets that could fund several countries. You follow me?"

"So far."

"My, uh, guys and I here are dedicated to exposing the real police state that the western world hides in plain sight. That means monitoring firms like T4S while slinking beneath the grid." He paused long enough to taste and savor his first sip of coffee. "The best way that we keep tabs on what happens is that we, as you know, float in and out of their complex systems without detection. I'm one of the best, hence my name." He pointed to his mug again.

"Ghost in the machine." She smirked.

"Right. So imagine my surprise this afternoon when you were mentioned *by name*, which is inexplicably bizarre and something that I've never seen them be so sloppy to do."

She sat staring at him, wondering if she'd missed a question in there somewhere. To be safe, she shrugged. "I don't know what to tell you."

"You know what I can't figure out about you?"

"What?"

He cocked his head. "You sure do heal fast."

She blinked. "What?"

"I've known you for what? A month and some change? And in that time you've been shot, hit by a speeding car, and tumbled down an embankment in the back of a fake ambulance, and look at you. Besides being a bit sweaty, you're the picture of health."

She stared back at him.

"You don't find that odd?"

"Trust me. I don't feel like the picture of health. Far from it."

Silence drifted between them.

"Kadir asked me something a few weeks ago."

She lifted a brow.

"He asked me what I knew about telekinesis. Do you know what that is?"

Abrianna sipped her water, not answering.

Ghost continued. "It's the ability to move objects through mind power. Still not ringing any bells?"

At her continued silence, he went on. "Kadir also said that at that party you guys crashed, you slammed a man against the side the house without laying a finger on him. Do you remember that?"

"This is nonsense," she protested, shaking her head.

"Is it?"

"Yes. Next you'll be telling me that Superman is my father."

He shook his head. "No. It would be more like Professor X. You're getting your comics mixed up."

"Whatever. The whole thing is ridiculous."

"Maybe." Ghost sipped his coffee while he evaluated her. "I'm going to do some more digging around. But something isn't jibing, in my opinion. Roger and the other guys think that you must still be caught in the White House's crosshairs. Maybe the order has something to do with that exposé you and your friend published, because her name came across the wire as well."

"What?" She sprung to her feet. "Then we got to go help her."

"Slow your roll," Ghost said, leaning back in his chair. "What do you think we are, the A-Team? And even if we were, we don't have the ability to be in two places at one time. I put my and my crew's neck out on the line as a favor to my man Kadir. I know that he would want me to keep an eye on you, if I can. The other chick isn't my problem."

"Then she's my problem," Abrianna said. "She's in danger because of me. I took my story to her, remember?"

"Yeah. And judging by the media blitz that she's

been on, she owes you at least a dozen roses and a box of chocolates."

"We can't sit here and do nothing," Abrianna snapped.

"Calm down," he told her. "Before I walked in here, we confirmed that your girl is back at her office. I sent Roger and Wendell to keep an eye on her for the next twenty-four hours. You might want to suggest to her the next time you talk to her that she might want look into hiring security until this whole thing blows over."

"When will that be?"

"I'm guessing not until there's a change in the administration."

"You mean if the president steps down?"

"It makes sense, I suppose. But it's stupid, if you ask me. If you and this reporter chick disappear, surely he'd be suspect number one. But, hey. Who says that you have to be smart to be president?"

"So what do I do until then?"

Ghost shrugged. "I can stash you back at my warehouse apartment. No one should think to find you there."

"What about my friends?"

"Hey, I'm not housing a fraternity."

"If I'm in danger then they are, too. Three of them have already been hurt."

He stared, and when it was clear that she was finished, he said, "Oh. I'm sorry, I was waiting for you to get to the part where this was my problem."

"Forget it. I'll stay with Shawn. Thank you very much." She turned to leave.

"And what are you going to do about these guys trying to take you out?"

"Not your problem, remember?" She reached the break room's door when she heard Ghost curse.

"All right. All right. They can stay there, too," he grumbled.

Abrianna stopped, plastered on a smile, and turned around. "Your hospitality is greatly appreciated."

"Bite me."

———————◆◆◆———————

Dr. Zacher arrived at what looked like a battlefield. T4S's cloned police cars and tow trucks hustled to clean up the carnage and haul the ambulance up the steep embankment.

Lieutenant Jessup Acosta spotted Dr. Z. climbing out of his car and stopped directing his crew to march over.

Dr. Z got straight to the point. "What the hell happened?"

"We were hit, sir," Acosta said. "Twelve of my men were wiped out."

Dr. Z growled. "I can see that you were hit. The questions are how and by who?"

"That, sir, I'm afraid I don't know. It was a simple extraction. Rushed, but we did the pickup with a two-car backup. The team made it within six miles of the facility when someone unleashed holy hell. Only one of my men had enough time to radio for help. The transmission was mostly of gunfire. It sounded like a goddamn war zone. By the time we got here . . ." Acosta shook his head.

"And the package?"

"Like I told you on the phone, sir. The package is MIA."

"That doesn't make any sense." Dr. Z stepped away and looked down the long embankment and then out into the surrounding trees. "Did you search the woods? Maybe she's hurt somewhere out there?"

"I got a team doing a grid search right now. If she's out there, we'll find her, but I don't think she's out there."

"Why do you say that?"

"Because whoever gunned down my crew clearly wanted to intercept your package. Do you have any idea who that may be?"

Dr. Zacher shook his head. "I have no idea what the hell is going on. But I better figure it out, and quick."

"What about your other package? Still want us to make a move on it?"

Dr. Z needed a moment. He didn't like making moves when he couldn't see all the chess pieces on the board, but time was of the essence.

"Sir?"

"Stick to the schedule," he told Acosta before turning and storming back to his waiting car with the cracked windshield. But before Dr. Z climbed into the backseat, he called out to Acosta. "Hey! I want everyone on radio silence. You never know, we could have a ghost in the machine."

30

Abrianna returned to Shawn's apartment with Ghost trailing behind her. Carving a huge smile, Abrianna explained to her best friend that they both needed to move out of the apartment for a little while, electing *not* to tell him about the whole getting hit by a car and kidnapping incident, but without it, her reasoning stood on shaky ground.

"You're not making any sense," Shawn said, eyeballing Ghost by the door. "And you haven't told me where you picked up the black terminator from."

"He's a friend."

He shook his head. "I know *all* of your friends, and he ain't one of them."

Sighing, she filled in a few more boxes. "His name is Ghost."

Shawn laughed. "He is aware that we can see him, isn't he?"

"I met him through Kadir. He helped us expose Judge Sanders and kept me and Kadir off the grid. I really can't tell you more than that right now. But I will eventually. Please. Can you trust me?"

Shawn drew a deep breath. "You know, I didn't listen to you once, and it landed me in this chair. So . . . all right. If you say that we have to move with your Suge Knight two point oh, then we'll move."

Ghost grunted.

Abrianna threw her arms around Shawn and squeezed. "Thank you."

"Now if you two are finished insulting me," Ghost said, "can we please get this show on the road?"

———◆◆◆———

Castillo told herself that she wasn't going to Dennis's place the entire time she was driving over there. When he answered the door, he was in his black boxers and an open gray robe. He took one look at her and sighed.

"You haven't been returning my texts."

"I know. I've been busy," she said.

"Busy breaking your arm, I see."

She shrugged. "Car accident."

"I know. I read the report." He took a swig of beer.

"Are you going to let me in?"

"See. That's the problem. I *keep* letting you in, on *your* terms and on *your* schedule. Right now I'm asking myself why."

"All right. Fine." She spun and marched away. She didn't have time for this.

Behind her, Dennis sighed and opened the screen door. "Gigi."

She stopped.

"C'mon in." He said it as if the words chipped off a part of his soul.

"Are you sure?" she asked.

"Hell, no."

Castillo turned around and saw the misery written on his face. She walked toward him, stopped with an apology on her lips, but then crossed the threshold without saying a word.

The house was wrecked. Empty pizza boxes, beer bottles, and discarded clothes littered the place.

"Had I known you were coming, I would have picked up," he said, closing the front door.

"Or at the very least call a hazmat team." She glanced at him. "What's going on?"

"Just more shit at the job." Dennis swigged his beer before adding, "Some high school kids partied with that fuckin' Cotton Candy shit."

Castillo's heart dropped. She knew that his department had been trying to get a handle on the designer street drug Cotton Candy. It was known for its pink coloring and its ability to produce something called a supernova high. A single dose could last for days and was often fatal.

Dennis shook his head to stop tears from leaping down his face. "Twelve souls, Gigi. Gone."

"Damn." She moved toward him.

He stepped back. "I'm sorry. This shit is fucking with my head. It's not just kids."

"You guys still have no leads about where this shit is coming from?"

"Honestly, Gigi, I have no idea why I even do this shit anymore. The streets are flooded with drugs, both legal and illegal. There's no end to it. And it's all walks of life. You know that shit was even at that crime scene at the Hay-Adams."

"I didn't know that."

"Yeah, well. At least there we know the drugs weren't what killed the congressman." He set the bottle down on the counter. "I don't want to talk anymore about this. Are you staying the night?"

"That depends."

"On?"

"On whether the bedroom looks like the living room."

He took her by the hand. "Why don't we go and find out?"

31

At midnight, the Dragons Templar came to order. The members, in leather masks and draped in black robes with fire-breathing dragons stitched in gold across their chests, chanted in ancient Coptic and bowed and passed a flame from wick to wick until the last. Golden emblems of a battling two-headed dragon hung around their necks.

The excitement was palpable. The second Saturday of the month was date night and everyone, including Cargill, couldn't wait to select a new beauty to share his and Lovely's bed tonight.

Cargill was a lucky bastard. He'd always known that. Born with a golden spoon in his mouth, everything was handed to him. Money, cars, boats, and planes, he hadn't hit a double-digit age before he discovered that money also bought people, people who'd do *anything* to please him. He had his father, Duke Lynnwood Parker, to thank for that, like he thanked his father for inducting him into the Dragons Templar. At nine, Cargill had been the youngest inductee. To this day, he relished the memory of his first date night. His father had watched as Cargill strolled around the dolled-up orphans with the instruction to find the one that he wanted to kiss the most. He thought it was silly until he stopped in front of a stunning, seven-year-old black beauty with eyes so dark that they made him feel funny inside. Her name was Abrianna. A strange name, he'd thought, but it was one that would stay with him for the rest of his life.

Cargill thought his father would be mad that he'd chosen a black girl. He'd never heard him say anything positive about black people. However, that night, Duke Parker was pleased and was only too happy to instruct Cargill on the right way to kiss and touch his new toy. He didn't like his father touching Abrianna. He made her cry, but by the time it was all over, Cargill was indebted to his father for the lifelong lesson. However, he did eventually anger his father when he insisted on playing with only Abrianna for months afterward. Cargill refused to pick another girl when new children arrived on date nights. After six months, his father took matters into his own hands and broke his black doll. She died with those big, dark eyes pleading to breathe and tears streaking down her face. Cargill had never fought his father before, but he did that night. He kicked, screamed, and raked at his father's hands, trying to loosen Duke's grip on Abrianna's neck, but Duke Parker didn't let go until Abrianna stopped moving.

Cargill cried for weeks after and then never again.

Putting away the memory, Cargill took to the lectern and welcomed his members and promised them all a great night, when a sudden cacophony descended into the room. "EVERYBODY, DOWN!" An army of federal agents charged into the hall, assault weapons drawn and pointed in everyone's faces. The costumed children screamed as grown men trampled them, racing for an exit.

Cargill raked off his mask and dashed off the stage. However, he didn't get far before an agent tackled him. His lungs emptied in a whoosh, but Cargill still wrestled to break free. He was almost successful when another agent pressed the barrel of an assault weapon at the back of his skull.

"Don't move!"

Cargill froze. "You're making a big mistake," Cargill gritted.

"Shut up, you sick fucker. You're under arrest!"

———— ··· ————

Ghost's warehouse apartment

"Breaking tonight, Billionaire Cargill Parker was led away in handcuffs tonight from the exclusive Lynnwood Club for running what the authorities have described as a sophisticated child sex-trafficking ring. More than two dozen children have been taken into custody. We're told that the arrests are the direct result of an anonymous tip to the FBI and Homeland security."

Abrianna stared at the television in the living room. Her father, head down, attempted to avoid the surrounding media cameras as federal agents led him to a waiting FBI van.

"Cargill Parker is the president and subsidiary holder of Parker Petroleum Industries, the third largest privately held company in the United States. He is a fixture in Washington, D.C., for his political advocacy and philanthropy."

"Bree? Are you all right?" Shawn nudged.

"Huh?"

"Are you all right?"

The reporter ended the report and handed off the next segment to the journalists at the studio.

Abrianna recovered. "Yeah. Yeah. Why wouldn't I be all right?" She powered off the television, but remained rooted before the blank TV screen. A knot hardened in her chest as her mind reeled.

"C'mon. It's me," Shawn said. "I know this shit bothers you. That asshole is going down—*and* on national TV."

Silence.

"Bree?"

She shrugged, determined to be indifferent. "It doesn't have anything to do with me. He's . . ."

"He's dead to you," Shawn finished. "I know. You've been saying that for years. But—"

Abrianna snapped, "But what?"

"The timing," Shawn said. "It's odd, no?"

"What do you mean?"

"I don't know. Maybe I'm paranoid. Getting shot kind of does it to you, but . . . the FBI and Homeland Security, busting him so soon after that exposé? It's fishy, if you ask me. The government raced around this city for weeks and couldn't find you or Kadir, but suddenly they get an anonymous tip on daddy dearest? You buy that?"

"I'm stunned that they arrested him," she said. "I always thought that . . . he was untouchable."

"He was . . . until his daughter tried to take down a president."

"What are you thinking?"

"I'm thinking the empire is striking back," Shawn said.

"And Darth Vader thinks that going after my evil father will get to me? Ha! They're barking up the wrong tree. They can fry his ass for all I care."

Shawn didn't respond.

"What? You think I should give a shit?"

"No."

The clipped answer agitated her. "Then what? Spit it out."

"What if they don't stop at your father? What if they keep digging until they find something or someone that you *do* give a shit about? The feds clearly still have you in their crosshairs. And no shade, Bree, but you got a lot of skeletons in your closet. They're going to bust down every one of them that you think is locked and hidden."

Her heart skipped. *Will this shit ever end?*

"All I'm saying is that you need to watch your back."

"That's all that I've been doing," she snapped.

Abrianna's cell trilled. She glanced at Shawn, and he wheeled himself over to the coffee table. "It's Tomi Lehane," he said, tossing the phone to her.

She caught it, hesitated, and then answered the call before it transferred to voice mail. "Hello."

"Bree, Tomi here. Have you seen the news? Your father has been arrested."

"Yes. I saw the coverage last night."

"Is there any truth to what they're saying?" Tomi pressed.

She didn't answer.

"Bree? Are you there?"

"Yeah. I'm here."

"So . . . does your silence mean what they're reporting is true?"

"Are you asking as a reporter?"

Tomi hesitated, "I guess that's a fair question."

"And your answer?"

"Okay. Off the record, but I need to know the truth before we do interviews. It's important that I know how many lions are waiting in the den. This has the potential to derail our plans to plea Kadir's case and get him released. The last thing we want is for the public to lose sympathy or start more unfounded conspiracy theories."

"We already gave them a video and a damn taped confession from the murderer."

"Yeah. But the propaganda machines are working overtime. People are suggesting the video was doctored and the confession coerced. We're not out of the woods yet. And if I know anything about this town, your father's arrest is no coincidence. The White House is playing a few cards."

Abrianna shook her head. "I don't know how they can make my father's situation have anything to do with me."

"Bree, you already have a few character strikes against you with your . . . profession. These charges against your father will make people question whether you're truly a victim or a criminal opportunist."

Abrianna flinched. *Victim* meant weak. "Are you finished?"

"I'm being real. You've never done press junkets. Trust me. They're going to do everything they can to strip the skin off your back and smile while doing it. Do you know whether there's any truth to this stuff about your father?"

"Adopted father."

"Bree . . ."

Abrianna sighed and then gave up the ghost. "Yeah. There's truth to it."

"Shit." Tomi pulled away from the phone for a long moment and then asked, "Are you sure you still want to do this?"

Abrianna's thoughts drifted to Kadir. "I really don't have a choice in the matter."

"Wrong," Tomi corrected. "You *always* have a choice."

Abrianna nodded. "I'm not changing my mind. I'm doing the interviews." She disconnected the call and then tossed the phone across the bed.

"Are you all right?" Shawn asked.

"I'm fine."

Shawn wheeled over to her. "Hang in there. You're stronger than you know."

"Humph." She shook her head. "Is this what we're reduced to, cheap sympathy clichés?"

"Would you rather I find you a Hallmark card? I'm sure there's a 'Sorry your father is a sadist fuck' section."

Abrianna chuckled despite there being nothing funny about the situation.

"Get some sleep." He kissed the side of her head and then wheeled off to his guest bedroom.

Abrianna stood and walked over to one of the long windows, thinking. She'd worked hard to put the past behind her. *I hope they give his ass the needle.*

A light rain drizzled across the windowpane. The chill from the glass seeped into her bones. When she closed her eyes, her brother's screams echoed across time and built into a crescendo in her ears. Before she knew it, she was back in that House of Horrors, hiding in her closet and praying . . .

"Stop! Stop! Stop! Please God, make it stop," nine-year-old Abrianna prayed.

But Samuel wouldn't stop screaming. It was differ-

ent this time. There was more than pain in his voice. It was torture, and she wanted it to stop. Why wouldn't anyone make him stop?

She had to do it.

That thought frightened her. What the hell could she do? She could never fight Cargill when it was her turn.

But Samuel was smaller.

Tears streamed down her face. She resented the half of herself that argued that she do something. If she crawled out of that closet, she was putting herself at risk. Why was she such a coward?

Where is Marion? Why didn't she ever help?

Her mother was likely passed out drunk or snorting that stuff that made her sleep all the time. She never did a damn thing to help either one of them. Why would she do so tonight?

Whack!

Samuel's voice hit a note that made Abrianna's head snap up. Then there was the steady banging of Samuel's headboard against their shared bedroom wall.

Unable to take it anymore, Abrianna rolled onto her knees and reached for the closet's doorknob. Once it was opened, she stuffed her fear down as far as it could go and rushed out with her heart in her throat to her father's downstairs study. She'd seen him show off his gun to a number of his friends and knew where he kept it. She also knew the passcode to open the safe. He always said it aloud when punching it in. After removing the gun, a power surged through her. It was amazing what a weapon could do, the confidence it instilled. She climbed back up the stairs, her heart hammering to get out of her chest. At his bedroom door, tears poured to the point she could barely see.

Abrianna reached for the knob, but the master

suite's door swung open behind her and Marion gasped, "Bree!"

She ignored Marion and threw open Samuel's bedroom door. Cargill's head jerked up. His sweaty, naked body hovered behind little Samuel. Abrianna stood frozen, staring.

"Come and join the party, Abrianna," Cargill said.

Sobbing, Abrianna aimed the gun.

"Bree, no!" Marion yelled.

Cargill stood and Samuel scrambled to get out of the way.

"I hate you," Bree cried, firing the gun until it ran out of bullets . . .

Abrianna pulled out of the memory, sobbing. She tossed herself across the bed and cried until her head throbbed and desperation filled her. She needed something; something to make her forget, something to numb the pain. Climbing out of bed, Abrianna dressed, crept through the apartment, and slithered out the front door in search of a fix.

32

Zeke folded Angel over like a taco and deep-stroked his way to paradise. He needed something to work out his frustrations. Abrianna had vanished like a fucking ghost. He'd interrogated every bitch at the Stallion Gentlemen's Club and even her neighbors at her apartment building. Nobody knew, heard, or had seen shit. He learned that Shawn White had been released from the hospital and tracked down his home address, but when he kicked in the door, the apartment was empty. This bitch and her friends stayed two steps ahead, and that crawled underneath his skin.

The heat was on after he promised Cargill Parker that he would find his daughter. But he caught a break. Parker had been arrested tonight. The news was a shocker. Nowadays, old money never got so much as a traffic ticket. The arrest meant Parker had some powerful enemies.

One of the three cell phones by his bed rang.

Annoyed, Zeke stopped in mid-stroke, twisted toward the nightstand, and grabbed the phone. "Hey." He reclaimed one of Angel's legs and resumed stroking and banging her head into the headboard.

"Yo, boss, uh. It's Flash here. Are those five stacks still up for that chick that used to dance down at the Stallion?"

Zeke stopped. "Why? You've seen her?"

"Not me. But my nigga Socks was talking shit about seeing her down her at the trap house on Benning. My man sold her an eight ball of that Cotton Candy. He said that it looked like she was partying solo. If you want, I can go back there and keep an eyeball on her until your crew swings through."

"I'll be there in twenty."

"You're coming yourself?"

"Yeah. Sit on that bitch until I get there." Zeke ended the call.

Disappointed, Angel groaned when Zeke pulled out and bolted from the bed. "You're leaving?"

"Yeah." Dick wet, he threw on some clothes. "Keep that pussy ready for when I get back."

"You got it, baby," she cooed, pulling up the sheets over her body while he snatched open the nightstand drawer and grabbed his gun.

"This shouldn't take long," he said. "Be back in about an hour." He strolled out of the bedroom and then raced out of the house. He signaled Spider and Defoe, who patrolled the estate, to get the car. Within minutes, they peeled out of the property and rocketed to D.C.

———※◆※———

"Bree? Can you hear me?" Draya asked, cradling her face in between her hands. "Bree?"

Abrianna ignored the voice while zooming across the vast galaxy inside her mind. The freedom was exhilarating and orgasmic. Every cell in her body burst with energy. She never felt so alive. If only she could stay in this pain-free zone forever.

"She's not waking up," Draya said.

"Guys," Ghost said. "I can't find a pulse."

"She's all right. Help me get her up."

Ghost shook his head. "How do I keep getting myself into this shit?" He lifted Abrianna from a corner of the dingy trap house, hoisted her over his shoulder, and proceeded to carry her.

Two menacing-looking men filled the doorway. "Sorry, man. But she's not leaving."

"What the fuck are you talking about?" Ghost barked. "Get the hell out of the way."

The guns came out, but before the dealers could take aim, Draya and Ghost had their weapons pointed at them.

"I *said* get the fuck out of the way," Ghost repeated.

The guys held their ground; but one could almost hear the rusted gears in their head grind against one another.

Ghost spoke up, "Are you boys hard of hearing?"

"We got strict orders to keep her here until the boss man shows up. So the bitch ain't leaving."

Two sliders racked before gun barrels were dug into the back of the dealers' heads and finalized the conversation.

"You were saying?" Shawn asked calmly.

The dealers' hands flew up in surrender.

"We'll take those," Julian said. He and Shawn seized the men's weapons. "Thank you."

"Man, you're going to fuck us up if that bitch ain't here when Zeke arrives."

"Zeke?" Shawn double-checked.

"Yeah. He wants that chick bad. We were guaranteed five stacks."

Julian said. "Tell you what. We'll do you a solid." He brought the butt of his gun down on the back of one guy's head. He dropped like a stone.

The other guy's eyes bulged and he swore, "Oh, shit."

Shawn cracked the back of the second dealer's head, and he collapsed next to his friend. "C'mon. Let's get the fuck out of here." He turned and strolled with his cane like a pimp.

Ghost shook his head. "I swear you muthafuckas stay mixed up in some shit."

Draya's gaze sliced toward him. "All right. I got your muthafucka in my left pocket."

"I didn't mean . . . uh . . ." Realizing that he'd shoved his foot into his mouth, Ghost put a cork in it. However, when they reached the van, a revved engine in the distance caught everyone's attention. "Let me guess . . . Zeke?" Ghost asked.

"Hurry," Draya ordered. "We got to get the hell out of here."

Ghost hustled to place Abrianna into the back of the van and hopped inside. Tivonté, already behind the wheel, cranked the engine. Once everyone was inside, he floored it.

———◆◆◆———

Zeke spotted the black van as it took off in the opposite direction from the trap house. Instinct kicked in. "Follow that van!"

Spider floored it, but the van had a good jump on them.

Anxious and fearful that the van would get away,

Zeke powered down his window, leaned out and started firing. Not to be outdone by the boss, Spider and Defoe followed suit. However, when the van's back door burst open, they were unprepared for the artillery fire that flew back at them.

"Holy shit," the three men yelled.

Spider yanked on the steering wheel.

Bullets punched across the windshield, sawing both Defoe and Spider in half. The SUV veered off the road as Zeke leaped for the wheel before the van plowed head-on into a utility pole.

Bam!

The impact sounded like an explosion, and the entire block went black.

33

*S*lap! Slap!

Abrianna felt sting after sting of someone's open palm across her face. But she'd be damned if she could rouse herself enough to care. In fact, she welcomed the pain. The punishment was nothing less than what she deserved . . .

Nine-year-old Abrianna stood in Samuel's doorway and lowered the weapon. She stared in quiet shock into Cargill's wide eyes.

Marion wailed as she bolted past Abrianna, bumping her shoulder.

Abrianna dropped the gun, smashing her bare foot. She didn't feel it or the throb in her wrists. In fact, she didn't feel anything. Finally, she freed her herself from Cargill's green stare and swept her gaze across the destruction she'd caused. There was so much blood; splattered on the walls, sprayed across the sheets, and soaking the carpet.

"Nooooo!" Marion sobbed, holding and rocking Samuel. "My baby. Noooo. I'm sorry. Please. Noooo!"

A switch clicked off in Abrianna's head, disconnecting her emotions from the morose characters as if they were all acting out an old black-and-white movie on a silver screen. She couldn't process this. Her mind refused.

"*I'm sorry. I'm so sorry,*" *Marion bawled.*

On the floor, Cargill made raspy noises, desperately fighting for oxygen.

Marion's weepy gaze swept away from Samuel and impaled Abrianna. "*Look at what you did,*" *she shrieked.*

Abrianna's heart dropped as something warm trickled down her legs. Embarrassment scorched her face when she saw the puddle on the floor.

"*You did this,*" *Marion hissed, wrenching Abrianna's attention back.*

Their gazes crashed.

"*You, evil, evil little girl. You killed him. It's all your fault!*"

Her mean words burst the protective bubble her mind had formed around herself. The film stopped, and reality returned in vivid color.

"*You did this,*" *Marion accused, her voice echoing in her head and down through the years . . .*

———◆———

Slap! Slap! Slap!

"Goddamn it. She's not waking up," Draya sobbed. "What the fuck did she take?"

"We've got to get her to a doctor," Ghost said.

"No," her friends thundered.

Abrianna's eyelashes fluttered as she cranked her lids open an inch. Blurred images moved and argued above her.

"Absolutely no doctors," Shawn declared.

Ghost tossed up his hands. "What the hell is with

her and doctors? The goal is to save her fucking life. I like the chick and everything, but she can't be dying up in my crib and shit."

"Doctors ask too many questions," Draya said.

"You mean like how did she die?"

"She's *not* dead! We just have to wake her up."

"How? Doing a séance or some shit? You've been knocking the crap out of her for hours."

"Shut up," Draya huffed and returned to Abrianna to smack her around again. "C'mon, Bree. Snap out of it. I know that you can do it."

Abrianna blinked.

Draya gasped, "Hey! Hey! Did you guys see that?"

Julian, Shawn, Tivonté, and Ghost crowded around and stared. "What? What happened?"

"She blinked," Draya said. "I saw it."

"No fucking way," Ghost countered. "She's not even breathing. You're seeing things."

"No. I'm not! She blinked. I'm telling you. I know what I saw."

They hushed and resumed staring.

Frustrated, Ghost huffed, "Look. I'm not trying to be an asshole or anything, but your girl is gone, and we need to figure out what to do because she can't be found here. We have to come up with a damn good story because that reporter chick keeps blowing up that burner. Not to mention, I don't know what to tell my man Kadir about this shit."

"She's not dead," Draya screamed. "Why can't you get that shit through your thick, muscled head?"

"She not breathing," Ghost roared. "She doesn't even have a pulse. I know dead when I fucking see it!"

Abrianna gasped, rolled over, and vomited. Luckily, she was in a bathtub.

"Bree," Draya and Shawn shouted.

Thunderstruck, Ghost tumbled backward, his eyes as wide as silver dollars. "How in the fuck?"

Abrianna emptied her belly and then dry-heaved until her stomach locked into a charley horse. She was gasping; her lungs rattled in her chest while her throat felt like she'd been drinking acid in her sleep.

A crying Draya stroked Abrianna's hair and consoled her, "It's okay. You're all right. Everything is going to be all right."

Tears splashed down Abrianna's face as she brushed Draya's hands away. Why was everyone always telling her that? It wasn't all right. *She* would never be all right.

Someone turned on the shower and washed most of the gunk off Abrianna's clothes and hair.

Ghost remained incredulous. "This shit ain't right. What the fuck am I looking at? Somebody gotta tell me something, goddamn it."

Draya snapped. "Can you chill the fuck out and help us get her out of this tub?"

"You evil, evil, little girl!" Marion's voice echoed in Abrianna's head, damning her.

Ghost swooped in and lifted her out the tub and carried her, still soaking wet, back to her room. The whole way, he grumbled about being out of the loop. However, he was gentle placing her onto the bed.

After that, Abrianna's clique kicked him out of the room.

Draya stripped off Abrianna's clothes while repeating the lie about how everything was going to be all right. She needed to get her warm. The next day, Abrianna woke up buried beneath layers of blankets and comforters. She dug herself out, confused as to her whereabouts. Angry voices outside the bedroom door drew her attention.

Groaning, Abrianna climbed out of bed and discovered that she was naked. When she spotted a bag on the floor, she remembered. *Fuck.* She threw on some clothes and then shuffled out of the room. The moment she opened the door, her friends shushed each other and smiled oddly when she entered the living room.

"Morning," she grumbled, her throat raw and scratchy.

"How are you feeling?" Draya and Shawn asked in unison.

"Like shit," she admitted. "Any coffee?"

"I can fix you some," Draya said, hopping up and rushing to do Abrianna's bidding.

"Thanks," Abrianna croaked.

Julian shook his head. *She looks like hell.*

Abrianna responded, "I look like I just woke up. What's your excuse, Jules?"

"Excuse me?" he asked.

"If you're going to talk shit about how I look, then fuck off."

Julian looked around to the others before addressing her. "I didn't say anything."

"I heard you," she snapped grumpily.

Shawn shook his head. "He didn't say anything, Bree." *Oh, my God. Now she's going crazy.*

"I'm not going crazy," she defended. "I heard him plain as day."

Shawn cocked his head and stared.

Ghost said, *What in the hell have I gotten myself into with this crazy group?*

"Fuck, Ghost. I'm not begging anybody to help me out. If you don't want us here, we can go." She slumped into a chair, swearing and propping her head in her hand. "My head."

Draya returned with her coffee. "Here you go."

"Thanks." She accepted the cup. Then Draya realized that everyone was staring at Abrianna.

"What did I miss?" Draya asked.

Shawn answered. "Nothing. Abrianna is arguing with herself."

"Whatever," Abrianna grumbled and sipped her coffee. The hot liquid aggravated her throat, but the caffeine was welcome. Her gaze landed on a book next to Ghost. *Telekinesis: Fact or Fiction?*

She glanced up, frowning.

"Research," said Ghost.

She shook her head.

He pushed his empty bowl away from him and leaned back in his chair. "Look. I'm tired of being dicked around," he began. "You and your friends have been trying to gaslight me into believing that I haven't seen what I've seen or know what I know. I'm fucking tired of it. I've put my neck out on the line, time after time. This shit is downright disrespectful. You got more muthafuckas trying to take you out than a Colombian kingpin."

"What?"

"Oh." He tossed up his hands. "You may *not* remember your friends saving you out of a trap house a couple of nights ago. When they brought you back here, I, frankly, thought that you were dead. It's usually the assumption when people aren't breathing and don't have a pulse. But lo and behold on the third day, your ass rose like Lazarus in the fucking bathtub, puking your guts out. Now, I'm no fucking doctor, and I don't play one on TV, but that shit ain't normal." He wagged a finger. "And too much shit about you ain't adding up. And to top it off, you're a fuckin' junkie. No offense."

The table was quiet, but everyone's gazes skittered around.

A phone trilled in the distance.

"And that reporter chick keeps calling. If she doesn't talk to you *today,* she threatened to call the police. And that shit can't happen," he warned. "Shit. I feel like a babysitter up in this bitch."

"I'll call her back," Abrianna croaked, climbing out of the chair with her coffee and marching back to the bedroom.

Ghost tossed up his arms. "That's it? You're really not going to tell *me* what's the real story is here?"

She ignored him and shut the door behind her.

Abrianna missed the call by the time she reached the phone. Recognizing Tomi's work number, she called her back.

"Where in the hell have you been?" Tomi demanded. "I've been calling you for days. Some guy named Shawn kept answering your phone and telling me that you were indisposed. I didn't know if I needed to call the police and file a missing person report."

Abrianna's heart leaped into her throat. "You didn't, did you?"

"No. But you can't be disappearing for days on me like that. I was beginning to think that . . ."

"What?"

"I don't know, that maybe that weird Charlie guy popped up or the president threw you into Guantanamo Bay. Hell. He's gunning for your father. Who knows what his desperate ass would do?"

"Well, I'm fine."

"Are you?" Tomi asked. "You don't sound like yourself."

"I'm good," she lied.

After a long silence, Tomi said, "The reason I was calling is because I booked your first interview. Well, I had to reschedule it now. But it's *The Greg Wallace Show* and they're willing to pay six figures. *The Filibuster* with Joy Walton also put an offer on the table, but it's to interview you *and* Kadir once he's out of jail. They are offering a cool million for an exclusive."

"Humph. We have to get him out first."

"That's the hiccup."

Abrianna sighed. "All right. I do need the money."

"Did you read those emails?"

"No. I . . . I haven't. Give me the date and time. I'll be there."

34

Kadir kept to himself.

At least that was the plan. He'd learned long ago not to clique up into any gang by the skin color bullshit that ensnared too many newbies. There wasn't a fool-proof way to avoid trouble, but the cost of protection is often too steep a price, and there was often no way out once you went down that road. Best to learn how to protect yourself and then let the chips fall where they may. Once word traveled about his fight with Precious, Kadir gained a lot of respect; he was left alone to mind his own business.

So it took him by surprise when a brother, broad as the side of a mountain, dropped his tray on the table in front of him and then took his time squatting down into the bench seat.

It took Kadir a second to know the big man had no interest in his lunch.

"Are you Kadir Kahlifa?" the mountain asked.

"Depends on who's asking."

"I got a message from Ghost."

Kadir lifted a brow. "I'm listening."

"He wants you to call him."

Kadir waited for the punch line, but there wasn't one. "Am I supposed to stand out in the yard and make smoke signals for this call?" he asked.

The mountain's lips twitched. "Bathroom, third stall. There's a loose tile by the base. Inside, there's a burner and a VOIP encryption number."

"A VOIP encrypt—are you a member of the revolution?"

The mountain smiled. "*Vive la resistance*, muthafucka. He's waiting." With that the big man lumbered to his feet, picked up his tray, and moseyed off.

Kadir finished his rubbery chicken and soupy mashed potatoes before stacking his empty tray with the other dirty ones and heading to the bathroom. Another prisoner occupied the third stall and was emptying his rotten guts in it, judging by the stench.

By the time he exited the stall, fanning the air, Kadir was sure his black-and-blue face now held an added shade of green. The disgusting part was watching the nasty fuck exit the bathroom without washing his damn hands.

Holding his breath, Kadir entered the stall and locked the door. When he knelt near the base of the bowl, he drew a breath and nearly passed out from the lingering toxic fumes. *I'm going to kill Ghost.*

Kadir found the loose tile. He grabbed the flip phone and a folded piece of paper.

Ghost answered, "It's about fucking time."

"How come I didn't know that you made moves on the inside like a crime boss?" Kadir asked.

"A ghost is invisible at all times." Ghost laughed.

"Then how come this is the first time I'm learning about it?"

"Let's me guess, you thought that you got through six years on the inside because you got six-pack abs and a winning personality?"

Kadir chuckled.

"Hey, you had my back in Afghanistan and I got you—and now apparently your girl."

Kadir sobered. "What do you mean?"

"The junkie stripper with the heart of gold is crashing at my play cousin's crib again."

Kadir's hand tightened on the phone as thoughts he shouldn't have crossed his mind.

"I can tell by the change in your breathing that you need to get your mind out of the gutter. We're boys for life, and I wouldn't do you like that."

"I know that."

"Do you?"

Silence.

"All right. Don't answer that. You're thinking about when I kissed Vaughn's girl in Las Vegas that one time. I get it. But this ain't that," Ghost said. "Ms. Parker is at my crib because the crew intercepted an extraction order at T4S over the wire. K-man, they mentioned her by *name*."

"What?"

"Yeah, and that's not all," Ghost said and then filled his buddy in on all that had happened before saying, "You were right, man. There is something very strange about your girl. She ain't normal. And what's worse is that I think that she's in denial. Her and her friends."

"T4S? Why in the hell are they interested in her?"

"You tell me and then we'll both know. I'm fishing around, and I'll let you know what I find. But it has something to do with that reporter chick, too. Tomi Lehane. Her name came across the wire, too."

"Then it has to do with the article." Kadir lowered

his voice. "T4S does a lot of government shit off the grid. Military work. Maybe the White House—"

"Yeah. That's what my crew thinks, too."

"But you don't?"

"I'm on the fence. On one hand, what y'all saying makes sense. But too much shit about your girl ain't adding up. You remember when you told me about seeing some guy fly against the wall?"

"Yeah?"

"I believe you now."

"You do?"

"Man, she was hit by a speeding car according to the 911 calls we intercepted. She rolled down a twenty-foot embankment in the back of an ambulance and is a hell of a shooter. And she's fine. While I was talking to her the other day, I tried to see how that bullet wound was healing up. I couldn't even tell where she was shot."

The floor shifted beneath Kadir. "What are you saying?"

"I'm saying it. Your girl is a freak—and not the good nasty kind either. She's a freak of nature."

35

Zeke refused to go to the hospital. It had been a miracle that he'd survived the wreckage and found help. Angel did what she could for him the first night, but when he coughed up blood and still refused to get help, she left. He'd lost ten pounds in three days and the constant pain turned his vengeance into an obsession. He promoted new heavies and placed them in charge of combing the city for Abrianna. However, the bitch was a magician or her people were loyal as fuck, because the streets weren't talking.

His people were talking. Zeke caught constant stares and noticed how muthafuckas slacked off. Money for the first time came in light in a couple of districts. This morning he sent out enforcers to make up the difference in collecting kneecaps. The shit won't come in light again.

Jermaine, his new number one heavy, entered the room with a knock.

Sitting in a pool of sweat, Zeke rolled his head in

the door's direction and had to blink hard to clear his blurred vision. "Yeah?"

"That Parker chick is on television," he said.

"What?"

Jermaine crossed the room, retrieved the remote, and powered on the television to the correct channel. "She's supposed to be coming up in the next segment. *The Greg Wallace Show*. You heard of it?"

Zeke pulled up out of his seat, his strength renewed.

Abrianna and Tomi settled into the guest chairs for Greg Wallace's show. A makeup artist buzzed around, powdering their faces, while a sound guy miked them up. "Are you sure that you're ready to do this?" Tomi asked.

Hell, no. The general public was cruel and judgmental. Since her story broke, the country had scurried into partisan corners. Part of the country believed that Abrianna was a pawn for the opposition party and that she'd set up or framed the president. Another part of the country declared her a hero, according to public polling. However, all agreed that this latest political scandal was bigger than Watergate, Monica Lewinsky, and Russian hacking combined. However, she wasn't doing this for herself. She was doing it for Kadir. "Bree?" Tomi inquired again. "Are you ready?"

"I'm as ready as I'm ever going to be," she answered.

Attorney Joseph Bowen rushed onto the set and took the last seat on Abrianna's right with a grunt. "Sorry I'm late, ladies."

The makeup girl turned her attention toward the attorney with a gasp.

Tomi put in her earpiece.

Abrianna saw her and did the same. The instant chatter in her ear caught her off guard. She followed instructions when a male voice told her to nod if she could hear them.

"We're live in two minutes," the producer said.

Tomi squeezed Abrianna's hand.

Abrianna smiled but her nervousness remained. This wasn't like stepping on a stage with a cocaine bump. It was far from it. On stage, she could pretend to be someone else. The customers were free to fantasize that she was anyone they wanted her to be. Baring your soul was far different than baring your body.

The two minutes it took before the camera's red light flashed on was the longest *and* shortest time that she'd ever experienced.

Greg Wallace blasted into her ear, "Joining us now via satellite is Ms. Abrianna Parker for her first live interview. As many of you know, Ms. Parker is at the heart of this latest D.C. scandal that involves the leader of the free world and his chief justice appointee Katherine Sanders plotting and killing the United States House speaker Kenneth Reynolds, all to avoid impeachment. It doesn't get any juicier than this, folks."

The host went on to summarize how Tomi's blockbuster story rocked the political world for his audience before he extended his greeting. "Ms. Parker, welcome to the show."

Abrianna cleared her throat. "Thanks. I'm pleased to be here."

Wallace continued, "I guess that I should start off by saying that this is one hell of a story. One, I'm sure, Ms. Lehane, has landed you solidly in the history books."

"It certainly belongs there," Tomi gushed.

"We should also let the audience know that you and Ms. Lehane have quite the history. Both of you are now the only survivors of serial killer Dr. Craig Avery. Is this why, Ms. Parker, you brought the story to Ms. Lehane?"

"I, uh, yes." Abrianna cleared her throat again. "I didn't know anyone else in the media to get my story out."

Wallace then took a moment to recap the Dr. Craig Avery case before asking, "In this President Walker scandal, can you please tell our audience how it is that you came to be in at the Hay-Adams Hotel the night House Speaker Reynolds was killed?"

"I . . . ." Cough. "I was hired," Abrianna answered.

"Hired? Meaning that you were . . . how should I say . . . a lady of the evening?" Wallace asked. "Is that fair?"

Another cough. "That's correct."

"Who hired you?"

"Mr. Reynolds was my client," she admitted. From there, she was drilled on every detail of that night. When they cut to commercial, Abrianna was handed bottled water, which she chugged greedily. Her nervousness must have been obvious because in her ear, the producer reassured her how well she was doing.

At the first opportunity, she pled her case for Kadir. "What is upsetting to me now is that Mr. Kahlifa is being held without charge. The man is a hero. He saved my life. To punish him for doing that isn't justice . . . or very American."

"With all due respect, Ms. Parker, I understand why *you* would feel this way. But there is the matter of the airport bombing that's still being investigated. That happened, according to your account, *before* you infamously dove into the backseat of his car."

"Yes. But Mr. Kahlifa was an Uber driver. He didn't know the two men that he'd dropped off at the airport. The fare was logged into his Uber account. A neighbor of Mr. Kahlifa has even stepped forward and admitted that he referred the Al-Sahi brothers to Mr. Kahlifa that morning. There is no ambiguity here. The FBI is looking for a scapegoat because for whatever reason, they have no answers to give to the public on who the Al-Sahi brothers were or to which terrorist group they'd pledged their allegiance. They only know that all the men were Arabs and, I guess, in their minds, they were all guilty."

"Whoa! That's a pretty wild accusation," Wallace said, clearly happy that she'd said something controversial on his program.

"There is no other reason, as far as I can see."

Attorney Bowen cut in and informed the audience that he and his partner were also representing Mr. Kahlifa and that the FBI weren't saying anything as to why they were still holding his client.

As the hour-long interview wrapped up, the host threw the speedball at Abrianna. "Ms. Parker, I would be remiss if I didn't take this moment to ask you about another scandal that, amazingly, involves another member of your family. Your father: Cargill Parker."

Abrianna froze.

"I'm sure that you've heard about him being swept up in a child-sex trafficking ring at the private Lynnwood Club. Is there anything that you can tell our audience about that?"

She blinked. An awkward and uncomfortable pause ensued live on camera.

"Ms. Parker," Wallace tried again, "do you care to comment? Have you been in contact with your father?"

Tomi stretched a hand out again and gave Abrianna another squeeze of support.

Abrianna drew a deep breath and injected steel into her spine despite the knots rolling in her gut. It was time to face one of the monsters.

"Yes. I heard about the charges against my *adoptive* father. I am . . . relieved that his money can no longer protect him. He's a sick man. And after all that I've been through these past six years, I've never regretted the day that I ran away from that house. I only regret that I haven't been strong enough to go after my adopted father myself." Her bottom lip trembled as a lone tear streaked down her face.

"Thank you, Ms. Parker," Wallace said in her ear. "I admire your strength for coming onto the program and sharing your story with us."

"My pleasure."

The camera's red light shut off. Tomi and Mr. Bowen congratulated her on her performance. She appreciated their praise; however, it was her own sense of accomplishment that made her proud.

<hr />

President Walker shut off the television after Abrianna's interview and unleashed a stream of expletives that burned Kate's ears. She, as well as Donald Davidson, knew that the beautiful Abrianna Parker had just won America's heart with that dynamic performance. The single tear streaking down her beautiful face at the end was an especially nice touch.

After a full minute of his temper tantrum, Kate grew bored and marched toward the door.

"And where the fuck do you think that you're going?" Walker barked.

She answered without stopping, "To get my measuring stick. I can start preparing to change these awful gold draperies."

36

The White House

For the second time in history an American president sat before a camera and addressed the nation with a resignation speech. Despite the coiffed hair, pressed suit, and lifted chin, devastation blanketed his face.

"Tonight, I come before the American people, not only as your president, but as a humbled man. I'm sure that, by now, most of you have heard the serious and unfounded accusations leveled at me in connection to House Speaker Kenneth Reynolds's death. It is important that the American people hear directly from me, regarding these *baseless* charges. I am as shocked as everyone to learn that my recent appointee to the Supreme Court, Chief Justice Katherine Sanders, had an alleged part in the speaker's murder, but the surveillance video that we've all seen on the news taken from the scene of the crime leaves little doubt.

"However, the wild confession tape of Judge Sanders obtained by the *Washington Post* saying that *I* or anyone in my administration are in any way connected to this horrific crime is preposterous. On that taped confession, I hear nothing but a desperate woman before taking her life. Granted, the chief justice is no longer here to defend or be cross-examined in a court of law, but we have no idea if this confession was coerced. I intend to *fight* these allegations. However, it is also clear to me that I won't be able to do this while serving the people here at the White House.

"Instead of putting the nation through a partisan impeachment trial, I've decided to resign from the presidency, effective noon tomorrow. At that time, Vice President Kate Washington will be sworn in as your president. I am both sad and disappointed that I will not be here to work on your behalf, but I am confident that the leadership of America will be in good hands . . ."

After hearing the president's speech, Jayson joked, "Microphone drop, bitches." He crumpled a wad of paper and tossed it for a three-pointer into the wastebasket in Tomi's cubicle.

Tomi smirked. "It's about time. He held on by his fingertips for as long as he could, that's for sure."

"Okay, Rock Star. Your story brought down a presidency. Your future is bright in this town. Your life is about to change. You're a big fucking deal now, baby girl." He held up a hand for a high-five.

"Baby girl?"

His smile waned. "I just . . ."

"I'm kidding. Lighten up." Tomi grinned and whacked him on the shoulder.

"Ow." He rubbed his shoulder.

"Don't start."

Jayson zipped his lips.

Tomi's colleagues broke out in applause as they clustered around her cubicle. Soon, red plastic cups filled with champagne were passed around for a toast. Many of her coworkers were sincere with their congratulations; most were jealous.

Tomi loved it and was on top of the world.

———•◦•———

Solitary confinement destroyed the weak minded. It never bothered Kadir. He used the time to pray, meditate, and read. When he wasn't doing that, he thought of Abrianna. What was she going through? How was she holding up? And was she still numbing herself with drugs?

His attorney told him about Abrianna doing media interviews to press for his release. He was pleased that she cared so much, but he held little hope that she would prevail, but Johnson said that public opinion was breaking their way. Still, Kadir refused to get his hopes up. When he had chosen to help Bree, he knew that he could land back behind bars.

A steady march of booted feet drew Kadir's attention. He lifted his head from the concrete floor and sat back onto his folded legs. Keys jangled into the locks and then the door slid open with a thunderous clang.

"All right, convict. On your feet."

Kadir eyed the two guards.

"Don't make me repeat myself," the barrel-chested guard barked.

Cautious, Kadir rose to his feet and then followed their added commands. Once he was cuffed, he was led out of solitary confinement. An hour later, he was being processed out and released.

Outside the federal prison, a horde of photographers barreled toward him. Microphones out and cameras pointed, they hurled questions a mile a minute. He couldn't make out a single one.

A horn honked.

Kadir spotted a black SUV at the curb. The back window rolled down and Abrianna's beautiful face appeared.

"Excuse me," he said, and then bogarted his way toward the SUV.

The reporters and cameramen followed with endless questions.

"Need a lift?" Abrianna asked.

When the reporters saw who was in the vehicle, they transformed into a mob.

Kadir muscled his way into the backseat and powered up the window. "Hey, you."

"Oh, my God," Abrianna exclaimed. "Your face looks worse." She slid across the seat and cradled it in her hands to examine the bruises.

Kadir hissed, "Easy."

"Sorry." She lightened her hold.

Kadir stared, marveling how she grew more beautiful every time he saw her. "It's okay."

"What happened?" Tomi asked from the front passenger seat, looking equally aghast.

"Hey, Ms. Lehane. Prison happened." He smirked.

Concern etched every inch of Abrianna's face, but he wasn't about to go further into it.

Julian spoke up from the driver's seat. "Where to?"

Kadir's smile expanded. "Oh, hey."

"Long time no see," Julian said.

"You can say that again."

Abrianna huffed. "I can't believe they kept you this long. Bastards. They should have released you a long time ago."

"Yeah, well. The FBI likes dick-swinging contests. The fact that we evaded them for as long as we did didn't go down too well."

Kadir realized that Julian was waiting for an answer. "I guess my place."

"Great. Mind sharing the address?"

Kadir chuckled and gave him the information.

Julian pulled away from the curb and the shouting reporters.

Abrianna drifted back to the other side of the seat. "I'm glad you're out of there."

"Me too." He cocked one brow. "How did you manage it?"

"Public pressure." She drew a deep breath. "Tomi and I must've gone on every news show in America, railing about how the government was treating you like a criminal instead of a hero. Tomi helped me build a social media movement and campaign." She shook her head. "It's been a lot of work in a short amount of time."

Touched, Kadir marveled, "You did all of that for me?"

Abrianna met his gaze. "You had my back, so I had yours."

A smile tugged at his lips. "Thanks."

"No need to thank me. It's what friends do."

He nodded. "Friends." *Just friends.*

Tomi spoke up. "I'm glad that you're out. I hope you don't mind giving me the first scoop on your release. Should only take a few minutes. We'll be finished by the time we arrive at your place."

"Nah. Not at all. Shoot."

Twenty minutes later, they arrived at the Park Flat apartments and, as Tomi promised, the interview was over.

The second Kadir stepped out of the vehicle, Mook shouted, "I know that ain't my man Kadir."

The neighborhood junkie rushed the SUV, but once

he was within a couple of feet, he reeled back. "Damn, man. Did you get the license plate of that truck that ran into your face?"

Kadir smiled. "Hey, Mook." He held up his hand and then slapped palms and bumped shoulders with him one time. "Good to see you."

"Yeah? Good to see you, too, man. At least the parts of you that are still recognizable. You know, I have just the thing to help you out with that busted lip." Mook shoved a hand into his oversize military jacket.

Kadir stayed the man's hand. "That's okay, Mook. I'm good."

"You sho'?" Mook jabbed a thumb over his shoulder. "I could run to my man working out of Kane's butcher's shop and get you a fat steak for that eye at least."

"Nah. Don't sweat yourself. I'll take care of it."

The SUV pulled off. Abrianna moved next to Kadir and grabbed Mook's attention as she stopped beside him. "Well, hello." Mook scratched his dry Afro as he eyed her up and down. "Aren't you a tall drink of water? K-man, is this all you?" Mook wormed in between them and beamed his buttery smile.

Abrianna's lips twitched in amusement. "Another friend of yours, Kadir?"

Mook answered instead. "You know it. Me and K-man here go way back—at least eight months." He cocked his head. "Hey. Haven't I seen your face before?"

She lifted a brow.

Kadir pulled the junkie aside. "Down, Mook. You're scaring her off."

"Oh. All right. I hear you talking." He lifted his fist for a bump.

Kadir took Abrianna by the elbow and escorted her toward his building.

"Oh. So it's like that?" Mook said, watching the couple walk away. "You're going to leave me hangin'?"

Kadir waved and kept it moving.

"You have a lot of *interesting* friends."

"Look who's calling the pot black," he joked. At his apartment door, Kadir snatched off an eviction notice and groaned. "I guess I can't be too surprised." He reached into his pocket. "Shit."

"What? Is there a problem?"

He checked his pockets again. "Look, stay here. Let me see if anyone is in the leasing office who can give me a key."

"You're joking, right?" she asked.

"No. It'll take just a few minutes. I'll be right back."

"No need," she said, shaking her head. "I got it." She unzipped her cross-body purse and removed a pouch.

"What's that?"

"A little sumpthin' sumpthin' that I try to never leave home without." She winked and knelt before the door. Kadir watched her slide two thin metal tools into the keyhole. "You're kidding me. You pick locks?"

She shrugged. "You hack into computers."

"That's not the same thing."

"Of course it is. I break into physical doors and you break into digital doors. Both are breaking and entering without permission. Same thing." The gear shifted with a click. Abrianna smiled, twisted the knob, and opened the door. "Voilà." Abrianna stood. "You're welcome."

Kadir shook his head. "You're full of surprises."

"Thank you."

———————◆◆◆———————

Offices of the Washington Post

Jayson rolled into Tomi's cubicle in an office chair, startling her. "Do you want to see something interesting?"

Tomi removed her hand from over her heart. "Jesus, Jayson. You startled me."

"I hate to pull you away from your next blockbuster story, but I got something that you'll find interesting."

"Oh?" she asked, turning away from her computer. "And what's that?"

Jayson plopped an open magazine on her desk. "Take a look at that."

Tomi glanced at the pages and shrugged. "What am I looking at?"

Jayson stabbed a finger at an article at the bottom. Beside it was a black-and-white photograph. "Look familiar?"

She blinked. *The guy in the black Mercedes.* Tomi read the name under the picture. "Dr. Charles Zacher. Doctor?" She shook her head and read the first paragraph. "Research and development director of T4S." She frowned. "Where have I heard that company's name before?" Her mind zipped through her mental database. She came up with the answer. "A security firm."

"A *paramilitary* security firm," Jayson corrected.

"A *private* security firm with *government* tags?" she asked.

Jayson shrugged. "If it makes *no* sense, then it makes perfect sense in this town."

But what would a guy like that want with me?

"Anyway, I remember that sketch you were drawing when I came across this. It's an old *Newsweek* issue. I swiped it from my dentist's office this morning. I thought that you'd be interested."

Tomi tuned Jayson out while she read.

He asked, "Did I do good?"

"Huh? Oh. Yeah. Good. Thanks. I appreciate you bringing this to my attention."

"Do you think that there is some kind of story there?" he asked, gauging her expression.

"I'm not sure. But I'll let you know as soon as I find out." She flashed a smile, hoping that he'd take the hint and leave so that she could finish the article. The phone rang, arresting her attention. "Hold on." She picked up the receiver. "Tomi Lehane."

"Hey, this is Sally down at the receptionist desk. You have a visitor."

"A visitor?" She wasn't expecting anyone. "Who is it?"

"She says her name is Marion Parker."

"Parker?"

"Yes. Hold on a sec." The sound was muffled, but then Sally returned to the line. "She said that you know her daughter."

"Oh?" Tomi blinked, caught off guard. This was an interesting turn of events. "Send her up." She placed the receiver back into its cradle.

"Another Parker?"

"Yeah. Bree's mother."

"Mother?" Jayson inquired. "Problem?"

"No. Well, I don't know," she answered. She couldn't imagine what the next twist would be in the Abrianna Parker saga. She stood from her chair and peered over the heads of her colleagues in time to see Marion Parker arrive on her floor. She recognized her instantly, not because she looked like her daughter; she didn't. Marion Parker was a honey-colored southern belle who apparently took her conservative style and fashion tips from a sixties *Vogue* catalog. Tomi recognized the woman from years ago after Tomi had been rescued from Dr. Avery's basement. Marion and her husband were on a desperate hunt to find Abrianna after she'd run away from the hospital.

"*That* is Abrianna Parker's mother?" Jayson asked.

Marion Parker stopped at the first desk she came to on the floor. A colleague pointed the elegant woman in Tomi's direction.

Tomi waved.

"Do you think that she's here regarding her daughter or her husband?" Jayson asked.

"We're about to find out." She pushed up a smile as Marion approached.

"Hello, are you Tomi Lehane?" Marion asked in a lyrical southern twang.

"Yes, I am. And you're Marion Parker?"

"I am." The women shook hands.

Marion's gaze went to Jayson.

"Oh! I'm sorry. This here is Jayson Brigham. He's a photographer for the paper . . . and he was just leaving."

"Huh? Oh, yes." Jayson also shook Marion's hand before reaching for his chair.

"Why don't you leave that here so Mrs. Parker can sit?" Tomi suggested. "I'll bring it back to your cubicle later."

"Oh. Sure. No problem." Jayson smiled again. "Nice to have met you," he said, exiting the cubicle.

Marion began, "Thank you, Ms. Lehane, for taking a few minutes to talk with me."

"It's no problem. Please, have a seat."

"Thank you," she said and then folded herself into the chair, back erect, legs crossed at the ankles.

Tomi marveled at how polished the woman was. There wasn't a single hair out of place. She was a real-life throwback picture of the sixties, right down to the strand of pearls wrapped around her neck. "What can I do for you, Mrs. Parker?"

"Please. Call me Marion."

"All right, Marion. How can I help?"

"Well, I hope that you don't find this too forward, but I have been following your articles in the paper lately. And I saw the interview you did with my daughter the other night. I was hoping that you could help me . . ." She took a deep breath ". . . get in contact with her."

"Oh," Tomi said.

"Yes. I know that this request is rather odd, but, you see, my daughter and I haven't been in contact for a few years. As you well know, she ran away from home when she was fourteen and . . . landed in quite a bit of trouble with that crazy man and . . . well, like I said, you know the rest. Now she's caught up with this whole political mess, and her father . . . Look. I know that I'm rambling. I wanted to ask whether you could help me, uh . . ."

"Help?"

"Yes. I want to reconnect with her," Marion said. "I don't mean to drag you into our family drama, but I don't know any other way to reach out to her." She fidgeted.

Tomi empathized with the woman.

"You're kind of like my only hope, really," Marion added, pouring on the guilt.

"Mrs. Parker, have you and your husband moved since the last time you've seen Abrianna?"

"We own several homes, but our main residence is the same since Abrianna left."

"I see." Tomi bit her bottom lip, figuring out the best way to proceed. "Not to be rude, but don't you think that if Abrianna wanted to return home, she would have by now?"

Marion sighed.

"I don't mean to be so blunt, but . . ."

"No. It's all right." She pulled another deep breath. "In truth, I don't know what to think. She may have been scared to come back; maybe she couldn't forgive herself for . . . some things. Or maybe that psychopath that snatched her really screwed up her head. All I know is that I want to make amends. I need her to know that it's okay now. There is nothing to fear now. Can't you pass along the message?" She opened her purse and pulled out a card. "Here. Can you give her this? It has my personal cell phone number. Tell her that I *really* want to talk to her."

Tomi accepted the card. "I can do that. I'll give it to her. Now can I ask *you* for a favor?" Tomi asked.

Marion said nothing.

"I'd really like to . . . interview you about, well, about everything that's been happening lately."

"How about we talk *after* you pass along my message? Fair?"

"Sure. Fair enough."

"Great." A smile bloomed across Marion's face. "Thank you. I can't tell you how much this means to me." She stood up. "I'll let you get back to your work."

Tomi stood as well, smiling.

"Thank you again," Marion added, offering her hand.

Tomi accepted it, noting how cold it was and how much it trembled in her grip. "It was nice meeting you, Mrs. Parker. Have a good afternoon."

"You too." Marion held onto her big smile for an additional awkward moment before pulling her hand from Tomi's grip and exiting the cubicle.

Tomi watched Marion's perfect walk capture nearly every male's attention as she strolled across the busy office before disappearing into an elevator.

Jayson returned. "Well?"

Tomi shrugged. "That's one hell of a crazy-ass family."

37

Castillo spent hours going back and forth working with Dennis and his contact down at the FBI and the Children's Protective Services. The understaffed departments were working overtime trying to identify and place the children who had been removed from the Lynnwood Club and they weren't having any success. The children weren't talking, and neither were any of the defendants from the Lynnwood Club.

Then Castillo got a hit.

"Hot damn." She punched the air in victory when she got the call.

Holder shared her enthusiasm. "You have no idea how happy this has made them over at the bureau today. This little girl was the *only* child that they've been able to make a positive ID on. It's like these kids materialized out of nowhere. It's been real disheartening the last couple of weeks. They've been ramming their heads into a wall every day."

"I get it," Castillo said. "I have a few dents in my

head, too, from working these cases. I can't wait to contact this little girl's mother. She's really bad off since she went missing out of her own bedroom."

"I've never met a parent who hasn't taken losing a child hard," Holder said. "But thanks for this win today. I'm sending her information up the ladder and over to the DOJ. I know that they're desperate for some good news, too. Word is that their case is sitting on shifting sand."

"How in the hell is that shit possible?"

Holder laughed without mirth. "When you're dealing with people who have more money than the GDP of a small country, there better not be a single i not dotted or t not crossed. These people have the kind of lawyers who graduated at the top of their classes at Purgatory Law. I heard they're challenging everything including the alleged anonymous phone call. The head douchebag Cargill Parker is laying the groundwork for a political persecution defense."

"Is that a real defense?"

"For the amount of money he's paying his lawyers, it will be."

"And who is supposed to be his political adversary?" The second the question left her mouth, Castillo knew the answer.

"The former president," Holder confirmed. "Parker is claiming that President Walker targeted him as some sort of payback for his daughter exposing his collusion in killing that congressman. It's a real-ass soap opera."

"And how does he explain the children?"

"The government brought them, of course. None of the children are saying anything. And the raid didn't actually catch anyone in the act."

"Surely a physical examination—"

"Only one showed any signs of sexual trauma, and that's your match. My guess is that the other kids were new to the market and our guys got there before an actual crime had been committed."

"That's good news on one hand."

"And pretty shitty on the other. It's a good chance this little secret club is going to get away with this. And their billions will make sure that none of their members will get so much as a ticket for jaywalking for the rest of their lives."

Castillo shook her head. "Justice is not blind."

"Not as long as you got enough gold to put on that scale she's always lugging around."

A minute later, Castillo ended the phone call with her victory high diminished to a low-grade buzz. It was the nature of the business. One step forward, twenty steps back. She thought about Cargill Parker and the few times their paths had crossed, and she had no problem believing him guilty of the charges leveled against him. She couldn't stomach the idea of him possibly getting away with this. She picked up the phone again and called her old friend at the Department of Justice. Leaning back in her office chair, she grabbed a case file of eight-year-old Lovely Belfleur and smiled. "At least you're going home, sweetheart."

The line picked up. "Kellerman."

"Hey, Skipper. Guess who," she said.

"Gigi! Long time no hear from."

"It's a couple of weeks before Christmas, so I figure this call could be your early Christmas gift."

He laughed. "If you really cared, you would come and see me in person."

"Ah. No can do. I don't break up happy homes."

"Who said anything about being happy?"

"Maybe you should file that under things to talk to your therapist about."

He chuckled. "I knew that I married the wrong sister."

"Yeah. Shannon's first husband said the same thing." She laughed.

"And the Gigi fan club grows. Are you still pretending not to be in love with that sap Holder?" he inquired.

"None of your fucking business."

"And we've come to the end of the small talk portion of our conversation. What can I do you for, *Ms.* Castillo?"

"Actually, this is more about what I can do for you."

"Are we flirting again?"

"No. Who's working the Cargill Parker case over there?"

"Oh. That's an all-hands-on-deck case. Why? Whatcha got?"

"It's not a what, but a who."

Laughing, Kadir stepped inside of his apartment and froze.

Abrianna followed and stopped beside him. "Nice place. Did you kill the maid?" She took in the destruction.

"It looks like a tornado touched down in here," he grumbled.

"Were you robbed?"

Kadir stepped over piles of overturned furniture. He stopped at the coffee table and set it back up on its four legs. "I doubt it. This looks like the feds' handiwork."

Abrianna closed the front door. "Damn. I'd hate to see what my old place looks like, then. The landlord is probably still digging bullets out of the walls. I can kiss that deposit goodbye."

"You haven't been there?"

"What's the point?" She glanced around. "Want some help?" she offered.

"Uh . . ." He smiled. "If you don't mind?"

"Not a problem, but . . . let's get something on that eye first." She maneuvered around the mess to make it to into the kitchen. However, the FBI tornado had hit in there as well. Cabinets were wide open, drawers were yanked out, and silverware along with pots and pans were strewn everywhere. "Goddamn."

"What?" Kadir joined her in the kitchen and sighed.

Abrianna shook her head and opened the refrigerator. "Did they jack your food, too?"

"Uh, no. I'd been meaning to make it to the grocery store before all of this happened."

Abrianna lifted a dubious brow, but let the explanation slide. In the freezer, she found a package of frozen peas. "This should do."

"Peas?"

"Yep. C'mon. Let's get you fixed up." She crossed back over to him and then led him into the living room. She placed the cushions back onto the sofa and told him to sit down. "Now hold your head back."

When the frozen peas touched his face, he hissed and flinched.

"Don't be such a big baby." She smirked.

"Who are you calling a baby?"

"One guess."

Kadir forced himself to remain still. "I'm not a baby," he grumbled jokingly.

Abrianna placed the peas on his face again. "There. See? That wasn't so bad, was it?"

"Nah. I got this." He smiled, even though his busted lips stung and throbbed.

"Your lips are bleeding," she observed. "Hold on." She sprang up and hopscotched over the mess and headed down the hall. "Which door is the bathroom?"

"First door on your right, but I can save you the trouble: I don't have any Band-Aids."

"What *do* you have?" she asked.

He listened to her open and close cabinets while shaking his head. "Not much." He sighed as the peas numbed his face.

Abrianna returned with a wet-and-dry towel. "Here, let's wrap those peas up so you don't get frostbite first."

Kadir resumed smiling as he watched her clean his lip and dab petroleum jelly onto it. Kadir enjoyed the pampering, even thought that he could get used to it. "You'd make a good nurse."

"Ha. Not likely."

"Why not?"

"It's a job that requires you to be a people person." She grinned.

"And that's not you?"

"Not by a long shot." She leaned back and admired her work. "There. All done."

"Yeah?" Kadir removed the thawing peas from his face and went to check in the bathroom mirror. "Holy shit!" He stared horrified at his reflection.

"What is it?"

"I didn't know that I looked this jacked up."

"Almost looks like a murder scene, doesn't it?" she

quipped and then added under her breath, "Smells like one, too."

Kadir jutted his head around the corner. "I heard that."

She raised a brow, prompting him to sniff under his armpits. "Whoa!" He reeled. "I'm taking a shower."

"The world thanks you," She waved the air. "I'll start picking up in here."

"Cool." Kadir returned to the cluttered bathroom, which suffered the least damage because there wasn't much in it. After turning on the shower to full blast, he stripped down and saw the black-and-purple bruises across his body. Maybe he did look like he should've been white-chalked at a crime scene. In the shower, the hot water was paradise, though he had to rush before the water heater clunked out and left him rinsing in subzero-temperature water.

In the living room, Abrianna got to work. After a few minutes of righting furniture and picking up scattered books and paper off the floor, she came across a broken picture frame. The image was hard to see through the shards of glass, so she took her time extracting the picture from the frame. It was a high school prom picture. She identified a smiling Kadir, though he was as thin as a twig and had wavy midnight hair flowing past his shoulders and . . . was he wearing braces?

Abrianna smiled, but then her gaze shifted to the pretty teenage girl holding a side pose. Actually, she was more than pretty. She was downright gorgeous in a gold-and-pearl gown that hugged her burgeoning curves. Her golden hijab drew the eye to focus on her flawless face. She looked like a young Arabian princess and Kadir her handsome Aladdin. She remembered a conversation she and Kadir had had two months ago.

"What was the longest relationship that you've ever been in?" Abrianna asked Kadir.

"Fifteen years," he answered. *"I have to say that it was the longest and only real relationship I had."*

"You're shitting me."

"No. She was the love of my life," he said.

Abrianna stared at the young beauty until she heard the shower shut off. She put the picture away, not wanting to be caught with it. The bathroom door opened. Steam billowed before Kadir stepped out with a towel wrapped around his hips. His hair dripped pearl-size drops of water down his back.

Abrianna smiled, liking his tapered hips and ripped abs, but the large ugly bruises splayed across his chest unnerved her. "Are you sure that you won those fights?"

"I won the first one. The other ones with the guards weren't even close."

She moved toward him, unable to pull her gaze away. "Maybe you should see a doctor?"

Kadir's brows shot up as he laughed and toweled dry his hair. *"You're* suggesting a doctor? I thought that you didn't care for doctors?"

"I don't . . . for me."

"Ha. Hypocrite."

"Call it what you want. But you really should get checked out."

"I'm fine," he said, winking. "I'm going to get dressed." He headed to the bedroom.

"Uh, yeah." She looked around. "Uhm. How about I order us some pizza? This is going to take a while, and I'm starving."

"Sounds great!"

Hours later, Kadir and Abrianna had made a dent in cleaning up Kadir's wrecked apartment and stopped to attack that pizza on the living room floor.

"So what's next?" Kadir asked, going for his third slice. "You've basically cleared your name—"

"Not quite," she corrected. "I haven't been charged with anything, but there are plenty of lunatics out there who still think I had something to do with it. Tomi thinks I could be dragged into Congress or into a deposition."

"So there *will* be a trial?"

"I'm assuming. Everyone is still waiting to see what the vice president is going to do. Pundits have been in a fierce debate on whether she's going to pardon her former boss. Some said that it would be a nail in her own coffin, especially if she plans to run for the office herself next year. Others say that having a former president convicted for murder would be bad for the country." She shrugged. "I get the sense that the media would like the spectacle of a trial."

"Wow. Sounds like you acquired your political training wheels while I was away."

"I never really appreciated the art of bullshitting before."

"Well. We are certainly in the right town to learn." Kadir shook his head. "I need to pay more attention to Ghost's crazy conspiracy stories."

"You and me both." Abrianna folded her pizza slice and took a huge bite.

Kadir chuckled at the spot of tomato sauce at the corner of her mouth.

"What?"

"You got a little tomato sauce on your face," he said, gesturing toward a corner of her mouth.

"Oh. Where? Here?" She touched the wrong side and left another smudge of sauce.

Kadir's chuckle deepened.

"No?" she asked, eyes sparkling.

"Here. Let me help you." He grabbed a napkin and stretched over the pizza box to dab the corners of her mouth. "There you go." He stopped and met her gaze.

She blushed and asked, "Did you get it all?"

Kadir stole a kiss. "There. Now I've got it all." He pulled back, but she stopped him.

"Hold on. Now you have some on you." They kissed again, longer this time, deeper.

Breaking away, he said, "Thanks for fighting for me. I was sure they were going to keep me in there for a few decades."

"I wasn't going to let them do that," she said.

"Humph." He cocked his head. "You're my ride or die chick now?"

She laughed. "I guess . . . you can say that. Truth is . . . you could've kicked me out of your car, left me for dead that first day. You didn't have to help me kidnap a woman or hack hotel files. I owe you my life." She leaned in for another kiss, but Kadir pulled back.

"So . . . what? Is this gratitude you feel for me or . . . ?"

"Huh? No," she said, shaking her head. In truth, she hadn't processed what any of this meant.

Kadir called her on it. "Are you sure?"

Abrianna closed the pizza box and pushed it aside. "I was attracted to you the first time you slid twenty dollars into my G-string at the Stallion." She crawled closer. "And then I was really turned on when I gave you that private dance in the VIP room."

The memory made Kadir smile.

She leaned within an inch of his lips and stalled. "What I feel for you is a lot deeper than gratitude."

His lips hitched upward while his gaze dragged from her eyes to her lips. "Yeah?"

"Yeah." Her breath caressed his cheek.

"Good." He captured her mouth with a moan. He'd forgotten how intoxicating she was. The world spun as he clutched her closer.

Their clothes came off in a flash before they pressed their naked bodies together. His bruises made it difficult to manage a few positions, but he powered through to enjoy her every curve.

Heaven. Abrianna didn't know how the man was able to do the things he did, but she loved every minute of it. His name tumbled from her lips when he entered her.

She twisted beneath his caresses and gasped when he drilled deeper. Lost in a wave of passion, Abrianna ceased to think. All that existed was this moment. Their breathing came hard and fast as something glorious unfolded within them and then spread like a wildfire.

Kadir held her hips, while his mind teetered precariously over the edge of insanity. It was as if everything was new to him—from the way her body massaged him to his need to possess her—all of her. He loved her groans and flushed face. She was beauty. She was love.

A cry tore from Abrianna's lips as an internal volcano erupted.

Kadir thwarted the cry by kissing her senseless until the tremors subsided.

It took Abrianna a while to regain control of her breathing and hammering heart, but once she did, she laughed.

Kadir propped himself up onto his side. "What's so funny?"

"Us," she said, grinning. "We were like animals."

"What? I think we did well. I wanted to throw you on this floor since the moment we entered the apartment."

"Then you should have. Could have saved us a lot of time."

He smiled and took the top position. "We certainly have plenty of time now."

38

Tomi hung up the phone, anxious for Abrianna to call back. Not only did she want to pass Marion's message along, she also wanted to revisit some information regarding the mysterious Dr. Charles Zacher. She'd read the article that Jayson had given her more than a dozen times and had spent an irresponsible amount of time at work researching all she could about T4S. However, the more she learned, the more questions she had.

There wasn't a whole lot of information about Dr. Zacher himself. His sanitized profile made it clear that he was a brilliant man with awards out the wazoo. There was nothing on the web that linked him to madman Craig Avery—other than the fact that they were both doctors. That thread was thin as hell. She spent hours delving into Avery's professional background and, for the first time, went beyond the man's LinkedIn information. She was stunned to find ancient articles announcing the young Avery as a seven-year-old Mensa member. The accompanying picture of a bright-eyed, tow-headed boy aroused conflicting feelings within her, mainly, because there was no trace of the wild-eyed, stringy-haired madman who had tortured her for ten months. There were a few more articles heralding the young Avery as a genius. He had been his high school's valedictorian and had graduated at the top of his class at Johns Hopkins, where he received his doctorate in biomedical engineering. When Tomi switched over to research Zacher again, there was nothing other than a thin biography that was listed in the lone article that Jayson had found. But then she came across a Ted Talk on YouTube.

"Imagine a soldier who can outrun any animal on the planet, carry hundreds of pounds with ease. Communicate telepathically with his squadron, go weeks without eating or sleeping or regenerate lost limbs on the battlefield, and be completely controlled mind and body by military technicians thousands of miles away. Does this sound like science fiction to you? If so, then you're not living in the real world.

"We are in a twenty-first-century arms race among a vast array of covert technologies that are presently under development. There will be a new kind of soldier, a genetically modified and artificially enhanced super-human fighting machine that dominates the battlefields of the future. The engineering of these super soldiers is not only a top priority for the Pentagon, with black budget projects with classifications so high that not even the president of the United States has the clearance to access."

"Holy shit." Tomi gathered her things and research papers and headed out. Her mind whirled. The dots were right in front of her. The *truth* was in front of her.

Shakily, she jabbed the elevator button and then paced while waiting for it to arrive.

"We were fucking government experiments," she concluded. She'd figured out that Avery had been some type of mad scientist years ago when she'd first discovered her little parlor trick of being able to move some things with her mind. Shalisa Young's murder case was her second clue. But discovering that this shit wasn't about a lone crazed scientist, kidnapping teenagers and turning them into freaks, but was really about some shadowy government genetically modifying them to create some sci-fi super soldier was madness.

The image of Dr. Zacher floated back to her mind.

"Muthafucker." At long last, the elevator arrived and she rushed forward and collided into Jayson.

"Whoa!" He reeled back with a laugh. "Where's the fire?"

"Sorry, Jayson. I can't talk right now," she said, jetting past him and stabbing the button for the lobby.

"Is something wrong?"

"No. I gotta . . . take care of something."

He frowned, but the doors closed in his face before he could fire off another question.

Downstairs, she bolted past security and jetted out of the building with a brain cloud circulating too much information. However, when she speed-walked into the parking garage, the hairs on her body stood as if a giant magnet had been turned on. She slowed down and glanced around.

Nothing.

She remained alert, not trusting her eyes. Someone was watching her. She resumed the beeline to her car, checked the backseat, and climbed inside. The moment

she slammed the door closed, she exhaled. After another glance around the near-empty parking lot, she
started the car. Ten minutes down the road, she relaxed.
After another five minutes, she laughed. All that T4S
shit had made her fucking paranoid. At the next light,
she made another call to Abrianna's phone and wondered if her paranoid friend had changed her cell
phone again. They were two peas in a pod now.

The Agency was in a building that looked as if it
doubled as a neighborhood tax preparation service.
The brick building had to be at least a hundred years
old and sat on a clean corner lot. The shades were
down, but the lights were still on. Tomi climbed out of
the car while wrapping her purse strap across her
shoulders and then grabbed her research papers and
crammed them into her tote bag. She felt like a bag
lady as she hurried to the Agency's front door.

"Oh, please be here." She pulled on the handle.
Locked. Tomi rapped on the glass door and then
tapped her foot while she waited.

Laughter punctured the silence. Tomi craned her
neck over her left shoulder to see a group of teenage
girls huddled together as they strolled unevenly in
heels too high. She watched their carefree gaiety as
they passed whistling and game-spitting brothers on
the street corner. When they didn't get any play, the
catcalling brothers fired off ugly and demeaning in-
sults at the girls' backs before the girls disappeared
into a corner pool hall.

Tomi shook her head and then returned her attention
to Castillo's locked door. *Is she here?* She knocked
again and attempted to make out if anyone was moving
around inside. At long last, she heard a noise and then
footsteps.

Castillo's recognizable figure approached the door.

Tomi relaxed.

Castillo pulled back a corner of the shades.

"Hey," Tomi said, waving.

Castillo frowned, but unlocked and opened the door. "What on earth are you doing here?" She glanced over Tomi's shoulder to gauge whether she was alone.

"Would you believe that I was in the neighborhood?"

Castillo arched a brow as she evaluated the reporter's mental state.

"Can I come in?" Tomi asked.

Castillo stepped back. "Sure. Come on in." After Tomi crossed the threshold, Castillo took another glance around outside before closing and locking the door. "How did you know I was still here?"

"I didn't," Tomi said. "I took a chance." She glanced around the office. It had an old forties *Maltese Falcon* kind of vibe. A large corkboard in the center drew her attention. It was filled with children's faces as well as three-by-five index cards loaded with information under each one. "Working on a case?"

"*Cases,*" Castillo corrected. "Pro bono work."

"Huh." Tomi moved over to the board and read a few of the cards. "Missing children?" She turned and looked at Castillo with a realization. "This is really a passion of yours, isn't it?"

Castillo shrugged. "Everybody got to have a hobby." She walked over to a lonely looking Mr. Coffee machine. "Would you like a cup?"

"Sure. Why not." Tomi glanced around for a chair that wasn't loaded up with notebooks and folders. There was only one, and Tomi had the distinct impression that it was Castillo's seat.

"Here you go," Castillo said, handing her a steaming Styrofoam cup.

Tomi clumsily shifted her broken tote bag to one arm and accepted the cup.

"Let me clear off a spot for you." Castillo went to one of the chairs and removed the piles of work.

"Your arm. I can do it."

"I got it." Castillo moved the clutter to a corner on top of a metal file cabinet. "Have a seat."

Tomi smiled and sat down. When Castillo returned to the coffee machine to pour herself a cup, Tomi thought about how she was about to broach the T4S subject. It turned out that there wasn't a good opening to tell someone that you were a walking, talking genetically modified quasi-government experiment. It didn't roll off of the tongue.

Castillo broke into her private musing. "Soooo. What *really* brings you out here this late? Are you working on another story?"

"There's always another story and always another deadline."

Castillo nodded. "Are you doing anything on Cargill Parker?"

"Uh . . . I'm working an angle."

"Oh?"

"Yeah, uh. Marion Parker came by the office to see me earlier. She wants me to help her get in contact with Abrianna."

"Oh?" Castillo leaned back in her squeaky office chair and propped her feet up on the corner of her desk. "I haven't seen her in ages. How is she holding up?"

"Mrs. Parker?" Tomi thought it over. "Perfect on the outside, but a wreck on the inside."

"Humph. So not much has changed." Castillo sipped her coffee.

Tomi followed suit but was stunned by the bolt of

caffeine that rocked through her veins. "Good Lord, this is strong. What is it?"

"It's made with Robusta coffee beans. It's not for the Starbucks lightweights."

"More for the walking dead crowd, huh?" Tomi set the cup down and backed away.

Castillo gulped it down like it was spring water. "I saw you and Abrianna on that Greg Wallace show. It took a lot of courage to go on there when her father is gobbling up as many headlines as she is."

Tomi nodded, but said nothing.

Castillo pushed, "Have you talked to Abrianna about this thing with her father?"

"We had a conversation. I know as much as the audience knows."

Castillo shook her head. "I suspected a long time ago that he was abusing Abrianna."

"You did?"

Castillo nodded. "Her X-rays from the hospital that night showed a lot of breaks that hadn't healed properly. When her father showed up that night, he was a grabby muthafucka that I thought I was going have to take down for a minute. Plus, Marion was skittish as shit and told me that it was okay if I was keeping Abrianna hidden from them. They didn't want to believe that Abrianna had run off again. I don't blame them. I could hardly believe it myself." She nodded toward the corkboard. "I've been running these kids' photos and info through the Children's Protective Service to see if any of them were swept up during the raid at the Lynnwood Club."

"Any luck?"

Disappointed, Castillo shook her head. "One."

"Damn. Well. That's good news."

There was that transitional pause again. Tomi still hadn't figured out a way to bring up what had brought her there.

"Soooo," Castillo said. "Should I kick-start the twenty-one questions, or are you going to tell me what brings you out here?"

"Maybe I should show you," Tomi said, opening her tote and pulling out the piles of research.

Curious, Castillo leaned over and picked up a few sheets. "What's this?"

"Research."

"On Craig Avery?" She looked up.

"Him and this guy who approached me a while back, a Dr. Charles Zacher."

"And who is he?"

"Craig Avery's partner."

39

Kadir woke in the middle of the night, pleased that Abrianna was still lying next to him. He inhaled her hair's floral scent. It had been a long time since he had a woman in his life.

He paused his ruminations and opened his eyes again. What was he doing? He had no idea how she felt about him. He had no idea how she felt about anything. Sure, they had chemistry. Damn good chemistry. The sex was hot—but what else was there?

She had his back—but what did that really mean? They were buddies? Friends? Friends with benefits?

Kadir's thoughts chased each other in a dizzying circle, killing his tranquil mood. His twin brother had often told him that he was too much of a romantic. He fell in love easily and hard. This time he had managed to do it with a damaged woman—who'd never been in a relationship that had lasted more than four months.

I still need to get my head examined.

Gently, Kadir eased his arms from around Abrianna and sat up. Before climbing out of bed, he stared at her.

She was still one of the most beautiful women he'd ever laid eyes on. She looked so peaceful—serene. Maybe too damn peaceful. *Is she breathing?*

Kadir leaned forward, unable to hear a sound. His gaze shot to her chest, but it wasn't moving up and down. "What the hell?" *Did she overdose?* Panicked, Kadir went to press a hand to the side of her neck to check for a pulse, but the moment he touched her, she moaned lazily and rolled over.

Relief whooshed out and deflated Kadir's lungs, but his heart pounded like a drum. When it returned to its normal rhythm, he chuckled at how he'd scared himself and climbed out of bed. He was still shaking his head over the incident after another hot shower and his morning prayer. While Abrianna slept late, Kadir resumed cleaning the apartment. As he worked, he worried about what his next step should be. He needed money, a job, and probably a new place to live. Those thoughts led him to his family. He needed to call and let them know that he was all right. He could only imagine the hell that he'd put them through during all of this.

No doubt his father would view it as another disappointment. He picked up the house phone, surprised that he still had service, and dialed their number from memory.

"Kadir!" Muaadh Kahlifa shouted after snatching up the line.

"Hey, dad."

What came next was a combination of praises to Allah and a steady weeping. At one point his mother wrestled the phone from his father and babbled a long stream of tear-filled questions. Soon enough, the conversation settled down and Kadir answered their questions: He was all right and yes, he was out of jail.

"You must come home," his father insisted. "America is no longer safe for Muslims. I fear the day when we get a call and they tell us that they have finally killed you. If you were going to die, I would prefer that you do it here—in our homeland among *our* people."

Kadir knew that this was coming. "I can't do that, Pop. I'm still on probation and . . ." He glanced off toward the bedroom door. "I still have a lot of . . . stuff that I'm working on here."

His dad didn't like that answer and argued with him about ways for Kadir to get around the laws and get on a plane.

"Sound like Baasim came by his radicalization honestly." Kadir chuckled.

"This is not a game, Kadir," his father snapped. "I want you here!"

Hearing Kadir's resistance, his mother's wails intensified.

Kadir loved his parents, but the phone call had turned back to their usual frustrations with one another. By the end of the conversation, Kadir abandoned the idea of asking his father for yet another loan. He would have to find a job as soon as possible—as well as get another car.

"All right, dad. I'll talk to you soon."

His father hesitated, but then grunted his consent and goodbye.

Exhausted, Kadir returned the phone to its port and then sank his head into the palms of his hands. That call had taken a lot out of him. Before returning to bed, he caught a few minutes of the news.

"In tonight's news," the reporter began with the word *pre-recorded* printed in the right-hand corner, *"more heartbreaking details of the child sex-trafficking ring involving oil and gas billionaire Cargill Parker.*

As previously reported, Mr. Parker's exclusive Lynnwood Club was raided two weeks ago after authorities received an anonymous tip about suspected illegal activities involving minors as young as five years old. The authorities continue to have a difficult time identifying a number of the children and predict that it may take a long time to comb through numerous databases across the country and internationally. Federal prosecutors argued that Parker was a flight risk and he was denied bail."

Kadir stared openmouthed at the screen. He'd seen Abrianna's father once before on Shawn's hospital TV. Then the man pled for Abrianna to return home. But that wasn't this. He didn't know what to make of *this*.

⬥

Castillo was well into her second pot of coffee when she finished reviewing all of Tomi's research on T4S. Leaning back in her seat, she stared at Tomi for a long moment while the information still processed in her head.

"Well?" Tomi asked.

"My brain hurts."

"Then we have that in common." Tomi shrugged, but quickly grew agitated. "I mean, what the fuck, right? We were fucking lab rats."

"I . . . know it may seem that way, but . . . maybe we're missing something."

"The man *said* that he wanted to talk to me about the powers Abrianna and I may have developed. What else could he have meant?"

"All those girls," Castillo said, devastated. She closed her eyes and rubbed the tension from her forehead. Like instant recall, the images of the lifeless teenagers she'd failed to save scrolled through her head. After all this time, she was still connected to each and every one of them. The long hours, sleepless nights, her total obsession with the case that nearly ruined her career was suddenly fresh in her mind. But never once did she detect anything other than some sick fuck with some medical training.

Castillo took a deep breath. "Okay. Let's say that you're right. What's our next step?"

"Our next step?"

"Well, we can't let him get away with it," Castillo reasoned.

"They have already gotten away with it," Tomi said. "Avery's dead and I doubt that we're going to wrangle a confession out of that Dr. Zacher guy—and what? You think I want the world to know that I'm some kind of freak? I'm not. I'm not!"

Without anyone laying a hand on it, Tomi's cold coffee toppled over and splashed onto the floor. "Shit!"

Castillo leaped to her feet.

"No. No," Tomi said, frazzled. "I'll clean it up. It's my fault."

Castillo eyed her wearily as Tomi rushed over to retrieve the roll of paper towels next to the coffeemaker. "I don't think that I'll get used to you being able to do that."

Tomi said nothing as she hurried to clean the mess, but it was clear that she was still upset.

"I don't think that you're a freak," Castillo clarified. "And nothing that happened to you was your fault."

Tomi stopped cleaning as a sob escaped her throat.

Castillo quickly went and joined her on the floor. When she put her good arm around her, Tomi turned and sobbed against her shoulder. "It's okay. We're going to figure this out." She actually had no idea what they were going to do.

A minute later, Tomi pulled away. "Sorry about that."

"There's no need to apologize."

"It hit me all at once, I guess. I'm fine." Tomi resumed sopping up the coffee.

Castillo realized that she was basically asking for her space. She stood and moved back to her chair. As she glanced at the paperwork again, she struggled with this new wave of helplessness. "So . . . what do you want to do? I'm not sure why you even brought this to me if the plan is not to expose it."

Tomi dumped the paper towels and the cup into the wastebasket and then shook her head almost hopelessly. "I don't know. I guess I needed to tell someone. I guess I could've told my dog Rocky—who I need to get home and feed, but . . ." She sighed.

"What about Abrianna?"

Tomi's gaze skittered around. "What about her?"

"Have you talked to her about any of this? I mean, can she move shit around too with her mind?"

Tomi hesitated.

Castillo leaned forward. "She can, can't she?"

"Not only that. She *knows* Dr. Zacher. He's been masquerading as some homeless guy in the park for the past six years. No doubt monitoring her process. When the whole Reynolds murder thing blew up and she disappeared on him, that's what made him seek me out."

"And you heard him talking to you in your head?"

Tomi nodded. "Shit freaked me out."

Castillo cocked her head. "Can you talk in people's heads?"

Tomi's expression twisted, but before she could dismiss the question, Castillo added, "Have you ever tried?"

"Well, no. But—"

"Try it." Castillo kicked back in her chair with a grin.

"What? Now?"

"It's as good a time as any," Castillo challenged with a grin. Why shouldn't they have some fun and experiment with this? It was better than trying not to be weirded out over it.

Tomi stared. "I wouldn't know how."

"Try to think of something really hard, I guess. Give it a try."

"Okaay." Tomi fidgeted and took a deep breath.

Castillo braced herself and waited.

And waited.

"Are you doing it?" she asked.

"I'm thinking loudly." Tomi asked. "You can't hear anything?"

Castillo listened and then concentrated. "I . . . don't think so."

Tomi gave up. "I feel stupid now."

"No. It was worth a try, right?"

"I better go. I've wasted enough of your time. I don't know why I brought any of this to you."

"No. I'm glad that you did. I . . . don't know what to do with this information now." She thought about it, and then her gaze swept to the children pinned up on the corkboard. "Do you think that they could still be engaged in doing this?"

Tomi followed Castillo's line of vision and then looked horror-stricken. "But . . . they're so young."

"We've got to find out more about these people. *And* we need to talk to Abrianna."

Tomi shook her head. "I think we need to hold off on telling Abrianna any of this. I talked to her briefly about that Charlie dude, and she didn't take it well. Maybe we hold off until we know for sure what's going on and whether we're still being monitored."

───◆───

Abrianna woke up in an empty bed. After she sat up and looked around, she heard the television on in the living room. Quietly, she climbed to her feet and wrapped the top sheet around her body before shuffling into the living room. She smiled at Kadir sitting on the couch, but then saw what had captured his undivided attention. "Catching up on the news?"

Startled, Kadir snapped to attention and shut off the television.

Abrianna leaned against the wall at the junction of the living room and hallway.

He looked as if he'd been caught watching porn in the middle of the night by a nagging wife. "Hey, I didn't know that you were up." He stood. "I was getting ready to come back to bed."

"Please. You don't have to on my account."

They stared at each other for a long moment.

Abrianna lowered her gaze to her feet.

"I've spent a long time trying to get away from that man, and it hasn't worked. I've done everything that you can imagine to blur him out and numb him away, but . . . he's one of the monsters that never go away. He laughs at me. He taunts me. But most of all, he hurts me. I'm not surprised that they dug him and his bullshit up. At least they managed to save those kids—something that I was too chickenshit to do." Abrianna sniffed, but didn't bother drying her tears.

Kadir took care of those with the pads of his thumbs. He half expected her to push him away and insist that she was fine when she was everything but. Instead she surprised him by melting against his chest and sobbing like a little girl.

"It's going to be all right," he said, wrapping his arms around her. He had no idea whether that was true or not, but he was going to do his best to protect her.

PART FOUR

Daddy Dearest

40

Scandal-riddled Capitol Hill kept political pundits working overtime. Everyone acknowledged that the time clock was ticking for whether the President Kate Washington would issue a blanket pardon for former President Walker, or would she allow a murder trial to move forward and wait until after a jury's decision before issuing the pardon? No one took the long odds bet on believing that an actual former president would be thrown behind bars.

No one.

James Crystal, a former political campaign manager who had never actually won a campaign, remained a staple on the Sunday morning talk shows spewing out predictions that never came true; he wasted no time telling the world that Walker would never see the inside of a courtroom.

"The feds have no case," he said, as he laughed at everyone's hysteria. "They aren't going to waste taxpayers' time by building a case around the word and supposed evidence produced by an ex-stripper-slash-call girl. What world are we living in?"

"But what about Judge Sanders's confession?" host Chuck Horton asked.

"The judge confessed that she *killed* Speaker Reynolds. She offered no proof other than her word that the White House was involved. And note that she *never* mentioned President Walker by name. She said the *White House*. Hell, there are hundreds of folks who work at the White House. It could be any one of them who didn't want to see the president impeached because of his alleged dalliances in Brazil. I'm telling you, the attorney general is probably pulling her hair out on this one. If President Washington goes ahead and pulls the trigger on a pardon, she can move on to the real big fish like Cargill Parker—father of said ex-stripper-slash-call girl." He laughed. "No one can make this stuff up."

Horton shook his head. "I'm going to have to agree with you on that one."

———

In the private quarters of the White House, Kate jabbed the mute button and bolted out of bed with a huff. "That damned James Crystal. He's always spouting off!" She paced angrily around the bedroom.

Davidson, reclined in the bed, slid his right arm behind his head and flashed her a goofy smile. "Will you relax? No one listens to Crystal's ass. He's the master chef of word salad. You're in the clear."

Kate shook her head, unable to ease the knot in her chest. This was usually a sign that she'd forgotten or missed something.

After watching her for another minute, Davidson huffed and climbed out of bed. He stepped in the path of her pacing and then pulled her stiff body into his arms. "You're overthinking things again. We're the only two people who know the truth. Relax. I say wait another week and issue Walker the pardon, and then focus on gathering your team for the election campaign in a couple of months. It's over. We did it."

She desperately wanted to believe him, but she was too much of a realist and perfectionist. She didn't want a single string left dangling. "I don't know about issuing that pardon so soon."

"Soon?" He laughed. "The whole world is wondering why you haven't done it already. Myself included."

Kate clamped her jaw tight.

"Now I know that you and Daniel used to have a thing that went sour and you may be reveling in a bit of schadenfreude right now, but if you ask me, it's time for you to get off of Team Petty and stop dangling Daniel in the wind."

Kate firmly pushed out of Davidson's arms. "Oh. Are you feeling sorry for your boy?"

He dropped his arms and sighed.

"Where was this prick of consciousness when you were worming your way into my bed?"

"My bad. I didn't know that you revered your position as the president's side chick so much, especially since so many were already wearing that uniform."

Kate slapped him.

Davidson sighed. He let the assault slide, but still spoke truth to power. "That right there is going to be your downfall," he warned.

Her chin came up. *Was he threatening her?*

"Your emotions," he added. "You need to get your emotions out of this and go back to thinking logically, strategically, and politically. Walker is defeated. Even if he lives to be a hundred years old, he will die in disgrace. That has to be enough."

Kate heard him, but she wasn't sure she was ready to listen.

41

Editor Martin Bailey looked up from his desk the moment Tomi's foot crossed into his office. "What do we know about Cargill Parker?"

"Excuse me?" she asked, caught off guard.

Bailey removed his reading glasses. "Cargill Parker—the escort girl's father? Next to your president's murder conspiracy—he's the second hottest story in D.C."

"Adoptive father."

He frowned. "Are we splitting hairs?"

"No . . . I was clarifying."

Bailey nodded. "Uh-huh. Anyway, like I was saying, hot story. We need to get on it."

Tomi sighed.

"What? What am I missing?"

"Don't you think that's it's a hell of a coincidence that all of this about Cargill Parker *happens* to come out *now?*"

"Nothing surprises me in this town, especially not

some entitled billionaire running a child sex-trafficking ring at an exclusive boy's club."

"Allegedly," Tomi said.

"You *are* splitting hairs with me," Bailey said. "Stop it. I need for you to put on your reporter's cap. There's another story here. You should tell the whole thing before somebody else does. Mrs. Parker was here yesterday, right?"

"Yeah."

Her editor waited for her to connect the dots.

"I've already asked Marion Parker for an interview."

"And?" he asked anxiously.

"And . . . she didn't say no. I have to do something for her first."

"Great!" He slapped his hands. "You're on a roll, Ms. Lehane. Keep it up. You'll be the first rookie reporter to win a Pulitzer. Every outlet wants to talk to Marion Parker, and she just waltzed in here yesterday and you didn't tell me anything. But I should've known that I could count on you."

"The story *is* the White House attempting to muddy waters by launching a character assassination. They wanted to shift public opinion on Abrianna—to something sick and seedy. If they can do that, then maybe you can cast doubts on her version of events. It's so transparent."

Bailey winked. "See? Now you're talking like a reporter instead of a lawyer. Get on it."

"Yes, sir."

"But interview Marion Parker first," he added before she could slip out of the door.

Tomi gave him a mock salute. "You got it, boss."

FCI Petersburg Low prison

An angry Cargill Parker strolled into a lime-colored cinder-block room in his bright orange jumpsuit to meet with his long-time, expensive lawyer, Peter Lautner.

Lautner, a mid-sixties Italian-American, met his stone-faced client with an affable smile and firm handshake. "Glad to see that you're in good health."

Cargill lifted a brow. "Why wouldn't I be?"

Lautner blanched even though his two-shades-too-dark spray tan did its best to cover it up. "I mean, the guards are treating you fair, right?"

That wasn't what he meant. Inmates who were accused of abusing children were pariahs and targets. Both were well aware of that. However, Parker's billions provided a hell of a protective layer.

"Why am I still here?" Cargill asked. "It's been two weeks."

"Politics," Lautner answered. His client always wanted shit straight, no chaser. "The climate is bad with this presidential murder scandal. Everyone is covering their asses to appear tough on crime and they aren't showing special favors toward a billionaire donor who put a few coins in their election pockets."

"I give them coins *for* special favors. That's the whole point. That's the system."

"I know. I'm working on it. The prosecution is getting a lot of mileage on your being a flight risk. You owning a jet and homes in countries that don't extradite to the U.S. also doesn't help."

Cargill was not accustomed to not getting his way. Heat rose and colored his face bright red. "The last time I checked your itemized overbilling, I don't pay for excuses or incompetence. If the prosecutor is the problem, then you get me another one. I don't care what it costs. I don't give a damn if you have to go all the way up to the U.S. attorney general. If it's the judge, you get me another fucking judge. I want a fucking successful bail hearing, or I'll get an attorney who can."

Lautner's chin came up from the verbal attack and threat.

Cargill wasn't finished. "And don't get too cocky thinking because you know where a few of my secrets are buried that you're irreplaceable. There is no such thing."

Conceding and tucking his pride back between his legs, Lautner flashed another smile. "Message received."

"Good. You have twenty-four hours." He stood, ending the conversation.

Lautner waited until Cargill reached the door before asking, "Aren't you interested in the latest with Abrianna?"

Cargill stopped short of knocking for the guard. "I saw her on TV for about ten minutes the other day."

"Yeah. She's been waging a press campaign to get this Muslim guy who helped her out while she was on the run released."

"I read about him in the paper. An ex-con, right?"

Lautner nodded. "He's supposedly some sort of computer genius turned hacker."

"I'm already bored," Cargill said. "Where is she?"

"Right now, she's with the Muslim. Her campaign was successful. He was released yesterday."

"Fuck. She's a better lawyer than you, Lautner. Maybe I should enlist her to get me out of here."

Lautner chuckled. "No offense, Cargill, but you have a better chance of seeing pigs fly. I'll stay on it, especially since she's alluding that abuse took place in her childhood. Surely it's a matter of time before prosecutors on your case are going to try and rope her in as a character witness."

"She wouldn't dare," Cargill dismissed.

"How on earth can you be so sure? She's not a child anymore. And not to speak out of turn, she hasn't been under your thumb for a while."

"I know my daughter. We share a special bond . . . whether she likes it or not. She'll keep her mouth shut because I'm not the only person in the family with buried secrets."

42

Tomi put all thoughts of T4S away and focused on her work. Right now she debated whether to tell Abrianna about doing an interview with her parents. It was her job to follow the story wherever it led. Every reporter in town was digging into the Parkers' luxurious closets. However, there was such a thing called loyalty, but did she owe it to Abrianna?

Tomi researched Abrianna's mysterious and allegedly criminal father. She learned that the oil tycoon Cargill Parker had earned his wealth and prestige the old-fashioned way: He inherited it. However, Cargill's father, Duke Lynnwood Parker, founder of Parker Petroleum Industries, was, up until he passed away, the richest man in Houston. Duke Parker was the embodiment of the American dream. After serving in the Korean War and putting himself through college on the GI bill, Duke took his first job in the energy industry in the late fifties. A decade later, he left the company with fifteen thousand dollars, two propane delivery trucks, and a dream.

When Duke died, his vast fortune was passed down to his son. Cargill owned a number of homes around the world and had all the billionaire toys: private islands, private jets, yachts, and privates country clubs. The one thing that interested him, outside of his big boy toys, was politics. Tomi found articles where Cargill entertained running for the highest office, but she couldn't figure out what had changed the oilman's mind to instead play political sugar daddy to politicians who advanced his political interests. When Tomi researched Marion Parker, she hit a brick wall. There were numerous trophy-wife pictures of her attending a fund-raiser or charity, some of her pleading for her daughter Abrianna's safe return, both six years ago and recently during the Reynolds murder manhunt. Other than those, there was nothing. She wasn't even included in Cargill's Wikipedia page . . . but neither was Abrianna.

The Parkers had six homes across the country and three outside of it. Cargill Parker had vast investments in companies and holdings, and then there was the ton of philanthropy and charity work that made him look like an upstanding citizen. There were reams of articles relating to his and Marion's desperate search for Abrianna. Tomi clicked through the sad pictures and press conferences they'd held over the years. But she could find very little on the exclusive Lynnwood Club and nothing at all on the Dragons Templar.

Tomi turned away from her computer, frustrated.

"No luck?" Jayson inquired.

"Nothing interesting that I can use."

"Go and interview the wife. I don't get what the problem is."

"Marion wants to see Abrianna first. That was the deal—and I can't get her on the phone."

"C'mon. You can bullshit your way through that."

"Yeah, but I can't shake the feeling that it would be crossing a line of trust with Bree."

"So you're not doing a hot story because you don't want to upset your friend?"

"We're not friends," Tomi corrected.

"Oh yeah? Then what are you?"

"We're . . ." She shrugged. "I don't know. Something in between acquaintances and friends? I have no idea what that space is called."

"Usually colleagues," Jayson said.

"What? You mean like us?" she asked, smiling.

"Not exactly like us." He shrugged. "I like to think we're more than colleagues."

Tomi's brow lifted.

Jayson's face reddened. "Yeah. I like to think we're *good* friends. Don't you?"

She grinned. "Of course, we're good friends. I wouldn't put up with half of your needling questions if we weren't."

Jayson's frown buoyed into a smile. "So are you going to call her?"

"Who?" Jayson made a face and she remembered their original topic. "Oh. You mean Marion Parker. I can't help but feel like I'll be picking at a scab if I interview or do an exposé on Marion behind Abrianna's back."

"You mean your non-friend's back?"

"All right." She retrieved Marion's social card and picked up the phone.

"That's my girl." Jayson winked and waltzed off.

Tomi's hand tightened on the phone while she waited for the line to connect. The sinking feeling in her gut warned that this was a mistake—but she'd been on a roll in breaking the Reynolds murder and the Sanders confession story—she couldn't let another reporter beat her to the punch for an exclusive on the Cargill Parker story. Abrianna would have to understand.

———◆◆———

Dennis Holder waltzed into the Agency in his chief's uniform and glanced around. "How is it that this is the place that I have to compete with for your time? It's a little more than a—"

"Don't say it," Castillo warned, smiling.

Holder zipped his lips.

Castillo's attention returned to the caller on the phone tucked under her ear. "Yes. I faxed over the photos and information an hour ago. I'm checking to make sure that you received them. Yeah? Okay. Uh. Do you know about when someone will get back to me? Twenty-four hours? Okay. Thanks." She hung up the phone, sighed, and then smiled at Holder. "You got something for me?"

"Maybe," Dennis teased, taking a seat across from her. "It depends on how much you want it."

"Oh. We're playing that game again." She laughed.

"Hey, I'll get it anyway I can with you."

"Should I break out the world's tiniest violin for this conversation?"

"I knew I wouldn't get much sympathy from you." He tossed over a folder. "Now tell me again why you're looking into this Dr. Zacher guy again?"

She snatched up the folder. "I'm looking into something for a friend. Is this it: name, address, and driver's license?"

"What can I say? The man keeps his nose clean, or better yet, I get calls from time to time to make sure that people from that T4S facility keep their noses clean."

"What is that supposed to mean?"

"Tell me what you're working on."

Dennis's sudden seriousness surprised Castillo. She leaned back in her chair and studied him. "You make sure their noses are clean. How come that sounds illegal?"

"It sounds like I follow orders," Holder countered. "The people over at that facility have some powerful connections. I don't want you getting into something that's way over your head."

"All you're doing is making me more intrigued."

"I was afraid of that." He sighed. "Dr. Zacher was swept up in the raid out at Zeke Jeffreys's birthday party."

"Really?" She searched her memory, but knew it was futile. She had had a one-track mind that night.

"The next morning, I received a call to erase all traces of his booking and another guy. A Ned Cox. I included his information in there as well. His record isn't as clean. He had two DUIs back in college."

"And a drug bust," she read from the folder.

"I figure that he must not be high enough up in the organization to merit keeping his shit buried." Holder studied her. "I mean it, Gigi. I don't like the idea of you snooping around those people. I've heard things."

"Things like?"

"Nothing good."

"Things like: having the power to make people disappear *permanently*?"

"Yeah. That's what I heard, too."

◆━━◆━━◆

Late that afternoon, Tomi arrived at the Parker estate's gate in Bluemont, Virginia. The beauty of the place blew her mind. She had always heard good things about the handful of vineyards in the area, but never considered visiting the city that was an hour outside of D.C. She made a mental note to come out more often.

"Can I help you?" a man's voice crackled over the speaker.

"Yes. I'm Tomi Lehane with the *Washington Post*. I'm here to see Marion Parker."

A long silence ensued. It was long enough for her to wonder whether Marion Parker had changed her mind about meeting. Then, the gate crept open, allowing her entrance. She drove through, still marveling at the place that screamed money. *Abrianna grew up here?*

There was another car parked in the circular driveway, with government tags. Tomi pulled up behind it and climbed out of her vehicle. She wondered who else was there while she rang the doorbell.

The door opened and a kind-faced gentleman greeted and allowed her entrance into the estate.

Smiling, Tomi crossed the threshold into a gold-and-white atrium and gawked. Heading her way were two serious-looking gentlemen in standard-issue FBI attire. The butler wished the men a good day and re-opened the door for them.

Tomi's mind raced to figure out what was going on. She waited until the door closed again before asking, "How long were they here?"

"This way, ma'am," the butler said, completely ignoring her question. He escorted her quite a ways across the immense home. She was shown into a salon and told that the lady of the house would be down in a few minutes.

Minutes turned into an hour.

"Ms. Lehane," Marion greeted, floating into the room in a pale pink ensemble that belonged on the cover of a 1965 *Vogue* magazine. As before, her hair and makeup were perfect and polished. She carried herself as if she'd spent a lifetime in charm schools. "Forgive me for keeping you waiting."

Tomi stood and offered her hand when Marion approached. "No problem. I wasn't waiting long. I appreciate you taking the time to talk to me. You must be flooded with phone calls."

"Just the usual smiling Judases." Marion glanced around. "Where is Abrianna?"

Tomi forced out a lie. "Abrianna isn't, uhm . . . quite ready to . . . see you . . ."

"I see." Marion's gaze shifted away. "I guess I should've known better than to hold out hope. So much time has passed and . . . I've failed her miserably."

Guilt hammered Tomi. She had no right to exploit this woman's pain. Yet she couldn't leave.

Marion recovered and asked, "Well, you didn't have to travel all this way to tell me that my daughter hates my guts. A simple phone call would've sufficed."

"Actually, I was hoping that I could get that interview."

Marion's shoulders deflated as she reevaluated Tomi. "Tell me truly," she said, "did you *really* pass my message on to Abrianna?"

"Yes, of course," Tomi lied, schooling her face to appear earnest. However, she suspected Marion's sharp gaze saw through her.

"Please. Have a seat." Marion gestured for Tomi to reclaim her seat.

"Thank you."

Marion glided to the chair adjacent to her as the tea arrived.

Uncomfortable, Tomi shifted around. Had she entered

a time warp? The house was filled with mannequin-like people, emulating human behavior. It disturbed her. "You have a beautiful home."

"Yes. It is lovely."

Okay, Mrs. Humble. "How long have you been married to Mr. Parker?" Tomi asked.

"Some days it feels like forever." Marion sipped from her teacup.

"Really?" Tomi cocked her head. "Excuse me, but you don't seem that much older than Abrianna."

"A true lady never tells her age," Marion quipped.

"Touché. But how are you holding up? I mean, with all that has been happening in the news recently with your family? First it was Abrianna and the whole president scandal, and now the allegations against your husband? It has to be taking a toll."

"I've discovered that there is nothing in this life that vodka and Valium can't fix."

"Together?"

"A lady never tells that, either."

They laughed before Tomi dove in. "Is there any truth to the government's charges against your husband?"

"Of course not." She rolled her eyes and took another sip of tea. "Cargill is a model husband and an upstanding citizen in the community. I have no doubt that these horrible allegations will go away."

Tomi noted the conviction. "What do you know about the Dragons Templar?"

"Nothing. I've never heard of it before it was printed in the paper. But I rarely believe anything written in the press. No offense."

"None taken," Tomi dismissed. "Could your husband be a member of a secret society without your knowledge?"

She shrugged, dodging Tomi's gaze. "I admit that I don't know *every* detail in my husband's life. He's a busy and important man. But no. He would never be a part of what they're accusing him of." Marion paused. "Personally, I believe that he, like my daughter, was framed."

Intrigued, Tomi leaned forward. "Your husband has enemies?"

Marion gave a look that questioned Tomi's sanity. "Powerful men have powerful enemies. However, in this instance, I believe these people are my daughter's enemies behind this chess move."

"The White House?" Tomi asked. "You think that the White House—the former president—was behind your husband's arrest?"

"It makes sense, doesn't it? It doesn't take a genius to figure out that the article you wrote angered *some-one* powerful enough to tear down my family."

"Still. It's an elaborate setup, don't you think?" Tomi pressed.

Marion smiled. "It always is, darling."

"And the children?"

She shook her head. "I don't want to talk about that. It upsets me."

Tomi's brows sprung up.

Marion grew antsy. She was about to shut down the interview.

"Why did Abrianna run away from home?"

Marion's ramrod posture slackened but then recovered.

"Abrianna was a spirited girl. It's not uncommon for teenagers to rebel against their parents. Unfortunately, she, uh, stumbled into a bad situation with that Dr. Craig Avery character. I'm sure that she suffered some irreparable psychological damages."

"Psychological damages?" Tomi echoed the sterile description.

"I'm sorry," Marion amended. "I know that you and Bree suffered horribly at the hands of that man. I don't mean to belittle it."

"Why didn't Abrianna return home after her *bad* situation?"

Marion set down her tea. "This has drifted way into personal territory, more so than I'm willing to discuss with you or your readers. Please know that I love my daughter and I support her during this difficult time." She stood. "Now. If you would excuse me, I have a busy schedule today."

"Oh. Of course." Tomi shut off her voice recorder and stood. "I really appreciate you talking with me."

"I only did so in hope that you'd come with my daughter," Marion stated bluntly.

"Right." Tomi gathered her things and then fell in step behind Marion's careful strut out of the salon. They passed a room with a piano. "Do you play?"

"I'm sorry?" Marion stopped and turned around.

Tomi jutted a thumb over her shoulder. "The baby grand, do you play?"

A genuine smile emerged, transforming Marion to near goddess status. "Why, yes. Do you?"

"I used to play when I was a kid." Tomi entered the room.

"Really? How wonderful," Marion said, impressed, following her.

Tomi waltzed around and admired the instrument. "Music was my first love. I used to dream of being a concert pianist like my aunt Helena. She was a concert pianist back in the nineties."

"What happened?"

Tomi stopped walking and gave her a look.

"Oh. That. I see."

"Yeah. Some of that irreparable psychological damage."

Marion glanced away.

Tomi sighed. "Anyway, I didn't mean to take up more of your time." She backed away, but then her gaze swept across a horde of silver-framed pictures sitting on top of the piano. Several were of a young, barely smiling Abrianna. "Wow." She picked up one. "How adorable."

Marion joined her by the piano. "Yes. Abrianna was eight years old in that picture. She didn't want to smile because she'd lost a tooth that summer." She sighed. "Still. The camera loved that face. So photogenic."

Tomi agreed. She cast her gaze among the other photos, which appeared to be a timeline of Abrianna's childhood. However, one picture stood out, a young black boy. "Who is this?" Tomi picked up the frame, but Marion plucked it out of her grasp.

"That's Samuel—my son." Her eyes shimmered as she set the picture back onto the piano.

"I didn't know that Abrianna has a brother."

"She doesn't. Samuel passed away very young." She turned.

"He looks like you," Tomi noted. "He was your biological son?"

Marion sighed. "Yes. He was. Now if you—"

"What happened to him?"

Marion folded her hands and stared, clearly debating whether to answer. "A gun accident." She drew a deep breath. "It's one of the reasons why I won't allow one in my house anymore. They don't keep families safe. Now this interview is over. I really must insist that you leave."

43

Kadir woke to a ringing phone. After cursing the caller, he peeled open an eye.

"Aren't you going to answer that?" Abrianna buried her head beneath a pillow and then bumped him with her ass, urging him to hurry.

"I take it that you're not a morning person," he grumbled, sitting up. "Or an afternoon person," he amended after seeing the time on the clock. When he reached for the phone, it stopped ringing. The call was sent to voice mail. Grumbling, he plopped down. He'd catch whoever it was later. Right now he shifted his attention back to Abrianna's lush ass.

She moaned when he cupped a firm cheek in his hand. She even emerged from beneath the pillow when he peppered kisses down the curve of her spine.

The phone rang again.

"Damn it," they swore together.

"Jinx," Abrianna called.

Kadir slapped her ass and left her with a good sting while he rolled over to answer the phone. "Hello."

"We need to talk," Ghost said.

"I'm good, man. Thanks for asking," Kadir said sarcastically.

"No time for niceties, man. When can you get your ass down here?"

"Uh, I don't know. Why? What's up?"

"Some explosive shit, man," Ghost said. "Is your girl around you right now?"

Kadir frowned. "Yeah."

"Then go somewhere else in the apartment so I can drop some knowledge in your ear."

That didn't sound good. "All right. Hold on for a moment." Kadir removed the phone from his ear, planted a kiss on the back of Abrianna's shoulder and whispered, "I'm going to make some coffee. You want some?"

"Sure. If it comes with some scrambled eggs and bacon, that would be great."

He chuckled. "It's past lunchtime and all we have is cold pizza."

Abrianna groaned, disappointed.

Chuckling, Kadir peeled out of the sheets and then shuffled to the kitchen. He tucked the phone back underneath his ear and resumed his conversation. "All right, man. This shit better be worth my ass leaving a beautiful woman in my bed. What's up?"

"Remember I told you that I was going to do some more digging into your girl and why the fuck T4S wanted her so badly?"

Kadir's dread intensified. "Yeah."

"Well, I ghosted around their system, but I didn't know what the fuck to look for, you know what I mean?"

"Okay."

"So I went back to where I saw the extraction order, and it came with what I thought was a random set of numbers, but after some digging, the numbers aren't random at all. They are ID and clearance numbers. Basically the employee who authorized the extraction order. You with me so far?"

"Yeah. So who ordered it?"

"A Dr. Charles Zacher."

The name hung over the line for a few seconds before Kadir asked, "Am I supposed to know who that is?"

"I didn't know who the muthafucka was either until I dug around some more. It was easier after I got his ID and clearance number. I can open all his files now. And guess who has a whopper of a file."

Kadir glanced over his shoulder. "Bree?"

"Bingo. Her *and* that reporter chick. It was a risk, but I made digital copies of everything that I could find. Kadir, it's wild, man. You need to get to the bunker and take a look at this shit yourself."

Kadir's curiosity skyrocketed. "Can you give me a hint?"

"Only that we were right about *everything*. Abrianna Parker isn't what she appears to be."

"I thought you were making coffee?"

Kadir jumped and spun around.

She chuckled at his reaction. "Okay. You're guilty of something. Who's on the phone?"

"Uh, Ghost," Kadir said.

"Ghost? Uh-huh." She smiled as she took the phone from his hand. "Hello."

"Hey, Bree," Ghost said overenthusiastically. "What's up?"

"Not much. I'm trying to figure out why your boy is acting so strange."

"Well. There's your problem," Ghost joked. "It's not an act."

"Good to know." She laughed and handed the phone back to Kadir. "Stop being weird." She shook her head and exited the kitchen.

Kadir waited until he heard her shut the bedroom door before placing the phone back under his ear. "All right. I'll see if I can make it over there somehow."

"No need. I'm right outside."

"What?" Kadir left the kitchen to go look out the living room window. "What are you driving?"

"Blue Mustang. You see me?" Ghost stuck his hand out of the window and waved.

"Yeah. I see you."

"Good. Now hurry up. Vampires aren't supposed to walk around in daylight."

———⊱◈⊰———

Cargill Parker climbed into the waiting Bentley while a horde of protesters and a few reporters screamed obscenities in his wake. He had ignored their ugly signs and threats of violence with his head held high. His ears rang after he shut the door and settled into the backseat. The five-man bodyguard team formed a protective line before his door while Lautner climbed in from the other side. The rabid protesters pounded and rocked the back of the car before the driver pulled away from the curb.

"Well, that was exciting," Lautner joked with his stone-faced client. "Aren't you happy? I made the deadline."

"You doing your job is expected, it's not the source of my happiness." He sighed. "Especially when my pockets are more than a billion dollars lighter."

"Understood, sir. But you said that you didn't care how much it cost. Turns out an appellate court commands top dollar."

Cargill grumbled, aware that this was only the first flock of crows that he would have to deal with. They always came in waves once they thought a body was lying dead in the street. But he was a master of this game, and he would show them all how it's played, including the ones who were cloaked with Secret Service and had brought about his downfall. He'd spent two weeks developing a plan. Now it was time to put it into action.

The hour drive to Bluemont, Virginia, passed by in a blur, but he was shocked to see there was another horde of protesters in front of his gated estate.

"You've got to be fucking kidding me," he mumbled.

Lautner shrugged. "Sorry, but you're a big fish in small pond out here."

"Have they been out here the whole time?"

"Nah. I'm sure that once word about you making the billion-dollar bail hit social media, it activated the activists."

The Bentley stopped before the gates. Protesters attacked, pounding and rocking the car like wild animals.

Cargill looked outside of his window and saw one demented woman raising holy hell and didn't waste a beat in giving her the middle finger. He regretted it after he noted the several cameraphones pointed in his direction. "The cameraphone generation and their fucking need to have every minute of their lives documented."

Lautner laughed. "A generation of narcissists. What can go wrong?"

Cargill counted to ten while the estate gate crept open and allowed the Bentley to pull through. He expected the crowd to pour through the gate behind them and follow all the way to the front door. Once on private property, he could shoot them and get away with it.

The car rolled to a stop in the circular driveway. Cargill climbed out of the backseat. The protesters' chants carried clear into the house.

"Cargill," Marion said, blinking and staring at him like she was seeing a ghost. "You're out."

He grinned. "Sorry to disappoint you."

"No. No. I guess that explains the crowd. I was about to call the police."

"Call them anyway," Cargill said and glanced around. "Where is James?"

"I, uhm, gave him the day off. I'm sorry. We weren't expecting you today." She glanced to Lautner.

"My apologies," Lautner said. "The fault is all mine. I should have called and given you a heads-up."

Marion recovered from her shock and pushed up a smile. "Well. Welcome home." She moved forward and brushed a kiss against his cheek. "I'll fix you a drink."

"Later," Cargill said. "First. I'd like to take a long, hot shower and then I'll take my paper."

"Of course. I'll get the water started for you right now." She gave him another peck and shared a flat smile with Lautner before scrambling off up the stairs.

Lautner watched her go with a growing smile. "Now that's a well-trained woman."

Cargill harrumphed. "Should there be any other kind?"

Abrianna had returned to the bedroom to grab a few things before jumping in the shower when her cell phone rang on the nightstand. She dove across the bed and answered it on the last ring.

"Hello."

"My God, Bree," Shawn complained. "Why is it every time you get a new man, you ditch your friends?"

"What? That's not true." *It is kind of true.*

"Uh-huh. Well, while you're out there being all brand new, have you seen the damn papers or the news?"

Abrianna's stomach dropped. "Oh God. What is it now?"

Kadir entered the room already dressed. "Uh, I have to make a run," he said, jabbing a thumb over his shoulder. "Ghost is outside, waiting."

"Wait. What?" She was confused and put Shawn on hold. "What do you mean Ghost is outside? When did he get here?"

"I shouldn't be gone too long," he said, already backing out of the door.

She couldn't stop him, but he was certainly acting weird. "Do you want me to come with you?"

"Nah. I'll be back soon."

Abrianna stiffened.

He crossed the room and planted a kiss on her cheek and then raced right back out.

She stood there, wondering what in the hell just happened. Belatedly, she remembered that Shawn was still on the phone. "Okay. I'm back. What were you saying?"

"I was saying that Daddy Dearest posted bail and your reporter friend has written another exclusive."

She sighed. "Tomi interviewed Cargill?"

"No. Marion. And the article is about Samuel," Shawn said.

"What?"

"I'm looking at the headline on the *Washington Post* right now. It reads and I quote: 'Whatever happened to Samuel Parker?'"

44

The Parker Estate

"You gave an interview?" Cargill Parker said, tossing his morning paper across the desk toward Marion. "Who the fuck gave you permission to open your big fucking mouth to the press?"

Marion stood ramrod straight with her hands folded in front of her and her gaze locked over Cargill's left shoulder. She'd learned a long time ago never to look Cargill in the eye, never to assume that she was in any way on his level.

"Maybe you thought that you'd gotten rid of me for good. Is that it?" he asked, cocking his head.

When she didn't respond, Cargill climbed out his chair and strolled slowly around the desk.

Her heart hammered but she didn't move, not until his backhand lifted her out of her Jimmy Choos and sent her crashing onto the hardwood floor and thumping her head off the corner of the fireplace. Marion had no idea how long she'd been knocked out, but like so many times before, pain surrounded her when she woke in the middle of her husband raping her. Disgust coiled in her soul as his pasty skin dripped rivulets of sweat over her ripped clothes and exposed body. He grunted like a pathetic animal who could barely keep it up. She knew why. She wasn't a child anymore. Her hips curved, her breasts had nursed a child. He was disgusted with her as much as she was with him. But while they were locked together in their golden palace with angry protesters surrounding the gates, he couldn't hunt for who he really wanted in his bed: some child that reminded him of his first Abrianna.

Growling and convulsing, Cargill flushed a bright scarlet color as he emptied his seed into her wombless body and then plopped over to lie next to her.

Silent and motionless, Marion listened as Cargill panted until his breathing found a normal rhythm.

"Get the fuck out of here," he ordered.

On command, Marion sat up. She ignored the dizziness as she made it to her feet. Calmly, she picked up her shoes and then left her husband's study as quiet as a mouse.

45

Tomi didn't come into the office until late in the afternoon, but her butt wasn't in the chair a full minute before she answered her phone and had an angry Abrianna blasting into her ear.

"What the fuck is this shit in the paper?"

"Oh. So you do know how to return phone calls. That's good to know."

"Cut the shit. Why are you doing an exposé with my mother and putting shit that doesn't have anything to do with Walker all on the front page?"

"First of all, Ms. Parker, I am a reporter. I go where the story takes me. Or the story that walks through the front door. Your mother came to the paper and reached out to *me.* You would know this if you'd pick up the phone every once in a while."

"I changed the number."

"And I'm supposed to know that how? Look, I'm not your personal assistant. I'm fielding as many phone calls and emails for interviews requests for you as I do for shit pertaining to my actual job. Speaking of which, your mother would like for you to call her."

"Yeah. Well, she can hold her breath for that phone call."

"Bree, I tried to give you a heads-up for *two* days. It's not my fault that you have this ridiculous thing about cell phones. If you want to tell your side of this story, we can sit down for another interview."

"Fuck," Abrianna swore. "I'm tired of slitting my wrist in front of the world to gawk while I bleed out. Samuel is off limits."

"And why is that? What happened to him? Why can't I find any record of him? If it wasn't for the one picture in your parents' house, no one could ever prove that he ever existed. I can't find a birth certificate or a death certificate. Was he adopted?"

"No. He wasn't adopted."

"What about you?"

"What do you mean, what about me? I told you that I was adopted."

"You still have a birth certificate filed somewhere, right? Was it an intercountry adoption or—"

"That is none of your or anyone's business. Let it go!"

"How the hell can I let it go when your father is being accused of running a child sex-trafficking ring? When you've already hinted to the world what happened to *you* in that house?"

"Shit," Abrianna mumbled.

"Tell me about Samuel. What happened to him?"

"He died, all right? That's all that you need to know."

"Fine. I'll let it go."

"Good."

"For now." Tomi glanced around her cubicle and

then lowered her voice. "And while I have you on the phone, my article isn't the only reason why I've been trying to call you. I've discovered some more information about your friend Charlie."

Silence.

"Bree? Are you there?"

"Yeah. I'm here." She sighed loudly over the line. "What about Charlie?"

"No. We can't talk about this over the phone. We need to meet."

"Are you kidding me? I want to punch you right now. This shit about my brother is across the line. He has nothing to do with anything."

"Oh? Not even your father?"

There was a brief pause. "What did Marion tell you?"

"About Samuel? Not much. But . . . she seems quite broken up about you, though."

"Ha. I highly doubt that. No doubt Cargill sent her to try and snoop me out."

Abrianna's bitterness was as sharp as a knife. Tomi felt sorry for her.

"Look. I promised your mother that I would pass her private cell phone number to you, so let me give it—"

"I'm not interested in anything Marion *or* Cargill has to say about anything. They're dead to me."

"Are you sure? It certainly doesn't sound like it. Anyone who controls your emotions controls you."

"Spare me the pseudopsychology."

"Take the number. I made a promise."

Abrianna sighed. "All right. Hold on." She disappeared off of the line and returned a minute later. "What's the number?"

Tomi quickly gave her Marion's number, fulfilling her end of the bargain. "Now. We still *really* need to talk about Charlie."

"Why?"

"Because you were right. He *did* work with Craig Avery." She made another paranoid look around before lowering her voice. "They both worked for a company called T4S. Ever heard of it?"

Silence.

"Bree?"

"Damn. You really are dropping one bomb after another today."

"So you have heard of it?"

"Yeah . . . but it's a long story."

"Well, so is mine. That's why we have to talk. You're not going to believe the shit that I've uncovered. I hired Castillo to do some more digging."

"Castillo?"

"Don't worry. She's cool. I'd already told her about some of the things that I can do. I figure that she could dig a little deeper since I do actually have a day job. So when can we meet?" When she sensed that Abrianna was still on the fence, she added, "Trust me, Bree. You want to hear this."

<hr />

Dr. Zacher couldn't stop the nosebleeds and had a hard time convincing himself not to panic. After all, he knew the risks when he started using the new experimental drugs. He was positive that he'd reverse-engineered a good hunk of Avery's work after studying Shalisa's bloodwork while she stayed in St. Elizabeth's. He knew that he was on the right track when his health improved in recent years. It didn't go unnoticed around the department how he seemed to have grown younger and stronger.

He had.

Now something was wrong. He had felt it for a long time. The constant headaches and nosebleeds were obvious indicators. He ignored them for as long as he could because, in the end, doctors made horrible patients. He drew and processed his own bloodwork; several times, in fact. He couldn't accept the first three results or the CT scans. But he couldn't remain in denial either. He had multiple myeloma, a blood cancer, and the shit was spreading fast.

There was a quick rap on his door. By the time he looked up, Ned was already poking his head into his office.

"They have a read on both Lehane and Parker," Ned alerted his boss, excited.

Dr. Z jumped to his feet and came around his desk almost in the same motion. "Do we have a team en route?"

"A three-man crew," Ned said, struggling to keep up with his boss's long strives. Low-key and undercover, like you requested."

"Good."

"Also, I got word from IT," Ned added once they reached the elevator bay. "Someone ran a criminal history check on your name."

"What?"

Ned nodded. "Someone from a police department."

The elevator arrived, and when they stepped inside, Dr. Z had to double-check. "The police?"

Ned nodded.

Dr. Zacher was stumped. How in the hell had he

flashed on anyone's radar? His thoughts flew back to the car accident with Abrianna. Had he screwed up?

———————◦◦◦———————

Shawn picked up Abrianna from Kadir's place and drove her to the Agency in an unfamiliar side of town. Entering the office, Castillo pulled out of the arms of someone they did recognize: the chief of police.

"Oh, hey." Castillo blushed while the cop grinned.

"Ms. Parker," Holder said. "You probably don't remember me. But I was one of the officers who helped aid Gigi in your rescue in the Craig Avery case."

"Gigi?" Abrianna glanced at Castillo again. She didn't look like a Gigi.

"It's short for Gizella," Castillo informed them.

"Ah. Well. Thanks for your help," Abrianna said, shaking Holder's hand.

The office door was pulled open again, and Tomi rushed inside. "Sorry I'm late. I had a devil of a time getting out of the office." She stopped and noticed Holder. "Hey."

Holder picked up his hat. "Looks like you have a full house. "I'll let you get back to work." He leaned over and delivered a peck on Castillo's cheek. "Have a good meeting," he told everyone and headed out.

All eyes followed his confident stride out the door. Once it closed, four sets of eyes zoomed back to an embarrassed Castillo.

"What?" She shrugged, cheeks darkening as she took her seat behind the desk.

"All right. You got me here," Abrianna said. "What is so important you had to see me today?"

Tomi and Castillo glanced at each other.

"Am I not going to like this?" Abrianna asked, narrowing her gaze. "If it's Shawn, it's okay. He's my best friend. He knows everything about me."

"Everything?"

"Yes. Everything."

"All right." Tomi dug through her bag and pulled out a huge stack of paper. "You should sit down."

Castillo nodded. "You're going to need to."

46

Kadir reviewed the T4S stolen documents for hours, trying to wrap his brain around what he was reading. Shock, horror, disgust, and anger whirled like a hurricane inside of him. It was more than the fact that an arms race for developing a science-fictional super soldier existed; it was the realization of the lengths these people went to to develop this madness. What happened to morality? Where were people's consciences?

Dr. Craig Avery, under the tutelage of this guy Dr. Zacher, somehow was able to murder more than a hundred people, whom they coldly referred to as test subjects, before the higher-ups pulled the plug on the experiment. Veterans, many suffering from PTSD from the country's endless wars in the Middle East, had volunteered for these experiments. Hot tears pooled in Kadir's eyes while reading the long, detailed descriptions of those veterans' painful deaths. There were descriptions of men clawing their skin off, organs liquidating, calcified bones, brittle bones, accelerated cancers, toxic brain disease, or sudden death. Nothing, it seems, deterred these bioengineers or made them stop what they were doing for years.

The project was terminated without documented explanation, and then two years later it restarted with a document dump of information from Dr. Zacher. It wasn't difficult to connect the dots. The project had continued off the books, and three test subjects were entered by name instead of by number: Shalisa Young, Thomasyn Lehane, and Abrianna Parker.

Ghost studied Kadir, waiting.

At long last, he pushed back from the computer with a loud huff. "Those muthafuckas."

"Ain't it some bullshit?" Ghost folded his arms. "This is some next-level shit, and your girl is right in the thick of it."

"Fuck," Kadir added and then unleashed a mother lode of expletives, none of which made him feel better.

"And the church says amen," Ghost said before returning to the matter at hand. "Any idea how you want to play this?"

"Play what?"

"Did you forget about the extraction order?"

"Shit." Kadir bolted to his feet. "I shouldn't have left her alone. They could be making another attempt right now."

Ghost restrained him by the arm. "Chill. She's good. I have Wendell and her friend Julian sitting on her."

"What?"

"Well, no offense, but your girlfriend is a bit hardheaded. Instead of arguing with her about where she can and can't go, I put a tail on her."

"Damn. I really have dragged you into my mess."

Ghost shrugged. "It's a fascinating mess, opening

my eyes even more to the bullshit that's going on. So far there hasn't been another attempt. My thinking is that their window of opportunity closed."

"What do you mean?"

"If Abrianna disappeared before the president stepped down, then folks would have suspected the White House of getting rid of her."

"Frame the former president?"

"Perfect scapegoat."

"But why?"

Ghost shook his head. "I forget how much you've been out of the loop. President Walker took a machete to the defense budget, which consequently affected private security contracts. Word on the wire is that whole mess that went down in Brazil with those prostitutes was a setup from jump street. The Pentagon and all these paramilitary guys wanted Walker gone. But he was a scrappy muthafucka and hung in there far longer than any of them thought."

"He made the impeachment go away," Kadir said.

Ghost shrugged. "Well, somebody did."

Kadir frowned. "What? Now you don't believe the judge's own confession that *we* taped?"

"I didn't say that."

"Then what the hell are you alluding to?"

"The judge said the conspiracy led to the White House. I think that part was true. But she certainly didn't mention President Walker by name. And I've always been a firm believer in listening to what muthafuckas *don't* say."

Kadir thought on that for a moment. "So . . . why not Walker? He certainly had the motive."

"He wasn't the only snake with a motive." Ghost shrugged.

"All right. You lost me."

"That's because you don't know that President *Washington* and Judge Sanders not only knew each other in college, they were roommates in their freshman year."

The light clicked on in Kadir's eyes.

Ghost chuckled and tapped the side of his head. "The matrix is real. All bullshit is connected."

"All right. So let's go with your theory and that the window closed to frame Walker. So that means that Bree is safe, right?"

"Depends on what they want her back *for.* Maybe they are worried about her abilities being exposed. She and the reporter chick stay in the news lately. Reading this guy's progress notes, he clearly knows Bree personally. I doubt that she even knows who the fuck he is and Lord knows she's in a state of denial. He even knows that she's self-medicating on street drugs to deal with the quote side effects unquote."

Kadir's head hurt.

"Let's review what we personally know about her. She clearly has some kind of telekinesis; that's how she threw that guy against the wall. She self-heals like a muthafucka, she is strong as fuck, and can appear dead for at least three fuckin' days. All evidence concludes that she's a walking, talking success story."

"So they wouldn't want to bring her in to kill her or anything."

"No. They may want to dissect her, and death could be another side effect. Or they want her ass to start working for them. Complete some military training and put her out in the field to see how all their hard work has paid off. Who the fuck knows with these people?"

"We got to tell Abrianna about all of this—somehow."

"We?"

Kadir gave him a sharp look.

"Do you think she's going to believe *you*? You think that she can handle it. I don't know how she or her friends have been in denial all this time. I mean, you should've seen them rail on me when I was trying to convince them that she was dead in that bathtub. I give it to them, they're loyal as fuck, but they know their girl ain't right."

Kadir sighed. "All right, then when we talk with her, we need to make sure her friends are there, too."

"Dead that *we* shit, man. This is all you. I'd like to stay out of all the emotional side of this shit. Interventions rarely go well. But you can tell me how it went."

"All right. Fine. *I'll* figure out how to tell her all this shit myself. But as far as this whole T4S, maybe it's best to go straight to the source."

Ghost cupped his ear. "Come again."

"We're the only variable not being calculated in their equation. Maybe we should use that to our advantage."

"Maybe . . . maybe not. They know damn sure that she had help escaping that extraction order. You were locked down, so yeah, they've probably eliminated you. But I'm sure that they've been looking for my ass for a minute."

"But there's nothing connecting her to you."

"I'd feel more comfortable if there were more than one degree of separation."

"I see your point," Kadir conceded. "But . . . sooner or later they are going to want their test subject back—both of them."

"Agreed. But how are we going to stop them?"

47

Abrianna finished reading and listening to Tomi about her search on T4S. The one thing she couldn't pull her eyes from was the magazine article with Charlie's picture staring back at her. The years of betrayal tied her heart into a knot. She really didn't want to believe that he had played a part in her own kidnapping, even when she'd put two and two together the last time she'd talked to Tomi. The shit hurt too much.

Over the years, he'd become a grandfather figure. He knew all about Shawn and her small band of friends. She told him everything: her trials of living on the streets, her heartbreak with a long line of boyfriends, and even her dreams of living on the French Riviera.

"I feel like a fool."

"Don't," Shawn said, sounding equally disgusted. "I've met him several times with you. He came across as a harmless old man."

"Yeah. Real harmless." She swiped her eyes. "Genetically modified? I don't . . . this is crazy. We were their fucking science experiment?"

"It's looking that way." Castillo offered her a box of Kleenex with her good arm.

She waved the box off. She didn't want to cry. She wanted to *punch* something.

Shawn said, "I've been telling you that you needed to go to a doctor and get yourself a complete physical for years. All those headaches . . . and how freakishly strong you are." He shook his head. "This makes sense."

"It's probably been best that you didn't," Castillo said. "I can't imagine that they would want whatever's flowing through your bloodstream to show up in somebody else's lab. I have it on good authority that the company has the ability to make people disappear."

"Now I'm starting to wonder what really happened to Shalisa," Abrianna said.

Tomi said, "I suspect that she was still a T4S lab rat. St. Elizabeth Hospital is a *federal* mental institution. They likely had carte blanche access to her. So when she died and then you disappeared, that's why this Charlie guy approached me."

Shawn elbowed her. "Are you going to tell them?"

"Tell us what?" Tomi and Castillo asked in unison.

Abrianna sighed. "T4S tried to kidnap me right after I saw you in Stanton Park."

"What?"

Abrianna exhaled a long breath and told them of the hit-and-run incident, followed by her heroic rescue by some friends-who-must-not-be-named.

"And you're fine?" Castillo asked, looking her over.

"I heal fast," she admitted.

Tomi and Castillo shared looks.

"Okay. I have to go." Abrianna stood. "I need some time to digest all of this."

"Don't we need to figure out what we are going to *do*?" Tomi asked.

"Survive." Abrianna laughed. "It's the only thing we can do. I would suggest for us to go underground, but that's hardly an option with my face splashed on every newspaper right now and your name as a by-line."

Tomi's shoulders slumped.

"I'm sorry. I wish I had something else to say." She shook her head and then told Shawn, "C'mon. Let's go."

Shawn stood and gave the other women an apologetic look.

Back in the car, he and Abrianna rode in silence. All the information that they had taken in weighed heavily on their minds. Then halfway through the drive, Shawn asked, "Are you going to tell Kadir?"

"I don't know. How do you think he'll react?"

"You got me."

"How would you react?"

"This is my reaction, shock. But it doesn't change anything between us. You're still my best friend. I'll still do anything I can for you."

"You would?"

"Of course. You know better than to ask."

"Take me to Stanton Park."

"What? What for?"

"Return to the scene of the crime. I don't know. Maybe I can smoke Charlie out. Maybe he doesn't know that I'm on to him."

"And then what?"

"I don't know. Maybe we should just ask."

Shawn shook his head. "I don't know if I like the sound of that."

"C'mon. We're both strapped, and I'm *freakishly strong,* as you said. Let's see."

Shawn sighed, but noted the seriousness in her eyes. "Shit."

"Thanks," she said, winking.

After a quick change in direction, Shawn headed out to Stanton Park. In the middle of December, it was freezing without the snow. The sun had set early, and the park was empty. Still, Abrianna and Shawn trudged to the park bench where she used to meet Charlie most weekdays for lunch and sat down.

"I sure hope that you don't plan for our asses to sit out here too long."

"Nah. I need a few more minutes to figure out how to tell Kadir all this shit on top of the other bullshit I got going on right now."

"You keep things interesting. I'll give you that." He kept glancing around like a deer on constant alert for hunters. "I don't know why I let you talk me into crazy shit like this all the time."

"Relax. I doubt he's out here anyway. I haven't seen him in months."

"Unless he was the one who ran you over."

She frowned.

"It's possible. And if he did, it means that he knew that you'd survive."

"This shit is fucking crazy."

"That's my whole point. Let's go. I can't feel my fingers."

A twig snapped.

They whipped their heads around and scanned the darkness.

Shawn sighed. "It's nothing."

Yet the buzzing in Abrianna's head told her other-wise.

"No. Someone is out there."

"Where?" Shawn asked, standing.

Abrianna shrugged. She didn't understand how any of this shit worked—especially now that she knew that she wasn't crazy.

"C'mon. No bullshit. We better go," Shawn urged.

Abrianna allowed him to pull her from the bench and then hustled her around a tall shrubbery where they collided with Zeke.

"Good evening . . . ladies."

Abrianna leaped back, dragging Shawn behind her.

"What are you doing here, Zeke?"

"Just out for a stroll in the park." He chuckled.

She looked him up and down and noted how awful he looked. He was much thinner and sweatier. "How in the hell did you even find me?"

Zeke shrugged. "It wasn't easy. You're harder to find than old Waldo. But then I got this genius idea to keep an eye out on your reporter friend from the paper. I followed her to that private dick agency and then followed you here."

Zeke's goons materialized behind his back. They looked much healthier.

"What do you want?"

"We need to talk."

"We have nothing to talk about."

"Oh, but we do. Things like you and your friends' kidnapping hobby." He cocked his head. "Ringing any bells?" Zeke latched onto her arm and squeezed.

Abrianna wrenched free. "I'm not going anywhere with you. All business dealings between us are finished. I don't owe you a damn thing. As a matter of fact, you owe *me*."

He laughed and then clutched at his side as if in pain. "How do you figure I owe you?"

"You have my *money* that you lifted off Moses."

"Oh. Aren't you the little detective?" He laughed. "Figured that out, did you? I always knew that you had a better head on your shoulders than that knuckle-headed nigga. I still don't know what in the hell you ever saw in him. But I'll tell you what: I'll keep the money to cover the service charge for putting a bullet in his head and getting rid of him for you. There. You're welcome."

Abrianna smirked. "Nah. Consider that a quid pro quo for your old-ass girlfriend who took that bullet in the gut and ruined her pretty dress."

Zeke's backhand rocked her head back.

"Hey!" Shawn went for his weapon, but goon number one tackled him.

Abrianna sprang forward, crashing her fist against Zeke's jaw.

A surprised Zeke dropped to one knee, and before he could recover, Abrianna attacked with a swift kick underneath his chin that physically lifted and reeled him back.

Goon number two snapped out of his shock and grabbed Abrianna from behind.

Shawn jumped onto his opponent's back and jammed his thumbs into his eyes sockets.

"Aaaaargh," the muscled man jerked around, trying to fling Shawn off. But he was like a crab, latched on and pounding the top of his head until the goon dropped like a stone.

Abrianna's opponent slipped both arms underneath hers and locked his hands behind her back. It pushed her head forward against her chest. She reared her head back, busting him in the lip, and then folded up-ward and flipped herself over the man's head. Now he was on his back, she crashed her elbows against the collar of his neck, dropping him next to his partner.

Click.

Abrianna and Shawn's attention snapped back to Zeke.

Panting, he stood with a gun leveled on them while blood trickled from his nose and mouth.

"What are you two, a couple of ex-WWE freaks?"

Abrianna hissed. "If you're going to shoot, shoot. I'm not dancing to your bullshit anymore."

"You'll dance until I say it's over. And I'm not . . ." The gun trembled in his hands. "What the fuck?" Zeke wrestled for control of his arm. He used his left hand to steady his right, but that didn't work. His right hand turned the weapon toward himself. "What the hell is happening?" Zeke yelled. "How are you doing this shit?"

Abrianna focused on the gun until it completed its turn toward Zeke's head. His wrist snapped before she forced his finger to pull the trigger.

Pow!

Zeke's head exploded as he reeled and crashed backward onto the ground.

Shawn stared at Abrianna. "You did that?"

The men at their feet groaned.

Abrianna glanced down, and before Shawn could stop her, she made their necks snap with a horrible crunch.

"Shit." Shawn jumped and glanced around at the three dead bodies in the center of the park. "How in the hell are we going to explain this?"

Abrianna was still in a daze.

"Your nose is bleeding," Shawn said.

"Huh?"

"We got to get out of here." Shawn tugged Abrianna's arm.

Abrianna's scalp tingled. "There's somebody else out here."

Shawn glanced around, panicked. "Let's go!"

The reality of what had happened hit Abrianna hard, but she allowed Shawn to pull her along before they took off running. A van appeared out of nowhere and flew up on the curb. Before Abrianna could react, the back door opened and a panicked Roger yelled, "Get in!"

Abrianna and Shawn didn't wait for them to tell them a second time and jumped into the back of the van.

Two witnesses to the carnage stepped out of the shadows and watched the van speed off.

"Did you see that, Dr. Z?" Ned asked, openmouthed.

Dr. Zacher nodded; his smile took up the lower half of his face. "I saw it, all right."

"What should we do?"

"First, we get a crew out here to take care of these bodies. Then I'm paying a visit to Spalding to let him know that there has been a change in plans."

48

Ghost's Warehouse

Kadir and Ghost listened as Abrianna, Shawn, Wendell, and Roger retold the evening's events with matching expressions of shock. When they were finished, a long, palpable silence hung over the room while everyone took a moment to process. Even after they did that, no one knew what to say.

Except for Ghost. "I'm starting to feel like God sent you here to test me."

"Trust me. God has nothing to do with any of it," Abrianna responded flippantly.

"Then it's the devil," he concluded and then looked to Kadir. "Anything you want to say to your homicidal girlfriend?"

"Uhm." He drew a deep breath, but words eluded him, so he shook his head.

Shawn spoke up. "There is nothing to say. As far as Zeke is concerned, and his hooligans, it was self-defense. And considering the asshole shoved a gun in my mouth a month ago, I have no tears for him. He can have all the seats in hell to himself."

Ghost looked to his guys. "And where were you two?"

"We hung back. I guess we were a little too far back. Sorry, boss."

Kadir's gaze remained locked on Abrianna, who was doing all she could to avoid his. "How are you feeling?"

She crossed her arms as a weak barrier of defense. "I don't know."

"You have no thoughts on all the stuff you learned about T4S, Craig Avery, and your friend Charlie?"

"Well, he certainly isn't a friend anymore, is he?"

Kadir pushed away from the wall and walked over and took her by the hand and proceeded to lead her out of the living room. "We'll be back."

The group said nothing, but watched them leave.

Kadir led her to the bedroom they'd once shared and shut the door. "There. Now you can talk."

Her arms folded back across her body again. "There's not much really to say."

"You had to have suspected *something* for a while, right?"

She shrugged. "I guess. Maybe I didn't really want to know."

"You never thought you should get help?"

"Help from who? Is there a specialist that can help me with my genetically modified body? You think after Avery I wanted to be poked and prodded like some alien? Even knowing what I know, I still don't want that. It is what is and I am what am now."

"True. But you and Tomi must be a gold mine to T4S. I can't imagine them letting you guys walk away. And now that you're under the spotlight, at least until we know what the justice department is going to do about President Walker, you're not going to be able to disappear."

"Well, I could, especially if we go on that show *The Filibuster*. They're offering a cool million to interview the two of us. We could take that money and fly off to the French Riviera—sun in our faces and sand beneath our feet."

"We?"

"I mean, if you wanted to come, I wouldn't stop you."

"You are . . . a handful of trouble."

"I've been told that." She grinned.

He chuckled.

"So . . . you're not weirded out about my . . . ability?"

"I am. I'm keeping it all inside at the moment. Plus, you're too pretty to break up over it. I do have *one* request, though."

"What's that?"

"That you promise not to use that stuff on me—like putting me through walls and shit."

Abrianna laughed and nodded. "All right. I promise."

"Good." He walked over and pulled her into his arms. "Then we'll take the rest of this one day at a time."

<hr>

Castillo spent a week reviewing the information Tomi had brought her about Dr. Zacher. She shared it with Dennis, who also didn't know what to make of any of it or what they were supposed to do about it. The Avery case was long closed, and the connections between the two doctors were tenuous at best and hard to prove.

Today, Lovely Belfleur was going home, and her mother had requested that Castillo be there when Children's Protective Service brought her that day. Castillo was honored that the mother had even made the request. Since she was in desperate need of some good news for once, she went.

She was welcomed into the Belfleur home with open arms, squeezed so tight by Penny Belfleur that by the time she was released, they streamed matching tears.

At the sound of another vehicle pulling up into the driveway, the waiting family members vibrated with excited nervousness.

Penny opened the door and led the crowd out onto the porch to watch the CPS workers help Lovely out of the car.

The waterworks went on full-blast when mother and daughter's gazes connected for the first time in a year. Castillo's heart exploded with joy at seeing the little girl race into her mother's arms. It was a good day.

<hr />

Abrianna and Kadir were shown onto the set of *The Filibuster*. The swelling had gone down on Kadir's face and makeup covered up the rest. Everyone at the studio put them as ease. Abrianna was relaxed, but Kadir was nervous. Neither really wanted to be on the show, but the million-dollar payday wasn't something either one of them could walk away from.

Standing off set, Tomi and Shawn gave them encouraging thumbs up.

Abrianna smiled, and when she saw Kadir's right

leg bouncing, she reached over and squeezed his hand. "You're going to be fine."

He covered her hand and winked.

Joy Walton settled into her chair and introduced herself. She put them at ease while being powdered and buffed. "You two make a good looking couple," she observed.

They smiled.

"We're on in five," someone shouted.

The host held up the okay sign and then returned her attention to her guests. "You two have been on one hell of a ride these past two months."

"That's putting it mildly." Kadir chuckled.

They engaged in small talk until the producer in their earphone counted them down, and then the show went live.

The Parker Estate

Cargill Parker threw his bourbon, glass and all, at the television. It hit the screen and bounced off to shatter on the floor. His inability to break the offending smart TV enraged him.

At seeing Abrianna's smug and self-satisfied image on the screen, he itched to wrap his hands around her neck. Who the fuck did she think she was? Did the bitch really believe that she was free of him? Did she think that he wouldn't beat these fucking charges? She must've forgotten who he was. He owned politicians, judges, and cops. The few that weren't on his payroll didn't have enough power to make a speeding ticket go away.

Needing another drink, Cargill pushed out of his leather armchair and stomped to the wet bar. Outside the window, protesters were still at it. He growled, "When in the fuck are those people leaving?"

Drink in hand, Cargill moved to the window and glared at their ridiculous signs. He'd love to grab an assault weapon and mow them down. He'd already had to step up security after a few of those crazy lefties climbed the iron gate and attempted to break into the house. Even now, he entertained having the damn gate electrified.

Abrianna laughed and recaptured his attention.

Cargill faced the television and at seeing Abrianna's smile, his chest tightened and his cock hardened. This time he couldn't pull his gaze away. She glowed. Then he realized why; the Arab guy sitting next to her. There was something between them.

The guy winked at Abrianna, and she blushed.

They're fucking. His glass exploded. Its sharp shards sliced open his hand, but he ignored it. He only had eyes for his daughter. He had to get her back by any means necessary.

"And we're clear," the producer declared. The cameras' red lights shut off.

Abrianna relaxed. She'd been more nervous than she'd realized while Kadir turned out to be as cool as a cucumber.

"You two were great," Walton praised, leaning and offering her hand. "I'm telling you. The camera loves you two."

"Thanks," they said in unison and then shared smiles.

Walton studied them. "Do I see love in the air?"

Abrianna and Kadir ignored the question while removing their microphone packs.

"Got it," Walton said. "It's none of my business."

She winked and stood. "Well, thanks again for coming on the show."

"It's been our pleasure," Kadir said. They engaged in a final round of handshakes.

Kadir gestured for Abrianna to take the lead while placing his hand on the small of her back. Together, they maneuvered around cameras and stepped over large cable and cords while exiting the set.

A sharp-dressed man in a navy blue suit smiled and cut off their path. "She's right, you know. You two *are* naturals on camera."

"Thanks," Abrianna said and waited for him to move.

He didn't.

"Is there something that we can help you with?" Kadir asked.

"Actually, yes. There is." He produced a business card. "I'm—"

"Melvin Kellerman," Kadir said, his expression stony.

Kellerman nodded. "Ah. So you *do* remember me."

"It's hard to forget the people who put you behind bars," Kadir said.

Abrianna asked, "Another one?"

Kellerman chuckled. "Unfortunately, we don't make too many friends down at the U.S. attorney's office."

He pressed the business card into her hand. "You're a hard woman to locate, Ms. Parker. We'd like for you to come into the office for an interview."

She accepted the card. "Only me?" She glanced over at Kadir.

"Yes. I'm sorry. This isn't about President Walker, but about your father, Cargill Parker."

She stiffened.

"Things are moving rather quickly, but we'd like to—"

"I haven't talked to my father in years." She attempted to hand back the business card.

Kellerman refused to take it back and instead shoved his hands into his pockets. "I understand that this may be difficult for you. But I implore you to *think* about the children we rescued from the Lynnwood Club. I've met most of them. They are scared—traumatized. They deserve justice. With your help, I know that we can get it for them."

Guilt engulfed her as she lowered her hands to her side.

Kadir's arm drifted around her hips and pulled her close.

Kellerman coughed and softened his voice. "At least think about it. I know that the media is making it sound like it's a slam-dunk case, but the truth is that we're dealing with some powerful and well-connected people who are lawyering up faster than the former president. To be frank with you—we can lose. Your father could walk. We didn't catch anybody in the act—and the children are either too scared or too traumatized to give us more than finger paintings that a first year law student could get thrown out of court. Hell, we're even having a hard time finding out who these children are and where they came from. We have a small—and I do mean small—window of opportunity—but it's closing fast. Think it over—but don't take too long." He nodded at Kadir and turned and walked away.

49

Lying in bed, Abrianna stared up at the ceiling while Kadir slept like a baby by her side. For two days, she couldn't get *"Your father could walk"* to stop looping in her head. The idea stressed her to the point her nerves felt like they were latched to a megavolt battery. The knots in her stomach multiplied.

You have to do something.

She cringed while resentment argued back. *Why do I have to do anything?*

Because it's the right thing to do.

"Aaargh." She threw off the covers and perched on the edge of the bed.

Kadir woke. "Are you all right?"

"Yeah. I'm . . . hot. It's hot in here."

"It's like fifty degrees. It's freezing."

It was. And nearly zero degrees outside.

"Well . . . I'm hot." She climbed out of bed and marched out of the room to check the thermostat. It read fifty-two degrees. Grumpy, she jabbed at the buttons, not sure which was doing what or why the damn thing kept beeping back.

Kadir leaned against the bedroom door's archway and crossed his arms. "Do you have any idea what you're doing?"

"Yes," she snapped. "What? You think I don't know how to work a damn thermostat? I'm not stupid."

Kadir lifted a brow and watched her stab the buttons some more.

Abrianna gave up. "I'm going to fix some coffee," she grumbled and marched to the kitchen.

Kadir followed, resuming the same position against the refrigerator while she opened and slammed cabinet doors.

"Where in the hell is the damn coffee?" she snapped, checking under the kitchen sink.

When he didn't respond, she glared. "Well?"

Kadir pushed from the refrigerator and strolled to the cabinet above the coffeemaker and removed the coffee and a package of filters. "Do you need me to get you a mug, too?"

"Don't be an ass."

"Oh? *I'm* being the ass?" He chuckled.

Abrianna hip-bumped him out of the way.

As he watched her prepare the coffee, his amusement morphed into concern. "Since it looks like we're going to be up for a while, do you want to talk?"

"About what?"

"Well, we already covered the weather. Why don't we talk about your going down to the U.S. attorney's office to talk about your father's case?"

"My adopted father."

Kadir cocked his head. He wasn't about to chase her around the rabbit hole.

Abrianna punched the brew button.

"Look, I'll support whatever you decide to do. But after all you told me about that asshole, I don't see what the conflict is here."

"Of course you don't," she grumbled.

"I get that it's hard, especially since you slammed the door on the past years ago, or at least you've tried." Kadir closed the distance between them and pulled her stiff body into his arm. "But, baby, this shit is much bigger than you. It's about those kids. Even if you walk away now, and don't get me wrong, I'll support you if you do, but if you walk way and that monster goes free, there will be more victims. His sickness will spread. Can you live with that?"

Abrianna couldn't lift her gaze any higher than his chest while she considered lying. She wanted to do the right thing. She wasn't horrible or evil, as Marion had accused. Bree was . . . scared. Couldn't she admit that she was fucking scared? All of her life, Cargill Parker was all the horrible monsters that lived beneath children's beds and in closets rolled into one. Fear was a part of her foundation, if not embedded into her DNA. For years, he'd told her that she would never escape and that he would kill her if she ever dared to try. Returning home after the Avery nightmare was never an option.

"He's only a man—flesh and blood. We can take him down," Kadir said.

She looked up into his dark gaze. "We?"

Kadir smiled. "I'm not going anywhere. I'm here for you. We're in this together." He kissed the top of her head. "Every step of the way."

Abrianna marched into the lion's den of the U.S. attorney's office in Alexandria, Virginia, with strength harnessed from Kadir through their braided hands. Her head screamed how much she didn't want to do this, but for once her heart ran the show. This was for those children who had been found and the thousands of children that the department knew nothing about.

The brick building off Jamison Avenue wasn't much to look at, but it still intimidated with its clean and almost minimalist décor.

A smiling, fresh-faced attorney greeted them and introduced himself as Grant Adams. A cluster of carbon-copy looking attorneys surrounded him. Where was Kellerman?

"We're glad that you decided to come," he said and then led them to a conference room where a buffet of baked goods and bottled drinks was offered.

Kadir whispered, "Their case must be really falling apart. In a minute they are going to offer us champagne and personal masseuses."

"I can always go for a massage," Abrianna whispered back.

Once everyone settled into chairs, the door flew open and an attractive and sharp African-American woman entered and strode to the head of the table with Kellerman trailing behind her.

"Ms. Abrianna Parker," the woman greeted, extending a hand. "It's great to meet you. I'm Attorney General Jaclyn Randall. You've already met the U.S. Attorney Melvin Kellerman."

"Yes. We've met." She accepted their handshakes and watched them take their seats, making it seven attorneys now in the room.

"I appreciate you coming in." Randall's gaze swept to include Kadir. "I know you've been quite busy with your press tour on the president scandal. You two are just good ole American heroes doing your civic duty, huh?"

A frost settled over the room.

Abrianna glanced to Kellerman and then back to Randall. "I was *asked* to come. I wasn't in the neighborhood."

Kellerman appeared uncomfortable as he shifted in his chair.

"You did want my help, didn't you?"

"Your help?" Randall said, venom dripping off each syllable. "You take down one president and now you're Nancy Drew?"

"You know what, lady? Fuck you." Abrianna pushed up from her chair. "I don't need this shit."

A confused Kadir followed Abrianna.

The other attorneys looked stricken.

Kellerman bolted to his feet and blocked their march toward the door. "Wait. No. Let's all take a deep breath and start over. We have *clearly* started on the wrong foot."

"We?" Abrianna countered. "Talk to Ms. Attorney General Bitch over there."

Randall spun in her chair, her smile a thin line.

"The fault is mine. I'm sorry," Kellerman said. "I failed to tell Mrs. Randall that you were coming in this morning and . . . again, I apologize. At the end of the day we all want the same thing, and that's to put Cargill Parker and his friends behind bars for a very long time."

Abrianna glared. "Then I wish you luck." She stepped around him.

"I apologize, too, Ms. Parker," Randall announced.

Abrianna kept walking.

"I was unprofessional and out of line," Randall added.

Abrianna stopped.

"Melvin is right. At the end of the day, we all want to put Cargill Parker and his secret society clan away. It has become increasingly clear that we're going to need all the help that we can get."

Abrianna lingered, waiting for the magic word.

"Please," Randall said.

Abrianna turned and assessed the woman's folded arms and stiff body language and knew what that apology had cost her. "I don't want to hear any more of that Nancy Drew shit."

"Deal."

Abrianna returned to her seat. The next three hours were like slicing open every vein on her body. She told them all that she could remember about the Dragon Templars, divulged the ugly rituals, and even told them about some of the children she remembered from years past. Kadir's hands squeezed hers tighter whenever she came to a particularly odious memory. But the one name she refused to mention was Samuel. She wanted to tell them, she wanted to tell Kadir.

But she couldn't. After all this time, her heart still wasn't ready.

"What about Marion Parker?" Randall asked.

Abrianna stiffened. "What about her?"

"What was her role in all of this? We've approached her. Right now she's maintaining that she knew nothing about her husband's sick double life. That can't be true, can it? And if it is, why did you never tell her about what happened to you at these gatherings and right underneath her nose in that house?"

"I was told never to tell," Abrianna said, which was the truth. She and Marion never once spoke about any of it.

"That's it? You were told not to say anything so you didn't?" Randall said.

"Marion had her ways of not acknowledging what was right in front of her."

"Meaning?" Randall pushed.

Abrianna took a deep breath and wondered at this sudden protectiveness that came over her. "Marion had her own hell to live through."

"She was abused?" Kellerman asked.

"Among other things," Abrianna whispered. "You should talk to her."

"We've tried. She's pretty good at stonewalling," Randall said.

Abrianna cleared her throat. "How much longer is this going to take?"

"A few more questions," Kellerman said. "Do you have any idea how this organization acquired the children?" he asked. "We're having a hell of a time finding anything on where they came from. Somebody is providing the children. Surely these men aren't out here kidnapping them themselves."

Stumped, Abrianna stared at them. "I don't know. I don't know where the children came from."

50

"*Abrianna Parker is back in the news today. She and Mr. Kadir Kahlifa were seen leaving the U.S. attorney's office earlier today. Many have speculated that this was a sign of the department moving forward with charges against former President Walker. However, anonymous sources within the department say that Ms. Parker may play a pivotal role in the child sex-trafficking charges against her father, Cargill Parker, who was arrested at his private Lynnwood Club a few weeks ago and is currently out on bail.*"

Peter Lautner set down his whiskey sour and heaved a long sigh. "This is not good. In fact, this is highly problematic."

"That fucking bitch," Cargill swore while nursing his second bourbon. He took several deep breaths to calm his nerves, but the protesters made it impossible.

Lautner continued, "The other members are already anxious. It is taking a herculean effort to make sure that everyone keeps their mouths shut and toes the line, especially the few members whose financial situations are built on quicksand."

"No need to pussyfoot around, Lautner. You can say the word 'politicians' in my presence."

Lautner grimaced. "I'd rather not. I have allergies, you know."

"How much?" Cargill asked, recognizing a shakedown when he heard one.

"It's not cheap. There are seven of them who are getting a lot of heat in their own districts since their arrests. They need guarantees. But with the collective contributing together, it's a pittance. You won't even miss the money."

Cargill frowned. "I miss it now, and I haven't even given it to you yet."

"Fair enough."

"How much are we talking about?"

"One million."

Cargill made the calculation in his head. "So a little over sixteen million?"

"A pittance for silence."

Cargill grumbled as he climbed to his feet and waltzed over to his safe. Out of habit he mumbled the passcode as he punched in the numbers. Once it was open, he removed the gun's lockbox and reached for the bundled stacks of cash near the back.

Lautner stuffed the cash into a leather duffel bag. "Now what about our other problem? I'm sure there's a new wave of members pissing in their pants and blowing up my office phones as we speak."

Cargill growled. Abrianna was certainly a problem now that she was no longer under his control. A part of him was surprised that she'd had the guts to even involve herself in this drama. He couldn't help but be turned on by her defiance. He saw it as a challenge whether he could bring her back to heel.

"Cargill?" Lautner probed, pulling him back to their conversation.

"I'll handle it."

"You have a plan?"

"Not yet. I'm still working on it." He thought about Zeke Jeffreys's offer to bring his daughter home. But now the man was missing in action. Strange how that kept happening.

"If you have a few more minutes, I have a suggestion."

Cargill returned to his seat and picked up his drink. "I'm listening."

"Well. If your daughter is going to play with the big boys, then we treat her like any other adversary, and we attack her weak spot."

"Samuel?"

Lautner nodded. "The papers are already asking questions. I say we give them their answer. Trust me. The prosecutor won't want her anywhere near their cases against you or any of the Dragons."

Cargill thought it over; however, the details of that night gave him pause. "I don't know. It's risky, especially if she convinces them of her version of events that night."

Lautner cocked his head. "Was there more to the story than what you told me?"

"Since when do you believe everything I tell you?"

"Okay. Maybe you should start from the beginning, and I'll figure out how we can spin it."

51

Abrianna took a nail-size bump of Cotton Candy and then tucked the rest of the drug in the back of the top drawer of her chest of drawers. She'd learned it only took a little to get what she needed to function; a little to make her feel good. When she stood, she caught her reflection in the bedroom mirror and froze. *What am I doing?* After a long moment, she closed her eyes. She was doing what she always did: screwing up.

"I *can* quit," Abrianna told herself.

"Baby, is everything all right?" Kadir called out from the bathroom.

"Everything is fine." She swiped under her nose and rushed to join Kadir, who was already soaking in a cloud of lavender bubbles.

He grinned when she entered. "I can really get used to this."

"You look ridiculous." She laughed, referring to the beard that he'd made out of bubbles.

"What? You don't find it sexy?"

"Actually," she said, approaching and peeling out of her robe, "you don't need any added help in that department."

Kadir swiped his face clean while his gaze caressed Abrianna's curves, and a smile exploded across his face. "Talking about not needing any help in the sexy department . . ."

Chuckling, Abrianna loved the way he looked at her. Over the years, men had gawked at her on stage, but there was more than lust in Kadir's eyes. She wanted to name it, but was afraid, just as she was afraid of the new feelings she experienced every time they were together.

When she stepped into the tub in between his legs, he leaned back and slapped on a silly grin.

"Shall I dance for you?" she asked.

He chuckled. "Do you, boo."

"Really? You want me to *do me*?" Abrianna rolled her hips and softly sang Rihanna's classic song "Skin."

Kadir leaned back and fell under her spell.

Feeling his gaze roaming over her body, Abrianna lost herself in the performance. By the end, she was on her knees, crawling through a cloud of bubbles and biting her bottom lip.

"Oh. You're good," he said.

"Yeah?" She draped her soapy arms around his neck and moved in for a kiss, but stopped short within an inch of his mouth. "Does that mean I'm going to get a big tip?"

"Oh, I got a tip for you all right."

She grinned as his hard-on stretched against her belly. "Hmmm. I can't wait."

Their lips sealed together as Kadir wrapped his powerful arms around her. For the next half hour, they made love among a rapidly vanishing bed of bubbles and ended up with more water on the floor than what was left in the tub.

Some time later, Abrianna lay curled against his chest, listening to his steady heartbeat while sleep eluded her.

"You want to talk about it?" Kadir asked.

"Talk about what?"

"It was a long session at the attorney's office. That was a lot of heavy stuff you unloaded." He caressed her hair.

She swallowed thickly. "I knew that going in."

"Still. It was a room full of strangers," he pushed. "Clearly, it wasn't easy."

"No."

There was a long silence. But it was a comfortable one. She felt protected—safe. And though he'd learned way more than she had originally shared with him about her past, there was no judgment. Outside of her small band of friends, she hadn't felt that way with anyone else. Certainly not any man she'd ever dated. This was new territory.

Abrianna sighed when Kadir's lips brushed the top of her head, but then a tear rolled from her eyes. "I never once thought about where those kids came from," she confessed. "Before Kellerman approached me, I never thought that much about anyone other than . . ." She couldn't say the name lodged in her throat. Suddenly, she questioned everything she felt a moment ago. *What if I'm wrong, and he does judge me for what I've done?*

More tears cascaded over her lashes.

"You couldn't have known," he said. "How could you have? You were a kid yourself."

"But . . . but . . ."

"Shhh." He kissed her head again. "You're being too hard on yourself. Children adapt to their environment. You were stuck in survival mode. Let it go." Another kiss.

"I have to do something," she whispered.

"You *are* doing something," he said. "You're going to testify."

She shook her head, worrying. "It's not enough."

"Of course it is." He tilted her chin up so that their gazes connected, despite the dark. "Don't put all of this on your shoulders. You're not being fair to yourself."

She sat up. "But you heard them. They are worried about their own case. If *they* are worried, then I should be worried. Cargill is not the man to fuck with on a normal day, let alone coming at him like this. And I'm sorry, but that group of pencil pushers does not fill me with confidence. I don't think you understand. He could really get off. If he does, he's going after those who tried to take him out. I'll be at the top of his fucking list. And I'm out in the open now."

"You're working yourself up." Kadir reached for her, but she swatted his hand away.

"You're not listening."

"I am listening. I don't understand what it is that you think you have to do."

"I *have* to make sure that he goes down. If I'm going into that court, I need for this to be a slam-dunk. We need an ace. We have to find out where the Dragons Templar get those kids."

52

Abrianna and Kadir called and gathered their friends for an emergency meeting at Castillo's detective agency. Tomi was the only one who couldn't make it. After Castillo apologized for the mess in her office and offered to make coffee, Abrianna started her speech.

"I guess there's no other way to start this other than to admit that I need your help." She looked at Ghost. "Yes, I'm well aware that I'm in constant need of help lately."

"How did you—"

"Anyway, you guys may have heard that I'm working with the U.S. attorney's office on their case against my father. The reason they approached me is because they believe their case is crumbling. Tapes of the raid have disappeared, they can't verify the anonymous tip, computers taken from the property have been compromised, and even the Lynnwood Club's surveillance has been erased or wasn't recording that night."

"Humph." Ghost shook his head.

"Our thoughts exactly," Kadir said.

Abrianna continued, "I can already see that I'm not just a character witness about my adoptive parents, but the feds expect me to be their star witness. The only problem with that is, well, my past. I'm a runaway. I'm . . . a drug addict," she admitted for the first time and paused before continuing, "I'm an ex-stripper and escort girl. And unlike with the president's scandal, I don't come bearing proof: a video and a taped confession. My father has deep pockets. It's not surprising that shit is disappearing—which means by now with my name being reported in the news as working with the prosecution, I'm in his crosshairs."

Shawn cut in, "So what do you need from us?"

"The children. That's how we're going to solve this."

Castillo sat forward in her chair. "What about the children?"

"Kellerman, one of the lawyers at—"

"Yeah. I know Melvin Kellerman. I'm the one who told him to talk to you. What is he saying?"

"That they only identified one child, and they have no clue where the others came from. Apparently my father and his secret club are claiming that the government framed them and that the kids weren't there before the raid."

"Weak." Castillo laughed.

"Not if you can pin it on a president who is already embroiled in a frame-slash-cover-up."

"Okay. Now it sounds clever," Castillo amended. "Walker framed your father to get back at you for exposing him for framing you. Do I have that right?"

"Exactly," Abrianna said. "So the key is to find out where or who traffics these children for the Dragons. They have to come from *somewhere*."

Castillo shook her head. "I like where your head is

but, and I'm speaking from experience in searching for lost children, your biggest problem is the clock."

"The information has to be stored somewhere," Roger said. "Phone records, files, computers."

Ghost nodded. "I can get my hands on the list of the other sickos arrested that night and comb through their shit as well. Somebody fucked up and told somebody something or wrote it down."

"So you guys will help?"

Draya laughed. "Are you kidding? We've been ready to help you take down that monster for six years."

Kadir looked around the office and hinted to Castillo, "You know, I need a place of employment to tell my parole officer."

Castillo smiled. "Then you're hired."

❖

The next day, while Abrianna and the gang set up shop at the Agency, she received a call from Bowen & Johnson. The moment the number displayed on her phone, she sensed that it wasn't good news. That feeling deepened when the receptionist danced around why her attorney wanted her to come into the office. After haggling over the time, she hung up and cast a worried glance at Kadir.

"What is it?"

"I'm not sure. But I need to get over to our attorney's office."

His face crinkled with concern. "I'll go with you."

"No. You have to check in with your probation officer. I can jet over there myself." His expression told her how much he didn't like that idea.

"I'll be fine."

"I can go with her," Draya offered. "As long as we

can swing by the MAC store afterward. I have a wedding party in the morning and I have to pick up a couple of blush palettes."

Ghost laughed. "No offense, but maybe someone who hasn't been shot should play bodyguard?"

"I don't need a bodyguard," Abrianna said. "Haven't you heard? I'm a genetically modified freakazoid."

"Yeah. You may heal fast, but you're no superwoman until bullets bounce *off* of you. As long as T4S, the former president, and now your crazy-ass daddy are out there, then you should have someone playing defense with you at all times."

She wanted to argue, but the squeeze of her hand by Kadir stopped her. "Fine."

"Good. Wendell can go with you."

An hour later, Abrianna entered the law offices of Bowen & Johnson with a stone-faced and strapped Wendell following behind. He was led to wait in the lobby while Abrianna was taken into yet another expansive conference room. However, the moment she stepped into the room, she wanted to bolt back out of it.

Peter Lautner sat at the head of the table, grinning. "Hello, Ms. Parker."

Abrianna cut her gaze to Marcus Johnson, who flashed her a nervous smile. "You know that you're fired, right?"

While Bowen's face fell, Lautner's rich laughter rumbled and filled the room. "Aw now. Don't blame Markie Mark there. We came here to talk. See if we can strike a deal."

Abrianna evaluated him. "Deal?" Then she glanced around the room. "And who is this 'we'?"

"Have a seat," Lautner said, gesturing to the two dozen chairs around the table. "Anywhere is fine."

Bowen leaned forward and whispered, "Maybe you should hear him out."

"Roll up your sleeve."

"What?" Bowen blinked.

"You heard me. You want me to sit, let me see your right arm."

His lips twitched. "We both know that's not necessary. You already know what's there."

Abrianna wanted to kick herself. All Dragons had a burn mark in the shape of a dragon on their right forearm. "You're a Dragon."

"For life. Now. Sit. Down."

She clenched her teeth as the conference room door slammed shut.

Bowen jumped, but Lautner simply frowned.

Telling herself to remain calm, Abrianna turned and took the chair on the opposite end of the table.

Lautner's smile returned. "Let me first start off by saying that it's nice to see you looking so well. I can't tell you how much your parents worried about you over the years."

"I bet."

"No. I mean it. Cargill, particularly, took it hard. He looked everywhere for you. Broke his heart."

Abrianna said nothing.

"You don't have to believe me. You should hear it from Cargill."

He turned, and Abrianna noticed the screen over his left shoulder for the first time. Lautner powered it on, and Cargill's smiling face came onto the screen.

Abrianna tensed while her heart rate sped up.

"At last," Cargill said, eyes sparkling. "There's my little girl. All grown up."

Against her will, Abrianna's confidence weakened.

Too many emotions flooded her all at once, and she couldn't process them.

Concerned, Cargill asked, "What's the matter? Don't you have anything to say to your dear old dad?"

Lautner offered his commentary. "I think she's overwhelmed."

Her father laughed. "I bet you're right."

Abrianna took a deep breath. "What do you want?"

Cargill's grin expanded. "Actually, I'd love for my favorite girl to pay her dear dad a visit. You have no idea how much I've missed you. At one point I was convinced that you were dead. I'm so happy to have been wrong about something."

"Go to hell."

He chuckled, but anger sparked in his eyes. "So it's true. You're still angry at me." He sighed. "That's unfortunate. Still, you should know that family affairs should remain within the family. This news I hear about you working with the U.S. attorney's office, I got to tell you, it troubles me."

"Good."

Cargill's brows lifted with surprise.

Even Lautner's smug smile shaved off a few inches.

"You do not want to mess with me on this, little girl," Cargill threatened. "You are in *way* over your head. You will tell those nosy feds that you had a change of heart, and you will shut up about all the things that you *think* you know—or you'll deal with me. Cross me and I'll come after you with everything I got. You're not invisible anymore."

She nodded as her heart pounded in a normal rhythm. "Do you know what else I'm not?" she asked coolly. "I'm *not* a little girl. I'm not afraid of you *or* your little Dragons. You want to dance, daddy dearest?

Then we can dance." With the clench of her fist, the computer screen exploded as if it had been shot.

Lautner launched out of his seat. "What the fuck?"

Bowen rushed for the emergency fire extinguisher in the corner of the room. By the time the minor chaos subsided, Abrianna had stormed out.

53

On *Face the Press*, Peter Lautner sat next to the equally arrogant pundit James Crystal. The fever pitch for Cargill Parker's arrest and conviction now required a public defense to combat the growing whispers of Abrianna Parker being a witness for the prosecution. Had Cargill not been such a public political donor who bought politicians to pass legislation that angered the activist left, Lautner's press offensive wouldn't have been necessary.

Chuck Horton greeted the audience, "Joining us today on the show is Peter Lautner, personal attorney for the now embroiled multibillionaire Cargill Parker. Parker is currently charged with operating a sex-trafficking ring with minor children out of his private and exclusive Lynnwood Club. Welcome to the show."

Lautner flashed his bright veneers. "Thank you for extending the invitation."

"Well, we're going to open the floor to you, Mr. Lautner. There is already a lot in the stew on this. The charges leveled at your client are quite serious."

"Yes, they are. And we have every confidence that our client will be exonerated on *every* count."

Horton looked incredulous. "That's quite a prediction, given the amount of evidence the prosecution has amassed."

"I know that the prosecution claims to have a lot of evidence, but they have yet to produce any of it."

"They're not in court yet."

"Exactly, which means that they can say anything they want to until the rubber meets the road."

"What about the children that were removed from the property?"

"We plan to argue that those children were not on the property prior to the unlawful invasion of the federal government. We plan to prove that this witch hunt was launched by the former president as a desperate attempt to lash back at Mr. Parker's estranged daughter."

"So you guys are going full conspiracy with this?"

"No. We're going with the truth."

"Then what do you say to the growing speculation that Mr. Parker's *estranged* daughter will be a top witness for the prosecution?"

"I guess that it makes sense if they're going to claim that Abrianna was there that night, too. One lie usually follows another."

"Whoa." Horton reeled back with an impressive smile. "I doubt they're claiming that Ms. Parker was there that night, but more likely she's being called to testify about her past experience in living with Cargill Parker. She pretty much alluded on a competing network that something nefarious went on in her home."

Lautner's smile turned oily. "Now we've come to an uncomfortable and unfortunate topic. It is well known Mr. Parker's daughter had gone through something very traumatic at the hands of serial killer Craig Avery.

I doubt many of us could even imagine the horrors she went through. But Mr. and Mrs. Parker fear that whatever happened to Abrianna in that madman's basement might have affected her memory. The Parkers are a very loving couple who opened their home to a child who was in desperate need of a family who could love her and provide a privileged life where she wanted for nothing."

Intrigued, Horton leaned forward. "If that's the case, why did Ms. Parker run away from home at fourteen?"

"Teenage rebellion." Lautner laughed. "Hell. I ran away from home when I was eight because my father took away my bike for a month. It's unfortunate that a small, *normal* childish action landed her in the hands of a madman."

"And that's really your client's position?"

"It's the truth. You know, Chuck, as parents you can do everything right and still end up with a willful child."

"So you're saying that Ms. Parker was a troubled child?"

Lautner shook his head as if he hated to be the bearer of such news. "Unfortunately, yes. When Abrianna was nine, she was involved in an incident that, uh, unfortunately led to the *death* of Mr. and Mrs. Parker's biological son, Samuel."

<hr />

"That lowdown, dirty muthafucka," Abrianna swore, staring at Lautner's smug expression on the television.

Kadir placed a comforting hand on Abrianna's shoulder. "Don't let him get to you."

She shook her head and backed away. "He doesn't think that I'll go through with it."

"Who, your father?"

"Yeah. He sent that slimy fuck onto that show as a warning to me. Talk and he'll tell the world what I did."

Kadir cocked his head. "And what exactly did you do?"

Abrianna sucked in a breath to calm down, but it didn't work. Her eyes burned, but she blinked back the tears. "This has got to stop. I can't let the past keep doing this to me. I can't." Suddenly, she was tired. Tired of running from what she'd done. Tired of feeling guilty and punishing herself. It had to stop.

"Bree?" Kadir pulled her into his arms. "Whatever it is, you can tell me. We'll work through it together."

She looked at him, her confession on the tip of her tongue when her phone rang from the bedroom. Abrianna welcomed the excuse to flee Kadir's intense gaze. "Hold on."

"Bree—"

"I'll be right back." She rushed out of the bedroom, swiping her eyes. When she reached the phone, she noted the call was from Kellerman. "Shit."

"Abrianna?" Kellerman asked.

"Yeah. It's me."

"Look. I saw a segment on *Face the Press*—"

"I know. My father's personal attorney was on there."

"What is he talking about? Who is this Samuel? I don't have any record of a Samuel Parker."

She shook her head. "No, you wouldn't."

"Abrianna, talk to me. Randall is going to have my head when she sees this clip. We have a lot banking on your testimony."

"Look. It's nothing. It's . . . a threat."

"A threat?"

Abrianna's head buzzed while the corners of her eyes twitched. "I'll take care of it."

"Take care of what? Take care of it how?"

"I'll call you later."

"Abrianna, we have to—"

She disconnected the call and then quickly searched for her purse and dug around. For a moment she feared that she'd thrown the number away, but then she found the folded piece of paper at the bottom. *I can't believe that I'm about to do this.* Abrianna took a deep breath and dialed the number. *Hang up,* her inner voice screamed while the line rang. She was tempted. Her hand even tightened on the phone. *Do I really want to do this?* She didn't, but suddenly she felt the need to see Cargill finally pay for all the hell that he caused, not only in her life, but for all those children that he and his secret boys' club herded through the Lynn-wood Club. In a short time, she'd gotten used to the idea of him being behind bars for the rest of his life or, even better, getting the needle. She couldn't give those fantasies up now.

"Hello."

Abrianna's heart stopped at the familiar voice that had haunted her for years. "Hello, Marion."

54

Despite Cargill's disapproval, Tina Bouchard and Marion Parker had been best friends for twenty-five years. When Tina was married to fellow Dragon member Jean Luc Bouchard, Cargill didn't have a problem. It was only after Tina's husband mysteriously dropped dead among strong whispers of having been poisoned that she lost Cargill's approval. In her only act of defiance, Marion succeeded in having covert brunches and the occasional dinner with her friend.

Today, Marion arranged a meeting with Abrianna to take place at one of Tina's rental condos in Wardman Towers. Marion arrived an hour early, paranoid about whether Cargill had placed a tail on her.

Tina, decked head-to-toe in pink Chanel, opened the front door, took one look at Marion's huge Jackie O glasses, and knew that her girl was hiding another black eye. "Why haven't you killed that bastard already?" she asked, shaking her head.

"Don't start. Can I come in?" Marion asked.

Biting and ruining her perfect red lip, Tina stepped back and held open the door.

Marion entered the condo, removing her shades.

Tina sighed. "Let me take your coat."

"Thank you for allowing me to use your place for this meeting."

"No need to thank me. You know I'll do anything for you." She hung up the coat in the closet. "Including acquiring a non-traceable poison to slip into your husband's bourbon bottle."

"Can we please have *one* afternoon where you're not plotting Cargill's death?"

"I guess—but it won't be as much fun." With a catwalk strut, Tina led the way to the living room. "I made cocktails. I figured your and Abrianna's *talk* would require alcohol."

"Thanks. I could use some right now. I'm so nervous."

"I can imagine." Tina handed her a Cinque Terre and took one for herself. "Bottoms up."

Marion sipped, but wished for something stronger.

"Are you really ready for this?" Tina asked.

"Hell no." Marion's hands shook. "I don't think I'd ever really believed that Bree would agree to meet. I hoped, of course. But . . . so much time and too much history has passed between us."

"Are you going to tell her the truth about—?"

"I . . . I can't." Marion shook her head. "Not yet."

"Have you not seen the news? Cargill's piece of shit lawyer dragged Samuel into this mess. It's the new shiny object in this political soap opera."

"I know, but I can't. It's too risky. She may use the information in court, and Cargill will . . ."

"Which leads us back to killing the bastard. *All* roads lead there, you know?"

A tear skipped down Marion's face. "You always make things sound like it's so simple."

"That's because they are simple. You overthink things. It's way past time for you to be a woman of action again."

Marion shook her head and moved toward the ceiling-to-floor window and stared out at the slate-gray sky while snow flurries dusted the landscape.

Tina remained like a rabid dog with a bone. "Think about it, Marion. Everything goes away with him out of the picture: the press, the protesters, the sex-trafficking scandal—everything. And then you'll have a *real* opportunity to be with your children. Don't you want that?"

"Stop it." Marion lifted her head in a silent prayer before admitting, "I'm not as strong as you are."

Tina came up behind her and squeezed her shoulders. "Nonsense. You're stronger than you know. You showed courage before. You can do it again."

Marion turned into Tina's arms a second before their lips brushed in a tender kiss.

A rap on the front door, and Marion broke away as if the police were hammering it down. "Cargill."

"What? Calm down." Tina turned for the door, but Marion grabbed her right arm.

"He may have had me followed."

"You're paranoid." Tina attempted to pull away. "It's probably Bree."

"No. It's too early."

"*You* were early." She wrenched free and headed toward the door.

Marion shook her head, frightened. She glanced around to note what other exits she could use, but unless she was going to throw herself over the balcony, she had no choice but to face whatever was coming her way.

Tina opened the door.

"Hello. I'm not sure if I'm at the right place. I'm looking for Marion Parker?"

At Abrianna's husky voice, Marion's fear downgraded from a ten to an eight.

Tina's lyrical voice floated throughout the condo. "Hello, Bree. It's good seeing you again. Please, come in."

Confused, Abrianna hesitated. After reassessing the elegant woman, she crossed the threshold. She glanced around with an appreciative eye at the place's sophistication.

"You don't remember me, do you?"

Abrianna frowned.

"I don't blame you. The last time I saw you, you were a lot smaller," the woman said, closing the door. "I'm Tina Bouchard. I'm a good friend of your mother's."

The name rang a bell, albeit a small one. "Is Marion here?"

"Yes. She's in the living room. May I take your jacket?"

Abrianna shook her head. "No. That's okay. I'm not staying long."

Disappointment rippled across the woman's porcelain face and then disappeared. "This way."

Abrianna followed behind the woman's rhythmic hips into a large living room where a nervous Marion stood by the window.

The mother's and daughter's gazes connected.

Butterflies Abrianna tried to ignore took flight while her heart pounded against her chest.

The corners of Marion's lips quivered. "Bree, it's so good to see you."

Abrianna's throat clogged.

"Cocktail?" Tina asked, extending a drink toward her.

Abrianna accepted the glass and then downed half of it before remembering to say, "Thank you."

Tina smiled. "I'll leave you two alone so that you can talk."

Abrianna caught the nod of encouragement that Tina sent Marion before strutting away.

Alone, Abrianna and Marion resumed their silent evaluation of each other. Abrianna had changed a lot, while Marion looked like she always had: elegant, polished, and failing at covering a black eye.

"Thank you for agreeing to come," Marion started. "I've dreamed about this moment for so long that—"

"I didn't come here to fulfill your dreams," Abrianna said. "I'm here because I want you to help me take down that monster that you're still pretending to be married to."

Marion flinched and then dropped her gaze to the deep pile carpet. "Bree, that's . . ."

"What? You're still too chickenshit to do it? Like you were too chickenshit to do anything when it comes to him? Let me guess: That black eye is another love pat from him? What did you forget to do—run his bathwater on time? Did you forget to have a drink ready when he walked in the door? Or maybe you didn't have his latest sex toy dressed in the right costume for playtime?"

"Bree, please. Don't be cruel." Marion sipped her drink.

"Cruel?" Anger flashed through Abrianna.

The cocktail glass in Marion's hand exploded.

Marion leaped backward, stunned. "Oh, God. I made a mess." She started to head off, to clean it up.

"Leave it," Abrianna snapped. "It can wait. You know you should be on trial, right along with Cargill and his Dragons, don't you? I don't know why I've covered for you."

Marion cowered from her daughter's anger. "Look. I understand you're angry and frustrated. I really do. And I had hoped that we—"

"No." Abrianna shook her head. "There is and there will never be a 'we.' You are *not* my mother and I am not your daughter. You're a coked-out, drunk bitch that let that man destroy so many lives. I can't even believe that you're still alive. You should have killed yourself a long time ago."

Tears skipped down Marion's face as she shook her head. She looked lost, broken.

Abrianna sneered, "No. You don't get to stand there and make me feel like shit. Like *I'm* the one who fucked up *your* life!" She paced while the hairs on her body rose.

"You didn't fuck up my life," Marion whispered. "It was fucked up the minute I came into the world. All I have ever done was try to survive it. I know that a lot of times I came off as cruel or indifferent—but nothing could be further from the truth."

Abrianna eyes narrowed, but she swept away the fleeting thought of throwing Marion out of the window.

"In order to survive I have always had to be as small as possible, to never make too much noise and to speak only when spoken to. I've seen and experienced too much. I'm so sorry that I've been nothing but a disappointment to you. I'm sorry that I'm a coward. I wish I wasn't. And I know that I said some things that night when . . ."

Abrianna steeled herself, prepared to hear Samuel's name, but of course Marion dodged it.

"I shouldn't have said those things. I didn't mean it. I was so angry and . . . I wasn't thinking. And in the days and years later, I should have told you that—"

"Stop," Abrianna said. "None of it matters."

"Of course it matters."

"Your being sorry doesn't change a damn thing! If you were really interested in stopping being a coward, you'd do the right thing *now*. The waterworks can't be just for *your* son. It has to be for *all* of those children Cargill and his friends have abused and destroyed and then tossed in the trash like they were nothing. Their lives matter, too."

"I know."

"Do you? I admit, I was a coward these past six years."

"No. You *tried* to do something that night."

"But I stopped afterwards. I'd toughed it out for a few more years before I got the hell out of that house. But I went from one frying pan to another one. After that, I was a complete coward. When I realized the cops were going to hand me right back to you and Cargill, I ran. And I kept running. I did like you. Stayed small. Didn't make too much noise. Stayed invisible. But that was wrong. It was a mistake, because Cargill and his Dragons were still trafficking those kids, month after month. Year after year. Now he's been caught. Whether it was because some sick muthafucka in the White House was trying to get back at me or not, I really don't give a shit. I want him gone. If I can't get him six feet under, then I'll settle for a lifetime behind bars."

"That's just it, Bree. He's not going anywhere," Marion pushed back. "Surely you know how *powerful*

Cargill is. You think a handful of government employees who if they aren't already on his payroll soon will be will really take him down? It's not going to happen. Absolute power corrupts absolutely. There is a reason why the one percent always wins against the government. It's because they *are* the government. They bought it lock, stock, and barrel a long time ago. This is a political dance to entertain the powerless. Nothing more. Let it go while you can, because now he has his sight set on you again."

Abrianna laughed. "I'm not scared of Cargill. Not anymore." She stepped back, shaking her head. "If you're not going to help me, then we really have nothing else to say to each other."

"Bree—"

"And if I have to take you down with him—so be it."

With that, she turned and left.

55

U.S. Attorney General Jaclyn Randall was livid as she hurled one expletive after another at both Kellerman and Abrianna.

"He's going to walk," Randall said. "I hope you know that!"

Abrianna had feared Randall would say this. Lautner's performance the previous morning tilted everything beneath their feet. "I'm sorry," was all she could think to say.

"She's sorry," Randall huffed, her smile tight.

"Jackie—"

"No. No. I get it. She completely wasted our time, but she's sorry."

Abrianna barely held her temper. "You guys came to *me* for help. Lautner is full of shit. He's talking out the crack of his ass because my father pays him extremely well to clean up his bullshit. He didn't say anything that I haven't already admitted to the public myself."

"Goddamn it. I have a damn migraine." Randall

slapped a hand over her head, but kept pacing. "I *knew* that this was a fucking mistake. I knew it!"

Kellerman drew a deep breath. "All is not lost, Jackie."

Randall lifted her head and speared Kellerman with a sharp look. "For once, Melvin, will you please take off those damn rose-colored glasses. Lautner annihilated our top character witness on a single talk show. I'm already quaking in my pumps on what the hell he could do to us in court. You know why? Because it *does* smell like a fucking witch hunt. Anonymous phone calls, missing surveillance tapes. We only identified *one* child. Agents with conflicting information, and now our ace in the hole: an estranged daughter who may have killed her brother and whose memories could be compromised because of another traumatic event. Why don't you put a 'kick me' sign on my back? Two of the biggest cases to roll through Capitol Hill, and she's tied to *both* of them."

Arms crossed, Abrianna spoke up. "I'm getting real tired of you talking about me like my ass ain't sitting right here."

Randall's narrowed gaze shifted to Abrianna. "And you . . . why didn't you tell us about Samuel?"

"You never asked."

"Really?" Randall slapped her hands down on the conference table. "*That's* the excuse that you're rolling with? We didn't *ask* you if you might have something to do with your brother's death? Why in the hell would we think to ask you that? You think that's a standard question we put on a questionnaire?"

"I don't have to put up with this."

"Oh. Is this the part where you threaten to leave again? Well, go! Don't let the door hit you where the good Lord split you!"

"Jackie!"

"No. Don't 'Jackie' me, Melvin. This is *not* getting through your thick head. We're fucked!"

"Why, because Lautner said that I have memory issues? How the fuck would he know? He's never examined me. He doesn't know anything about me. And he definitely doesn't know the truth of what happened to Samuel, either. My father put him out there as a threat. He thinks that I'll shrink and slither back into my closet and hide like I used to. But I want to make it crystal clear that my days of hiding are *over.* I'm not scared of him or his cronies anymore. He doesn't want what happened to Samuel played out in any courtroom any more than I do, but if he wants to call my bluff, then I'll show the world my card and he will not come out clean."

Randall's hard features softened. "What are you saying?"

"I'm saying that he wants you to drop me as a witness."

Randall held Abrianna's gaze while she evaluated her, then she addressed Kellerman. "What do you think?"

"I think that we're still standing on quicksand," Kellerman answered honestly. "Sorry, Ms. Parker. But we're going to need to know the full story before we put you on a stand. And even if Cargill Parker is bluffing, we're going to be reduced to a he-said-she-said situation. Your father had a sterling reputation, until recently, and if he can convince a jury that this is nothing more than a witch hunt by a desperate ex-president, which is very attractive to the growing anti-government crowd, he's golden. Then there's you, who has lived the last six years on the streets, hustling for every dollar. And unlike with President Walker's situation, you don't have a video and a taped confession."

Abrianna sat, thinking.

"What? What is it?" Kellerman asked, watching Abrianna's face.

"There is one *other* person who knows what happened to Samuel and knows all Cargill's dirty little secrets."

"Who?" Randall leaned forward. "Is it Marion? Are you now saying that Marion *did* know about Cargill's activities with the Dragons Templar?"

Abrianna drew a deep breath and weighed how badly she wanted Cargill behind bars. "Yes."

56

Castillo marveled at the work her little agency was getting done. Draya, outside of her occasional makeup artist bookings, acted as the office's receptionist and bookkeeper. Kadir and Julian had helped clean and organize the place before staking claims on two of the desks and combing through the list of Dragons Templar who were arrested the same night with Cargill Parker. They also worked through back channels with Ghost and his crew to perform some duties about which she preferred to have a little plausible deniability.

But for the many hours that they put in finding Cargill Parker's trafficker, it felt like they were spinning in place. The men in this secret society were extremely careful. Then she had the thought: "Maybe we should try to interview Lovely Belfleur ourselves?"

Abrianna didn't look up from the piles of research. "Randall and Kellerman said they couldn't get her to talk."

"I know. But I'm pretty good with kids, and I have a relationship with the mother. It couldn't hurt to try and talk to her ourselves, would it?"

Abrianna looked up. "I guess not."

———·—·———

"Are you sure can do this?" Tina had asked as she handed over a vial that contained the deadly toxin *Clostridium tetani.* *"I can do it,"* Marion had assured her. But now she wasn't so sure. She was frightened. What if she got caught? What if something went wrong?

But the memory of an angry Abrianna denying her forgiveness and turning her back on her helped Marion to cement her resolve. It was time to stop being scared and time to do the right thing. When she returned from her late brunch with Tina, she was surprised that Cargill had actually left the house and there was a telephone company van parked out front.

"Where is Cargill?" she asked James.

"He left to go skeet shooting with Mr. Lautner soon after you left this morning," James said.

"Oh." She guesstimated that she likely had only a short time to do what must be done. "And why is the phone company here?"

"We're having some trouble with the phone lines. They arrived rather quickly and should be about done now."

"I see." She removed her coat. "Thank you, James."

Careful not to draw the staff's attention, she climbed the steep stairway to the second floor in her usual, measured pace and then strolled to Cargill's upstairs salon with her heart lodged in her throat. She jumped at seeing two phone company men working.

"Oh! Hello."

The larger of the two men looked up, smiling. "Good afternoon, ma'am. We're wrapping up." He picked up a clipboard. "Are you the lady of the house?"

"Yes."

"If I can get your signature here." He walked over.

The second man stood and gathered their tools.

Marion signed and handed the grinning man's pen back. "There you go."

"Thank you."

Marion closed the door behind them and rushed over to the bar. She opened her clutch and carefully pulled out the delicate handkerchief that Tina had wrapped around the small vial. Her hands trembled as she opened it and the crystal bourbon decanter.

A noise outside the window caught her attention. Marion's heart leaped. *He's back.* She dumped the poison into the decanter and then quickly returned the vial and the handkerchief to her clutch bag. With her heart still pounding in her throat, she raced back across the salon and flew out of the door.

There was a commotion in the house with Cargill thundering at someone.

"You can't come in here. I know my rights! Who the hell do you think you are?"

Curious, Marion strolled back to the staircase so she could get a better look at what was going on.

"Marion," Cargill roared.

Marion automatically picked up the pace. She was unprepared to see the team of FBI agents pouring into the house.

Cargill roared again, "Marion, get Lautner on the phone, right now." He looked up and spotted her standing and gawking. "Did you fucking hear me? Call Lautner!"

An agent spotted her as well. "Are you Mrs. Marion Parker?"

Fear seized her, but she nodded.

He waved her down. "Mrs. Parker, could you please come down here?"

Her heart stopped. *They know!* But how could they have known?

"Mrs. Parker," the agent threatened.

Cargill calmed down. "What in the hell do you need *her* for?"

Swallowing, Marion descended the stairs on shaky legs. Then she remembered that she was still carrying the vial and handkerchief. At the bottom of the staircase, she casually set her clutch bag on the atrium's table next to a vase of cream-colored roses.

In the next second, two agents grabbed and spun her around. She shut down at the sudden violence.

"Somebody tell me what the hell is going on," Cargill demanded.

He was ignored, and Marion was placed under arrest. She said nothing as the cold metal bit into her wrist, nothing when her arm was jerked so hard it felt as if it came out of its socket. The tears didn't come until she was placed in the backseat of a car and hauled off from one set of bars to another.

Abrianna and Castillo drove out to the Belfleur residence. She was uncomfortable with this plan the whole way out, but Abrianna figured what in the hell did they have to lose?

Penny Belfleur greeted them at the door with a smile and then offered both something to drink after they were seated in the living room. To avoid being rude, they accepted the offer of water and then waited for her to join them after they were served.

"So how is she doing?" Castillo asked.

Penny's smile wobbled before she confessed, "We're taking everything one day at a time. She's definitely not the same bubbly child she used to be. But I'm hoping that in time, she can heal from all of this."

Abrianna lowered her head and sipped her water. She knew as well as Penny that it was unlikely that her daughter, Lovely, would ever heal. Cope, yes. Heal, no.

"Is it all right if we talk to her?"

Penny hesitated. "I don't know if it will do any good. There have been at least a half a dozen child therapists out here, and Lovely hasn't talked to a single one of them.

"I know you," a voice said, startling the adults in the room.

Lovely Belfleur had entered the living room without anyone noticing. But it was clear whom she was talking to.

"Lovely, you spoke," Penny said, shocked.

Abrianna locked gazes with the child.

"You're Abrianna," Lovely said.

Stunned, Abrianna smiled back. "Why, yes. I am. And you must be Lovely."

"He used to make me pretend to be you."

Abrianna's heart dropped.

Penny rushed to her daughter's side. "Who, baby?"

"The monster. He made me call him daddy."

Office of the Washington Post

By the time Tomi arrived at the office, the news of Marion Parker's arrest had gone viral. Bailey was in

Tomi's cubicle before she'd powered up her computer. "In my office," he said and kept moving.

Jayson popped up. "That doesn't sound good."

She frowned, wondering what in the hell she could've done now. Quickly, she put her stuff away and raced to catch up with the boss. The whole time, she hoped that she wasn't about to be canned.

"Yes, sir? You wanted to speak with me?"

"Yeah. Have a seat," he said.

"Okay." She drew a deep breath, plastered on a smile, and then took a seat.

"You got a problem," Bailey said bluntly.

"I do?"

"Yep. I received word that we've been bought out. Effective Monday morning, we're going to be under new management."

"Uh. I didn't know the paper was up for sale."

"It wasn't," Bailey said. "But the owners were offered a deal they couldn't refuse. You want to take a guess on who is the new owner?"

Tomi had no idea, but judging by the way Bailey looked her, she should. She thought about it and then the answer hit her. "Cargill Parker?"

"Bingo."

"Shit." This was surreal. "He can do this?"

"No law against buying a paper."

"All right. So . . . am I fired?"

"No."

She sighed, relieved.

"At least not yet," Bailey modified. "And I'm including myself in this calculation."

"I see."

"Don't sweat it, kid. You can pretty much write your own ticket in this town. Probably even get your own book deal, too."

That didn't make her feel any better. "All right. So maybe if I keep my head down, he'll forget about me."

"You can try to do that," Bailey acquiesced. "Or . . ."

"Or?"

"Or you can write something worth getting fired for." He peered over his glasses. "That's if you catch my drift."

———※———

Abrianna and Castillo left the Belfleurs' driveway and dialed Kellerman's office from the car.

"Guess who is your new best friend," Castillo teased.

"Gigi." Kellerman laughed. "What are you talking about? I thought that we were already best friends?"

"That's because you live in an alternate universe," Castillo countered.

"Nope. In my alternate universe, you're Mrs. Kellerman instead of your ball-breaking sister."

Abrianna cut Castillo a look.

"He's joking," Castillo told her.

Kellerman sobered. "What? Is someone on the call with you?"

"Relax. It's not Shannon. You're on speakerphone, and I have Abrianna Parker with me."

"Gee. Thanks for the heads-up," he grumbled.

"Sorry. My bad. But hey, I wanted to tell you the good news. We just came from the Belfleurs' place and believe it or not, we finally got Lovely to talk."

"No shit? Is she saying anything that can help us nail this asshole?"

"Oh, yeah. Specifically Cargill Parker and the sick role-playing games that he made her participate in."

"I don't believe it. This is great fucking news," he said. "Holy shit. Wait until Randall hears this. How the fuck did you get her to talk? We must've had like seven child psychologists go out there."

"Actually, it was Abrianna who did it." She flashed a smile to Abrianna. "Lovely took one look at her and spilled her guts."

Abrianna smiled and was proud that she had been able to get Lovely to open up, but guilt also crashed within her at learning that Cargill had other children pretend to be her. His sickness knew no bounds.

Kellerman said, "Look, I'm a hit you later. I'm going to tell Randall the good news. Good job, ladies. Bree, I hope you will to go back out there with one of our guys so we can get the proper documentation."

"Of course. I'm willing to do all I can to help end this madness."

"Great. I'll talk to you ladies later."

The women disconnected the call and gave each other a high-five. When they returned to the Agency, everyone in the office looked glum.

Abrianna sighed. "What is it now?"

Everyone's gazes shifted to Kadir, their faces clearly urging him to be the one to tell them the bad news.

"It's Marion," Kadir said. "She has been arrested."

57

"We interrupt this program for breaking news: Former President Daniel Walker has died this afternoon in Dallas, Texas. He was discovered unconscious by his wife, Nancy. He had apparently lapsed into a deep coma after suffering a massive heart attack. He was rushed to Baylor University Medical Center but then died at 5:42 this morning. He was fifty-six years old. This news comes as the former president was embroiled in a Capitol Hill murder that many have called the political scandal of the century."

Home from her and Rocky's morning run, Tomi stared openmouthed at the morning's breaking news on TV. Within minutes, her house phone and her cell phone rang. Somehow, she snapped out of her trance and caught the cell phone caller before it was transferred to voice mail.

"Yeah."

"Can you believe this?" Jayson asked, sounding as stunned as she felt.

"I'm waiting for someone to pinch me right now."

"President Washington has got to be sighing in relief. This spares the country a trial and the eventual presidential pardon that would've tanked her in next year's election."

"There's that," Tomi said, shaking her head. "But a heart attack at fifty-six? He always seemed so fit."

"Might've been genetics," Jayson said. "Can't alter that."

Tomi almost laughed. "Some might disagree with you on that."

"What?"

"Nothing." She finally shook off the morning shock. "I'll see you in the office. I have to jump in the shower and then feed Rocky."

"You got it."

They hung up, and she headed off to the shower, marveling at the latest news. "A heart attack?"

⇒•⇐

President Kate Washington was a wreck when she received the news of Daniel's death. Initially, she was in shock, and then she was convinced that there had been a mistake.

There was not a mistake.

She excused herself from a meeting with President Zuma of South Africa to retreat to the White House's private quarters. She ignored her husband, who was entertaining guests, and hid in her room until her chief of staff came looking for her.

A speech was expected in the Rose Garden about Daniel. For about a half an hour, she honestly didn't know whether she could do it. Guilt besieged her. Daniel was dead because of *her* ambition. It wasn't enough that she had taken his job, but the added stress of her not immediately issuing a pardon to avoid charges of co-conspiring to murder was no doubt the cause of his massive heart attack.

Eventually, she dried her tears, looked in the mirror, and reminded herself who she was: the president of the United States. She owed no apologies to anyone for making it to the top. By the time she returned to the West Wing, there wasn't a trace left of her distress. When she stepped out into the Rose Garden, for the first time she truly felt like the most powerful woman on earth.

58

The Bunker

On off hours from the Agency, Ghost and Kadir ghosted around the T4S system, using Dr. Zacher's ID and passcode to access and copy files. Between his full-time hours at the Agency and the T4S probing he did with Ghost as a part-time job, Kadir was borderline sleep deprived. Tonight, their debate was on how they wanted to get the information out to the public without attaching Abrianna or Tomi Lehane's name. Thus far, there was no way to put the information out without the average reader connecting the dots to the women.

"We have to respect their wishes to remain private," Kadir argued. "Neither of the women wants to have this scab ripped off in public. We can remove *all* the names or change them."

"Then it's not the whole truth, man," Ghost countered. "I'm in the truth business. Without the real names, it's fan fiction."

Roger put in his two cents. "If you ask me—"

"Which we didn't," Ghost countered.

"Go on," Kadir said.

"Releasing the information redacted or otherwise will force T4S to erase their tracks. Right now, it's more like they want to monitor Abrianna closely. The idea of exposing the program and associating them with Avery's serial killing may force them to eliminate all evidence."

"Erase? You mean they'd kill her?"

"I don't see where they'd have a choice. Do you?"

Kadir's hard gaze swung to Ghost.

Ghost sighed. "All right. We *don't* release the information."

"Thank you."

"For now," Ghost said. "But we have an obligation to the truth."

Kadir agreed and understood. He would like nothing more than to storm the place and lay everyone out for what they'd done not only to Abrianna but to all the teenagers and test subjects in their labs. It was wrong, unethical, and inhumane.

"Wait a minute," Kadir mumbled under his breath.

"Whatcha got?" Ghost asked.

"Dr. Zacher has a personal lab file."

Ghost rolled his chair over to read Kadir's computer screen. "What do you mean?"

Kadir couldn't believe his eyes. "He's testing this shit on himself."

"You're fuckin' kidding me."

"No. Look." He pointed to where he was looking, but reading the most recent notes made his heart drop. "He's dying."

Another night and Abrianna couldn't sleep. This time, she didn't even try. She stayed up in her and Kadir's new two-bedroom apartment, pacing before the television, watching alternating top stories between President Walker's surprising heart attack and Marion's arrest. "She's in there because of me," she kept repeating.

Kadir arrived home. "You're up worrying again." He shut the front door, shaking his head. "Come on. Let's go to bed." He tossed his house keys onto the counter.

"I'll be there in a moment," Abrianna said, blowing him off.

Kadir saw what she was watching on the television. "It's not your fault," Kadir said. "She knew what was going on. I don't understand why you're beating yourself up over this. Given the circumstances, you can't be concerned about being labeled a snitch. The goal is to shut this shit down. If she's a part of it . . . ?"

"You don't understand."

"I'm trying to understand. Honest."

Abrianna stopped pacing and cupped her forehead; however, her head's constant buzzing wasn't the only thing bringing tears to her eyes. "How about this, what makes Marion any different than me? I know I gave her hell when I last saw her, but really, what's the difference? Why isn't she a product of her environment the same way that I am?"

"I don't follow."

"Really? How did you feel when you were locked up and all your freedoms were taken away from you? How did it feel as a man to have to ask for *permission* to do such basic human needs as go to the bathroom? You're told when to eat, sleep, and shit. Someone is watching your every move, and you better believe there are severe consequences if you don't do as you're told. A lifetime of that may lead you to block out atrocities, to secretly drink or get high." She lowered her head. "A lifetime like that, you'd train yourself how to get as small as you possibly can and pray that nobody notices you."

Tears leaped over her lashes. "I was angry, and I shouldn't have said some of the things I said to her."

"Shhh." Kadir pulled her into his arms. "I see your point. I don't know Marion. I just hate that she didn't protect you better. I shouldn't judge."

Abrianna placed her head against Kadir's chest. "I've been judging her for a long time. Marion once said some horrible things to me, and now . . . I don't think she meant them. She was heartbroken that I had . . . that I . . . *killed* Samuel."

"What?" Kadir took a half a step back and peered down at her.

Her heart clenched tighter. *Here comes the judgment.* "I was nine. Cargill was . . . abusing Samuel and . . . he was screaming. It sounded awful. I can close my eyes at any time and still hear that scream. As usual, I had hid in my closet, hoping . . . praying that it would stop. That Cargill would stop, but . . . he never did. None of us could stop him. But that night, I thought I could do it. I told myself that I had to." Needing to breathe, Abrianna pulled out of Kadir's arms. She swiped beneath her eyes once and then let the tears flow, but this time she was determined to get through this.

To his credit, Kadir stood patiently, ready to listen.

"Finally, I couldn't take it anymore. I crawled out of the closet and went and took Cargill's gun out of the safe. I had to stop him. Nobody else was going to do it. But then I entered Samuel's room and . . . once I started shooting, I couldn't stop. I hit Cargill, but I also hit Samuel." She choked on a sob, and before she knew it, she was back in Kadir's arms.

As she'd secretly prayed, he resumed whispering, "It's all right. It's okay."

"No. It's not all right. He's dead because of me."

Kadir was speechless, but continued to hold her.

Abrianna sobbed. She may have confessed, but she would never forgive herself. Never.

Tomi needed to come at Cargill Parker hard, but what could she dig up that she hadn't already learned through Abrianna? She spent most of the afternoon trying to find out the official charges that Marion had been arrested for, as all Capitol Hill reporters were doing at that moment. Of course it *had* to be something to do with her husband's charges. Had Marion known what was happening the whole time? She had to have known—common sense. But why hadn't Abrianna said so? And why was Samuel off limits?

Lautner alluded that Abrianna had something to do with his death, but Marion had said that the kid was killed in a freak firearm accident, hadn't she? For a while, Tomi tried to make one plus one add up to something other than two. But alternative facts weren't going to help her with the truth that was staring her in the face.

Did Abrianna kill her own brother—by accident? She had to add the mental tag because she couldn't believe that it could've gone down any other way.

She returned to her numerous files on the Parkers, and she dug again in all the states that the Parkers owned property, and still she couldn't find a death certificate or even a live birth certificate for a Samuel

Parker. Then she thought maybe Marion was Samuel's birth mother, but Cargill wasn't the birth father, so she dug for Marion's maiden name. She couldn't find that, either. It was hours before she found one certificate for a Marion Parker in Puerto Rico. She almost dismissed it, because what were the chances of her maiden name being the same as her married name? She clicked on the public record and was surprised to see Duke Parker's name listed as the father on the certificate. She paused, rolled the information around in her head for a while. But it was another one plus one equation.

"It can't be, could it?" Tomi asked her computer screen. "Marion Parker isn't Cargill's wife, but his sister?"

Cargill was fit to be tied over Marion's arrest and beyond pissed that Lautner had been unable to do anything about it.

Lautner sighed and told his client yet again, "We knew that this could happen."

"Get her the fuck out of there. Now!"

"You're upset, but I need for you to keep a level head. We both know that Marion won't talk. If anyone knows the rules of this game, it's Marion. She won't dare cross the Dragons."

Cargill nodded, but he couldn't dispel a lingering bad feeling. Marion had been acting . . . off, lately. For example, she gave an interview to a damn *newspaper* when she knew better.

"Cargill, are you still there?"

"Yeah. I'm here." He walked over to the wet bar; the protesters outside briefly caught his attention.

"I'll call down there and see if I can speed up the arraignment. They aren't giving me an explanation to why she wasn't arraigned this morning, but I'll have her home soon."

"She was never supposed to be arrested. You assured me."

"No. I've always maintained that it was a slim possibility."

"I don't like it." He reached for the bourbon decanter, but then changed his mind and went for the brandy.

"I know. But to be honest, for appearance's sake, it's good that she's been arrested. We need to check all the right boxes for this defense. Everything is going according to plan, especially with Walker out of the way."

He'd almost forgotten. "Yeah. It's still all over the news along with Marion's arrest." Cargill sighed. "Massive heart attack. Nice touch."

"Thank you."

"I'd rather the asshole had suffered, though."

"Suffering leaves evidence and raises too many questions," Lautner reminded him. "But, uh . . ."

Cargill tensed. "But what? Spit it out."

"I'm handling it, but . . . I spoke with Randall. There are a couple of hiccups."

I knew it. "We've spent a fortune getting her to lose and erase evidence. How much are these hiccups going to cost me now?"

Lautner hesitated.

"That much?"

"Randall claimed that she had had a heated argument with Kellerman. It was bad enough for her to think he'd quit and might go directly to the press about suspicions of her sabotaging the case."

Cargill drained his brandy. "If it's not one thing, it's another."

"Agreed."

"Then take care of him."

"I don't think it's that simple, and neither does she. Apparently, Abrianna and a detective . . . Castillo? I think I'm pronouncing that right."

"Castillo?"

"Do you know her?"

"We both do. She's the ex-cop that rescued Abrianna years ago."

"Oh."

"Damn it! I *knew* that bitch was lying. She knew where Abrianna was this whole time."

Lautner cleared his throat. "They paid a visit to a little girl named Lovely Belfleur. Do you know who that is?"

Cargill's chest squeezed.

"If you don't, apparently this little girl remembers you. According to this Kellerman fella, the little girl took one look at Abrianna and spilled her guts."

"Fuck!" Cargill threw his glass across the room. It shattered against the portrait of his grim-faced father.

"I'm going to take that as a *yes,*" Lautner said, sighing. "Anyway, I think you see the problem. Randall told Kellerman that she didn't want to risk putting the little girl on the stand, and he lost his mind on her. President Walker was a big get, but if we start dropping too many bodies, it will be the same thing as planting a big red guilty flag in your front yard. I got to tell you, I'm surprised Abrianna is turning out to be a woman of her word. She's determined to take us off the dance floor."

Cargill surprised himself by laughing. "Hardly."

"So what do you want to do?" Lautner asked.

Cargill made himself another drink and processed

everything. "We don't need to drop a trail of bodies. "We need to drop the right one."

"What are you thinking?"

"I think that little Lovely has outlived her usefulness. We take her out, and Randall's shoddy case continues to fall apart, and that other fella has nothing to report to the press. But we have to take care of it swiftly."

"You got it." Lautner laughed.

"Good. But make sure you get Marion out of jail first. If Abrianna decides to pay her a visit, I don't want her to all of sudden get diarrhea of the mouth, too. I want Marion where I can keep an eye on her."

***

Castillo couldn't believe her ears when Kellerman called. "What do you mean your boss doesn't want to use Lovely as a witness? She's your star witness. I recorded most of the interview on my phone. Do you want me to send you a digital file so you can take it to her and convince her?"

"Send it over to my personal email in case I no longer have a job and can't access my computer in the morning."

"She fired you?"

"Not exactly. I may have quit. I'm not sure. I was so mad, I may have blacked out and said some things that may affect my being able to pay the mortgage next month. But something is going on. I think I accused Randall of personally sabotaging our case during that rage blackout, too. But I will take this to the press if I have to."

"I don't fucking believe this," Castillo groaned. "This is . . . beyond."

'What is it?' Abrianna mouthed to her.

"All right, Melvin. I'll send that recording over. *Please* do what you can." She hung up and looked at her curious crew. "The attorney general doesn't want Melvin to put Lovely on the stand."

"Why?" Abrianna asked, shocked.

"He's not really sure, but he thinks that she's trying to sabotage the case."

"Shit. Of course." Abrianna groaned. "This is like Bowen again. Randall is probably on Cargill's payroll, too. In fact, I'm willing to bet my life on it. The missing surveillance, erased files, and Randall's initial anger at Kellerman bringing me onboard. It all makes sense. There's nothing that man's money can't buy. I wouldn't even be surprised if he's somehow behind what happened to President Walker."

Castillo laughed as if that was a bridge too far. "I doubt that he has the power to take out a president—former or otherwise. They are always surrounded by Secret Service."

Abrianna gave her a look that made her reconsider her words.

"That sounded incredibly naïve, didn't it?"

Abrianna nodded and then turned away and headed to the door.

"Where are you going?" Kadir asked, looking up from his terminal.

"To see Randall. I'm gonna give that bitch a piece of my mind. Whoever's turn it is to play babysitter needs to come on."

Kadir climbed out of his seat and raced to catch up.

Castillo shook her head when she noticed Draya's pensive look. "What is it?"

"If that attorney chick really is on the take and she

now knows that the little girl is talking, doesn't that mean that Cargill knows that she's taking?"

Castillo's heart dropped, but she sprang to her feet.

Julian looked up from his pile of research. "Do you need a babysitter, too?"

"You got a weapon?"

"Never leave home without it," Julian said.

"Then come on, if you're coming," Castillo said.

Feeling left out, Draya grabbed her purse and scrambled from behind her desk. "Wait for me!"

59

Abrianna and Kadir marched into the Department of Justice building off Constitution Avenue and drew wide-eyed stares when she demanded to see Randall.

"I'm sorry, but the attorney general—"

"Never mind, I'll look for her myself," Abrianna snapped.

"Wait. Ma'am, you can't go back there!"

Abrianna ignored the woman and stormed through the place until she found Randall's name printed on a glass office door and then entered without knocking.

"It's okay, Suzanna. There's no need to call security," Randall told the receptionist and then hung up the phone. "Please." She gestured toward two chairs in front of her desk. "Have a seat."

"I'd rather stand and curse you the fuck out."

Randall leaned back in her leather chair, arms crossed. "Oh, really?"

"Humph." Abrianna smirked. "You really had me fooled. That faked passion about locking Cargill up. Hollering about your and everyone's career being on the line and blah, blah, blah. I mean, really. Fuck those Hollywood bitches. You got the acting game on lock."

"I see you're pushing a lot of hot air around, but you're not saying shit."

"Then let me be clear. You're on the take. You're on daddy's payroll. You've been sabotaging your own case this whole time."

"That's a very serious charge, Ms. Parker. Have you been talking to Kellerman?"

"I don't know why it didn't hit me sooner. But that whole bit about no video surveillance. It's bullshit. My father made it his business to always know what was going on at all times—on all his properties. Cargill is a watcher. He watches—everything. It's why I spent a lot of time in a closet growing up. I was always trying to hide from his prying eyes. Where are the tapes?"

"Sounds like a question that we need to ask your father."

"See. That's just it. He doesn't have them."

"Okay. Now I'm confused. You tell me that your father records everything, but he doesn't have these mysterious recordings."

"No. You do."

Randall laughed. "We're going around in circles. I already told you that we don't have surveillance from the club. None of the cameras were operating that night."

"Yeah. I know what you said, but a lie ain't nothing for a bitch to tell. You have those tapes and you're blackmailing him for a nice payday. In fact, you're making a whole lot of shit disappear, including where those children came from. You'll drag this shit out until the whole case collapses, guaranteeing that Cargill will walk."

"You"—Randall stood—"have a *damn* good imagination. And a big set of balls to come charging into my office and hurling wild and unfounded accusations. What? Are you wired again? Am I suddenly supposed to break down with a deathbed confession?"

"No. I'm not wired. But I will do you a solid and warn you."

Randall stopped within inches of Abrianna. "Warn me?"

"Yeah. You have no idea who you're fucking with."

"Humph. Correct me if I'm wrong, but that sounds more like a threat and not a warning."

"Take it any way you like it. But it's not me who you need to look out for it. It's Cargill. You're a fool if you think he'll ever let anyone get the best of him, especially a woman."

Randall glared. "You know, Ms. Parker, I don't think your services will be needed after all. Mr. Lautner may be right about you. You're simply not a credible witness for us to put on the stand. You know, with the Avery trauma and your heavy drug use. I hope you understand."

Abrianna smiled. "Fuck you, Ms. Randall."

"No. Fuck you, Ms. Parker. And I don't advise that you repeat that wild diatribe to anyone in the press or I will bring the full force of this department to raid through your closet of skeletons. In case you didn't know, there is no statute of limitation for murder."

A heat wave rolled over Abrianna's face.

Randall's eyes bulged as she rasped for air and clawed at her neck.

"Don't you *ever* threaten me!" Abrianna stepped back.

Randall dropped to her knees, face darkening as the veins in her neck bulged.

"Bree, stop!" Kadir grabbed her by the shoulder.

"Ohmigod," Suzanna gasped, rushing into the office toward her boss. "Ms. Randall, are you all right?"

Her concentration broken, Abrianna released her invisible grip on the attorney general's neck.

Randall raked in a huge, ragged gulp of air and then choked on it.

Suzanna scrambled to retrieve her boss's bottled water from her desk.

Abrianna waited until Randall cast her frightened eyes up at her. "I'm glad that we had this talk." She smiled and left the bewildered attorney on her knees.

———— ⋙•◦•⋘ ————

Castillo, Julian, and Draya were engaged in an old-fashioned stakeout, complete with junk food and stale coffee to keep them awake.

"Maybe we're overreacting," Julian suggested. "That's always possible, isn't it?"

"Anything is possible." Castillo sighed, scanning the Belfleurs' neighborhood's dark streets.

"So how long are we staying out here?" Draya asked. "I mean, we can't hang out forever."

"You're more than welcome to leave if you want. Nobody is holding a gun to your head."

"I'm not complaining," she lied. "I'm stating a fact. We have to have some kind of plan."

Two patrol cars turned onto the street. As they approached Castillo's car, they slowed and rolled down their windows.

Castillo did likewise. "Good evening, gentlemen. What can I do for you?"

"Are you Castillo?" the cop asked.

The question surprised her. "I am," she said, reaching for her weapon.

"Holder said that he'd like to see his girlfriend sometime and sent us to take over the stakeout of the Belfleurs."

Draya mumbled, "Thank God."

"He did, did he?" Castillo relaxed.

"We're just the messengers." They rolled past her and parked a few feet down the road.

Castillo grabbed her phone.

"I take it your replacements have arrived," Dennis said.

"They have, and thank you. I don't think my new partners are cut out for this kind of work."

Draya and Julian protested.

"Well, call it a night. I'll move some numbers around and keep the Belfleurs under police protection for a few days. Now dump your partners and get your ass home. I'm tired of waking up in an empty bed."

"Aye, aye, Captain."

* * *

The Bunker

Ghost laughed and kept wiping tears from his eyes.

Annoyed, Kadir stood stone-faced and waited for his friend to get a grip. "Are you finished?"

"No. I wish I could have been a fly on the wall. That shit sounds hilarious."

Abrianna shrugged. "I thought so, too."

"It's not," Kadir insisted. "You can't go around choking people like that. Whatever happened to keeping a low profile? That woman is probably burning sage and putting up crucifixes in her office right now."

"Good. Her crooked ass deserved it. All of this work that we are doing is a waste of time if Randall is sabotaging the case. We may as well give up now."

"No. We're not going to give up," Kadir said sternly. "We're doing this for the children, not for her. Besides, you promised."

"No. I promised that I wouldn't use my abilities on *you*. I never said that I would never use it on anyone else. Besides, I can't always control it."

"What do you mean?" Ghost asked.

"I don't know. *Lately,* whenever I get upset things . . . happen."

"Things like what?" Kadir asked, intrigued.

"I don't know. Things . . . break."

"Explain."

"Well, like the first time it happened. I was here. I broke the bathroom mirror by just . . . staring at it."

"So that's what happened to it," Ghost said.

"Then, I remember I got upset once at the hospital and the television exploded, and then it happened again at Bowen's office. It didn't used to happen."

"I wonder why the change," Ghost said, thinking.

Abrianna thought it over. "Really. Ever since the . . ." *The weekend at the Hay-Adams.*

"Bree?" Kadir cocked his head.

A montage of events sped through her head. The times when her abilities were heightened and the times the buzzing became a stream of voices. "It's the Cotton Candy."

Kadir leaned forward. "Excuse me?"

She looked up. "Uh, nothing. I . . . I'll try to be more careful," she said, wanting to change the subject. Kadir would hit the roof if he knew that she was self-medicating again—albeit a much lower dose with the Cotton Candy.

"What all can you do?" Ghost said, still intrigued. "Do you even know?"

She shook her head. "Not until I do it. Like tonight,

I was so angry that I *wanted* to choke the shit out of Randall. The next thing I knew, she couldn't breathe."

"And you got that Zeke dude to shoot himself in the face," Ghost reminded her.

Kadir added, "And you threw that one guy up against the house. Maybe we should perform our own set of tests on your abilities."

"If I don't want to be a government lab rat, what makes you think that I want to be yours?"

"It's not for us," Ghost said. "It's for you. Don't you want to know what you're capable of? Hell, the way trouble keeps finding your ass, the shit is valuable information."

Kadir nodded. "I agree for once."

"I'll think about it."

"Can't ask for more than that," Ghost said. He looked to his crew. "You guys ready to rock and roll?"

"What's going on?" Abrianna asked.

"Well, as you know, we've been narrowing down the list of possibilities of who's been helping Cargill traffic the children. We've been hitting a couple of places, rummaging around the homes or offices for something concrete. Nada, of course. We hit that Peter Lautner cat's crib last night. So tonight we figured we go to his office downtown."

"Yeah?" She turned excited eyes toward Kadir. "Mind if I tag along?"

"I-I, uh?" He looked to Ghost.

"Sure. Why not? We're packing light, though. You got your piece on you?"

"Of course."

"Great. You can be out in the van with Roger and Wendell."

"Wait. What?"

"Take it or leave it."

"Fine," she huffed. "I'll take it."

———◆———

The old breaking and entering gang was back together again. The mark was Lautner's D.C. law office.
This time Kadir and Julian would work to jam the
building's security system while Ghost and Wendell
broke in.

"I don't get why we have to change up," Kadir complained.

"You're on parole," Ghost reminded him.

"What damn difference does that make? If we get
caught, we're all going to jail."

"Good point. Fine. Me and you."

"I should be doing *something*," Abrianna said.

Ghost grinned. "Look at you. You do one break-in
and then you're already hooked. Maybe when you're
finished playing detective with that ex-cop, you can
come on over to the dark side and join the revolution."

Kadir groaned. "Oh, God. Not the revolution again."

"Really? Your mutant girlfriend there is a byproduct
of the man, and you still aren't a believer?"

"I didn't say that—"

Abrianna snapped, "Are we going to do this or
not?"

Ghost and Kadir killed their quarreling and slid on
their backpacks of tools.

Wendell and Julian mouthed "Thank you" to her.

"Cameras are down," Wendell said. "Delaying backup signal. We got ten minutes, aim for eight."

"All right," Ghost said. "Let's rock and roll." He
slid open the side door as the van slowed near the law
office, and Kadir and Ghost jumped out.

Roger kept driving while Abrianna slammed the door closed again.

Kadir and Ghost hustled toward the glass front door.

Ghost produced a small tool set, much like Abrianna's, and got them through the first door within seconds.

Abrianna crossed her fingers. Getting into the place and bypassing the security system wasn't a problem. She worried about searching, finding, breaking into an unknown safe, grabbing everything, and making it out in eight minutes. It sounded impossible.

Rogers parked three blocks down and killed the lights. Out of view, but still in range of their video/audio connection on the computer.

Abrianna huddled behind Wendell in the back of the van, watching the video feed from the camera strapped on Ghost. Two minutes into the caper, Ghost and Kadir made it into Lautner's office. But then the camera cut out.

"What in the hell happened?"

"I don't know." Wendell's fingers flew across the keyboard. "Fellas, can you hear me?"

"Yah. What's up?" Ghost asked.

Abrianna sighed in relief.

"We lost visual," Wendell told him.

"We're good. Found th—" Ghost's voice mixed with a lot of static feedback blasted over the line.

Abrianna frowned.

"Ghost, man. Are you there?" Wendell checked.

A weird noise buzzed on the line, and there was nothing.

"Looks like we lost audio as well."

"That can't be good," Abrianna fretted. "I got a bad feeling about this."

"It's all right. Calm down," Wendell told her. "Don't forget this isn't Ghost's first time at the rodeo. He knows what he's doing."

The third minute passed.

Fourth minute passed.

"Maybe we should circle back around and make sure the coast is still clear front side," she suggested.

Roger glanced at Wendell, who shrugged and left the decision up to him.

"Let's give it another minute."

The next sixty seconds were torture, but the instant the clock on the computer rolled into the fifth minute, she snapped, "Go, go, go!"

Roger spun around and started the van to circle around to the law office.

"Hey, where did those cars come from?" Abrianna gasped, pointing.

"Oh, shit," Roger grumbled. "Wendell, do you have a feed yet?"

"No bueno," he said shaking his head.

"Let me out," Abrianna demanded.

"What?"

"You heard me, let me out."

"No way," Roger said. "Ghost would kill—"

Abrianna glanced down at the brake pedal, and the van screeched to a stop.

Roger gasped. "What the fuck?"

She threw open the van door and jumped out.

"Hey," the guys yelled.

With no time to argue, Abrianna took off toward the building; when she pulled on the door, it was locked. A scorching heat rolled through her veins, and when she touched the door again, the glass exploded.

———◆———

Chris Lautner jumped. "What in the hell?"

Kadir threw back his elbow and nailed Chris in the chest.

Chris's gun fired, nailing one of his three cohorts in the neck.

That guy's gun also went off, firing a round into Ghost's chest. He stumbled back, but thanks to a bullet-proof vest, the shot only succeeded in pissing him off.

"Muthafucka!" He launched forward, fists whaling on the man. Next to him, Kadir and Lautner went at it. The bloody lawyer turned out to be an experienced fighter and a good adversary. He blocked and landed as many body blows as Kadir dealt.

———◆———

As she heard gunfire, Abrianna's panic escalated. She raced in its direction. In her haste, she ignored the buzzing in her head and was blindsided when something crashed against her skull and then she took second blow to the head when she hit the floor.

Ghost and Kadir were winning their matches, when the fourth man returned to the fray, dragging in Abrianna by one arm. "That's enough, ladies," the man thundered.

Kadir froze and missed his chance to duck before Lautner's fist connected to his chin. His knees buckled as he tumbled to the floor.

Ghost ignored the fourth man and kept swinging on his opponent. The fourth guy fired up into the ceiling and finally won Ghost's attention. He stopped pummeling his opponent and released him to collapse against the floor.

"Step back," the fourth man ordered.

Ghost stepped back.

Panting, Lautner looked at Abrianna. "Ahhh. Now I

know where I've seen you before," he said to Kadir and smiled, showcasing a rack of bloody teeth. "Cargill has been itching to meet you." He picked up his gun and crossed over to his desk. "This coup should earn me a nice bonus." He glanced at his fourth man. "Is she dead?"

He knelt and felt for a pulse. His stony expression collapsed into concern. "Shit."

Lautner stopped dialing. "What is it?"

"I can't find a pulse."

Kadir's heart dropped. "What?" He sprang forward, but the fourth guy leveled his weapon straight at him. "Ah. Ah. Ah. Back up!"

Kadir stopped on a dime.

The redhead grinned, "All right, Mr. Hero, back up and stand next to your boyfriend over there."

Chris shook his head. "If she's dead, then so much for that bonus." He picked up the phone and referred to his downed man. "Vince, how about Scotty?"

Vince knelt with his gun still trained on Ghost to check his partner.

"Scotty's gone."

Chris sighed. "Damn." He looked at Kadir and Ghost. "I liked Scotty."

Ghost shrugged. "*You* shot him."

Chris's eyes narrowed. "All right, smartass. Why the fuck are you guys in my uncle's office? What the hell were you looking for?"

Abrianna moaned, startling the redhead.

"Holy shit!"

Chris perked up. "Well. Looks like that bonus is back on the table." He looked back to Kadir and Ghost. "Things still don't look too good for you two, though. But before we kill you, I still want to know what the hell you were looking for. Money or . . . ?"

Neither Ghost nor Kadir responded.

"How about this? If you tell me, I'll make sure that we kill you quick. If not, Red over there does some really good knife work—and he likes to take his time."

Silence.

"No?" Chris double-checked. "Too bad. Red?"

Red grinned. "I was hoping to get to carve up a little girl this week, but I guess you two will do." He reached into his jacket with his free hand and removed a tactical bowie knife.

Kadir gulped, but despite his racing heart, he held onto his stony expression.

Chris said, "Last chance, boys."

Kadir shook his head and then watched Red grip the blade, a clear indication that he was going to launch it at him. "Bree, if you can hear me, I can really use your help right about now."

Red frowned and then laughed. "Don't worry, man. I'll tell her how you died screaming like a bitch." He launched the knife.

"Duck," Ghost yelled, moving to shove Kadir out of the way, but miraculously the knife shifted direction and nailed Vince in the center of his forehead.

Lautner and Red jumped back. "What the fuck?"

Vince remained standing for a few seconds, slow to realize that he was dead. The men marveled, but then finally Vince slammed to the floor.

"Shit." Chris dropped the phone and rushed toward Vince, but the moment he came around the desk he went flying backward, crashing out of the window.

At the same time, Red flew up toward the ceiling, twice. His neck cracked with a sickening crunch before he flopped onto the floor.

Abrianna sat up and sneered at Red. "Teach you to fucking hit me on the back of the head, *bitch*."

Ghost gave her a slow clap while Kadir raced to her side to check on her.

"Are you all right?"

"I think so. Yeah."

He frowned. "Your nose is bleeding."

"Huh?" She swiped her nose. "Oh."

Ghost grabbed their bags. "We got to get out of here. We're waaay past eight minutes."

"What happened?" Abrianna asked.

"Apparently, Lautner's nephew sometimes falls asleep in the office," Kadir said. "His heavies showed up within minutes of our breaking in to the office. By that time, Lautner already had the jump on us."

"Did you find the safe?"

"Yeah," Kadir told her. "But nothing but money and gold bars. We left it. We're not those kind of thieves."

The sound of rushing feet drew their attention. Seconds later, Wendell rushed inside, assault weapon in his hand. "What's going on?" He peeked into the office and saw the three bodies.

"Well, it's about time," Ghost said.

"Bree said for us to keep circling. When we saw a body fly out of the window, I figured maybe you needed one more backup."

"A body out of the window is the universal sign for help." Kadir chuckled. "Let's get out of here."

⸻

"Do you know what time it is, Peter?" Cargill grumbled into the phone while swiping sleep from his eyes. "It's oh dark thirty. Please tell me you have a damn good reason why you're calling me at this ridiculous hour."

"We had a break-in."

"We?"

Peter grumbled. "*I* had a break-in, and now I have a dead nephew who's been thrown out my office window downtown."

Cargill sat up. "No shit?"

"Would I fucking kid about something like that?"

"What the fuck happened? What did they take?"

"That's just it. It doesn't look like they took anything. Whoever they are. Right now this place is crawling with cops."

"You're not making any sense. Why the hell do you think that this shit has anything to do with me?"

"Because whoever broke into my law office, they were smart enough to kill the security cameras. And considering the people I pay for this shit, it had to be someone who knows what the fuck they're doing—which makes me think about that ex-con your daughter is hanging around with lately. If memory serves me correctly, he did time for doing shit like this."

"Fuck. They're fishing."

"Of course they're fishing. I believe I warned you that Abrianna was unpredictable now that she's no longer under your thumb."

Cargill cursed a blue streak as he snatched the covers off and climbed out of bed. "Please tell me that you were not dumb enough to leave any incriminating evidence about me or the Dragons down at that office!"

"Of course not. I'm not a fucking amateur. Right now I'm trying to figure out what I'm going to tell my sister about her kid."

Cargill sighed. "Focus. I only give a shit about how this mess affects *me*. If you're sure nothing was taken . . ."

"Consider this a heads-up. I'm going to reach out to the other members on your behalf and let them know to burn all incriminating evidence from all devices in their possession. If this muthafucka is bold enough to hit your law office, all bets are off on where they're going to fish next."

"Right. Right. Smart. Get on that right now. Don't wait until sunlight. Who knows how many steps behind we are with this unknown wild card."

60

After Castillo dropped Julian and Draya off at the Agency so that they could part ways, she couldn't shake a bad feeling settling in her gut. She appreciated Dennis trying to help her out tonight, but she didn't feel right going home to Netflix and chill while Lovely's life was in danger.

Cargill Parker was as evil as they came. There was nothing the billionaire wouldn't do to protect his reputation and his sick lifestyle. "Maybe I should swing back by and double-check on the guys," she told herself, missing her exit to head toward Dennis's crib. When she returned to the Belfleurs' neighborhood, there was no trace of the squad car that had relieved her less than an hour ago.

"Fuck!" Castillo scraped her tires as she pulled up next to a curb. She killed the headlights and climbed out of the car. Crouched low with her weapon gripped firmly in her good hand, she rushed toward the Belfleurs' to survey the area. The house was quiet. In fact, the entire neighborhood was as silent as a grave-yard.

I'm overreacting. It was possible. The guys could've checked out for a coffee run—or been called to a crime scene. It's no secret what the recent slash in the city's budget was doing to the department on manpower. More crime, less cops. What could go wrong?

For a full minute, Castillo debated ringing the door-bell. She was sure that Penny wouldn't appreciate a midnight scare, especially if Lovely was sound asleep in her bedroom.

A pair of headlights swung onto the quiet street be-fore a car rolled forward doing less than five miles an hour.

Castillo moved toward the hedges lining the side of the Belfleurs' home. The back doors of the mysterious vehicle were thrown open and two lean characters, dressed head-to-toe in black, sprung out without the car stopping.

Fuck! Castillo's heart shifted to run on octane and was close to hammering its way out of her chest. She had seconds to decide on a play. The one thing that she knew for sure was that it would be over her dead body that these goons would get their hands back on Lovely. When they were within ten feet of the house, she made her only play.

"Freeze," she shouted, springing out of the hedge. Not big conversationalists, they opened fired.

Lights clicked on up and down the small neighbor-hood as Castillo returned fire. The world shifted into slow motion as Castillo felt the Grim Reaper's scythe hiss behind her neck. *Any second now,* a voice whis-pered. How could it not? She was outmanned *and* out-gunned. But was she crazy, or were the bullets just grazing past her as if she was huddled behind some invisible shield? But then her right ankle buckled. As she fell in that same slow motion, she saw another pair of headlights swing onto the road. It belonged to a van.

A van she recognized.

Julian.

More bullets joined the fray.

One of Castillo's attackers pivoted toward the van only to have his head explode like a watermelon.

Castillo fired off her last bullet just as she crashed to the frozen ground and blew a new hole in her last attacker's groin. The howl that came out of the man's throat was loud enough to wake the dead. He hit the ground, his weapon forgotten, as he writhed and begged for help.

The van stopped, and Draya raced from the passenger's seat with her weapon trained on the dickless gunman. "Gigi? Are you all right?"

"I think so," Castillo said, panting and rubbing her ankle. "How did you know I was here?"

"Julian had a hunch. Plus, it did seem kind of odd those cops popping up like they did." Draya looked around. "By the way, where are they?"

That was a damn good question.

———◈◈◈———

Ghost and his men didn't know how to behave around Abrianna. None of them had ever seen anything like tonight, and each was at a different stage of processing.

"It's like having our own real-life superhero in a nice, curvy package," Roger said, a grin carving his face. "It's pretty fuckin' cool."

Wendell nodded while staring at Abrianna.

Abrianna ignored them. Her head pounded like she

had a million jackhammers running wild, not to mention her nose seemed to have sprung a leak. She went through a box of Kleenex before she jumped up and excused herself to the bathroom.

Kadir followed. "Are you all right?"

"I'm fine. I . . . I don't know." Abrianna unwound a wad of toilet paper and clogged up her leak. But she bled through the toilet paper.

Kadir ordered, "Put your head back."

She did as she was told and allowed Kadir to play doctor. By the time the bleeding slowed, Abrianna was curled up against him and light-headed.

"I guess it's still useless to suggest you see a doctor."

She smiled. "I'm afraid so."

Kadir returned a half smile. "I figured as much." Concern seized his dark gaze.

"Hey, it's fine. Haven't you heard? I heal fast."

He chuckled. "Yeah. It's been brought to my attention."

They lapsed into silence, even though it was clear that Kadir had plenty on his mind.

"Thanks for saving my life back there tonight," he said.

"Don't mention it. You've saved mine a few times, too. It's what we do."

"Yeah. It does seem to be that way."

They drifted back into a strange silence. Abrianna was sure he hadn't finished all that he had to say.

"What is it? Spit it out."

"Nothing," he lied, but then covered. "It's just that . . . that no pulse thing that you do. I'm not a fan."

He'd truly been scared, she realized. "Don't worry. You're not losing me any time soon." She kissed him.

When she pulled back, his eyes shimmered. "I'm going to hold you to that."

Ghost knocked on the open bathroom door.

Abrianna and Kadir looked up.

Ghost jutted a thumb over his shoulder. "Julian and Draya are on the back channel. Said someone made a move on that Belfleur kid tonight."

"What?" Abrianna and Kadir jumped to their feet and rushed to hear the latest saga in this long nightmare.

Castillo answered the cop's questions for the umpteenth time while demanding where the hell the two idiot police officers had been when they were supposed to be watching the Belfleurs' home. Of course, they thought they could use a donut and coffee run. Both swore they'd only been gone ten minutes, but Castillo wasn't buying it. And why the hell wasn't Dennis answering his damn phone?

It was another couple of hours before she'd arrived at his place to give him a piece of her mind. A big piece.

She knocked on the screen door and then grew impatient when he didn't answer. *Maybe he's asleep.* That irritated her even more. While she was out here dodging bullets, he's flying high in dreamland. Sighing, she grabbed the extra house key hidden underneath the planter on the porch. She was supposed to keep it, but she'd never felt right accepting it from him. It was too much of a commitment.

It turned out that she didn't need the key. The door wasn't locked.

Entering the house, Castillo instantly felt that something was wrong. The house was stuffy—hot, which didn't make sense, since it was in the middle of winter. The living room was a wreck—as usual. She bypassed it and climbed the stairs. However, her steps slowed as the hairs on the back of her neck rose and it grew harder to breathe.

"Dennis?" Her weapon was in her hand without a thought. When there was no answer, her heart clawed into her throat. *He could be asleep.* It was possible, but intuition said otherwise. At the bedroom door, she used her left foot to push it open instead of using her injured arm. Even before the door swooshed open, Castillo knew. But seeing Dennis lying a pool of blood took her breath away.

———◆———

"Is it done?" Dr. Zacher asked.

"Yes, sir," Ned informed him, closing the doctor's office door behind him. "A clean hit. I'm sure that he didn't feel a thing."

Dr. Zacher nodded and wiped his bloody nose. "Good. And did you see anything in his place about T4S or . . . myself?"

"No, but . . ."

"But?"

"I didn't get much time to search the place completely. He had a visitor pop up—so I had to cut the search short. But I'm fairly sure that he didn't have anything about you or the organization."

"Fairly sure?"

Ned nodded.

"But you *are* sure that he's dead?"

"Well, yeah. I shot him."

Zacher took a deep breath. "People survive gunshots every day."

Ned blanched.

"Well? Was he dead?"

"I . . . I think so."

Zacher stared. "You didn't check?"

"No. Like I said, someone drove up to the house."

Silence hummed in the space between them before Dr. Zacher growled. "I don't like a job done half-assed."

Ned's eyes bulged when he suddenly couldn't get air into his windpipe.

Dr. Z stood from his chair and quietly stalked toward his gasping assistant. "I needed to know *exactly* why that cop was digging around in my files. Now how am I to know just how bad our exposure is if you didn't do your job correctly?"

Ned dropped to his knees while his manicured nails clawed at his throat.

"I can't afford another screwup filtering its way to Spalding."

Ned stared up at his boss as if he was looking into the eyes of the Grim Reaper.

Zacher didn't doubt that he looked like him, either. The experimental drugs had broadened his face, thickened his skin, and made the veins in his eyes damn near glow red. "It's bad enough that you're sneaking formulas out of my lab so that you and your friends can make that ridiculous street drug Cotton Candy as a side hustle."

Ned's face purpled.

"What? You think I'm an idiot?"

Ned shook his head.

"Can't trust any damn body to do a simple-ass job anymore." Zacher's veins throbbed visibly against his temples. "I have zero margin for error. Do you understand that?"

Ned nodded and then toppled over.

"Good." Zacher released his mental hold around the kid's neck.

Ned choked on his first drag of oxygen.

"You better hope that nosy cop is the end of it. Now." Zacher drew a deep breath and reclaimed his composure. "About Ms. Lehane . . ."

61

THE PARKERS: INCEST AT FIRST SIGHT

Kadir's eyes bugged as he read the headline on his cell phone. "Holy shit!"

Abrianna looked up from her bowl of cereal. "What is it?"

Kadir kept staring at the screen, his jaw dropping lower by the second.

"Hello?" She waved her hand in front of his face, breaking the spell.

"Uh?"

"What are you reading?" she asked, smiling.

He stared at her.

"Okay. Now you're scaring me."

Kadir handed over his phone. "I'm sorry."

Abrianna took the phone and read the digital edition of the *Washington Post*. Her spoon slipped from her fingers and clanked against the bowl. Her gaze zoomed across the article. There it was in black and white, the other half of the Parkers' dark secrets for the whole world to see.

"Bree, are you all right?"

Instead of answering, her gaze drifted to the byline. "The fuck?"

The dining room table bounced on its legs.

"Whoa." Kadir gripped the table, attempting to settle it, but instead started vibrating along with it. "I'm going to kill her."

"No. No, you're not," he said. "Bree, look at me. Bree!"

Her gaze shot up.

"You need to whoosa this shit right now." To be a sport, he led by example and drew a deep breath and then slowly exhaled. "Now you. Breathe," he said, rolling his hand for her to follow along.

He looked ridiculous, but she joined him on the third breath.

"That's it." He smiled when the table settled down. "There. Don't you feel better?"

"Not really," she admitted and popped out of her seat.

"Where are you going?"

"I'm going down to that paper and give Ms. Lehane a piece of my mind. See? This is why I don't trust people. They latch on and suck the damn blood out of you!"

"I'm sure that's not the case here."

Abrianna's hands settled on her hips while she gave him an old-fashioned cobra neck. "Exactly whose side are you on?"

"There's no side."

"Oh. There's muthafuckin' sides and right now, it looks to me like your ass is Team Tomi, so why don't you pack your shit and do your rah-rah cheerleading at her fuckin' crib?"

"Whoa. Whoa." Kadir picked up a napkin and waved it. "White flag. Time out."

Abrianna's hands went from her hips to fold across her chest. "Don't play Switzerland with me."

Kadir tried again. "If there's a side, I'm riding with you. Know that. I'm tryin' to get you to take a couple of things into consideration."

"Like what?"

"Like Tomi's a reporter. She's doing what reporters do. Report shit. You said yourself several times that you two aren't friends—and even if you were, is she supposed to stop doing her job?"

Abrianna wrestled with her nerves. "First of all, she's dead-ass wrong for not *at least* giving my ass a heads-up. Second, I told her ass when she did that first interview with Marion to back the hell off. She wants to report on Cargill and the Dragons, fine. It's all good. But for her to rummage for shit like that after she carries on and on about not wanting anyone to know that *she* is a freak? She doesn't want anyone to know about what T4S has done to her—to us. But it's cool to put *all* my business on Front Street? Nah. The bitch is dead-ass wrong—and she knows it. That's why the fuck she didn't call. And that's why the fuck she needs to catch these hands."

"And then what? She's likely to be as strong as you are and probably can do all the things that you can. Fighting her isn't going to change anything."

"It'll make me feel better."

"Let it go. Don't fuck with her anymore. There are other reporters out there who will help us once we crack how Cargill traffics those children. She's not the only game in town. Far from it. We have other contacts, like Joy Walton and Greg Wallace. Fuck her."

She nodded. "Yeah. Fuck her."

Kadir grinned. "You still want me to pack my shit?"

"Depends," she said stubbornly.

"On what?"

"Are you going to stop playing Switzerland?"

"For now."

"Then you can stay . . . for now." She grinned.

———◆◆———

"What the hell is this?" Cargill stared at the *Washington Post*'s morning headline. Like a cartoon, he took both fists and rubbed his eyes as if they needed a good cleaning. He took another look. The headline remained the same. "Holy shit." He jumped up from the dining room table, abandoning his breakfast to race to his study. He turned on the television to see the words "Breaking News" emblazoned across the bottom of the screen along with his own damn paper's morning headline.

Cargill's arm tightened, and then the sensation stretched across to his chest toward his racing heart. He stumbled back a few steps and wondered if *he* was now having a heart attack. But a minute later, the pain subsided, and the air he had locked in his lungs burst free. The scare was over; he rushed to the phone and dialed Lautner. For the first time in twenty-five years, Lautner didn't answer his call, and he was transferred to voice mail.

"Goddamn it, Peter! Where the fuck are you? Have you fucking seen the damn papers? This is a nightmare! Get your ass over here right now!" He slammed the phone down and flinched at the tingling that lingered in his fingers.

Eternity was twenty minutes, Cargill discovered. That was how long it took for Lautner to call him back. "It's about goddamn time! Where the hell were you?"

"Cargill, I have some bad news," Lautner said gravely.

"No shit. It's all over the paper and on my television. What the hell is going on? Is Marion in that damn jail giving out more interviews? What the fuck has gotten into her?"

Lautner's sober tone remained steady. "Marion isn't giving any interviews—now or ever."

"What in the hell does that mean?"

"I'm sorry, Cargill, but Marion is dead."

Cargill's knees gave out and plopped him down into his desk chair. "What?"

"I'm down here at the prison. They are saying that she hung herself in her cell."

Silence.

"Cargill?"

He slammed down the phone and then chewed on his anger. "That bitch."

Abrianna couldn't stop crying. She fell apart the moment Marion's death was reported on the news. None of Kadir's well-intentioned and soothing words penetrated her cocoon of depression. The fact that she'd always thought she hated Marion didn't matter. There had always been bonds between them. Bonds of tragedy. Bonds of pain. Bonds of regret.

For two days, Kadir and her friends left her alone to grieve.

Tomi called several times, but Abrianna refused to take the calls. Tomi then tried to contact everyone in Abrianna's circle, including Castillo and, out of loyalty, they refused to take her calls, too.

Other media outlets called endlessly as well. Everyone wanted to know her response to Tomi Lehane's hit job and whether Abrianna believed that Marion had taken her life because of it.

News dribbled out about Cargill being enraged, and many suspected that he would be suing the *Washington Post*, but then the shocker of Cargill Parker being the new owner of the paper threw everyone into a tailspin.

There had been an unexpected dust-up when it had come time to claim Marion's body. According to the paper, Cargill tried to have the body cremated, but Marion's long-time friend, Tina Bouchard, emerged with documents, a will, and a mean-ass lawyer who helped her take possession of Marion's body.

Marion would get a proper burial at Ebenezer Cemetery.

The day of Marion's private burial, Abrianna surprised herself by climbing out of bed and announcing to Kadir that she was going. She didn't care that Cargill and reporters would be there. She had to say her final goodbye and do what she should have done weeks ago: forgive.

The trek out to Ebenezer Cemetery was a circus for the small group of friends that Marion had managed to collect despite Cargill's hawkish surveillance. The media weren't there for Marion, but for Cargill and Abrianna Parker, should they show up.

They did.

When Abrianna stepped out of the car with Kadir by her side, Cargill stood less than twenty feet from her. With her red eyes safely hidden behind a large pair of dark sunglasses, Abrianna ignored Cargill and walked with her head held high. The preacher said a few words and then Tina stunned everyone with one of the most powerful and soulful voices Abrianna had ever heard. The song "Trouble of the World" triggered a memory of Marion singing the song at the piano. She was always singing about an invisible God who was going to save them, and it never happened.

Abrianna resented him for that. God didn't save her or Samuel or even Marion in that cold cell. But by the time Tina reached the last line—*I'm going home to live with God*—Abrianna broke down.

Kadir helped lead her back to the car and then into their apartment.

Later that night, she recovered some and shared memories with Kadir and Shawn. Memories she'd long forgotten. They were always from when Cargill wasn't around, and most of them involved her and Marion around the piano. She'd forgotten how much Marion loved music.

"It's funny. I didn't remember before, but the first time I came to the Parkers' house Marion and Tina were at the piano, singing."

"You remember that far back? How old were you?" Shawn asked.

"I couldn't have been more than . . . five, I think."

Shawn looked at her oddly. "Cargill and Marion were never married, so . . . didn't the adoption agency check them out?"

"Money allows you to break all the rules." She paused as a thought occurred to her—to all three of them.

"It's an adoption agency!" they declared in unison.

"I don't believe it. The answer has been right in front of us the whole time," Abrianna gasped.

Kadir popped up and grabbed his laptop. "Do you know the name of the adoption agency? There are thousands, if not millions around the world."

Abrianna shook her head. "I-I have no idea. I've

never possessed any of my adoption papers." Then she remembered, "But I think I know someone who may know."

⸺◆⸺

An exhausted Tomi arrived home to an excited and hungry German shepherd dancing by the door. The doggy door in the laundry room saved her from returning to ruined carpets and floors. However, the longer hours lately made the German shepherd twice as excited and aggressive. Tomi made it no more than a couple of feet into the house before her big baby had knocked her down and slobbered all over her face.

"Okay, boy. Get off of me."

Of course, he didn't get off. They laughed, rolled around, and played for a while.

Thump!

Tomi and Rocky froze.

"What was that?" she asked.

Rocky's ears pointed up as he cocked his head from side to side.

She pushed the dog off of her and climbed to her feet. Had the sound come from upstairs or the basement? She looked to Rocky, but he just stared back. "You're a lot of help, you know that?"

Leaving her bag and purse on the floor, Tomi reached for the .38 holstered at her back. "C'mon, boy." She and the dog crept to the basement door.

Heart pounding, Tomi turned the knob and then cringed when the rusted hinges announced to the whole world that she was opening the door. She hit the light switch, but it lit the top of the stairs and not the basement.

In the three years that she'd lived in the townhouse,

she'd only been in the basement three times before. A psychiatrist wasn't needed to tell her why. Of the three Avery survivors, Tomi had been huddled in the mad scientist's basement the longest. Ten months. Ten months of hellish torture, watching other teenage girls die around her, and being scared every second that she would be next.

He's not down there. It was silly that she even had to say that as she coached herself down each step, determined to conquer her fear. At some point, she'd stopped breathing. She was sure of it. However, her heart sounded like an African drum in her ears as she crept along. At the bottom of the stairs, she hit the second switch and flooded the room with light.

Nothing.

Other than boxed summer clothes and home tools, the coast was clear.

Relieved, Tomi sighed and lowered her weapon. "I'm going crazy." She rolled her eyes and marched back up the staircase.

Rocky sat on his haunches at the top of the stairs, panting happily at her return. She closed the basement door.

"Thanks for having my back."

Rocky barked.

"Yeah, yeah. I'm going. I'm going." She holstered her weapon and headed to the kitchen. As she crossed the living room, she noticed the lace curtains billowing, the sliding glass door open. "What in the hell?" She shifted direction from the kitchen to the dining room.

A disappointed Rocky whined.

Tomi palmed her weapon again and performed another slow creep. The closer she got to the open door, the louder Rocky whined. When she reached the door and glanced out into the backyard again, she didn't see anything. She relaxed, but then her entire scalp tingled. Instinct made her duck. The sliding door exploded and became a cascade of shattered glass. Rocky barked wildly. Quickly, Tomi crawled out of the dining room.

However, her shooter wasn't outside. He was in the house.

She heard another suppressed gunshot.

Rocky cried out and then hit the floor, hard.

Tomi's scream died in her throat when she was gripped by the back of her head and snatched to her feet. A needle was jammed into her neck. Her eyes widened as the plunger emptied its drug. A poisonous fireball roared through her veins, closing off her throat and shutting off her oxygen. She dropped her weapon and slumped into the man's arms. She heard more gunfire. Her attacker released her to return fire.

She hit the floor with a *thump!* Eyes still wide open, Tomi had an unobstructed view of Rocky's still body. Her big baby. Were they now going to watch each other die? Tears swelled and blurred her vision. Smoke. Fire. Her townhouse was going up in flames.

Before losing consciousness, she was aware of her body being picked up and carried out of her townhouse and into a waiting van. The last faces she saw were Dr. Zacher and Jayson Brigham.

62

Tina Bouchard opened her door with surprise, but then graciously allowed them to enter her home.

"I'm sorry for popping up like this," Abrianna said.

"No. It's no problem." Tina closed the door behind her and Kadir. "I'm thrilled that you came. Can I take your coat?"

"Sure." Abrianna slid out of her leather jacket.

Kadir also removed his coat.

"Please, go in and sit down."

"Thanks." Abrianna waltzed in with butterflies in her belly. Of course, she instantly remembered the last time that she was there and was again filled with remorse.

"Can I get you two something to drink?"

"No. That won't be necessary," Abrianna said, taking a seat. "I hope you don't mind, but I came to ask a few questions."

"Okay." Tina took a seat across from them. "I take it that they are questions you didn't get to ask Marion the last time you were here?"

"Yes. I'm afraid so. You have no idea how much I regret that day."

"I think I have a pretty good idea," Tina said. "What's your question?"

Abrianna looked to Kadir first, who squeezed her hand in encouragement. "The last time I was here you said that you hadn't seen me since the first day I came home from the adoption agency. I remember that day now. You and Marion were sitting at a piano."

Tina smiled. "Yes. Your mother and I bonded over music."

"You wouldn't happen to remember the name of that adoption agency, would you?"

Tina's brows lifted with another wave of surprise, but then a small smile crept across her face. "Do you mind if I ask you why?"

Abrianna met Tina's gaze. "Because I'm going to take Cargill and the Dragons Templar down if it's the last thing I do."

"Now that sounds like music to my ears. I'm glad that you have the balls to actually do something. The last time Marion was here, I thought that she'd at least come to her senses, but . . ." She sighed. "Anyway . . . I don't know the name of the adoption agency."

Abrianna's hopes deflated.

"But I'm sure that Marion wrote it down. Heaven knows she was always writing things down in her diaries."

"Diaries?"

"Loads of them. I'm sure that they're all fascinating reads."

"But . . . where are they?"

"She placed them where she knew they would always be safe until the time was right. Looks like that's today."

"And where is that?"

"I have them."

———◆◆◆———

Abrianna didn't assemble the whole crew to help read through the trunk full of beautiful gold-trimmed diaries. That would be too insensitive and an invasion of her privacy. However, she did ask Shawn and Kadir, the people she trusted the most, to skim through the books. Three hours into it, everyone was emotionally exhausted reading through the horrors that were written in perfect penmanship.

"Abrianna, have you seen this?" Shawn said, lifting one of the diaries and scooting closer.

"What is it?"

"Well, according to this: Samuel wasn't Cargill's kid."

"What?"

"No. He wasn't," Tina said, drawing their attention to the bedroom door. She leaned against the doorframe with a full wineglass in one hand and a near-empty wine bottle in the other. "Asshole Cargill was too damn stupid to realize that he was shooting nothing but blanks all these years."

Tina was drunk.

"I don't understand," Bree said.

Shawn answered, "Says here that she had an affair with some guy named Michael back in '98."

Pain rippled across Tina's face. "Yep. Granted, it was before we were . . . you know. Still hurts, though." At Bree's confusion, she added, "It's always painful when someone is able to give someone you love something you can't."

"Oh." Bree lowered her gaze to the diary Shawn held. "But who was this Michael guy?"

"Just some lobbyist who used to work off of K Street. For a few playful months, he and Marion snuck around D.C. under Cargill's nose. Frankly, I think Cargill finally got hip to the game because one day Michael just '*poof*.' Vanished without a trace. Marion didn't want to believe it, though. I don't know what she told herself had happened. I just know that I was forbidden to ever mention his name again."

"So Samuel wasn't Cargill's?"

"No. Thank God for small blessings."

Abrianna frowned at Tina dragging God back into the picture. Then she thought about her first day from the adoption agency again. "I got it," she shouted. "The Lifeline Adoption Agency." Excited, she threw her arms around Shawn and Kadir and danced around in a circle. "Quick, get Castillo on the phone. We're about to make her fucking night!"

———❖———

The protesters were gone. They left the day Marion died and hadn't returned. Cargill poured himself and Peter Lautner each a bourbon. "Here's to Randall closing the case." Cargill clinked their glasses together. "When will the press release go out? The sooner this mess is in my rearview mirror, the better."

The phone rang.

"Hold that thought," Cargill said, and then strolled over to the phone on the corner of his desk. He didn't recognize the number but answered anyway. "Hello."

"Hello, daddy dearest."

There was pause while a slow smile eased across Cargill's lips. "Abrianna," he said. "What a pleasant surprise."

Lautner also lifted a surprised brow.

"To what do I owe this pleasure? Are you finally coming back home?"

"Bluemount is *not* my home. And it's not going to be your home much longer. Have you not seen the news?"

"No. Should I have?"

"The Lifeline Adoption Agency is being raided as we speak."

"What?" Cargill powered on the television. "Breaking News: Lynnwood trafficked children found" scrolled at the bottom. "The hell?"

"Yeah. Did you know that Marion kept diaries?"

The question threw him while he tried to split his attention between her and the television screen. "Diaries? What are you talking about?"

"She left a whole trunkload of them with her friend Tina. She wrote down every dirty secret on these beautiful gold-rimmed pages; she wrote all about the Lifeline Adoption agency. And this time, I made damn sure that these books don't disappear. The FBI, the attorney general, as well as a few *media* outlets have copies of the books most pertinent in putting you behind bars for the rest of your life."

Eyes wide, Lautner sank into one of the leather chairs before the screen.

Police sirens whirled in the distance.

"What's that?" Cargill rushed to the window to see the glow of blue lights. "What the hell is going on?"

"Sounds like that's your ride coming."

"You little bitch," Cargill raged.

Abrianna laughed. "Goodbye, asshole. I hope you burn in hell." She hung up.

The blue lights drew closer.

Cargill gulped down his drink, and immediately a

fire scorched his throat, but before he could gasp for air, his windpipe closed off. He turned toward Lautner for help, but Lautner was on his knees and clawing at his throat.

Cargill hit his knees, too. His head felt like it was growing like a balloon.

Lautner keeled over. His body writhed violently as a bloody foam bubbled from the corners of his mouth.

Poison. Scared and confused, Cargill realized that he was going to die. His fear escalated as he raked his nails down his neck and drew blood. At long last, he collapsed while a thick foam of blood eliminated that last route for oxygen. Seconds later, his heart stopped.

63

Out of all the many ways that President Washington wanted the whole Walkergate to end, the police finding billionaire Cargill Parker and his lawyer dead by poisoning was *not* one of them. Capitol Hill and talk radio was turning her young administration into mincemeat with headlines like: "Who killed Cargill Parker?" All morning, she fielded calls from members of her own party, begging her not to run for election. If she insisted, she would be primaried.

"Can you blame them?" Davidson asked.

"Shut up," she snapped, pacing a hole into the Oval Office's carpet. Having a dead billionaire on her hands was bad enough, but for the last hour, news coverage shifted to reports of U.S. Attorney Jaclyn Randall being arrested for sabotaging the Cargill Parker case and her first assistant attorney Kellerman accusing Randall of being behind the attempted murder of a child witness. Apparently, an old city hero and ex-police lieutenant, Gizella Castillo, had saved the little girl. It seemed Castillo also discovered the city's police chief Holder near death in his home on the same night.

"The whole damn town has gone mad," Kate seethed.

"This is Washington," Davidson joked. "It's your circus now for the time being—unless you're still crazy enough to run to keep this loony bin of an office next year."

Kate nibbled on her bottom lip.

Davidson shook his head. "My God. You are, aren't you?"

———⟫•⟪———

Abrianna placed a bundle of flowers over Marion's grave. Emotions rioted through her as she read Marion's name and life span engraved in the gray marble tombstone. She wished she could go back in time and change so many bad decisions. When she stood, Kadir wrapped his arm around her shoulders and pulled her close for the long walk back toward the car.

Tina Bouchard stood waiting. "Hey," she said, smiling with shimmering eyes. "I hoped I'd see you here today."

"You really loved her," Abrianna said. "I'm glad that someone was there for her over the years."

"I did. And I still do. That's why I need to show you something."

Surprised, Abrianna tossed a look at Kadir.

He shrugged, showing that he didn't have a clue to what this was about either.

"You guys can tail my car."

They agreed and followed Tina's white Mercedes across town to Howard University. They parked near the stadium. Various groups of students were in different stages of stretching or running up and down the field.

Abrianna's confusion only deepened as she and Kadir climbed out of the car. "Why are we here?"

Tina smiled and waved for them to follow.

Kadir and Abrianna fell in line behind Tina's distinctive walk. Abrianna snuck a peek to check where Kadir kept his gaze. To her amusement, he concentrated too hard on making sure that his eyes stayed glued to the back of Tina's head and not her hips.

She gently elbowed his side and laughed.

"What?"

She shook her head.

They reached the bleachers and had a clearer view of the athletes.

"All right. What gives? Why are we here?"

Tina smiled and searched through the runners. "There he is," she said, pointing.

Abrianna followed the direction of Tina's finger.

"Do you see the handsome guy running with the bright orange sneakers?"

"Yeah."

"They're his lucky sneakers," Tina said proudly.

"Okay."

"Don't you recognize him?"

Abrianna frowned and took in the young man's fit form and handsome face. Something tickled in the back of her memory, but she couldn't quite place the face. "No. I don't think so."

Proud, Tina proclaimed, "It's Samuel. Your brother."

Incredulous, Abrianna's gaze shot to Tina.

"What?"

"That night when you tried to rescue Samuel, it's true that Marion thought, in that moment, he was dead.

But when both Cargill and Samuel were taken to the hospital in separate ambulances, they were able to detect a faint heartbeat in Samuel. When it was clear that Cargill would survive, too, Marion had her first burst of courage. She—along with my checkbook—paid off a lot of people to hide the fact that Samuel had survived.

"My brother and his wife in Atlanta were unable to have children, so they were thrilled to take Samuel. He chose to come here for college. He's a smart kid. Marion wanted to tell you, but she couldn't risk telling a soul."

Abrianna returned her attention to Samuel. He was a handsome young man, grinning at his teammate. He looked so . . . happy. Tears flowed down Abrianna's face. For the first time in a long while, her shoulders were lighter. "He's alive."

"Yes. In the end, your bravery that night really did save him. When you had initially run away, Marion was happy for you—then when she heard about the Avery situation, she was devastated. But once that was all over—she really hoped that you'd found your way to some measure of happiness. She really did."

"Does he remember . . . ?"

Kadir slid an arm around her waist.

"Does he remember you?" Tina smiled. "He does. We never lied to him. Which is why I know that he can't wait to see you again."

Abrianna's heart fluttered. "Really?"

Tina nodded. "Really. Come on." Tina whistled and waved to Samuel before leading the way onto the field.

Kadir pressed a kiss to Abrianna's head. "I'm so happy for you, baby."

Abrianna lit up as she and Kadir fell in step behind

Tina. As they drew closer to the track field, Tina shouted, "Sam!"

He stopped and looked up, shielding his eyes.

Abrianna reached for Kadir's hand. He grabbed it and held it as they completed the walk.

Samuel towered over all of them. He was a lean six-four with a dust of brown sugar coloring and hazel eyes. When he smiled, Marion's dimples winked back at her. He was definitely *not* Cargill's son.

Tina made the introductions while the brother and sister smiled and drank each other in.

"Hello," Samuel said in a baritone made for late night radio.

"Hi." Abrianna's graze raked him up and down. "My gosh. You've grown so tall."

They laughed, and then suddenly Samuel snatched her up into his arms and swung her around.

Kadir's face nearly broke in half from smiling. A buzz in his right pocket broke the spell. He scooped the phone. Looking at the unknown caller ID, he was certain that it was Ghost and just made a mental note to call him back later. But as soon as he returned the phone to his pocket, it started buzzing again. *This can't be good.*

Sighing, Kadir stepped away and turned his back to the happy brother and sister reunion. "Hey, Ghost. This isn't a good time."

"We fucked up." Ghost cut to the chase.

"Wait. What?" Kadir asked, confused.

"T4S struck again. They have Lehane."

"How? When?"

"They took her the other night. Her face is plastered all over the news as missing. They even burned her townhouse to the ground."

"Fuck?" Kadir pivoted back toward the happy reunion.

Ghost asked, "My boys are ready. We're strapping up and going in after, right?"

Kadir raked his hand through his hair, thinking.

"Kadir, you there? It's not over, right?"

DON'T MISS

Conspiracy by De'nesha Diamond

On sale now

After a harrowing abduction, Abrianna Parker is
forced to repay a debt that she never owed. Her only
option is to trade working the gentlemen's clubs for
an elite escort service. But getting framed for a high-
profile murder isn't what the cool-headed beauty
signed up for . . .

1

A scared and hungry fourteen-year-old Abrianna Parker stepped out of Union Station and into the dead of night. The exhilaration she'd felt a mere hour ago evaporated the second D.C.'s blistering wind sliced through her thin leather jacket and settled somewhere in her bones' marrow. A new reality slammed into her with the force of a ton of bricks—and left her reeling.

"Where is he?" she whispered as she scanned the growing crowd. Abrianna was more than an hour late to meet Shawn, but it couldn't have been helped. Leaving her home had proved to be much harder than she'd originally realized. After several close calls, she'd managed to escape the house of horrors with a steel determination to never look back. Nothing could ever make her return.

Now it appeared that she'd missed her chance to link up with her best friend from school, or rather they used to go to the same high school, before Shawn's father discovered that he was gay, beat the hell out of him, and then threw him out of the house. Miraculously, Shawn had said that it was the best thing to have ever happened to him. Over the past year, he'd found other teenagers like him living out on the streets of D.C. His eclectic group of friends was better than any blood family, he'd boasted often during their frequent text messages.

In fact, Shawn's emancipation from his parents had planted the seeds in Abrianna's head that she could do the same thing. Gathering the courage, however, was a different story. The prospect of punishment, if she was caught, had paralyzed her on her first two attempts and had left Shawn waiting for her arrival in vain. Maybe he thought she'd lost her nerve tonight as well. Had she thought to charge her battery before leaving the house, she would be able to text him now to find out where he was.

Abrianna's gaze skimmed through the hustle and bustle of the crowd, the taxis and cars. Everyone, it seemed, was in a hurry. Likely, they wanted to meet up with family and friends. It was an hour before midnight. There was a certain kind of excitement that only New Year's Eve could bring: the tangible *hope* that, at the stroke of midnight, everyone *magically* changed into better people and entered into better circumstances than the previous year.

Tonight, Abrianna was no different.

With no sight of Shawn, tears splashed over Abrianna's lashes but froze on her cheeks. Despite a leather coat lined with faux fur, a wool cap, and leather gloves, Abrianna may as well have been butt-ass naked for all the protection it provided. "Goddamn it," she hissed, creating thick frost clouds in front of her face. "Now what?"

The question looped in her head a few times, but the voice that had compelled her to climb out her bedroom window had no answer. She was on her own.

Someone slammed into her from behind—hard.

"Hey," she shouted, tumbling forward. After righting herself on frozen legs, she spun around to curse at the rude asshole—but the assailant was gone. She was stuck looking around, mean-mugging people until they looked at her suspect.

A sudden gust of wind plunged the temperature lower and numbed her face. She pulled her coat collar up, but it didn't help.

The crowd ebbed and flowed, but she stood in one spot like she'd grown roots, still not knowing what to do. And after another twenty minutes, she felt stupid—and cold. Mostly cold.

Go back into the station—thaw out and think. However, when she looked at the large and imposing station, she couldn't get herself to put one foot in front of the other. She had the overwhelming sense that her returning inside would be a sign of defeat, because, once she was inside, it wouldn't be too hard to convince herself to get back on the train, go home and let *him* win . . . again.

Icy tears skipped down her face. *I can't go back.* Forcing her head down, she walked. She passed commuters yelling for cabs, huddled friends laughing—some singing, with no destination in mind. East of the station was bathed in complete darkness. She could barely make out anything in front of her. The only way she could deal with her growing fear was to ignore it. Ignore how its large, skeletal fingers wrapped around her throat. Ignore how it twisted her stomach into knots. Ignore how it scraped her spine raw.

Just keep walking.

"Help me," a feeble voice called out. "Help!"

Abrianna glanced around, not sure from which direction the voice had come. *Am I losing my mind now?*

"Help. I'm not drunk!"

It came from her right, in the middle of the road, where cars and taxis crept.

"I'm not drunk!" the voice yelled.

Finally, she made out a body lying next to a concrete divider—the kind work crews used to block off construction areas.

"Help. Please!"

Again, Abrianna looked around the crowds of people streaming past. Didn't anyone else hear this guy? Even though that side of the building was dark, it was still heavily populated. Why was no one else responding to this guy's cry for help?

"Help. I'm not drunk!"

Timidly, she stepped off the sidewalk and skulked into the street. As vehicles headed toward her, she held up her hand to stop some and weaved in between others. Finally, Abrianna stood above a crumpled old man, in the middle of the road, and was at a loss as to what to do.

"I'm not drunk. I'm a diabetic. Can you help me up?" the man asked.

"Uh, sure." She knelt, despite fear, and asked, *What if it's a trap?*

It *could* be a trap, Abrianna reasoned even as she wrapped one of the guy's arms around her neck. Then, using all of her strength, she tried to help him to his feet, but couldn't. A Good Samaritan materialized out of nowhere to help her out.

"Whoa, man. Are you okay?" the stranger asked.

Abrianna caught a glimpse of the Good Samaritan's

shoulder-length stringy blond hair as a passing cab's headlights rolled by. He was ghost white with ugly pockmarks.

"Yes. Yes," the fallen guy assured. "It's my blood sugar. If you could just help me back over to the sidewalk that would be great."

"Sure. No problem," the blond stranger said.

Together, they helped the old black man back across the street.

"Thank you. I really appreciate this."

"No problem," the white guy said, his teeth briefly illuminated by another passing car as a smoker's yellow.

Once back on the sidewalk, he released the old man. "You two have a happy New Year!" As quick as the blond savior had appeared, he disappeared back into the moving crowd.

The old guy, huffing and puffing thick frost clouds, wrapped his hand around a NO PARKING sign and leaned against it.

"Are you sure you're all right?" Abrianna asked. It seemed wrong to leave him like this.

He nodded. "I'm a little dizzy, but it will pass. Thank you now."

That should be that. She had done what she could for the man. It was best that she was on her way. But she didn't move—probably because he didn't *look* okay.

As she suspected, he started sliding down the pole, his legs giving out. Abrianna wrapped his arm back around her neck to hold him up. "I got you," she said. But the question was: for how long?

"Thank you, child. Thank you."

Again, she didn't know what to do next. Maybe she

should take him up to the station. At least, inside, she could get him to a bench or chair to sit down. "Can you walk?"

"Yes. I—I think so."

"No. No. Not back there," he said, refusing to move in the direction of the station. "They done already kicked me out tonight and threatened to lock me up if I return."

His words hit her strange. "What do you mean?"

He sighed. "Let's just go the other way."

With little choice, she did as he asked. It took a while, but the man's stench finally drifted under her nose. It was a strange, sour body odor that fucked with her gag reflexes. "Where do you want me to take you?" she asked, growing tired as he placed more and more of his weight on her shoulders.

When the old man didn't answer, she assumed he hadn't heard her. "Where are you trying to go?"

"Well . . . to be honest. Nowhere in particular," he said. "Just somewhere I can rest this old body and stay warm tonight. I read in one of the papers that it's supposed to dip down to nine degrees."

It hit her. "You don't have anywhere to sleep?"

"Well—of course I do. These here streets are my home. I got a big open sky as my roof, some good, hard concrete or soft grass as my floor. The rest usually takes care of itself." He chuckled—a mistake, judging by the way it set off the most godawful cough she'd ever heard.

They stopped when the coughing continued. Abrianna swore something rattled inside of his chest.

"Are you all right?" she asked. "Do you need a doctor?"

More coughing. *Are his lungs trying to come up?*

After what seemed like forever, he stopped, wheezed for air, and then wiped his face. "Sorry about that," he said, sounding embarrassed.

"It's okay," she said, resuming their walk.

"I really appreciate you for helping me out like this. I know I must be keeping you from wherever it is you're trying to get to. It's New Year's Eve and all."

"No. It's all right. I don't mind."

He twisted his head toward her and, despite the growing dark, she could make out his eyes scrutinizing her. "You're awfully *young* to be out here by yourself."

Abrianna ignored the comment and kept walking.

"How old are you?" he asked.

"Why?" she snapped, ready to drop him right there on the sidewalk and take off.

"Because you look like my grandbaby the last time I saw her. 'Bout sixteen, I'd say she was."

Abrianna jutted up her chin.

"She had a beautiful heart, too." He smiled. "Never could see any person or animal hurting."

The unexpected praise made her smile.

"Ah, yeah. A beautiful smile to boot."

They crossed the street to Second Avenue. She'd gotten used to his weight already, appreciated the extra body heat—but the *stench* still made her eyes water. *Did he say that it was going to get down to nine degrees tonight?* Abrianna had stolen cash from her house before she'd left, but hadn't had time to count all of it. Maybe she could get a hotel room—just for the night. After that, she would have to be careful about her finances. Once the money was gone—it was gone. She had no idea on how she and Shawn were going to get more.

Still walking, Abrianna pulled herself out of her

troubled thoughts to realize that she and the old man had entered a park—a dark park—away from the streaming holiday crowd.

"Where are we going?" she asked, trying not to sound alarmed.

"Oh, just over there on that bench is fine." The old man pointed a shaky finger to their right. When they reached it, he dropped onto the iron bench like a sack of bricks and panted out more frosted air. "Whew," he exclaimed.

"That walk is getting harder and harder every day."

"You come here often?" Abrianna glanced around, catching a few figures, strolling. "Is it safe?"

"That depends," he said, patting the empty space next to him.

She took the hint and plopped down. "Depends on what?"

"On your definition of safe," he chuckled and set off another series of hard-to-listen-to coughs.

Abrianna wished that he'd stop trying to be a jokester. His lungs couldn't handle it. She watched him go through another painful episode.

At the end, he swore, "Goddamn it." Then he was contrite. "Oh. Sorry about that, sweetheart."

Smiling, she clued him in, "I've heard worse."

He nodded. "I reckon you have. Kids nowadays have heard and seen it all long *before* puberty hits. That's the problem: The world don't got no innocence anymore."

"Doesn't have any," she corrected him.

He chuckled. "Beauty and brains. You're a hell of a combination, kid."

Abrianna warmed toward the old man.

"Trouble at home?" he asked, his black gaze steady on her.

"No," she lied without really selling it. Why should she care if he believed her? In a few minutes, she'd probably never see him again.

"Nah. I didn't think so," he played along. "You don't look like the type who would needlessly worry her parents."

Abrianna sprung to her feet. "Looks like you're cool here. I gotta get going and find my friend."

"So the parents are off limits, huh?" He nodded. "Got it."

She stared at him, figuring out whether he was working an angle. Probably. Older people always did.

"It's tough out here, kid." His eyes turned sad before he added, "Dangerous too."

"I'm not looking for a speech."

"Fair enough." He pulled in a deep breath. "It's hypothermia season. Do you know what this is?"

"Yeah," Abrianna lied again.

"It means that folks can freeze to death out here—and often do. If you got somewhere safe to go, then I suggest you go there tonight. I'd hate to see someone as pretty as you wind up down at the morgue."

"I can take care of myself."

"Yeah? Have you ever done it before?"

"You sure do ask a lot of questions," she said.

"Believe it or not, you're not the first person to tell me that—bad habit, I suppose. But I've gotten too old to change now."

"What about you?" Abrianna challenged. "Aren't you afraid of freezing to death?"

He laughed, this time managing not to choke over his lungs. "Oh, I *wish*—but the devil don't want nothing to do with me these days. I keep expecting to see him, but he never comes."

"You talk like you want to die."

"It's not about what I want, little girl. It's just time, that's all," he said quietly.

Abrianna didn't know what to say to that—but she did know that she could no longer feel her face. "Well, I gotta go."

He nodded. "I understand. You take care of yourself—and if you decide to stay out here—trust *no one*."

She nodded and backpedaled away. It still felt wrong to leave the old guy there—especially if that whole freezing-to-death stuff was true. At that moment, it felt true.

The hotels were packed—or wanted nearly three hundred dollars for *one* night. That was more than half of Abrianna's money, she found out. At the last hotel, she agreed to the figure, but then they wanted to see some sort of ID. The front desk woman suggested she try a *motel* in another district—or a shelter.

An hour later, Abrianna was lost. Walking and crying through a row of creepy-looking houses, she had no idea where she was or where she was going.

Suddenly, gunshots were fired.

Abrianna ran and ducked down a dark alley.

Tires squealed.

Seconds later, a car roared past her.

More gunshots fired.

The back window of the fleeing muscle car exploded. The driver swerved and flew up onto a curb, and rammed headlong into a utility pole.

Bam!

The ground shook and the entire row of streetlights went out.

No way the driver survived that shit. Extending her neck around the corner of a house, Abrianna attempted to get a better look at what was going on, but at the sound of rushing feet pounding the concrete, she ducked back so that she could peep the scene. She counted seven guys running up to the car. When they reached the driver's side, a rumble of angry voices filled the night before they released another round of gunfire.

Holy shit. Abrianna backed away, spun around, and ran smack into a solid body.

The pockmarked Good Samaritan materialized out of the shadow. "Hey there, little girl. Remember me?"

Abrianna screamed. . . .

Connect with Us

Visit us online at
KensingtonBooks.com
to read more from your favorite authors, see books
by series, view reading group guides, and more.

Join us on social media

for sneak peeks, chances to win books and prize packs,
and to share your thoughts with other readers.

**facebook.com/kensingtonpublishing
twitter.com/kensingtonbooks**

Tell us what you think!

To share your thoughts, submit a review,
or sign up for our eNewsletters, please visit:
KensingtonBooks.com/TellUs.